THE SUPERSTRUCTURE

THE SUPERSTRUCTURE

JACK BELMONTE

Voltaire Publishing

The Superstructure

Published in the United States of America by Voltaire Publishing.

Cover art by Boomer Rucker.

ISBN: 978-0-9891775-2-8

Library of Congress Control Number: 2014957799

For Mohamed Bouazizi, and all those who resist

Chapter 1

Johnny Luca sprang to his knees at the flash of 0100, the terrain a vapor of night-vision green. He maneuvered in a crouch, his ski mask grazing the low ceiling, his boots crunching into the bed of rocks. He seized a ruptured chain link, bent the fence towards him, and yanked himself through the opening.

Johnny stood up, clad in black in the December night, the wind dusting snow through his prey's backyard. His eyes darted at one neighbor's house—lights out, no one at the windows. Then they glanced at the other—the same.

The twenty-five-year-old Anti-Subversion Authority agent reached under the porch from which he had just emerged, where he had sat coiled for four hours after secreting himself within at 2100 hours, and pulled out a black bag. Johnny was in the middle of a postage-stamp backyard in Staten Island, standing in the shadow of a duplex at 1:00 A.M. a couple of weeks before Christmas 2023.

Inside that duplex was one of the men who killed his father.

Johnny zipped his black down coat all the way up, fiddled with his ski mask, and crept up the porch steps. *Time's up*, he thought.

He knelt before a sliding-glass door and pulled a glass-cutter and masking tape from his bag. The subject had stuck a block of wood in the inside track of the door to keep someone from sliding it open; Johnny had noticed that the first time he reconned the place a month ago. He stretched black electrical tape across the glass, tracing the length of the block inside, until there was a rectangle of solid black. Then Johnny scraped along the four sides of the rectangle with the glass-cutter, carbide scoring glass like chalk on a blackboard. He tapped on the tape—which absorbed the sound—until the glass popped. He nudged the glass with his thumbs, broke out the rectangle and pulled it free, then reached in and pulled out the block. Track clear.

Johnny reached inside, pointed a transmitter up at an alarm contact on top of the door, and pushed a button until the transmitter blinked. Alarm out.

Then Johnny pulled out a tool, jabbed it into the door, and jimmied. Lock picked.

He slid open the door a crack, slipped inside, and slid it closed. He stepped into the subject's darkened kitchen, now officially a man apart.

Johnny set a transmitter on the kitchen counter and pushed a button until it beeped, knocking out all Wi-Fi and mobile phone signals in the house. He crept through the kitchen, around a table burning infrared green, towards a flight of stairs. His subject lived alone in the house—Johnny had eavesdropped on the house for weeks to make sure of that—and was sleeping in the upstairs bedroom, about to answer for Giovanni Luca, Sr.

Johnny laid a foot on the first step. He knew everything now. He knew they'd murdered his detective father two years ago and made it look like suicide. He knew they'd blasted a bullet through his father's throat for figuring out that rogues within the Anti-Subversion Authority had been staging terror attacks through its proxy, a terror group called Brigade 910, and were plotting a massive false-flag attack that would usher in a coup. Johnny's father died trying to stop that coup, and Johnny and his unit finished his work last May when they halted Brigade 910's Operation Reichstag attack and arrested Shepherd Moloch, one of the Authority rogues responsible.

Those seven months ago, a bullet meant for the President of the United States had singed into Johnny's shoulder at nine hundred feet per second as he tackled one assassin and took a shot from another. The bullet was to be a trip-hammer that would trigger the worst terror attack in American history, but instead it just damn near killed Johnny and left a hell of a scar. And now there would be justice, justice for everyone responsible for his father's death.

Johnny glided up the steps, deeper into the valley of green. Just a few more steps, then a right turn, then down the hallway and into the bedroom. The house settled behind walls and creaked beneath floors.

Johnny now knew that a Brigade 910 terrorist named Jack Gaines, codenamed Hyperion, had pulled the trigger those three years ago. Now Gaines, just two years older than Johnny, was the operational commander of Brigade 910 and deep underground.

Tonight Johnny was after Sergei Ivanov, a thug who was in the room when Gaines shot Giovanni Sr. He was on the Brigade 910 periphery, less dedicated to the overthrow of the government than he was to making money as hired muscle. He'd abducted Johnny's father that night, cracking his skull with a blackjack, throwing him in a trunk, and dumping him at a Brigade 910 safe-house. He then stood guard as Gaines executed Giovanni Sr.

Johnny reached the top step and looked down the hall each way—all clear. He fingered his holstered Glock and edged towards the closed door at the end of the corridor.

It had taken a lot of work after hours, and away from his supervisors' prying eyes, to reach this point. He'd begun over the summer, by hacking into Authority files on Brigade 910 informants, and then started buying intel with his own cash. *Open mouths get fed*, he'd tell informants. Then Johnny moved on to breaking into Brigade 910 terrorists' homes, planting bugs and imaging their hard drives. He worked from the bottom up and the outside in, identifying first those who'd heard of the murder, then those who knew who was responsible, until he learned the identifies of Gaines and everyone else in the room that night.

Johnny grasped Ivanov's doorknob. He'd finally breached that room, the safe-house basement where Gaines had stuck a gun under his father's chin, his hands tied behind his back. Johnny was about to step into November 2021. Outside was December 2023—his mother struggling to keep a job and pay the rent, his boss working hand-in-hand with the President to hunt down the last of the rogues and to dismantle the Authority, the bombings that continued to strike American cities because Brigade 910 had come unhinged from the Authority—but behind Ivanov's door was justice.

Johnny twisted the knob, nudged open the door, and peered inside. His eyes lasered towards the bed, fixed on the figure bulging beneath the sheets. He crossed the room, tiptoeing across hardwood, yards melting to inches as the last grains of Ivanov's time ran through the glass. He reached for the sheet, but that wasn't Ivanov, it was—

Metal exploded across Johnny's back, hammering him to the floor, the hardwood bursting green as he crashed into it. He looked up at Ivanov wielding a baseball bat, about to axe it towards his face. Johnny rolled out of the way as the bat blasted into the floor.

Ivanov had stuck pillows under the sheets, he realized. *Goddamn rookie mistake.*

"Who sent you?" Ivanov yelled, stalking him. He raised the bat. "Who sent you!"

Johnny swept his foot behind Ivanov's ankle, dropping him. He turned on his side, squared up, and kicked him right in the face. Then he pulled himself up and dove on Ivanov as he thrashed, seizing the hand holding the bat and punching him in the face. Ivanov's grip loosened; Johnny knocked the bat away.

"I'll kill you!" Ivanov yelled, bench-pressing Johnny off of him.

Stronger than I thought, Johnny thought, *much stronger—*

Ivanov wrenched him up by the neck, locked him in a headlock, and dragged him into the bathroom. He smashed Johnny's face against the glass shower door, the night-vision goggles' frame bashing into his forehead, then opened it and threw him into the bathtub. Johnny was bleeding inside his ski mask.

Ivanov pulled a handgun out of his waistband and snapped it against Johnny's head. "Who sent you?" he said again.

Through the green blur, Johnny saw Gaines jamming the gun under his father's chin in full color, Ivanov hulking by the door in that filthy basement.

Johnny looked up at Ivanov, his two hundred thirty pounds sagging in a sweatshirt and track pants, his nose broken, his balding scalp bleeding. *I won't die here. Not tonight.*

Johnny narrowed his eyes. "Hyperion sent me," he said.

Shock registered in Ivanov's eyes. "How do you know him?" he asked.

Johnny didn't bother to answer. In three motions, he slapped the gun out of Ivanov's hand, jumped to his feet, and bashed his face into the shower door. He stepped out of the tub, a year of elite Authority training firing through his nerves as he kicked out Ivanov's legs from under him, smashed an open palm into his already-broken nose, and flipped him onto his stomach. Johnny lashed zip-ties onto his wrists, stepped back, and then leveled a kick into his rib cage.

He glowered at Ivanov. "Get on your knees," he ordered.

"My friend," Ivanov said, his voice shaking. "Just tell me how you know Hyperion. I want no trouble—"

"Shut up. Get on your knees." Johnny picked up Ivanov's gun and forced him to his knees. "How did you know I was coming?"

"I never sleep, man. Nightmares. Always somebody coming for me. I heard you downstairs and I get ready."

Johnny stepped back. He had him now. He was way too fast for Ivanov to pull any moves. "Nightmares about what? Not enough blini to eat?"

"Blood on my hands." Tears slipped down Ivanov's face. "But I'm right with God, no one knows, I straighten up and I'm right with God…"

Aren't we all. "Good. You can meet him now." Johnny cocked the gun. "Open your mouth."

"Please, my friend, my mother needs me—"

"Open your mouth. I won't say it again."

And for the first time all night, Johnny began to tremble. He'd sworn to kill them all, but he'd never killed anyone. Before tonight, he'd never even attacked anyone before, for anything, ever.

Ivanov opened his mouth, and Johnny pushed the gun inside. His heart pounded, blood racing through his veins, flooding his face. He swallowed hard.

"Did you know," he said, "that someone I loved got killed because of you?"

Johnny had recited these words in front of the mirror before he left his apartment tonight, but now they came out forced, wooden. *I have to believe in this. This guy killed Dad, I have to believe this is right.*

Ivanov shook his head, sobbing.

"We'll make it look like a suicide," Johnny said. "Shoot you with own gun, real quick. Enjoy hell."

His finger curled around the trigger. *I can take a life*, he thought, looking into Ivanov's eyes. *I can take this life…*

He jammed the gun farther into Ivanov's mouth, until the Russian began to gag. A chasm opened in Johnny's stomach; his arm wavered. He steadied the arm, his eyes fixed on Ivanov's.

Chapter 2

Two hours later, Johnny lay awake in his bed, clutching the Glock as he stared into black.

He hadn't pulled the trigger. Instead, he'd smashed another open hand into Ivanov's nose, then jammed a syringe into him and held it until he was unconscious. He fished Ivanov's bank and credit cards out of a wallet on the dresser, then ran a scanner over them so that Ivanov would beam a record out to Johnny every time he used them after tonight. Then he bundled Ivanov's laptop under his arm, spit on the Russian, and headed out. Ivanov was a heroin dealer; he wouldn't be calling a cop.

I can take a life, Johnny thought again, glancing at a sliver of streetlight that slipped into his Newark studio. He raised the gun, his finger curling around at the trigger at the thought of Ivanov prone on his knees, and then shook his head and laid the gun on the bedside table. *I have to. They've taken so many.*

Johnny sat up in bed. He traced his hand over one laceration that snaked across his back, then another near his eye. *How the hell am I going to explain this to everyone?*

Seven months after saving the President's life and becoming a legend to the handful of people who knew about it—including to the President himself—and here Johnny was, chasing shadows and breaking laws. By day, he was a rising star in an elite unit tasked with tracking down the bitter-enders of Brigade 910. And by night—burglary, armed robbery, and attempted murder.

Johnny reached for his mobile and pulled up a text he'd received while he was at Ivanov's. *Yo Lead Mag*, it read. *I know what you're up to. Let it go.*

It was from Julius Fullerton, his partner, the man who'd saved his life twice. "Lead Mag," of course, was short for "Lead Magnet," since Fullerton found it endlessly funny that Johnny had been shot. Johnny rolled his eyes at the nickname. *Smartass.*

He considered the message. He didn't doubt that Fullerton knew. He'd probably known since the beginning, since the first job Johnny had pulled. And Johnny was pretty sure that Fullerton hadn't reported him for it.

But eventually he will. If I keep on like this—he will.

Johnny went back to his inbox. He'd missed a few other texts during tonight's op. *Did you know…* the first one read. Johnny smiled. Then the second: *That you are the most handsome man I have ever laid eyes on (even if you ARE a Yankee fan), and I am totally, hopelessly in lurve with you?* And the third, sent two hours after the first two, around midnight: *Goodnight, Gio. I miss you.*

They were from Lizbeth. Lizbeth Heathrow was Johnny's girlfriend of seven months, his best friend of seven years. After taking the bullet last spring, Johnny had confessed his love to her just as she was about to move to Phoenix with her douchebag Red Sox fan boyfriend. *I came a long way to see you tonight*, he'd told her as he took her in his arms in the rain that night. *And I'd like to tell you all about just how far I came.*

Johnny switched on a digital photo frame, bathing the room in pale light, and glanced around his studio. Laundry lined the floor, crumbs from tonight's frozen pizza were scattered across a paper plate sitting on the kitchen table, and a crooked dart stuck in the bull's-eye of the Red Sox dartboard on the wall. He'd told Lizbeth that he worked for the Authority—it would be impossible to keep telling her that he worked for the FBI—but he'd fed her the same ruse he fed his mother and brother, that he was just an office support technician. He'd wanted to tell her the truth—more than anything—but he couldn't.

Why not?

Johnny took the digital photo frame in hands and gazed at a picture of his father burning in the dark. Because his work wasn't done, that's why. Where was he supposed to begin? By telling Lizbeth that her Gio really belonged to a secret strike team that had prevented "Nine-Eleven squared" and saved the President's life? By explaining that thugs had murdered his father and that Johnny planned to kill them all? How could things ever be normal between them after that?

Johnny sank into the bed, still holding the photo frame, his five-foot-ten, one hundred seventy-five-pound body throbbing in pain from the fight with Ivanov. A siren wailed outside, Newark's finest out to bust the degenerate of the minute. Soon Johnny would be moving, because he didn't want Lizbeth braving a war-zone to come see him.

But that was nothing, just a token gesture. Johnny risked Lizbeth's life every nanosecond he was her boyfriend, and moving to a nicer neighborhood wasn't going to fix it. He was making enemies by the day, among both the terrorists he hunted on his nine-to-five job, and the goons he stalked after-hours. They were killers, and everyone close to Johnny was a target. His mother and brother were stuck with this—they were his blood. But Johnny *chose* to drag Lizbeth into it.

Johnny stared in at the picture of his father hoisting him on his shoulders in the bleachers at Yankee Stadium. *I can't let this go, Dad. Not until Gaines eats a bullet for what he did to you.*

He turned over in bed, grimacing as the laceration from the bat blow shot a bolt of pain up his back. He toggled to another picture, Lizbeth kissing him under the tree at Rockefeller Center, from just last week. Some tourist had agreed to snap it for them, and just before he did, Lizbeth pecked Johnny on the cheek, her red mittens tugging at his lapel.

Johnny smiled as the picture bathed him in light. *I love you so much*, he thought. He shook his head. *But how am I going to keep you safe?*

He powered off the frame and shut his eyes. Sooner or later he'd have to learn how to kill—because his enemies already knew how.

Chapter 3

"Total war," President Reed Wilkins said to Hunter Peterson and Wilson Sharpe. "It's the only way. Total war, until we destroy them."

"We're talking about men who'll do anything," Attorney General Sharpe said. "Gunfights in the streets. Terror bombings every day. They'll wade in blood to beat you."

"Which is why we have to fight them, Will. Just for that reason."

"When you say total war, you'd better be ready for just that," Peterson said. "Because they're going to give it to us. Whoever they all are, they're ready."

"But are we strong enough?" Sharpe asked. "Can your presidency withstand this?"

"Are you my A.G., or my campaign manager?" Wilkins said, choking back exasperation. "Are you going to wipe out a gang of thugs when I tell you to?"

"This isn't some drug cartel. This is a military-grade force."

They were talking not about Brigade 910, but rather about the rogues within the U.S. government who'd unleashed that group on America, the gangster syndicate headed by former Authority Director Alexander Bryson. Brigade 910, it turned out, was not an autonomous terror group, but rather was Bryson's brainchild, sketched to life by him and controlled by him since its inception. Last spring, Bryson had deployed Brigade 910 in Operation Reichstag, a massive false-flag terror attack intended to culminate in Wilkins's assassination and the institution of a police state in America.

But thanks to Peterson and his young agents, Wilkins had survived the assassination attempt, and now was rousting to smash Bryson. And what was more, Wilkins now knew that there was someone above Bryson, the one who had started all of this, the one Wilkins would have to destroy in order to win this war and save the republic—a figure known as Octavian. *Octavian*, Wilkins thought. *The man who's named himself for the first Roman emperor after the fall of the Republic. The man who has to kill me to become the first American emperor.*

Wilkins surveyed Sharpe and Peterson as they sat across from him at a coffee table in the main lodge of Camp David. He would be riding with these two generals into the fight of his life.

Sharpe, fifty-eight years old like Wilkins, African-American like Wilkins, had been Wilkins's best friend since college, the best man at his wedding, practically a father himself to Wilkins's children. He was the only black man in his Cabinet, and, Wilkins always thought laughing to himself, the only other mustachioed man in politics, besides himself. He was skinny, bespectacled, bookish, the damn best lawyer in the country. In law school, he'd always been the A to Wilkins's A-minus, and that was exactly how Wilkins felt about him as a man.

Peterson had headed Wilkins's protective detail in the Secret Service years ago, and then, as Special Agent in Charge of the Newark Field Office of the Anti-Subversion Authority, had saved Wilkins's life by striking down Operation Reichstag. He was forty-nine, six-foot-two, nearly two hundred pounds. Silver shone across his light brown hair. Wilkins had appointed Peterson as Authority Director last spring.

Wilkins bent forward in the brown leather sofa, stared into the weathered mocha coffee table, and traced his fingers over his U.S. Army coffee mug. "You're right," he said to Sharpe. "Whoever these people are—we have to assume we're about to do battle with a state, with all the resources of a state."

"Well I'm ready for this war, if that's the plan," Peterson said. "Like I've told you, I've put together a good team. Small—but loyal. And goddamn good."

Wilkins nodded. He knew he could count on Peterson—he was always up for a fight. That's why he'd reached out to him in late 2022, why he'd told him, *We're in trouble, Hunter. Trouble of the worst kind.* There was a plot against Wilkins, and Wilkins knew it—Bryson was planning to have him assassinated to make way for passage of the Total Information Awareness Act, the most draconian counter-terror law in American history. Over several midnight meetings at Arlington National Cemetery, Wilkins, Peterson, and Kevin Chan—the now-deceased former director of the Secret Service—planned to outmaneuver Bryson. Only at the end did they discover that the plot was so much worse, that Bryson had been pulling the strings of Brigade 910 since it formed, that he was planning to stage a massive false-flag terror attack that would kill thousands of Americans and turn the United States into a dictatorship. At zero hour last May, Peterson and his "goddamn good" team had neutralized Bryson's operatives all over the country, and one brave, lucky, incredibly quick young agent had tackled Wilkins just before his would-be assassin shot him.

Wilkins looked at Sharpe. "And you?" he asked. "Are you ready for this war?"

There was a reason why Wilkins had reached out to Peterson and Chan last year, but not Sharpe, even though his Attorney General had the entire Justice Department at his disposal. Sharpe was pragmatic, a consensus-builder, a rule-of-law type who'd negotiate to the last. He'd have been the Neville Chamberlain of Operation Reichstag. And more than that, Wilkins knew that Sharpe would let his love for his best friend interfere. For that, he could never blame him. Wilkins would die for Sharpe.

"I'm ready to do whatever you order," Sharpe said.

Wilkins nodded. "I'm not a poet. I make some fancy speeches sometimes, but I'm not a poet. If I were, I'd be able to tell you much it means to me that you're both at my side for this." He sighed. "Now hang onto yourselves, both of you. You should know that Bryson has proposed a deal."

Wilkins saw the vein on Peterson's head instantly bulge. "A *deal*?" Peterson said. "What kind of deal?"

Wilkins held up a hand to calm Peterson down. "Now think of where we are right now, Hunter. We dealt them a hell of a blow last spring. Moloch is in custody. We've dismissed Bryson as director and publicly executed a search warrant at his home. We're dismantling Brigade 910 by the day. They're all on the run."

"Which makes this the perfect time to chase them all down and annihilate them."

"We should at least hear it out, Hunter," Sharpe said. He turned to Wilkins. "How did Bryson offer you this deal, anyway?"

"Through backchannels," Wilkins replied. "I've got my backchannels."

"Don't go all Richard Nixon on us, please," Peterson said.

Sharpe laughed. "Or Dick Cheney," he added.

Wilkins smiled. "This is what former Authority Director Bryson is prepared to offer. First, he's promised to guarantee my safety, and my family's. I can keep the Secret Service as my protective detail—I don't have to hand protection back to the Authority." He turned to Peterson. "And they'll give you amnesty, Hunter. You and your agents."

"*Amnesty*?" Peterson said. "We caught them trying to overthrow the government, and they're offering *me* amnesty?"

Wilkins nodded. "I'm to restore Bryson as Director, and let him implement Total Information Awareness. They know that we know about Brigade 910, and they're willing to let you chase all the rest of them down and wipe them out. But after that, they want Bryson's control over domestic security to be absolute. And Will, they want you to dismiss the prosecution of Moloch immediately."

Shepherd Moloch was the former Special Agent in Charge of the Authority New York Field Office, Bryson's right-hand man and logistical leader of Operation Reichstag. Posing as a Brigade 910 commander one night, he'd helped torture Agent Luca, the kid who ultimately saved Wilkins's life. Peterson himself had arrested Moloch after a fistfight atop the World Trade Center in New York, and he was currently incarcerated at a military prison.

Wilkins looked away for a moment as his men considered the offer. It sounded genuine. Considering the enemy's position, it was exactly what they'd offer—an appeal to Wilkins's personal interests, a forgive-and-forget with Peterson, and a solid push of Brigade 910 under the bus. In return, Wilkins would release Moloch, cease all investigations into Bryson's intrigues, talk the American public down from its latest conspiracy theory ledge, and stay the hell out of Bryson and co.'s affairs.

Wilkins turned back to face them. "What's the latest with the Moloch situation?" he asked.

"Any day now," Sharpe said. "The judge will order him released any day now, if not outright, then into civilian custody. We're keeping him on a military base, for Christ's sakes. Even under the broadest interpretation of Total Information Awareness, that violates half the Constitution."

"Only half?" Wilkins grinned. "Well what good is passing a draconian law if it doesn't give me dictatorial powers?"

Total Information Awareness, of course, wasn't meant to be enjoyed by Wilkins. It had passed a few weeks before the attempt on his life. Bryson's plan was that Wilkins would veto it, and then after he was killed, an outraged Congress would override the veto to give his successor the tools to crush the terrorists responsible. Wilkins had vetoed it, all right—but survived the assassination attempt. An outraged Congress had overridden his veto all the same, "For your own good, Mr. President," as the Speaker of the House had said. And now Wilkins was wielding all of the law's power against Bryson and his cronies.

Sharpe grinned back. "I expect the judge to transfer Moloch to a federal prison. He'll have a hell of a lawsuit against us one day."

"Well if anyone deserves a damages award against the United States government, it's Moloch," Wilkins said. "He should sue us for emotional distress." He paused. "So what do you all think?"

"No deal," Peterson said. "No way, never."

Wilkins and Peterson looked at Sharpe. After a pause, Sharpe threw up his hands. "They're going to put this country through hell if we stand up to them. But no. We can't make a deal with them. We're going to have to fight."

Wilkins smiled. "I appreciate your counsel, gentlemen," he said. "But that was only a test. I made up my mind the second I heard the offer. We're not making any deal. You can't make a deal with people like this. First of all, I can't trust them to hold their end of any deal we make. And second of all…" Wilkins gestured to an American flag in the corner of the room. "There's your second of all. No deal, ever. We'll execute Bryson for treason, do the same to whoever Octavian is. We're going to crush them all and keep this democracy safe."

"They'll wade in blood, like I said," Sharpe said.

"Then so will we," Peterson said.

Sharpe frowned. "That's easy to say in the abstract, Hunter. But we're decent, and they're not. They don't really care who they kill. And… we do, don't we? We've already lost Chan. We lost a lot of good agents last May. And…" Sharpe looked at Wilkins. "We almost lost a good buddy, POTUS here."

Wilkins held up a hand again, this time to ward off Sharpe's worry. "You know, lately I've been thinking a lot about this recording," he said, "from one of the Nine-Eleven flights."

"Which?" Peterson said.

"It was from Flight Ninety-Three. The one that crashed in Pennsylvania."

"What about it?" Sharpe asked.

"Well, you know, they rose up against the terrorists, and they started to take the plane back. The hijackers crashed the plane. And one of the last things you hear in the cockpit recording is a voice outside the door yelling: 'In the cockpit! We die if we don't!'" Wilkins stared hard at his Attorney General and Authority Director. "Just think about that. They knew that if they didn't take that plane back, they were dead. And so were lots of people on the ground, at the Capitol." He paused. "And that's what we're facing. If we don't unmask Octavian, if we don't beat these folks…we're dead. Democracy dies, and so do we. We die if we don't."

"Then we unmask Octavian," Peterson said. "We keep trying."

"That's right. We keep trying. This is war, like I said. And I'm going to tell them no deal. They can all surrender if they want. That could spare them the death penalty, maybe—even Octavian. But no deal. We're going to destroy every last one of them." Wilkins turned to Peterson. "Hunter, it's been seven months now. And we still have no idea who Octavian is."

"We'll do everything we can, Mr. President," Peterson said. "Everything. We'll get him."

It had been seven months since the attempt on Wilkins's life and Operation Reichstag. They'd arrested Moloch, executed the search at Bryson's home, hinted that there were rogues within the government. Wilkins had addressed the nation last May and suggested that it wasn't only Brigade 910 who was to blame for the attempted terror attacks—that there were also "unknown interlopers who pull the strings of terror and hide in the shadows." But it all had to be a gradual process. He couldn't just tell three hundred fifty million Americans that traitors inside their own government had been staging terror attacks and had tried to carry out Operation Reichstag. There'd be riots in the streets; it would devastate the national psyche. Wilkins needed proof, the hardest proof. If he made a false move, Bryson and his confederates would accuse him of conspiracy theory lunacy.

"We're going to have help," Wilkins said.

Sharpe's eyes lit up. "From who?"

"Gordon Bragg."

"Gordon Bragg?" Peterson asked. "What does he have to do with this?"

Everything, Wilkins thought. Bragg, the billionaire media mogul, was one of the few media bosses with the guts to confront Bryson, and his publications had savaged the "fascism" of the Authority in the months leading up to Operation Reichstag. So after the assassination attempt, Wilkins invited him to the White House. *I need your help*, Wilkins said. *We have to stop Bryson. You know that. And we have to hit him now, while he's on the run. But there's only so much I can do, so much I can say.*

Anything you need, Bragg had told him. *Just say the word, and I'll give you anything you need.*

And so Bragg had, ordering his publications to ramp up their focus on the Authority and on Bryson.

"I've been working with Bragg over the last few months," Wilkins said. "We've needed his resources in going after Bryson, someone in the media who can really hammer the bastard. And now we're going to need his help in figuring out who the hell Octavian is."

"We'll take all the help we can get," Sharpe said.

Wilkins nodded. *Damn right we will.* "I want you to take a look at this," he said. He pressed a button on a remote, and a flat-screen television flashed to life on the wall. "MASSIVE DEMONSTRATIONS ROCK NEW YORK CITY," beamed a graphic on the cable news channel.

The three craned their necks to view the broadcast. The broadcast carried live video of protesters in Times Square waving placards that read "*Repeal Total Information Awareness Now*," "*Give Us*

Jobs, Not Jail Sentences," "*Wilkins Is the Bankers' Assassin,*" and "*Authority Agents Are Nazis.*" A crowd of thousands, pulsating as it thumped placards, boomed a chant of "*Down with the Authority!*" in unison, followed by "*I am a subversive, make your move!*"

The broadcast then cut away to a counter-demonstration of lesser thousands, cut off from the larger set by barricades and nervous-looking NYPD officers, hoisting placards that read "*Aid and Comfort to Terrorism Is Terrorism,*" and "*Destroy the Enemy Within—Wipe Out Subversives.*" The counter-demonstrators chanted "*Wilkins, where are you? Send in the Authority!*"

Wilkins turned off the television. "This has been going on for weeks now," he said. "Demonstrations and counter-demonstrations, in every major city in the country. Getting closer and closer to an explosion. And I haven't ordered in the Authority, because we aren't supposed to be using them for crowd control anymore." He breathed deeply. "But make no mistake, this is Octavian at work. This is Octavian playing both sides, whipping people into a frenzy. He owns the subversives and the ultra-nationalists both, and neither side knows it." Wilkins shook his head. "This is what fifty percent youth unemployment gets us. And we're just a short step away—just a lit match thrown on some dry wood—just a short step away from a complete insurrection, a living hell for this country. The total breakdown of order and unity everywhere. Which is exactly what the son of a bitch wants."

Wilkins looked at Sharpe and Peterson. "We have to unmask Octavian," he said. "We die if we don't."

Chapter 4

"*Down with the Authority!*" the crowd chanted in Times Square. "*I am a subversive, make your move!*"

"Maybe someone should take them up on it," Johnny said as he walked hand-in-hand with Lizbeth. "We'll see how tough they are after a couple of tear gas canisters head their way."

"How fascist of you," Lizbeth said, rolling her eyes. "I think this is pretty awesome, actually. An uprising."

Johnny looked out at the crowd, bathed in the electric red and blue of the video screens beaming through the square. It was much bigger than he expected, at least a couple of thousand on a frosty December night. The protesters were young, between his brother Paul's age and his own, in their early to mid-twenties. They were all sorts, in hooded down jackets and sneakers, in smart overcoats and leather gloves and dress shoes, a mass of people, no different from the crowd swirling through the city at night, just now penned into Times Square and passionate and angry and edgy. Johnny regretted his "tear gas" comment.

He thought back to last December, when a girl had tried to recruit him to join a few dozen protesters, and all Johnny could do was crack a couple of jokes and offer to set her up with Paul. Later that night, a car bomb ripped through her "Freedom Now!" stand, and he'd watched as EMTs carted a covered stretcher from the scene.

Johnny winced at the memory. *And now there are thousands of protesters,* he thought.

He squeezed Lizbeth's hand. "I hope you're hungry," he said, leading her towards an Italian restaurant. "We're celebrating tonight."

A few minutes later, after breezing in courtesy of Johnny's reservation, they were sitting in the dining room. Lizbeth held up her glass, the pinot grigio sparkling in the chandelier light. "To me being awesome," she said.

Johnny smiled. "I'll drink to that," he said, holding up his glass with one hand and crossing his fingers with the other.

Lizbeth slapped away the crossed fingers. "Shut up. I had to stay up all night fabricating my resume to get this job. I stole it fair and square."

"To Darnell Williams and his fixings," Johnny said.

Lizbeth rolled her eyes, then laughed. "You're such a weirdo." She clinked Johnny's glass. "To Darnell Williams and his fixings."

Darnell Williams was the star of one of Lizbeth's articles when she was covering high school sports for the *New Jersey Tribune. Darnell Williams doesn't care much for turkey this Thanksgiving,* she'd written. *But the Linden High star quarterback cares about the fixings—fixing to lead his team to a championship, that is.* Johnny had teased her about the lead ever since.

And now here she was, a newly minted investigative journalist for *Rebellion*, a new online publication that was all jazzed up over stamping out corruption and battling tyranny. Its principal backer was Gordon Bragg, a billionaire who'd resolved to make a stand against the "creeping surveillance state being forced on us by the Bryson-Authority axis."

Johnny lowered his glass and took her hand in his, his eyes gliding up to hers. Lizbeth was still the same beauty who'd bewitched him the first week of freshman year, five-five and slim in her black dress, her brown hair falling to her shoulders in ribbons, her emerald eyes dancing behind black rectangular glasses.

"So let me tell you about my first assignment," Lizbeth said.

Johnny grinned. "Let me guess." He leaned in close. "Dork convention."

Lizbeth tickled him under his chin. "No, darlin'. No one wants to read about your fantasy baseball draft." She sipped her wine. "It's about the assassination attempt last year."

Johnny arched his eyebrows. "The assassination attempt… on the President?"

Lizbeth raised an open hand, striking a faux-celeb pose. "That's the one. But maybe I shouldn't say more. I can't share Pulitzer material with the general public."

"You going to make me beg?"

"I always do!" Lizbeth winked. "Well, you remember how it all happened, right? How that guy ran up to the stage and tackled the President right before the bullet hit?"

I might know something about it. "I remember."

"And you know how no one knows who he is? And it's this big mystery? I mean, he's such a hero, and the government is covering up his identity."

"Don't you think that's for his own good?"

"But what does the government have to hide?" Lizbeth asked. "I mean, he did his job. The public has a right to know who saved the President's life."

Goddamn it. "And you're going to find out who he is?"

Lizbeth smiled. "We're launching a full investigation starting tomorrow. And it's my story."

Awesome. Johnny raised his hand to signal the waiter. "Jack and Coke," he said.

Chapter 5

Hours later, Johnny reached for his father as he walked towards a wall blasting light. They were at the mouth of a long, formless corridor, and Giovanni Sr. was walking towards the light at the end. "Don't!" Johnny yelled. "I can get us out of here!"

His father's large frame ambled on, but then his shoulders heaved with indecision.

"Come back," Johnny said, choking up. "Please, Dad!"

Giovanni Sr. stopped walking. The light throbbed in the corridor as Johnny held his breath. And then his father began to turn around.

But just before Johnny could see his face, the corridor exploded in light, and he woke up.

He snapped awake in Lizbeth's bed, sitting up. Two years since his father had died, and he hadn't seen his face in a dream once.

"Are you all right, Gio?" Lizbeth mumbled, half-sleep beside him. "Did you have a bad dream?"

Johnny stroked her hair, then leaned down and kissed her on the forehead. "It's okay," he said. "Go back to sleep, sweetheart." Lizbeth snuggled back to sleep.

Johnny sat back up, gazing at the streetlight glow that poured through her window. Outside, the Hoboken street rang out with the occasional drunk incoherence of barhopping twenty-somethings yelling at each other.

He traced his finger over his shoulder, along the groove of the scar the assassin's gunshot had carved last spring. *Shoulder surgery,* he'd explained to Lizbeth. *From a two hundred-pound chick slamming into me at the plate in softball.*

Johnny unconsciously clenched his fist as he looked at the window. *You're out there somewhere, Gaines. And I'll never get rid of these nightmares until I find you.*

He looked down at Lizbeth, her shoulder exposed to the December night, and pulled up the sheet to keep her warm. He smiled. *This beautiful girl who's going to be investigating me starting tomorrow.*

"How did we ever live…" Lizbeth said, half-asleep, rustling the sheets next to him.

Johnny stroked her hair again. "What's that, sweetheart?"

"How did we ever live… before we found something so perfect?"

Johnny lay back down and wrapped his arms around her. "I don't know," he said, kissing her. "But we'll never have to live any other way again."

"Promise?"

Johnny stared at the window again.

"Promise me, Gio."

Johnny held his gaze on the window. "I promise," he said.

Chapter 6

Alexander Bryson strode through the bowels of the military prison, his heels clicking on the spit-shined floors as he walked past empty cells. Approaching the commanding officer, he wondered how much longer he'd wield this power that he'd spent a lifetime amassing.

A trifle, a turn of the screw, separated the power to walk through this corridor from the powerlessness of serving a sentence behind the bars that flanked him. Shepherd Moloch, his former right hand, languished in one of these cells tonight, while Bryson acknowledged a salute from his jailer. Moloch, the muscle behind Operation Reichstag, faced Wilkins's justice while Bryson, the architect, had slinked free.

"Colonel," Bryson said to the commanding officer. "Take me to the prisoner."

The colonel nodded, then about-faced and marched deeper into the gray cellblock, illumined by blotches of yellow electric light.

Bryson studied him as he followed. As of yesterday, this colonel was loyal to Wilkins. Not even Bryson could turn him. But Octavian saw to that. Octavian—who'd seen to everything from the beginning—made sure the colonel threw open the prison doors to Bryson.

It was Octavian who'd rescued him last spring, Octavian who'd pulled him from the rapids, Octavian who had given Bryson enough breathing room within the government and the media to survive Wilkins's onslaught and fight back politically. It was Octavian who had given his life meaning all those years ago, after Bryson returned home from years of special ops spent trying to avenge his wife's and daughter's deaths aboard Flight 11, which crashed into the World Trade Center on September 11, 2001.

Bryson was now in the fight of his life. After federal agents raided his home last May, Wilkins had addressed the nation and announced an investigation into "unknown interlopers who pull the strings of terror and hide in the shadows." Wilkins had not named Bryson, but the media was whirring with speculation after Moloch's arrest and the raid on Bryson's home.

So Bryson lunged for Wilkins's jugular. Wilkins had coddled Brigade 910 for years, he charged, and now was using the attacks as a pretext to settle a political score against Bryson. Wilkins was cementing his power through a national tragedy, through the near-massacre of thousands of his countrymen. The media, through Octavian's manipulation, provided Bryson cover to level his counter-charges, while Wilkins hesitated to move decisively against him until he had an airtight case.

As Bryson followed the colonel, Moloch came into view at last. The colonel approached two guards who clutched machine guns as they stood in front of Moloch's cell. They immediately stood at attention. "Open the cell and admit Director Bryson," the colonel ordered. He then about-faced to face Bryson.

Bryson nodded at him as he walked past. *Director Bryson.*

Wilkins had ousted him from the Authority last May, and replaced him with Peterson. Bryson then sued to regain his office. The case was now tied up in the courts as Bryson was relegated to the role of political commentator, haranguing Wilkins on cable news and in speeches before ever-swelling crowds. But here in this military prison, Bryson's writ ran.

Moloch arched his eyebrows, but didn't rise from his bench. "Seven months is a long time," he said.

Bryson considered the salutation as the colonel and guards left them alone. Moloch wore his detention well: he still had all of his jet-black hair, his body was still sculpted of sinews that had smashed roundhouse kicks into Peterson's face last spring, and murder and sadism still flashed in his beady brown eyes. In fact, they were flashing up at Bryson right now.

"On your feet," Bryson ordered.

Moloch didn't move. "Only if you're showing me out of here."

Insubordinate. "Well, that depends. I'll have to debrief you first."

Moloch glared at Bryson. "And what would you like to know?"

Bryson paused. "Tell me how they're treating you in here."

"Twenty-four hour solitary. No counsel. Sometimes Wilkins's people drop in to question me."

"And what have you told them?"

Moloch grinned. "That I'm going to eat their children when I get out of here."

Bryson didn't grin back. "What have they been asking you?"

"The better question is what they've been *telling* me, Bryson."

"And what's that?"

"That they have a nuclear-bomb-proof case against Alexander Bryson for sedition. And that I can either testify at the trial of the century, or die alone in this hole."

Bryson weighed that. Maybe they'd built their case; but he was betting they hadn't—not yet. "Tell me what they've been asking you."

"Little holes in Operation Reichstag—how this person knew that person, how the funds moved, all that. But they have it all. Just not all the links in the chain, not yet. That's what they need me for." Moloch sharpened his gaze. "And there's one other thing they're after."

"What's that?"

"Octavian. They want Octavian."

Bryson nodded, surprised. So they'd figured out that someone had been giving Bryson orders. And they were going to risk everything to go after Octavian and take down the whole superstructure.

Bryson smiled at the idea. *That'll be their undoing.* "When was the last time they were here?" he asked.

"Just a few days ago."

"And you've told them nothing?"

"Not a word."

Bryson nodded. "You've done well, Moloch. And now you've earned your reward."

He whipped a handgun from his waistband and blasted a bullet between Moloch's eyes, splattering his brains on the cell wall. Moloch hit the floor and thrashed. Bryson stood over the former Special Agent in Charge of the Authority New York Field Office, glowering at him through ice-gray eyes as he perished. He then dropped the handgun and turned to the guards.

"Attend to Mr. Moloch's suicide," Bryson ordered.

The guards rushed to Moloch as Bryson exited the cell and walked up to the colonel. "Execute the operation like we discussed," he told him.

Without another word, Bryson strolled away as the colonel and the guards set about the task of "suiciding" Moloch. A forensic expert would be along to reconstruct the scene: Moloch had lunged at a guard; there'd been a struggle; he'd then grabbed the gun and shot himself. And the video footage, of course, would be scrubbed.

A moment ago, Moloch was the only person in America besides Bryson who could identify Octavian. It had taken seven months, but Bryson had finally penetrated the prison and punished him for his failure against Peterson atop the World Trade Center last May.

Soon Bryson would penetrate the White House and punish Wilkins for his crimes—and wipe out Peterson, Fullerton, and Luca along the way.

Chapter 7

"Good afternoon, court eunuchs," Gordon Bragg said as he stood at a lectern, heckling the gaggle of old-media lackeys who were covering the press conference he'd called to roll out his new publication, *Rebellion.* Clutching a sledge hammer in one hand, he winked at his ravishing blonde wife, Courtney, then gestured to a red curtain behind him that cloaked a sheath of plate glass. "So glad you could make it."

Bragg grinned at the hacks who had assembled in the ballroom of the Prescott Hotel, the same room where assassins had attempted to murder President Wilkins last May. "Court eunuchs" had been his preferred term for these idiots of late, these shiny Ivy League denizens of the Washington-New York corridor, defenders of the corrupt media complex that Bragg would vanquish for once and for all. These journalists were "court eunuchs," he'd concluded, because they defended any member of the Beltway elite, regardless of party, who fed them stories and invited them to Georgetown cocktail parties—Alexander Bryson chief among them. They had gone beyond slanting the news; this was something else, something far more vile, far more rotten. This was a conspiracy of silence in favor of a monster who had tried to kill thousands of Americans last spring.

"So today, we launch a publication that I've named *Rebellion,*" Bragg said. "You'll soon regard it as a menace. *Rebellion* will do the one thing you cannot do, that you will not do: It will tell the truth. We'll report the affairs of the day from the bottom up, in all its unvarnished imperfection, as you continue to peddle received wisdom from Washington chieftains who shower leaks on you if you prostitute yourselves sufficiently. With the financial backing of Bragg Enterprises, and more importantly, with the relentless determination of the army of citizen journalists that I've recruited to beam the truth to the world, we'll change the face of media in this twenty-first century. Today I stand athwart you all, and I launch a rebellion—a rebellion against fascism, against the tyranny of the self-appointed elite. Today I launch *Rebellion.*"

Bragg threw his shoulders back in anticipation of the first question. He stood before his antagonists as a captain of industry, a general in Wilkins's war against tyranny. He was sixty-one years old, six feet tall, and slim. His straight silver hair was layered in a Caesar fringe, silver stubble peppering his tanned face, his blue eyes exploding with vitality. He wore an Italian charcoal suit with a starched white shirt, no tie.

Bragg had fought through childhood and adolescence in a rough-hewn corner of Brooklyn in the 1960s and 1970s, pulling himself up into the Ivy League in the early 1980s, dropping out in his sophomore year. He then threw himself into the Information Age technological revolution that would alter the course of history. He had a brilliant mind for technology, but an even better mind for business, and had a knack for picking winners. As one investment after another paid off, he found himself meeting other difference makers of the age; Bragg was a principal backer of key ventures in the personal computer revolution, the internet revolution, the high-speed internet revolution.

In the 2000s, Bragg had figured out the meaning of it all, had figured out how his investments of the last two decades could be channeled into technologies that would democratize the planet. He was a key backer of Google, Youtube, and Facebook, the iron triangle of the era.

And in the great Arab revolutions of 2011 that convulsed the Middle East and North Africa, Bragg saw the death of the mass media, the ossification of newspapers and television networks that had told people what to think. It occurred to Bragg that the world had reached an end of history of sorts, a dreamed-of epoch in which the people would tell their own stories, bottom-up rather than top-down, through citizen reporting, the unfettered flow of information, and the exposition of truth.

In the latter part of the 2010s, Bragg, already a billionaire, found his celebrity. He led the charge in harnessing the energies of the citizen-reporting movement into profit-making enterprises, his brand of online publications overthrowing the old dailies in every city in America and penetrating markets around the world. His reporters were the hardscrabble gumshoes of the 1920s, not the over-professional eggheads of the 2000s, and they were relentless in their pursuit of the littlest and the grandest corruptions, from the graft-taking cop to the seditious Director of the Anti-Subversion Authority. Bragg became a figure of global renown, personally flying his private jet to the Horn of Africa to deliver famine aid, showing up unannounced to sundry "Occupy" protests in the world's metropolises to deliver perorations against the excesses of greed. In time, he made plans to launch *Rebellion*, an anti-fascist publication, and to build his own renegade cable news network.

And in the darkest hours of 2023, Bragg found the crusade of his life, pledging his life to Wilkins's cause of opposing Bryson's machinations. Bragg's imprints called for the abolition of the Authority and the defeat of Total Information Awareness, savaging Bryson and seeking to halt his rise in politics. Bragg toured the country delivering addresses to that effect, and his wife Courtney, twenty-three years his junior and beaming at him beside him on stage today, worked the subject into her Best Supporting Actress acceptance speech at the Academy Awards. But ultimately, Bragg had failed to move the needle of public opinion much; Bryson was inexplicably, supernaturally powerful, and after years of extolling the virtues of "bottom-up", Bragg struggled to turn the tide of public opinion against Bryson and the Authority. But *Rebellion* would change that at last—and President Wilkins had taken notice, inviting Bragg to the Oval Office to discuss stopping Bryson.

Bragg pointed out the first questioner, some blond pinhead in the first row who wore a pink tie. "Marcus Finch, *New York Times*," the reporter introduced himself.

"Ahh, Finch," Bragg said. "Good article on urban poverty last week. How's life on the Upper East side?"

Finch grimaced, then gestured towards Bragg. "The sledgehammer," he said. "And the red curtain. What's going on?"

Bragg smiled in triumph. "I'm glad you asked," he said. "Today I'll do what you all should have done years ago. Jessica, the curtain, please."

Bragg's secretary pulled a rope, and the curtain fell. It yielded to an eight-foot-tall panel of plate glass bearing the seal of the United States Anti-Subversion Authority.

"Today I'll swing a hammer at the glass wall you've erected in front of this country's most disgusting secrets," Bragg said. He turned to the glass panel and squared up, gripping the sledgehammer like a baseball bat in a left-handed batter's stance. "Down with the Authority!" he yelled. "I am a subversive, make your move!"

Bragg hurled the hammer at the glass, which shattered into shards on impact.

Chapter 8

That night, Bragg pondered his glass of scotch as he leaned back in his chair on the patio outside his Malibu home. The laughter of his wife's Hollywood friends, drinking the night away inside, danced over the murmur of the Pacific waves tumbling onto the beach below.

He glanced up at the panels of floor-to-ceiling windows fronting the patio, at the partygoers holding forth in his living room. There was his wife Courtney, her exquisite body poured into a little black dress, her long blonde hair shimmering, laughing at what no doubt was the wittiest joke ever told. Making her laugh was Josh Saxon, an A-list director she used to screw, whose latest blockbuster portrayed a team of Authority agents busting up a Brigade 910 cell. Next to him was the leading man who played the hero in that film, a muscle-bound meathead with a fondness for snorting powder up his nose. Across the room was a music industry titan whose bag was auto-erotic asphyxiation, introducing his latest signing—some tatted-up L.A.-based DJ whose beats were going to revolutionize the world of hip-hop—to a gaggle of coked-up female admirers who were batting the eyelashes of their saucer-shaped eyes.

They fluttered through the room, like grains of sparkle dust—the actor who cut PSAs promoting gun control, but appeared in movies where he gunned down bad guys by the dozen; the producer who wanted to tax "the rich" at ninety percent, but hid all of his assets offshore; the actress who lectured her fans on the urgency of climate change, but flew her favorite sushi in from New York on private jets twice a week; and the hangers-on, so many hangers-on, selling themselves for a few minutes of access.

Every single one of them had pledged fealty to Taylor Quade, governor of Indiana, who was running for president against Wilkins on a platform of healing the nation's wounds, bringing everyone together, and showing empathy for all—and little else, as far as Bragg could tell. He was the front-runner for his party's nomination.

Bragg raised his glass and winked at Courtney; she winked back. She was a good woman with a good heart, better than the creeps in the room, and he understood that these were the kinds of friends she had to have, the kinds she'd always have. But it had all gotten to be a little much tonight, and he'd excused himself to go sit out on the patio.

Bragg walked to the edge of his balcony overlooking the Pacific. He sipped his scotch as he watched waves of moonlight glide into the beach.

This country's in trouble, he thought. *Deep trouble.*

The grandees in his living room had the star power, and the money, to propel Quade to the presidency. And if Quade ousted Wilkins, America would be over, finished.

There would be nothing to stop Bryson if Quade prevailed, certainly not Quade himself, who was too fixated on building up his cult of personality. *Bryson would win!* Bragg wanted to scream at the vapid automatons in his living room, *Bryson would win if you idiots make Quade president.*

But what did they care? Sure, they all mumbled about "civil liberties" every now and then, but not a single one of them gave a damn about Bryson, the Authority, or what was at stake. What did it matter to them? Was there anything about the Authority—its snooping on private citizens through their laptop microphones, its monitoring of their web surfing and debit card transactions, its beating of protesters—that would get in the way of their movie deals, their clubbing, their drugs, their awards shows where they all congratulated each other for enlightening the unwashed rubes who consumed their "art"?

They'd be hip for backing Quade, who himself would become hip in the process. It was like a brand extension for them—a "hip" president. And blue-collar Wilkins, who'd nearly taken a bullet to stop Bryson's dictatorship, would be tossed on the ash heap.

It could happen, Bragg thought. *Quade could actually win.*

The American people were scared, weary, worn-out. Brigade 910's rampage had terrorized them over the last few years, and the attempted Project Orion attack had whipped that terror into a frenzy. The economy was weak, with high unemployment and an unfathomably massive debt, the servicing of which was now so expensive that local governments couldn't deliver basic services, such a drag on the budget that the country's infrastructure was decaying. And along had come Quade, spouting bromides, playing the white knight.

Bragg shook his head. *The walls are closing in on Wilkins*, he thought. *He has to make a move. If he wants to beat Bryson, he'd better make a move.*

Chapter 9

"And God bless us, every one," Johnny said, running the carving knife over the fork as he stood over the Christmas turkey. He glanced at Paul. "Even porcupine-head over here."

Paul grinned. "Good one," he said. "Shouldn't a guy be unwrapping your package right now?"

Marissa grimaced, then smiled politely at Lizbeth and Paul's girlfriend Julia, seated beside her. "What a lovely blessing," she said. "Just cut the damn turkey."

Johnny sliced the turkey into hunks. "I was just kidding," he said as he heaped a helping on Paul's plate. "There's nothing wrong with that spiky hair of yours. I mean, you could kill a man by head-butting him. That's pretty cool."

"You really have to excuse Johnny," Marissa said to Julia. "He's a moron."

"I'm not a moron," Johnny said, doling out turkey. "I'm just full of the Christmas spirit. There's nothing like Christmas with the family… even the Paulinator here."

"I can think of better things," Paul said.

Johnny sat down and winked at Lizbeth. *Christmas 2023*, he thought, *and goddamn, am I lucky to be alive.* He thought back to last Christmas—he was nursing a cut on his head from an Authority officer beating the shit out of him in Manhattan for jumping the barricade at the scene of a car bombing. *A box fell out of the closet and hit me*, he'd explained to his mother and brother.

And then in the months after Christmas—he'd survived a shootout with Brigade 910 at a safehouse; abduction and torture at the hands of Sigma, a Brigade 910 leader; a grenade thrown into his SUV the morning of Operation Reichstag; and of course, the gunshot to the shoulder. And just two weeks ago, a brawl with Ivanov.

Johnny smiled at Marissa and Paul. His mother was five-four, her blue eyes vital, her hair in a short bob, so much younger than her fifty-five years. And Paul was nineteen now, a sophomore, skinny with spiky brown hair and his mother's blue eyes.

I could pack it in right here, Johnny thought. *Forget about Gaines, forget about those terrorist punks, just go to law school or something and enjoy life… maybe go into business with that fat bastard Billy, now that he's back from Miami. And every Christmas, I could chill with Lizbeth, Mom, and Paul, and not think about how many times I died during the year.*

Johnny studied his brother's girlfriend. She was petite, five-one and skinny, her brown hair cropped short, a stud adorning her nostril.

"So Julia," Johnny said. "I'm dying to know, what moves did Paul pull on you to win you over? Did he temporarily blind you or something?"

Lizbeth slapped his arm.

"Well," Julia said, smiling at Paul. "He's the smartest guy in class."

Oh man, she digs him, Johnny thought. "The smartest… guy in class. What class, history of Pokemon?"

Johnny was just being an asshole now. Paul was a genius, especially at math and science—the top of his class in high school. He had appalled the graduation crowd by calling President Wilkins an "ass jockey" during his valedictorian speech. And now he was in his sophomore year at college, excelling at chemistry.

Johnny began to wolf down his turkey and pasta. He was just giving Paul a hard time. If someone was going to buy Luca stock, investing in Paul was the smart move. Johnny could be dead in a week; Paul would probably be a rocket scientist someday. Paul was way smarter, gentle, and easygoing. He'd make something out of the family name, while Johnny was screwing around with Gaines and other low-lives.

"So Lizbeth mentioned that you guys checked out the protesters the other night," Paul said. "Did you see us there?"

Johnny nearly choked on a piece of rigatoni. "No," he said. "I didn't know you were down with the cause."

"Well, I have an IQ over eighty and a conscience. So of course I'm down with it."

"And why's that?"

"Because this Total Information Awareness Act is bullshit, man. It's—"

"Language," Marissa said. "Christmas language."

Paul collected himself. "It's bull feces," he said. Marissa groaned. "It's totally fascist," he continued. "All they're using it for is to keep surveillance on kids my age, to keep us down because we're standing up to them, because we're sick of the bankers hoarding money while no one can get a job. You should quit the Authority, man. Go fix printers for someone else."

"I don't fix printers," Johnny said. "I—fix printers and clean guns."

Marissa shot him a glance. *Yes, I know you don't believe me, Mom,* Johnny thought.

"You should join us," Julia said. "It's totally a nonviolent movement. All we want is for them to repeal the new law and lay off the fascism. We didn't start this whole war, Brigade 910 did. And now because of Brigade 910, they look at everyone under twenty-five like they're a terrorist."

"You're telling me there are no Brigade 910 sympathizers out in that crowd with you?" Johnny asked.

"I haven't met any. Even if we believe in a lot of the same things, none of us want to do this violently."

"If anyone gets violent, it won't be us," Paul said. "Remember that."

"Well *I* think the whole thing is great," Lizbeth said. "Someone has to make a stand."

"And what about the counter-protesters?" Marissa asked.

"They're sick," Paul said. "Real Nazi types. Bryson is their hero. If they had their way, we'd all be in jail."

"But they can't all be Nazis," Johnny said. "You and Julia, and all of you out there, you guys aren't part of Brigade 910, are you?" *The answer is always somewhere in the middle, right?* he thought.

"They're total fascists, dude. Believe it."

Johnny shrugged. "Just try not to get mixed up in it. If you want to make a difference, go win a chemistry Nobel Prize or something."

Paul shook his head. "God, you're old, dude. Did you know you've got a couple of grays on the side of your head?" He grinned. "Lizbeth, check it out. Your boyfriend totally has gray hairs."

Lizbeth giggled. "It makes him look sophisticated," she said.

"I don't have gray hairs!" Johnny said.

"And ear hair, too," Paul said. "They flare out of your ears when you get mad, like a party favor."

"Eat a dic—"

"Christmas language," Marissa said. "I think your gray hair and your ear hair make you look handsome, Johnny."

Johnny shoved pasta in his mouth. "I hate Christmas," he said, his mouth full.

"Anyway, you need to come party with us this semester," Paul said. "You and Lizbeth. Relive the glory days. Play flip cup with some actual college kids."

"We'd love to," Lizbeth said. "Maybe it'll turn Johnny's hair back to brown."

Johnny rolled his eyes.

After dinner, Johnny stayed behind in the kitchen as Lizbeth, Paul, and Julia piled into the living room to watch Christmas movies.

"You should've seen the look on your face when Paul said you have gray hair," Marissa said. "You do, you know." She started clearing the table.

"Sit down for a minute," Johnny said. "Don't worry about the dishes. I'll take care of it."

Marissa sat down, sipping a cup of tea. "What is it?" she said. "It must be a matter of national security, if you're actually going to do the dishes."

Johnny looked at her for a moment. "I want you to take this." He passed a check across the table.

"What's this?" Marissa slipped on her reading glasses and studied the check.

"Rent."

Marissa passed the check back. "Johnny, you know I can't—"

"Yes you can, Mom. It's been months since you were laid off. Just take the check so I can sleep at night, please."

"I'll find something, sweet pea. It's just a matter of time."

"I know you will. But until then, let me help you out. Then we can call it even for you giving birth to me."

Marissa laughed, nearly spitting out her tea. "You'd have to give me ten million dollars to make up for *that* childbirth."

Johnny passed the check back. "Just for now. Until you find something."

Marissa took the check and studied it again. "Just until then," she said. "Where are you getting this money, anyway?" She narrowed her eyes, then frowned. "Must be all those printers you've been fixing. Or whatever else you do."

Johnny looked her in the eye. "That's all I do," he said. But they both knew it was a lie. The Authority had compensated Johnny pretty well over the last year, paying him bonuses out of a secret slush fund for his troubles in carrying out black bag operations and nearly getting killed a few times.

Marissa returned the volley with her blue eyes. "Sure you do." She paused for a moment, then gestured to the living room, just as Lizbeth was laughing at the movie playing inside. "I really like her, Johnny," she said. "I think you've found your girl."

Johnny smiled. "I think so, too."

"Which means you need to be responsible. Put away childish things."

"I know."

Marissa brushed her hand over Johnny's. "I remember that conversation we had last spring. When you came to me after you finished reading your father's diary. *I'm gonna kill them all*, you said."

"Mom—"

"I think about it all the time, actually. Because I believed you when you said it. And I think you might actually be trying."

Johnny shook his head. "I'm not a killer, Mom."

"That's right. Not yet. And I'm telling you now: Don't become one." Marissa sipped her tea, her hand shaking the cup a bit, clinking it against the saucer. "Revenge is like poison, Johnny. It'll turn you into someone you're not, someone different from my son or Paul's brother or Lizbeth's boyfriend. Someone different from Giovanni Luca's son." Marissa gestured towards the living room again. "The stakes are higher now. Don't go down that road. Just live a normal, boring life. That's the best way to get back at them—to be the man your father wanted you to be."

He wanted me to be someone who'd do justice, Johnny thought. "I'm working on it," he said, as Lizbeth and Paul whooped at the movie in the living room. "I'm doing the best I can, Mom."

Chapter 10

He gripped twelve o'clock on the steering wheel with his left hand, his left shoulder muscle bulging under his polo shirt, his right hand clutching a handgun and resting on the passenger seat. He furrowed his eyebrows beneath the nylon stocking that clung to his face, his eyes looking through the tinted windows of the SUV.

They're taking too long, he thought as he glared at the bank. *Amateurs.*

A moment later, three of them came tearing through the bank's exit, clad in black with nylon masks, brandishing machine guns and hauling duffel bags. They jumped in the truck. "Go, go!" screamed the one that jumped into the passenger seat.

The driver didn't respond, or flinch. He snapped the gear into drive, spun the wheels, and rocketed down the street.

As he ripped through the thoroughfare, he pulled out his mobile phone and dialed a number; a second later, a bomb exploded in the bank, incinerating the lobby and devastating the structural integrity of the building. He dialed two more numbers, detonating a bomb in the town's police station and in a secret FBI post across town.

"What the fuck are you doing?" one of the robbers yelled from the backseat.

Again, the driver didn't answer. He arced hard left, racing down another street, then swerved right, headed towards the Texas highway that would taken them straight to the Mexican border.

A few minutes later, he snapped off the highway onto an exit for a campsite, bounding along a dirt road and boring through brush until he came to a clearing.

"What the fuck—" the passenger started to say, until the driver put a bullet through his head.

Without a word or hesitation, he turned to the two in the back and blew each of their brains out. He slipped out of the driver's seat, grabbed the duffel bags, and loaded them into the trunk of a sports car he'd deposited at the campsite. He yanked off the nylon mask and tossed it into the SUV, then dropped into the sports car and sped off.

As he drove, he pulled out the phone again and dialed. The SUV exploded.

He pulled onto the highway, headed for the border. At the checkpoint, a guard on his payroll would wave him through, and in Mexico, loyalists would launder the money in the duffel bags.

The money would go to more guns, more bombs, more minions on the payroll. A revolution was coming.

As he blazed towards the border, he gripped the wheel tightly for a second, his shoulder muscle bulging again. He thought of Johnny Luca.

Luca was after him, to avenge his father. He'd gotten as far as Ivanov and would soon visit the others. And when he was through with them, he'd come—he'd surely come.

Jack Gaines—Hyperion—smiled as he drove on. What Luca didn't know was that he had him under full surveillance, and he'd be waiting. And when Luca came at last, he'd die, just like his pig father.

Chapter 11

"Now don't fuck this up, Lead Mag," Fullerton commanded into Johnny's headset.

Johnny fingered the microphone at his chin. "The only thing I'm going to fuck up," he said, "is your face, if you call me that one more goddamn time."

"Do you or do not have lead in your shoulder, sucka?"

"They removed the bul—"

"Ladies," Special Agent in Charge Wolfe thundered over the headsets. "Am I the commanding officer on a counterterrorism operation, or am I babysitting a couple of damn kids?"

Johnny clutched his shotgun and crept towards the subject's hovel, the driveway swallowed in darkness, the rotting front door laid bare in the glow of his headband flashlight. "He started it," he said, the 1:00 a.m. January wind lashing him.

"Aw, Wolfe," Agent Kleibeck called behind Johnny. "Luca's just scared because it's his first time through the door. He's got a bad habit of catching bullets."

"Shut up, Kleibeck," Johnny said. "Let's do this."

"The kid wants to get down to business, sir," Agent Austin said over the headset. "So I think you should give the order."

"All right, on my mark," Wolfe said. "Remember—we don't knock, and we don't announce. Total Information Awareness, all the way up the ass." He paused. "Ready?"

"Ready," Johnny said.

"Ready," Fullerton said.

"Ready," said Agents Kleibeck, Austin, Miller, and Lundquist, one after the other.

These were seven of the agents Peterson had deployed to halt Operation Reichstag last spring, housed on Colonel Shay Rutherford's army base in the days leading up to the attack, handpicked more for their loyalty than their abilities. Peterson had thrown them up in desperation against Bryson's best thugs, and they'd risen to the occasion, surviving a grenade attack and a rooftop sniper, and in Johnny's case, storming to a hotel ballroom stage to tackle the President's would-be assassin the instant before she shot him.

Now Peterson had welded them into his core counter-terror force, hunting down and apprehending Brigade 910 terrorists, dismantling the group one operative at a time. Wolfe, who had replaced Peterson as Newark Special Agent in Charge, was a forty-five year old black man, a former Secret Service Agent thick in the shoulders and thin on the scalp. Last May, he led the unit tasked with identifying the President's assassin in the hotel ballroom.

Kleibeck was thirty-seven, redheaded, wiry, and quick, on loan from the FBI; Austin, thirty-five, ruddy-faced, an ATF sharpshooter; Lundquist, also thirty-five, built like a bouncer with a shaved head and goatee, an Afghan War vet most recently busting heads for the Secret Service before this assignment; Miller, thirty-four, a U.S. Marshal with a knack for hauling in fugitives; and the babies, Fullerton and Luca, twenty-eight and twenty-five, the kids who'd saved the world last spring.

Tonight they were all clad in black, stalking towards the Plainfield, New Jersey home of Brad Chase, a Brigade 910 grunt who'd become a bit too close to going operational. The team had lifted as much intelligence from him via surveillance as they could, and whatever diminishing returns he could provide at this point weren't worth the risk of the spoiled rich kid reject detonating a car bomb to strike at the "crypto-fascist Wilkins regime."

Johnny crept towards the front door, the wind whipping him again, Kleibeck and Austin bearing battering rams behind him. They were to break down the front door, and Johnny was to rush inside, risking a bullet as the first man in, and apprehend the subject. Lundquist and Miller were to break down the back door, with Fullerton rushing in.

"All right," Wolfe said. "Breach the doors."

The pit opened in Johnny's stomach. His first time through the door... and he was, after all, a lead-mag.

Kleibeck and Austin charged past him and slammed the battering ram into the door, splintering it off the frame, and then nailed it again, breaking it down. Johnny hurled a stun grenade inside, waiting a moment for its percussion blast of light and smoke, and then surged inside. "Anti-Subversion Authority!" he yelled, every hair on his body sticking up like wires of a steel brush. "You're under arrest!"

I guess it would help if I could see the subject before I told him he was under arrest, Johnny thought. The living room looked as if the sun had exploded inside.

And then the subject emerged through the light and smoke in all his frat boy glory, a twenty-one-year old white kid. Johnny raised the shotgun. "On your knees, douchebag, and hands in the air," he said.

Chase sank to his knees, but did not raise his hands.

Fullerton burst into the living room, Lundquist and Miller in tow. "Put your hands in the air before I count to zero," Fullerton said. "Three. Two. One—"

"Fascist *fuck*!" Chase yelled, pulling out a knife and slashing Fullerton's shin.

"Motherfucker!" Fullerton screamed, falling back and clutching his leg.

Johnny's reaction was automatic. He cracked his shotgun butt into Chase's skull, knocking him to the floor. He kicked the knife away, yanked Chase up, and then punched him in the eyebrow, his knuckles smashing into Chase's eyebrow ring and splitting the skin. He then flipped him on his stomach, plunged a knee into his back, and zip-tied him. Then Johnny stood up and kicked him in the ribs.

"Luca, relax—" Miller said.

"Check on Fullerton," Johnny said, breathing heavy. "And someone load this scumbag into the truck."

"I'm fine," Fullerton said, pulling himself to his feet and limping towards Johnny. "Congratulations," he said.

Johnny trained his shotgun on Chase. "For what?"

"For not catching lead through the door!"

Johnny whirled around to his partner and best friend as Lundquist yanked Chase to his feet and frog-marched him out the door. Fullerton was taller and thicker than Johnny, his head shaved, a black man from the Newark ghetto. "Fuck off, Fullerton," Johnny said, smiling. He leaned into the microphone.

"Wolfe, I'm sending Fullerton out to you. He got cut up in his leg a little bit. We should check on him."

"Don't listen to this punk, sir," Fullerton said. "Don't worry about me. We got Chase. Lundquist's taking him out to you right now."

"Good," Wolfe said. "We'll take him in. You'd better get out here too, with that leg of yours. Luca, Kleibeck, Austin, Miller—effect the search."

Fullerton rolled his eyes. "The leg's fine, boss," he said. He groaned. "It's Luca's damn fault, anyway. He should've shot him." He smiled at Johnny. "All right, superstar. Time for you to do some evidence collection like the rest of us common folk."

"Catch you later, knife-mag," Johnny said, chuckling. *I'm the man*, he thought.

Fullerton shook his head. "Keep trying, Luca. Try and crack one good joke by the end of 2024." He limped away.

Johnny headed towards Chase's bedroom as the others fanned throughout the house. He pushed open the door and clicked on the light, and Chase's bedroom revealed itself in all its bachelor-terrorist ignominy. *I don't think this dude gets laid much*, Johnny thought, grimacing at the carpet strewn with dust balls and boxer shorts.

In the corner was the only piece of evidence worth seizing, Chase's laptop, a screensaver bouncing across the monitor. Johnny would pack that up last, after poring over every drawer and shelf in the house. He'd done enough of these searches now to know that the rote search would turn up nothing more than the odd bag of pot, and that everything they needed would be on the computer.

Johnny slid open the top drawer and swept his hand through Chase's underwear; nothing. *I hope this dude does his laundry*. He shook his head. *Underwear duty*.

Just then, the laptop screensaver danced across the corner of his eye. *That's funny*, he thought.

Johnny crossed the room to the computer, and a pit burst open in his stomach. "Jesus Christ," he said.

It wasn't a screensaver on the screen; it was a photo slideshow. Johnny watched as a photo of the outside of his apartment building glided across the screen. His shoulders stiffened as a photo of Johnny bounding out the front door slid across the screen in its place. *What's going on?*

The photo yielded to a shot of Johnny and Lizbeth out in Manhattan a few weeks ago, which gave way to a snap of just Lizbeth, outside her office building, which gave way to an image of Marissa leaving her garden apartment.

Johnny stabbed the pause button on the screen, halting the picture of his mother in place. "Fullerton," he called. He clicked on his microphone. "Fullerton," he called again. "Get over here now."

"We're trying to get a band-aid on Fullerton here," Wolfe said. "What is it?"

Johnny sat down on the bed, his eyes fixed on the picture of his mother. "I… I found something in the bedroom, sir."

A moment later, Kleibeck, Austin, and Miller appeared at the door. "What is it?" Kleibeck asked.

Fullerton hobbled in. "What is it?" he echoed.

Johnny pointed at the screen, his hand trembling, then turned to face them. "My mother," he said. "And he's got more. Pictures of me, my place. A picture of me and my girlfriend out in the city a couple of weeks ago."

Fullerton looked at the others, then limped in front of them, anguish in his eyes. Johnny knew that look. It was the same look Fullerton wore when he ran up to Johnny after he'd been shot.

"We have a lot to tell you, Luca," he said. "There's something you need to know."

Chapter 12

"When are we going to have a meeting about good news, for a change?" Johnny asked Peterson and Fullerton as they sat in Peterson's office. "Like world peace? Or me getting a raise?"

"Those bonuses weren't enough for you?" Peterson said. "If the Authority weren't an unconstitutional proto-fascist agency that has to be destroyed, I could've been fired by the inspector general for that… if we had an inspector general."

"Base comp, boss. It's all about the base comp."

Fullerton laughed, a pair of crutches propped up on the chair next to him, his right trouser leg thick from the wrapping around his wounded shin. "If he gets a raise, then I get one," he said. "Federal lockstep, boss. Plus I deserve a premium for being better at dodging bullets than he is."

"I really don't think you should allow him to joke about me getting shot," Johnny said to Peterson. "It's creating a hostile work environment."

"I'll take it under advisement," Peterson said, grinning.

Johnny studied his boss. He was the Authority Director now, living in Washington, though he still kept an office in the Newark Field Office. In ways his life had to be easier now, since he wasn't fighting Bryson in the shadows and leading a secret life. At least he was a public figure now, holding press conferences and all of that. That seemed like a good way to keep himself, and by extension Johnny and the rest of the team, alive—by being a public figure. But it also had to be pretty stressful—he was the director of an agency full of people still loyal to Bryson, and now he had to play the D.C. political game. Johnny didn't see much of Peterson these days.

"So those pictures you saw on Chase's computer," Peterson said. "They're building a dossier on you. We've known this for awhile. That's part of the reason we hit Chase last night—not only because he was a Brig 910 about to go operational, but because we knew he was one of their intelligence guys keeping tabs on you."

Johnny nodded. "How come no one told me this before we went in last night?"

"Well, we didn't expect Chase to have a goddamn slideshow of you as his screensaver. We figured we'd just evaluate the evidence and see how much they had, and then tell you on a need-to-know basis. And besides, with the way you've been acting lately, you might've killed him if you knew beforehand."

"What do you mean, 'the way I've been acting'?"

"You roughed him up pretty good," Fullerton said.

Johnny turned to him. "So?"

"So that's not how we do business, now that I'm the director," Peterson said. "That's how Bryson's men work, not us."

"The guy cut Fullerton! He had a knife!"

"You know the protocol, Luca. You went beyond disarming him. They had to pull you off him."

Johnny shook his head, but he couldn't argue. He glanced around the office for a moment, cooling off. It was a big room, with Peterson's desk at one end and a small conference table at the other. The pictures on the wall showed Peterson in his Secret Service days, aboard Air Force One, at White House press conferences, escorting the Pope. In a cabinet behind Peterson there was a Russian officer's cap, a plaque from Tel Aviv police, and an I-shaped clock from Egypt, with the crouching figure of a lion with a pharaoh's face sitting on top.

"So why are they building a dossier?" Johnny asked.

"You're very interesting to Brig 910," Peterson said. "Which means you're interesting to Bryson, and he's filtering it down to the group through Gaines. First of all, it's because Bryson knows that you're the one who stopped the attack last year, which must have Bryson thinking you're some kind of super agent."

"Of course, we know the truth," Fullerton said. "You're just a lucky-ass fool."

Johnny held a hand up. "That's no way to talk to a superstar."

"And *besides that*," Peterson continued, "it's because of your father's work in investigating them, and because of what you know about your father, and the motive for revenge you have." Peterson's eyes bore into Johnny's. "And also because you're actually out *seeking* revenge."

"What are you talking about?"

"Come on, Luca," Fullerton said. "We *know*."

"We haven't kept close tabs on you, because we're trying to treat you like a responsible adult," Peterson said, "and because you haven't actually killed someone yet. But I know what you're up to. And lo and behold, if you go around breaking into terrorists' homes and conducting your own covert operations, they start thinking of how to deal with you. And they start thinking of how to deal with your family and your girlfriend too."

"You'd want to get your hands on Gaines too, if you were me," Johnny said.

"But Luca—I *do* want to get my hands on him. And I *do* want to kill him. But let him die by lethal injection after a jury convicts him. Or if it has to be violently, then let him die in a shootout if he's resisting arrest. But we don't do vendettas, and I won't permit you to carry one out."

We'll see about that. Johnny squared his jaw. "Then let's bring him in, boss. The Authority bulletins say he pulled that bank job in Texas a few days ago. Everyone knows he's working out of Mexico, out of the border down there. Send us down there and we'll collar him."

"Worry about your jurisdiction—not Texas. If we had actionable intelligence, we'd make a move on him. Believe me when I tell you that I want to bring him in as much as you do—not only is the asshole financing terror attacks, but he's embedding Brig 910 with these protests going on and agitating everything, stirring up unrest. But the reality is, we've got nothing concrete on his location. And if we did, we'd deploy a hundred agents to bring him in—not just you and Fullerton."

"What do you know about Gaines, Luca?" Fullerton asked.

Everything. "He calls himself Hyperion," Johnny said. "He's twenty-eight, turning twenty-nine this year. He took over operations for Brigade 910 after we killed Sigma. He's a smart guy—a Harvard dropout. And he was in the Army."

"Luca, he was an *Army Ranger*, man. Special forces. Remember, I was undercover inside Brigade 910 for a minute—I know this shit. Gaines has been deployed in Afghanistan and throughout Central Asia, and he's trained to live on his own in the wilderness and kill al Qaeda guys with his bare hands. We know of at least a few covert ops he pulled when he was on our side, and it was some serious shit. And he went to Harvard—think about that. He's smarter than you or me, or Sigma, or Bryson. He's got a genius-level IQ. On top of all of that, he believes in his cause. He thinks he's leading an anarchist revolution, and that he's the only one who can lead that revolution. He's named himself Hyperion, who was the lord of light, the father of the sun and the stars."

"And a few days ago," Peterson said, "Gaines pulled a bank robbery in which he murdered all of the other robbers, set off three bombs in the town—including a secret FBI post no one should have known about—and made it over the border into Mexico. If you try to confront him yourself, he will kill you. No question, he will kill you. You're smart, and you're tough, and you've picked up some martial arts from Fullerton here and you're close to a sharpshooter with firearms—but if you take on Gaines one-on-one, you're dead."

Johnny's face flushed, not from fear, but at the thought that a super-soldier like Gaines had tortured and killed his father. "You have to let me be part of the group that brings him in," he said to Peterson.

"I don't *have* to do anything," Peterson said. "But if you prove to me that you can control yourself, I will. I promise you that I will."

Johnny nodded. "I don't want you to think that I'm a loose cannon or something, that you can't trust me. It's just—I'm burning. That's the only way I can describe it. I'm burning inside, and it won't go away until he's dead."

Peterson looked at Fullerton for a moment, then back at Johnny. "Listen," he said. "You two haven't heard me talk about my wife Patricia much, because it's none of your business. She died six years ago—cancer. I know how that burning feels, Luca."

"I'm sorry," Johnny said.

"Don't be. That's life. But the thing is, she suffered, and she died, right before my eyes. I was a Secret Service agent, I had all the world's best training, I could break down a door and raid a room full of bad guys—but I couldn't save my wife, I couldn't arrest cancer, I couldn't arrest the pain she had. I know how it feels to be bottled up like you are, to have a gun and a badge and not be able to use them to make your pain go away. But you want it to go away, Luca? Then do what I do—your goddamn job. You're luckier than ninety-nine point nine percent of people in the world—you're working in a job where you can actually do some justice and change the world. Just focus on that. It'll get you through the day. And I promise you that the burning will go away. It gets better."

Johnny wanted to believe him, he had every reason to believe him—but he was the one having nightmares about his father every night, not Peterson or Fullerton. "What are we going to do about this surveillance on me?" he asked.

"We already did most of the work by hitting Chase. He was a node for them, a conduit for the Johnny Luca file. Now we'll see what he knows and what they're up to. He's already talking—these Brig 910 punks are easier to crack than you think, because a lot of them are poser rich boy wannabe revolutionaries. And now that we've got him, and he's chirping, I think that'll shut down their surveillance operations for a while. And now that you're going to stop carrying out your own personal black bag ops, they'll probably lose interest in you because they've got bigger fish to fry."

"But my mom, sir. And my brother, and my girlfriend—are they in danger?"

"It's going to be all right once we bust up this ring that's been keeping tabs on you, go on the offensive, make some arrests. We need to be aggressive, push Bryson back on his heels. If Bryson's in the fight of his life, he's not going to dedicate resources to getting revenge on you." Peterson paused. "I'll tell you what, Luca. When we're ready to make some arrests, I'll send you out to bring these people in. Consider it a test—if you rough them up, you fail. Clear?"

They'd better not resist arrest. Johnny nodded. "Clear."

"Good." Peterson smiled. "Well, there's one more thing. With Fullerton hobbled for awhile, you're going to have someone new to work with." He picked up his phone and dialed an extension. "Neely, come in."

Johnny and Fullerton looked at each other. *Neely?* Johnny mouthed. Fullerton shrugged.

A moment later, the door opened. "Sir?" a girl's voice called.

"Neely" stepped into the room. She was petite, about the same age as Paul, streaks of orange in her cropped brunette hair. She wore jeans, red sneakers, and a t-shirt that read: "Nuke the Whales" under an image of a mushroom cloud exploding over the ocean. There was a hoop in her nostril, and she wore a spiked bracelet on each wrist.

Christ almighty, Johnny thought.

"Neely McLain," Peterson said. "Meet Johnny Luca and Julius Fullerton. Get to know each other. Have fun arresting terrorists together."

"Nice to meet you," Neely said, holding her hand out to Johnny. "I hear you got shot once."

Johnny looked up at Peterson. "Isn't there a dress code around here?" he said.

Peterson smiled. "Come on, Luca," he said. "You haven't ironed your shirts for the last year."

Fullerton stood up and crutched his way over to Neely. "Nice to meet you," he said, shaking her hand. "Don't mind Luca here. He hasn't been the same since he was shot. In fact, let me tell you what his nickname is, which I want you to call him every time you guys are out on an op together—"

Johnny sank in his chair. *Where's a Jack and Coke when you need one?*

Chapter 13

"Riots have engulfed the streets of Chicago," the blonde correspondent reported. Behind her, a young man in a balaclava smashed a store window with a steel pole. "A crowd calling for the overthrow of the federal government has overwhelmed riot police and is rampaging through the Magnificent Mile and Near North Side."

President Wilkins grimaced as the images flashed across the Situation Room television: cars exploding in flames; young men in ski masks smashing sidewalks with hammers to break off stones to hurl at police; rioters surrounding luxury cars driving down the street, smashing windows and pulling drivers and passengers out; black-clad riot police ducking behind their shields, whipping their batons at rioters, then turning tail as crowds of hundreds surged at them; protesters thumping placards that read: "The People Want the Capitalist Regime to Fall," and "Down with Fascist Banker Overlords," and "Arrest Wilkins for War Crimes".

Wilkins turned to Peterson and Sharpe. "This is sedition," he said.

"It's Hyperion," Peterson said. "Gaines. He's running what's left of Brigade 910. He's got his operatives mingling with these protests, stirring up violence."

Wilkins gazed past Peterson and Sharpe, across the 5,000 square-foot Situation Room. The conference room table stretched down an alley of flat-screen televisions, black leather chairs, and briefing books. This was the command-and-control center of the U.S. government, the seat of authority of the most awesome force in the history of the world, the American superpower.

He looked up at the television again, then shook his head and turned back to his confidantes. "This is more than Brigade 910. I'm telling you, this is sedition."

"You're talking like Bryson," Sharpe said.

"I'm calling it like it is. Look at what's happening. Have you ever seen anything like this? It's more than Gaines and Brigade 910 and the terrorists. It's getting into the American bloodstream.

Bryson and Octavian are gaining power, not losing it. They're winning."

Peterson shook his head. "Sir, that's not true. We've got them on the run."

"You don't understand. We might have the *terrorists* on the run. But their *message* is catching on." Wilkins paused. "I'm failing the people. The unemployment, the rising prices. The country is breaking apart. People are splitting into camps, into tribes."

"The haves and the have-nots," Sharpe said.

"No, Will. It's not like that." Wilkins measured his words, as if he were rolling out a new policy on the campaign trail. *How do I make them understand?* "On one side, you've got people who want to take the whole system down, who want to blow it all up. And on the other side, you've got people who want to defend the country so much that they'll fight and kill their neighbors—people who want Bryson to be the next President, people who want to change the country forever and turn this place into a security state. Two radicalized extremes. And caught in the middle are the millions of normal people who just want to live their lives." Wilkins shook his head. "It's not the haves and have-nots. It's people who want to rule with guns and mobs, and people who want to live under the law, who trust the system. And more people are taking refuge behind guns and mobs because the system is failing them—and because Octavian and Bryson and Hyperion are whipping them into a frenzy. The fringes are eating up the middle." Wilkins looked down. "I'm presiding over the disintegration of America."

Which only leaves me one option, Wilkins thought.

He looked back up. "Send in the Authority," he said to Peterson.

Peterson leaned forward. "Sir?"

"You heard me, Hunter. Send them in. Break up the protests."

"But using the Authority was the one thing we said we wouldn't do."

"Don't you think I know that? But we have to do something. They're rampaging through the damn streets. They'll burn down half the city if we don't stop them. And we owe people more than that. We owe them a normal way of life." Wilkins turned to Sharpe. "What do you think, Will?"

Sharpe's answer now mattered more to Wilkins more than his own instincts. Since the day Sharpe took office as Attorney General, he'd been the one who stood up to Bryson in Cabinet meetings, who counseled Wilkins to uphold the citizens' civil liberties, to resist Total Information Awareness. He was Wilkins' conscience.

"Send them in," Sharpe said. "Chicago police can't contain it. Maybe the National Guard can, maybe they can't. But we've got command of the best crowd-control force in the country. And it's ours, not Bryson's. I say we use what we've got."

"We'll send in the Authority Uniformed Division," Wilkins said. "Back them up with Illinois National Guard. I'll talk to the governor. Hunter, you go to Chicago to lead the operation."

"Yes sir," Peterson said. "But if we make this move, I don't think we're going to be able to contain the protests in the other cities. It's going to break wide. We'll be battling them in at least ten different cities today."

"If that's what it takes, that's what we'll do. Bryson and Octavian want power more than I'm willing to wield it myself. They know that. Look at what they're willing to do, how far they'll go. They just hit Moloch, deep in our most secure prison. They walked right in, shot him, and like they always do, made it look like suicide. And their press lackeys on the payroll are making it look like suicide. Now we've lost our best case against Bryson, the Octavian trail's gone cold, and we have to explain to everyone why we arrested Moloch in the first place, why we drove a good man to suicide." Wilkins clenched a fist. "We have to show some resolve. Think of what Lenin used to say: 'Probe with a bayonet. If you meet steel, then stop. If you meet mush, then push.' Octavian is probing us with a bayonet. We have to show him he's meeting steel."

"I understand, sir."

"Good. The helicopter's waiting to take you to Reagan. Fly to Chicago and take care of this. Show me how the Authority works under Hunter Peterson."

"We're just receiving word," the blonde correspondent announced, "that a bomb has ripped through the Chicago offices of media tycoon and philanthropist Gordon Bragg."

"Christ," Wilkins said. "Jesus Christ. Get on that helicopter, Hunter. Establish order."

Chapter 14

Peterson monitored the operation from the office of the Special Agent in Charge of the Chicago Field Office, ninety floors up in the Willis Tower. He'd commandeered the office from the Chicago SAIC, one of the few remaining Bryson loyalists in a senior position within the Authority. Peterson would purge him soon.

He stood at the window and saw smoke rising over pockets of America's second city. As he'd feared, the protesters were fighting back—and the riots were spreading. But that was no matter, at least in terms of who'd rule the streets. The rioters may have been able to overwhelm Chicago police, but they were no match for the Authority shock troops, the most awe-inspiring crowd control force on the face of the earth.

Armored personnel carriers rumbled through the streets, spewing out Authority officers clad in black, cloaked in Kevlar and body armor, helmets and visors snapped shut over their faces. They surged towards the crowds, firing tear gas canisters and rubber bullets, brandishing batons and ordering demonstrators to disperse. Each personnel carrier hatch was manned by a gunner blasting tear gas as the vehicle bulldozed along.

God forgive us, Peterson thought.

At the very least, he could console himself that he'd forced some humanity on the storm troopers. Under Bryson, they'd have been whipping through crowds on motorcycles, swinging chains, running after demonstrators with batons drawn and clubbing anyone they could grab.

But maybe it was a distinction without a difference. Sending in the Authority, viciously or not, was permanently radicalizing this Chicago crowd, and as Peterson had predicted, things were now spiraling out of control in other cities.

As he stood at the window, he gazed out at the Chicago skyline, standing majestic over Lake Michigan. He looked farther out, deep into the sleepy reaches of the Midwest. Just then, an el train streaked through the cityscape.

There wasn't much time left. Even with everything they'd accomplished the year before, the fabric of the country was still pulling apart, starting to give way, to tear. Wilkins had given an audacious speech last May, had called out "unknown interlopers who pull the strings of terror and hide in the shadows." But he didn't tell the country everything he knew—and while Wilkins and Sharpe were building the case of the century against Bryson, Bryson and Octavian were regrouping. They'd murdered Moloch, setting the good guys back by orders of magnitude, and now they were stirring mayhem in the cities. Their endgame was clear, at least to Peterson: the election of 2024.

Wilkins never mentioned the election, but it was obvious that's what Octavian was after—the presidency, through Bryson or some other lackey. They couldn't kill Wilkins last year, but they could make things miserable enough that he'd lose the election. And that would be that.

"Mr. Peterson?" a voice called at the door.

Peterson turned around, and there was the Chicago SAIC's secretary, a young brunette girl about Luca's age. "Yes?" he said.

"Gordon Bragg is here to see you."

What? Peterson knew Bragg had survived the explosion in his office—he wasn't there at the time. But Bragg was here?

Peterson straightened his suit jacket, smoothed his tie. "Send him in, please."

A moment later, Bragg entered. "Mr. Peterson," he said, extending his hand. "It's an honor to meet you."

Here was Gordon Bragg, the oracle of an age, a billionaire, one of the President's confidantes. Peterson shook his hand. "Mr. Bragg," he said. "Please sit down." He led Bragg to the SAIC's desk and sat across from him.

"So the son-of-a-bitch finally tried to kill me," Bragg said to Peterson across the desk, his eyes smoldering.

"Brigade 910 claimed responsibility within minutes," Peterson said. "They said—"

"It doesn't matter what they said. It's just words. You know that. It was Bryson—that bomb killed a couple of secretaries in my office, two innocent girls who have nothing to do with any of this. Bryson made his move."

Peterson nodded. "It looks that way."

"Something's up. Things are happening, pieces are moving. The escalation of the protests, the killing of Moloch. They're going to make a move soon, and for all we know, it could be checkmate this time."

Peterson nodded again, a pit opening in his stomach. *The thought had crossed my mind*, he thought. "I don't know what the move is, Mr. Bragg."

"Well I do. The President has to move against Bryson. It doesn't matter whether the evidence is good enough to convict him. Wilkins has to move against him publicly, decisively. Take him down."

"I agree with you, but Sharpe doesn't. And Sharpe's the one who's got his ear. And even if Sharpe didn't feel that way, I know that the President himself is very hesitant to make a false move. It's a minefield. One wrong step, and we all get blown to bits."

"Well, today I was almost literally blown to bits. And two of my employees *were* blown to bits. What's the plan here? Sit around and wait for Bryson to kill us?" Bragg gestured to a bottle on the desk. "That your bourbon?"

Peterson grinned. "Sure is. Right from the Oval Office, actually."

"Well, you'd better pour us a couple of fingers. Because I've got an idea."

Peterson arched his eyebrows. *I hate it when people have ideas*, he thought, pouring bourbon for each of them. He passed the glass to Bragg. "What's your idea?"

"Not only do we make our move against Bryson," he said. "But we move against Octavian."

Peterson sipped his bourbon. He knew that Wilkins had taken Bragg into his confidence; he must've told him about Octavian. "And how are we going to do that?"

Bragg threw back some bourbon. "I'm prepared to dedicate the full investigative powers of my publications into identifying the bastard. It'll be the investigation of the century. The last great thing I do before I croak, the last thing of any significance." Bragg leaned forward. "One last ride, for all of us. We take down Bryson, pull the mask off Octavian, and destroy the whole goddamn superstructure. For once and for all." He held up his glass.

Peterson clinked his bourbon glass against Bragg's. "I'll drink to that," he said.

Chapter 15

The flat-panel monitor on the wall flashed to life. Alexander Bryson appeared on the screen in liquid crystal, the transmission cloaked in military-grade encryption.

"Wilkins just made the biggest mistake of his presidency," Bryson said.

Octavian nodded at the screen. "He's finished," he said. "Everything is coming together, Nightfox."

Bryson nodded back. "The demonstrations are going to overwhelm the Authority before long. And when they do, Wilkins will either have to crush them with full force, or pull back. Either betray his own cause, or unleash mass disorder on the country. Either way, we'll be inaugurating a new President next January."

Octavian nodded again. "And how is Project Scorpion coming?"

"Right on schedule, sir. It'll be ready for full deployment when the time comes."

"Good. That's what I like to hear. After last year's setbacks—I like to hear that everything is right on schedule." Octavian grinned as Bryson shifted uncomfortably on the screen. "Of course, Nightfox, last year at this time Operation Reichstag was right on schedule. So if any of your men need extra motivation, I'll be happy to supply it."

Bryson nodded, and for a moment Octavian saw defiance in his eyes. "I'll let you know if that's necessary, sir."

Come on, Bryson, Octavian thought. *Just try and challenge me.* "But you didn't let me know it was necessary to motivate Moloch, did you?"

"It was a judgment call. Based on what he told me when we spoke in the prison. I had to decide what to do with him, and I did."

"But I told you I wanted him *alive*, Bryson. I don't care what Wilkins's lapdogs may have been asking him about me. I'm the one who got you into that prison, and I'm the one who decides who lives and who dies in all of this—not you." Octavian sharpened his eyes. "But Moloch was just an animal, and he died like an animal.

He was nothing to me, or to our cause. I just care about the chain of command here. I care about Alexander Bryson, and whether he's performing as the general I know he can be. For the good of his country."

"I understand, sir. You can count on me."

"I know I can." Octavian nodded. "I want you to give another of your speeches. Make the case for the strong hand of law and order. Emphasize that Wilkins has encouraged these leftist groups on the one hand, and then ineptly deployed the Authority against them on the other." Octavian paused. "But take it a bit further than that."

Bryson considered that. "Further?"

"That's right. It's time. It's time to start insinuating that Wilkins has gone beyond encouraging leftist positions, that the Administration itself may have connections to Brigade 910 terrorists. Gentle, Nightfox, and subtle. The mirror image of the speech he delivered to the country last May. Pick the right audience, the right setting, the right tableau. Sell it as a major address. It will move the national conversation in the right direction. And we'll see what it does for you politically."

"With the early primaries passing us by," Bryson said. "We'll have to decide soon. I can launch a primary challenge against Wilkins, or jump in on the other side, or even run as a third party. But we'll have to make a move soon."

"And we will. We just need to survey the landscape, see where the angles are. We have ways of bending the arc our way, no matter when you declare. Just be patient, and do everything I say."

"I will, sir."

"Good. I'll be in touch."

Octavian terminated the transmission, and the screen went black. He was now sure of two things, neither of which were Bryson's business at this time: first, Wilkins would not be standing for election in November; and second, neither would Bryson.

Wilkins was far too dangerous—incredibly too dangerous—to be allowed to run for reelection. Even with the exploding protests, the cratering economy, the media savagery, and formidable opponents—there was something about him that rallied the country, something intrinsic to him, something beyond any residual sympathy people felt for a man who nearly took a bullet. Wilkins was a leader, and a fighter—and even worse, Octavian had discovered, a tactician besides. Octavian would not allow him to run for reelection, and he need not reveal to Bryson his way of accomplishing this until the time was right.

As for Bryson, Octavian didn't need him in the White House, and now didn't want him there. His little streak of willfulness with Moloch in that military prison had cost him the presidency. Octavian needed absolute fealty from the next president, and if Bryson couldn't provide it, then he would never be president. Octavian was better off propelling some empty-vessel huckster—who would be easy to control—to the presidency than a nationally revered tough guy who had a single brain cell's worth of independent thought. And in any event, there was no guarantee that Bryson could get elected—Wilkins had inflicted massive damage on him politically by raiding his home last May and delivering that speech.

In fact, Octavian had found his empty-vessel huckster, a glossy governor named Taylor Quade who was well-positioned to sweep the early primaries. And if Quade wasn't the horse, there were others, so very many other ways to skin this cat for once and for all.

The United States of America was now the property of Octavian. He owned it, all of it, and the lives of three hundred fifty million—of eight billion around the world—were in his hands.

It was simple: Octavian was fit to rule others, and others were fit to serve him. And through a confluence of events—a global depression, national unrest, his own capabilities—he was in a position to grab the grail of power and make this reality. Year after year, he had positioned himself for power. Not money, not fame; those baubles were for the Gordon Braggs of the world. No, Octavian was after power. And now his moment was at hand.

Octavian believed in one creed only: the supremacy of himself. Not conservatism, not liberalism, not capitalism, not communism, not Christianity, not Islam. He couldn't even call himself an atheist, because he believed himself a god. He was so superior a force on the face of the earth that he was now a heartbeat away from absolute power in the most powerful nation in the history of the world. Octavian was only taking what he deserved, nothing more, nothing less.

He would accomplish it by a *strategia della tensione*, a strategy of tension. That was the doctrine of Italian neo-fascists in the 1970s, when they massacred hundreds of civilians in a series of brutal bombings, setting things up so that leftists would be blamed. They'd intended to drive the public into the arms of the far right, who would protect them from rampaging communists. That was the *strategia della tensione*—turning citizen on citizen, preying on his basest fears and dividing the body politic so that it was easy to conquer. It all culminated in a vicious bombing of the Bologna rail station in 1980, when the neo-fascists were finally caught in the act and the *strategia della tensione* was bared for all to see—as well as a Europe-wide neo-fascist plot known as Operation Gladio that even the European Parliament itself eventually had to acknowledge publicly.

Octavian would perfect the strategy of tension in America, circa 2024. Americans were making it easy for him, increasingly sorting themselves into two extreme camps, with Brigade 910 and the anti-Authority protesters on the left, and the law-and-order ultranationalists on the right. Both sides served Octavian in his strategy of tension, but the left was far more important to him than the right. If the right were to engage in excesses, it would turn the public against Total Information Awareness and the national security state. But if leftist radicals were rioting and bombing in the name of anarchy, then terrified citizens would demand protection, would embrace the fascism they needed.

Operation Reichstag had been too top-heavy, too ambitious; Octavian now acknowledged that. But if Wilkins believed he had caught Octavian and Bryson red-handed *a la* the Italian neo-fascists in Bologna 1980, he was about to get the shock of a lifetime.

And now Octavian knew he didn't need any grandiose attacks—he just needed both camps to keep tearing at each other, to keep tearing at the fabric of the republic. Octavian's power was filling the vacuum they were creating, mending every inch of the fabric they tore.

And now it was time to remake America in his image. For a time, he'd be content to be the power behind the throne, to own the next President of the United States as a chattel. But when the time was right, that president would step aside, and Octavian would emerge as emperor, to the worship of three hundred fifty million starving, terrified citizens begging for a superman to rule them.

This was why Wilkins had to be eliminated, why Bryson had to be marginalized, why a bomb exploded in Gordon Bragg's office today. Octavian was too close now, and nothing would stop him. An empire for an emperor. His birthright.

Chapter 16

"You can't smoke that in here," Johnny said, narrowing his eyes as Neely lit up a cigarette in the passenger seat of the SUV.

"Why not?" Neely said, taking her first drag and poking the cigarette out a sliver of open window.

I don't need this aggravation, Johnny thought. The two were parked on an empty street at some ungodly hour, reconning a Brigade 910 prick named Richards in north Jersey. "Because I said so. Put it out."

Neely laughed. "It's not gonna kill you, dude. I'm blowing it out the window."

Johnny powered the window up, slicing the cigarette out of her hand as she scrambled to keep her finger from getting crushed. "Not anymore, *dude*."

Neely wrenched her hand away from the window. "What the hell, man?"

Johnny studied the orange-haired munchkin. *Where do we find these people?* "I'm gonna make some rules here, McLain," he said. "Rule number one—don't ever open the window on an op. Rule number two—don't ever smoke on an op. And rule number three—don't piss me off."

Neely turned to gaze out at the night sky. "You're the boss!"

That's a new one, Johnny thought, adjusting his headset. Tonight he was in Fullerton's old position, manning the driver's seat as the two pulled a graveyard shift, a handgun holstered at his waist. Neely was unarmed.

Neely turned back to face him. "So we're gonna bust this guy tonight, right?"

Johnny grinned. "What are you gonna bust him with, a water gun?"

"Your gat, of course!" Neely smiled. "If something goes down, you call it in, and I'll go break down the door and collar the dude."

Who is this chick? "If something *goes down*," Johnny said, "then *I'll* call it in, and *I'll* break go down the door while you sit here and radio Fullerton at the duty desk." *And that's an order.* "But I don't think we'll see any action tonight, McLain. The guy hasn't made a peep all night."

"Except for when he was jerking off before."

Johnny shook his head, letting a laugh slip. "I admit there may have been some masturbatory sounds earlier," he said. "Lots of these Brigade 910'ers are pimply little geekboys who can't pick up chicks. But all we heard on the mic was some suspicious rustling. And anyway, wanking isn't a crime."

Johnny gazed out at the night sky. *Back on the surveillance beat.* Earlier in the day, Kleibeck and Austin had planted microphones throughout the subject's apartment, and now Johnny and Neely were manning the recon truck across the street, with Fullerton overseeing the operation from the duty desk back at the field office. The subject, Richards, was one of the assholes involved in running surveillance on Johnny.

"You've seen some action out on these surveillance ops before, haven't you?" Neely said.

Johnny turned to face her. "You're already forgetting rule number three," he said. "But yeah, I've been through some crazy stuff on these."

Neely giggled. "In fact, Peterson used you as an example of what *not* to do on an op."

"For what?"

"When you were doing surveillance on that professor last year. You followed the vehicle fleeing the scene."

Johnny shook his head. "You know, sometimes I think I'm the only one with a heart around here. Those sickos killed a dude in his sleep, with his two kids in the next room. I couldn't let just let them leave."

"But you disobeyed orders, dude. Fullerton says you have to leave your heart at the door in this business."

"Good luck with that. Sometimes it isn't so easy." Johnny studied her again for a moment. She really was just a petite kid about Paul's age, with goddamn orange streaks in her hair and a goofy hoop in her nose. "How old are you, McLain?" Johnny asked.

"I'm twenty."

Are you kidding me? "Shouldn't you be in school or something?" Johnny asked.

"Dropped out." Neely fiddled with her cigarette pack.

"Dropped… out? You can't do that."

"What do you mean? I dropped out."

"How did you end up with us?"

Neely grinned. "Job fair in the quad at school."

Johnny grinned. *Wiseass.* "How did Peterson recruit you?"

Neely winked at him. "That's classified, sir."

Johnny shook his head. "You're serious."

"No joke, brotha. You'll have to ask him."

Johnny rolled his eyes. *I really need to get into a normal line of work.*

"So how's it going, kids?" Fullerton said, crackling over the radio. "Luca ain't putting the moves on you, is he, McLain?"

Neely laughed and picked up the transmitter. "If he is, then they're the worst moves I've ever seen."

Fullerton chuckled. "No surprise there! We all know how he likes to use his pimp hand on himself."

"Give me that!" Johnny said, grabbing the transmitter from Neely. "Fullerton, you should be thanking me for filling in for you while sit on your ass with sick leave."

"Excuse me, Lead Mag, but you're the one who took a whole month off last year."

"Yeah, after they pulled a bullet out of my shoulder that just missed my neck. It wasn't from a paper cut like yours."

"It was a deep gash, Luca. Could've bled to death. So now I get to boss you around from the duty desk, instead of in person." Fullerton laughed to himself, and Johnny could just picture him patting himself on the back. "You two holding up all right out there? Anything going on?"

"Nada. We had a possible masturbation incident earlier, but that's about it."

"Well, you'd be the expert!" Fullerton said. "All right, then. Just checking in. Try and maintain some radio contact for the rest of your shift. It gets lonely up here."

"You're breaking my heart," Johnny said. "Piss off, Fullerton."

"Copy that!"

Johnny rolled his eyes as he stuck the transmitter back in place.

"You guys are close, aren't you?" Neely said.

Johnny turned to Neely. "Don't believe everything you hear, McLain."

"Come on, dude. You guys are like brothers."

Even more than that. Johnny nodded. "Well, we've seen a lot."

"He saved your life twice."

"And I saved his once—did he leave that out?"

"He said that doesn't count—you got lucky."

Johnny thought back to the time he shot someone from behind a door as Fullerton crawled on the floor, blinded by a stun grenade. *I guess I sort of was lucky there.* Johnny laughed. "His fiancée probably thinks it counts," he said.

"You started out in my position, didn't you?" Neely asked.

"Sure did."

"And how did you move up?"

Johnny smiled. "You tell me. You know everything about me, right?"

Neely shrugged. "Just what your personnel file says."

"My *file*? How the hell did you read that?"

"Well, you're kind of a big hero with the guys, the way you saved the President and all that. Peterson thinks of you like a son. So I got curious and read your file."

"You just read the file—like that?"

Neely nodded. "Yeah, pretty much. It wasn't hard. I'm even better at working a computer than you are at getting shot, Luca."

I'll let that slide. "So what does the file say?"

"It's classified."

"But it's *my* file!"

Neely grinned. "I'd be committing a federal crime if I told you what it said."

Johnny groaned. "So how did I move up the ranks, then?"

"*Well.*" Neely cleared her throat, as if she were about to give a presentation. "You scored way high on your investigative skills entrance exam, but you were doing dead-end surveillance ops for a year until you chased that truck from the scene of the professor's murder. Even though you broke the rules, you impressed the boss.

He paired you up with Fullerton, who trained you on search-and-seizure and martial arts. You guys witnessed a murder on a surveillance op upstate, but you had to let the killers get away. Then you two rendered a Brigade 910 terrorist and blew up his safehouse."

"Which is when I saved Fullerton's life," Johnny said.

"Yes, even though the recoil from the shotgun knocked you down the first time you fired it."

"What the hell is *that* doing in the file?"

Neely ignored the question. "Eventually, a Brigade 910 leader known as Sigma abducted and tortured you," she continued. "And that's when you figured out that Shepherd Moloch was really the operations leader of Brigade 910. Fullerton rescued you, and Peterson stuck the two of you on Colonel Rutherford's base while you prepared to stop Project Orion. Which you did, when you saved the President's life by tackling the girl who was going to shoot him."

Goddamn. "McLain," Johnny said, putting his hand on her shoulder. "You can't tell anyone any of this, ever."

Neely looked down at his hand as if it were a foreign object. "I took the same oath as you, man. Anyway, all of the guys know your story. Peterson put me on the team. You can trust me."

Johnny pulled his hand back. "Yeah, but I haven't gotten to look through *your* file."

"Because it's classified." Neely winked.

Johnny shook his head. "You are one annoying Paddy McSullivan O'Mick. Shouldn't you be home baking soda bread or getting oppressed by the British right now?"

Neely laughed. "Except I'm not Irish," she said.

"Of course you are. *Neely McLain.* You couldn't be more Irish if I found you face-down in the gutter outside a bar on a Monday night."

"And I heard they made a nice tomato sauce out of your blood when you got shot," Neely said. "Easy on the racism, my guinea guido friend. I'm Syrian."

Bullshit. Johnny studied her for a moment. "Syrian. Hmm." He paused. "No, I don't believe you."

"You must've cheated on that investigator's exam, Luca. I'm adopted. My first name is Neelah. My *mick* parents, as you might call them, nicknamed me Neely, and I've loved the name ever since I was ten years old."

"Which was three years ago, right?"

Neely rolled her eyes. "The guys were right, man. You suck at jokes."

Johnny beamed. "I'm the *best* at jokes. Real genius is never appreciated in its own time, you know."

"Except by your mom and your girlfriend, right?"

"Right." Johnny paused. "I guess my girlfriend was in the file too?"

"No, Don Corleone. Just a lucky guess."

"And what about you? Is there a Mr. Neely McLain I should know about?"

"Hell no, man. No relationships for me. That's not how I operate."

"That's not how you operate?" Johnny chuckled. "Then tell me how you operate."

"Well, it's like the movie *Heat*, with Pacino and De Niro. Never get yourself into something you're not prepared to walk out on in ninety seconds flat when you feel the heat around the corner."

Who is this chick? "And what heat are you going to face? An overtime shot in beer pong?"

"Whatever Peterson gets me into," Neely deadpanned. "I've got some things I need to accomplish."

She's serious. "Classified?" Johnny asked.

Neely nodded. "Strictly." She studied Johnny. "So? Does your girlfriend know how you spend your nights?"

"How I spend my nights?"

"Right. How you chase bad guys for a living, serve as a magnet for lead, et cetera. What you *do*, man. Does she know?"

"She doesn't need to."

"What did you tell her about the gunshot?"

"We weren't dating then, McLain. When I saw her with my arm in a sling, I told her I got hurt in softball."

Neely burst out laughing. "Softball—that's priceless!" She laughed some more, doubling over, clutching the glove compartment to gain her composure. "Damn, that was the best laugh I've had in awhile. *Softball.* And she bought it. What's her name?"

"Lizbeth." *A Jack and Coke would hit the spot right here.*

"Hmm. Lizbeth. And you weren't dating her when you got shot, but she saw you right afterwards. So what was the deal? You picked her up in a bar that week? And even though you were the biggest hero in America, your pick-up line was that you got hurt playing softball?" Neely chortled.

"Actually, smartass, we were already friends then. And when we got together, yeah, I was in a sling. I could've told her, but I didn't."

"Aww. So when you got shot, you realized you loved her. And you won her over."

"Something like that. I used my guinea charm."

"So you've been dating eight months. Don't you think you should tell her what the deal is?"

I think about it all the time. "Don't you think you should mind your business?" he asked.

"I'm an agent for the top domestic spy agency in the United States," Neely said. "Everything's my business."

Johnny shook his head. "Let's get something straight, McLain. You're not an agent. You're a surveillance technician. If you put the work in, and manage to do so in a less annoying manner, Peterson *might* make you an agent."

Neely smiled. "I'm an agent, dude. Check out the creds." She passed Johnny her Authority identification.

Peterson really did made her a goddamn agent, Johnny thought, studying the ID. "Peterson made me wait a year for those creds. You don't even carry a weapon!"

"Not yet. But Fullerton's training me on firearms. He says I'm a young Johnny Luca." Neely winked again.

Johnny grinned. "That would make you the luckiest person in the world," he said. "In fact—"

"You're late," a male voice came through on Johnny's headset.

"I got held up," said a second man, younger and less resolute in his voice.

Johnny put his hand to Neely's elbow. "Pay attention," he said. "Check the recorder. Make sure we're getting every second."

"Check," Neely said.

Peterson had ordered the team to set up IMSI-catchers, which were dummy base stations of a subject's mobile network, to recon Richard's mobile phone conversations.

"What held you up?" the authoritative man asked.

"Things are heating up," the younger man said. "Walls are closing in."

"That's Richards," Johnny said. "The guy who just spoke. That's Richards."

"And who's on the other end?" Neely asked.

Johnny shook his head. "Don't know."

"Closing in how?" the older man asked.

"Lots of our men taken in for questioning, or arrested," Richards said. "Chase—they got Chase. Who knows what he's saying now. And Luca hit Ivanov last month, took his computer."

Johnny and Neely looked at each other. *Ivanov,* Johnny thought. He may not have called the cops, but he did tattle to his Brigade 910 buddies.

"Ivanov?" Neely asked.

"Classified," Johnny said.

"There's never too much heat for you to get in touch with me when I tell you to, is that clear?" the older man said. "You set the revolution back, and you wasted my time. Nothing is more valuable for the revolution than my time."

"But these phones aren't encrypted, they're wide open—"

"That doesn't make any difference to me. The pigs could be listening to our conversation right now. They'll never find me. And if they find you—you'll keep your mouth shut, for the revolution. Especially if you want to live."

There was a pause, and then: "Yes, Hyperion."

The hairs rocketed up straight on Johnny's neck. "Gaines," he said.

"Gaines," Neely repeated. "Gaines."

Johnny reached under his coat, fingered the handgun at his hip.

"I expect you to play your part in this," Gaines said. "No matter where it ends for you—prison, or at my side as Washington burns. Either fate would be your reward. Even death would be."

Johnny realized that he'd unholstered the handgun, was clutching it at his hip.

"I'll worry about the pigs," Gaines continued. "The revolution is here. Do you know what that means?"

"It means that the fascist regime is about to fall," Richards replied.

"Right. That's right." Gaines paused. "But it means something else. We haven't heard from Sigma since Project Orion last year—the pigs neutralized him somehow. So there's no one else. No one can lead this revolution besides me. The time is *now*, this minute, on the streets of Chicago, New York, Los Angeles, everywhere. You see how big the demonstrations are getting now—and you see how Peterson moved into Chicago with his storm troopers. It's all going to explode now, in every city. This is what we've been working towards from the beginning—the tipping point. No more slavery to the banks, no more living under the boot of the dictator Wilkins or the vampire captains of industry sucking windfalls out of our bloodstreams. This is the moment, now—when every city burns, and the dispossessed in this country rise up to rip down the rotten cage locking them in."

He actually believes this stuff, Johnny thought. *This is worse than Bryson and Moloch pulling Brigade 910's strings. This is a lunatic—a true believer—waging a terror war on the U.S.*

Then another thought jolted him. *The phone. We need to get Richards's phone. I—need to get Richards's phone. We're using rogue IMSI-catchers to intercept the conversation. We don't know what number Richards just dialed to reach Gaines. I need that phone.*

"Fullerton," Johnny said, clicking the radio. "We've got Richards on the line with Gaines."

"With *Gaines*?" Fullerton radioed back. "Hyperion? Gaines?"

"Jack Gaines. The most wanted terrorist in America."

"What are they talking about?"

"Their revolution. No details yet." Johnny paused. "Fullerton, permission to apprehend Richards when the call is finished."

"Denied."

"But we need that phone. We set up our own monitoring of this call. We don't know what number Richards just dialed or what other contacts he has."

"Do we have a warrant?"

"Do we ever need one?"

"Well, *you* do, Luca. You either need a warrant issued by a neutral magistrate, or one issued by Julius Fullerton. You're getting neither."

"Why not?"

"Because I want you to record this call, record anything else that goes on there, and finish out your shift. The whole team will figure out steps forward once we review the recordings. Peterson wouldn't appreciate breaking down this dude's door without his approval."

"Well someone had better start issuing these warrants, Fullerton," Johnny said.

"Someone had *better* start?"

"That's right. We're talking about the most wanted man in the country. And our subject is chatting him up on the phone."

"And when the time is right, we'll make a move on him. Not when the time is right for *you*, but when the time is right from an operational perspective. You capture whatever they're saying right now, bring the audio back, and we'll review it."

Johnny pulled the radio close. "Copy, Fullerton. You're the C-O."

Gaines and Richards carried on, with Gaines mostly lecturing on the virtues of the revolution. Richards was not to delay in contacting him again. Gaines, after all, was invulnerable to wiretaps, to hear him tell it.

At some point, Johnny stopped clutching the handgun. Fullerton had denied him permission, and he was standing down.

But in the end, if this went on long enough, Johnny would be the arbiter, not Fullerton or Peterson. He would track down Gaines, and Gaines would answer for Giovanni Sr. They'd meet somewhere that wasn't governed by search warrants, or revolutions, or Wilkins or Bryson or capitalism or whatever the hell else this was all about. Johnny and Gaines would meet in a place governed by justice. And in the end, Gaines would die—and Johnny didn't give a goddamn what Fullerton, Peterson, or anyone else thought about that.

Chapter 17

"To our last night in Newark," Lizbeth said, holding up a glass of wine as she sat up in Johnny's bed.

"To the last night in the pimp's lair," Johnny said, walking over and clinking her glass.

Lizbeth grimaced. "That name is so stupid."

"Take it up with Paul. I didn't make up the name, I just lived it."

"Whatever!" Lizbeth threw a pillow at Johnny, then laughed, her eyes dancing behind her rectangular glasses. "Anyway, Paul seems to have a different opinion of your sexual orientation these days."

"Yeah, but he's just projecting. I'm all man, babe." Johnny turned to take in the sight of his Newark studio apartment, all boxed up. "Ahh, the pimp's lair. It's the end of an era."

Johnny had lived here for two years, and this little studio had been home for some of the most important nights of Johnny's life: the night he and Fullerton blew up a Brigade 910 safe house in Irvington, when Johnny collapsed into a heap in his bathroom after nearly being killed; the night Johnny finished reading his father's diary and learned that Giovanni Sr. had been murdered; the night that Sigma's crew abducted Johnny. And there were better memories, the light on shadow: the night Lizbeth fell asleep on his couch, after surprising him in the lobby to cheer him up on the anniversary of his father's death; the first night they made love. Johnny had moved in as a bright-eyed kid bounding off to his first real job after college, and he was moving out as… something else.

And he was moving on up: into a snazzy apartment in Jersey City, in some new development where yuppies shopped for organic food, drank vanilla soy mocha lattes at Starbucks, and did whatever the hell else they did. Somehow Johnny was getting Lizbeth to swallow that he could do this on his office support technician's salary, when in reality he was living large off the hazard-and-nearly-murdered-by-terrorists-pay that Peterson had secured for him. But he wasn't living large for the hell of it. The neighborhood was much safer for Lizbeth to visit, and the particular building was important to Johnny—it provided direct underground access to the train station, so that no one could see him enter and exit the place.

Johnny turned back to Lizbeth and kissed her, then sat beside her in bed. They'd be living a few minutes apart once he moved, and when all this was over—when Gaines was dead, when Bryson and Octavian were in a Supermax in the Rocky Mountains—Johnny would propose, they'd move in together, get married, and live their forever together. He knew it; he *knew.* Maybe then he'd do something stable and sensible with his life, like apply to be general manager of the Yankees or something.

"Check this out," Lizbeth said, handing Johnny her tablet computer.

"What's this?" Johnny said, taking the tablet.

"Look at it."

Johnny nearly dropped the tablet. The screen shimmered with an image of him tackling Wilkins on the stage last year, at an odd angle, his face obscured as the two crashed to the ground. A pit exploded in Johnny's stomach; his face kindled. "What's… what is this?"

"You don't recognize it?"

"Recognize it?" Johnny swallowed hard. "I… No. I don't."

Lizbeth paused, then narrowed her eyes. "You don't recognize this?"

"Well—yeah. I do. It's… this is when they tried to kill the President." Johnny furrowed his eyebrows. "But I thought they destroyed all the pictures? They—they said they destroyed all the pictures." *They said they destroyed all the pictures.*

"Every one except this one!" Lizbeth said, holding up the tablet. She smiled. "Every one except this one, Gio. This is my big break. We're going to get a ride on Mr. Bragg's corporate jet out of this."

"Where did you get it from?"

"You know I can't reveal my sources. It was just… someone who was there. They couldn't have destroyed *all* of them. Something always gets smuggled out, leaks out."

"Then why hasn't it come out until now?"

"Because they've been afraid until now. The way they locked down the place, interrogated everyone for hours, collected everyone's cell phone. They were scared. Lizbeth slapped Johnny's arm. "This is a huge break for me!"

It sure is. "I'm proud of you." Johnny forced a smile. "But don't you think they kept it secret for a reason? To protect the guy?"

"But he's a hero! What does he need to be protected from? Anyway, if the Authority is keeping something a secret, then it's automatically shady. You know it too, Gio. I know you work for them and all, but—you know how I feel about them. And with the speech that the President gave after the assassination attempt—it just sounds shady. If the Authority is keeping a secret—any secret—it should be exposed."

Fan-fucking-tastic.

Lizbeth looked at him for a moment. "Can I ask you something?" she said.

Johnny's heart was pounding. *No*, he thought. "Anything."

"Did you ever hear anything about this…on the job?"

You're going to make a liar out of me, Lizbeth. "No, never did." Johnny took her hand in his. "Whoever this guy is, he must have been one of the President's protective detail guys. Those guys are out of DC, they're super elite. That's not my scene."

Lizbeth nodded. "I thought so. I'm sorry, I shouldn't have asked you about something so confidential to help me with the story. I just really want it, you know?"

Johnny kissed her hand. "I know you do."

"I want to show you something else.

What next? "What's that?"

"Look." Lizbeth reached into her pocket, then produced a key. "It's a key to my place. You should have one." She smiled. "You know what they say—what's mine is yours, what's yours is boxed up in a studio in Newark."

Johnny took the key, then kissed her. "So this means I can pop over for dinner whenever I want, right?"

"Of course, I need my own personal chef!" Lizbeth grinned.

"So when you move into your new place…" She glanced at the key. "Well, you know. It's up to you."

Johnny let the moment pass, then deftly changed the subject. He could never give Lizbeth a key to his apartment—not as long as long as terrorists were keeping tabs on him—and he didn't want to lie to her again. He was in too deep already.

Chapter 18

Johnny glanced sideways at the elderly man nodding off at the front desk of his new building. *Well look who it is.* He lay down the box he was carrying and trotted up to the man, slamming his hand on the desk. The old man jolted awake.

"Hey, I know you!" Johnny said. "But the last time I saw you, you were falling asleep at my building in Newark."

It was the security guard from his old building, who had quit some months ago. Johnny surmised that he'd died or something, probably in his sleep, since that's all he ever did on the goddamn job. He knew the old man was powerless to prevent Sigma's crew from bursting into his apartment last year, but he still didn't appreciate the thought that the dude was snoozing at the front desk at the time.

The old man blinked a couple of times, fiddled with his glasses, and then his eyes flickered with recognition. "I remember you… You're the little guinea from the old building!" he said.

"You should watch your mouth," Johnny said. "But you're right, I was in your old building. Let me know if you need me to bring you a coffee maker down here."

He hoisted his box back into his arms, strolled through the lobby, and took the elevator up to his floor.

Johnny walked down the hallway, lined in a patterned red carpet, and pushed open his door. White carpet rolled from his feet to the sixth-floor windows in the living room some forty feet away, the New York skyline poking through the haze in the distance. To the left, the granite countertops gleamed in his sleek kitchen, shimmering in the electric light. And off to the right, in a separate room—a *separate room*—was his bedroom.

Johnny threw his keys on the countertop. *I need to get shot more often.* He set the box down and walked into the bedroom. It was empty, save for more boxes and a mattress resting on white carpet—he'd ordered new bedroom furniture. Soon he'd sleep with Lizbeth here, and soon—not soon enough—they'd have a normal life here, make a home here. He had a good feeling about this place.

Johnny crossed through the bedroom to the right and opened a white door that gave way to a walk-in closet. *Fancy*, he thought. He yanked the door open and stepped inside.

Hanger-racks wrapped around him in a horseshoe shape. And in front of him was a safe nearly as tall as he was, fitted with two doors like an armoire.

Johnny swiped his fingerprint over a reader, and after a beep, the safe popped open. He yanked on the doors, which snapped open like a bank vault as they folded out. The safe automatically lit up within.

He studied his arsenal. A shotgun, a machine gun, and two handguns were racked on the doors. On the shelves were boxes of ammunition, a taser, a Kevlar vest, and a police scanner. There was also a computer producing read-outs from various IMSI-catchers, GPS trackers, remote microphones, and other surveillance that Johnny had set up on subjects of interest.

He knew he was a man apart now; he didn't care. The weapons were black market and the surveillance illegally planted, but none of that mattered. Johnny wasn't an assassin—he was an avenger, and he was up against killers far better-armed than he was. When this was over, he'd be happy to throw the safe into the Hudson and forget the whole thing.

But until then, he'd be armed and ready. The computer generated daily reports that were zeroing in on Gaines cohorts, and maybe even Gaines himself. And the weapons—well, those were for self-defense, and for just a single act of offense, the only one Johnny would need to carry out.

He surveyed the safe for a moment more, then forced it shut. He would keep it drowned in clothes, secreted behind a couple of boxes.

But even if Lizbeth found it and had questions, it wouldn't matter. Johnny would come up with whatever explanation he needed. And anyway, she'd have to fire a tank shell at the safe to open the damn thing.

Johnny studied the safe for another moment, then exited the closet and bounded out of the apartment. He crossed the corridor back to the elevator, then punched a button that took him three floors beneath street level.

Johnny stepped out of the elevator into the parking garage. The yuppies' slick cars brightened the damp concrete landscape.

He nodded with approval at the sign for the Jersey City train station. The garage provided him direct access to the train station, and better yet, it was a dead spot for mobile signals. Johnny could get in and out of his apartment building, and across the river to New York City, without anyone on the street seeing him.

Johnny scrutinized the garage for a moment more, then rode the elevator back up to the lobby. He shook his head as he walked past the guard, the old man's eyes fluttering shut. *I need to get this dude's job.*

Johnny pushed open one glass door, controlled by RFID access, then crossed the vestibule and pushed open a second glass door. He strolled out into the January blue-black twilight, crossing the street to his new local bar.

Johnny stepped inside, then gulped at the sight of Mets memorabilia on the walls. *Not a goddamn Mets bar*!

He stepped up to the bar. "Jack and Coke," he said to the bartender. "Shaken, not stirred." The middle-aged bartender didn't crack a smile. *No sense of humor.* "What's with all the blue and orange?" Johnny asked him. "You realize they haven't won the World Series since 1986, right?"

"At least we don't buy our players, like the Yankees!" the bartender said, pouring the drink.

Keep telling yourself that, little jabroni.

Johnny gulped the Jack and Coke. *So this is what it's come to. Renting an apartment with an underground passage to the train station, and setting up an armory in my place. This is what I took a bullet for—for the same terrorist douchebags to be running my life.*

Johnny threw back more of his drink, then spit out some at the sight of a blonde drinking a beer with a friend across the bar.

"Take it easy, lover boy," the bartender said, wiping up the mess. "She don't like Yankee fans."

"You know her?" Johnny said.

"I wish I did. Do *you*?"

Johnny nodded. "I used to. A long time ago."

It was Justine, his ex-girlfriend. They'd dated for a few months last year, right before Johnny almost got himself killed. In fact, Sigma's minions had pretended to be delivering a package from Justine when they forced their way into his apartment.

"Do me a favor," Johnny said to the bartender, throwing a few bills down on the bar. "Send her a round from me. I owe her one." Justine had, after all, bought Johnny a round the night they met, back when she was a destitute law student.

"It'll never work, buddy," the bartender said. "She's out of your league."

"What are you, a scout for male models? Just give her the damn drink.

The bartender glanced at Justine for a moment, then pulled a Corona out of the refrigerator. "You Yankee fans," he said, shaking his head. He brought the drink over to Justine just as Johnny whipped out his phone and pretended to be reading something.

He looked up from his phone for a second, and he knew she knew. Justine was looking him over, gesturing to her friend, and then pretending not to look.

And then she pulled a Justine move: She walked around the bar, right up to Johnny.

"What's the meaning of this, Mr. Luca?" she said.

Johnny grinned. "I'm just supporting a local establishment," he said.

"Local?"

"That's right. I just moved in across the street, into the Dickerson Building."

Justine shook her head. "Well there goes the neighborhood, Luca. *I* live across the street, a few buildings down from you."

Of course you do. Johnny held up his drink. "To being neighbors?"

"Not quite," Justine said. "I don't toast guys who dumped me unceremoniously."

"But it wasn't unceremonious. It was… ceremonious." *Nice one, dumbass.*

"*Anyway.* I'm going back to my friend. Welcome to the neighborhood." Justine stepped away.

"At least tell me what's new with your life… since we're neighbors and all."

Justine stopped mid-step. "I don't think you have the right to know, *neighbor.*" Then she shook her head and groaned. "I'm working in the Manhattan DA's office."

"A prosecutor! Just like you said you'd be." Johnny held up his glass again. "Here's to not representing scumbag defendants!"

Justine didn't reciprocate. "Anyway. You might actually be interested in what I'm working on."

"What's that?"

"Terrorism. Project Orion, to be specific."

"Project Orion? How?"

"You don't read the news, do you? DA Stevens would like to know exactly what happened last year, since we don't take the Authority's story at face value."

"But that's a federal investigation, Justine." *Isn't it?*

"Tell that to Stevens."

"What exactly are you investigating?"

"I can't tell you anything more than what's already in the news. The DA doesn't accept the official story, and we're investigating further. We neither confirm nor deny that a grand jury has been convened."

"Which means that there's a grand jury," Johnny said. "Be careful, Justine."

"What are you talking about?"

"I'm just saying—be careful with this one. It could get messy."

"Messy how?

Where do I begin? "Messy like, certain people are going to do everything in their power to stonewall you."

"Nothing new there," Justine said. She paused. "You know something about any of this?"

Johnny threw a hand up. "I don't know anything about anything. You know that."

Justine smiled. "Your specialty, Luca. Anyway, you do your job, and I'll do mine. Welcome to the neighborhood." And with that, she flipped her hair, then walked back to her friend.

Johnny held up his drink, then hoisted back some more. *You see this, Dad?* He looked up at the ceiling. *My girlfriend and my ex-girlfriend are investigating me at the same time. You proud of me yet, old man?*

The bartender walked over, grinning. "Didn't give you the time of day, did she?" he asked.

Johnny threw back more Jack and Coke, then smiled. "They never do!" he said.

Chapter 19

"Looks like we've finally got the bastard," Peterson said.

"So what's the move?" Fullerton asked.

"We do our jobs. We bring him in."

"A-S-A-fucking-P?"

Peterson nodded. "Absolutely." He held up Richards's phone. "This is a direct result of hollowing out Brigade 910 over the years, you know. We pick off enough of their operatives, and now they have clowns like Richards leading us straight to Gaines."

Immediately after Johnny and Neely reconned Richards, Fullerton had presented the audio recordings to the rest of the team and pressed for Richards's arrest. *There's no sense stringing this out to build a case,* he'd explained. *We've got the case already. And we can't wait for Richards to lead us to Gaines—he's already led us far as he's gonna get. Gaines has no faith in him and thinks he's disposable. So let's seize the phone and see what we find.*

And so Fullerton led the team, under Wolfe's supervision. Wolfe was the graybeard calling the shots from the truck, but it was Fullerton, his leg healed after last month's stabbing, running the op on the ground, directing Kleibeck, Austin, Miller, and Lundquist around the perimeter and giving the mark. Within five minutes, Wolfe and Kleibeck were driving Richards back to the field office, and Fullerton was supervising the inventorying of the home, starting with the phone. A spotless op.

So spotless, in fact, that Fullerton had time to think while they were searching the premises. And what he thought about was Luca.

The op just didn't feel the same without his best friend riding alongside him. But Peterson had insisted on excluding him, with good reason. Johnny had come unhinged, had slipped from emotional to unreliable, from the President's savior to a vigilante.

And it was all Fullerton's fault. Fullerton had known, since the moment Johnny's arm was out of its sling, what his partner was up to. But he hadn't intervened hard enough, hadn't thrown him against a wall and told him to either get professional or get ready to spend years in prison for what he was doing.

And now Fullerton was sitting in Peterson's office, drawing up a strategy to bring in the man who had consumed Johnny's nightmares, had become his obsession. Jack Gaines, Hyperion himself.

"Right under our noses," Peterson said. "All this time, holed up upstate."

"Not quite all this time," Fullerton said. "He was in the Southwest for awhile, running back and forth over the border, raising money. But he's gotta be around this area sometimes, gotta stay in touch with the local Brig 910's around here. He wants the New York protests to explode way worse than Chicago, to turn all of this into the Battle of New York. It's what he's wanted from the beginning."

Fullerton knew all too well. Three years ago, he'd been deep undercover in Brigade 910, had met Gaines and Sigma, had learned that they really believed in the revolution they were fomenting and were willing to kill anyone to bring it about. And with protests now boiling in every major city, the moment was at hand.

"I know you appreciate what this means more than anyone," Peterson said. "More than even Luca would. This'll be a tremendous victory. The entire Brigade 910 group could collapse after this. For all of the car bombs and the guns, it's all about human capital. They could have all the best chemists building bombs, all the craziest nut-jobs willing to get in shootouts with the cops, but without someone who can run an operation like Gaines can, they're nothing. If he were sane, he could've been a four-star general, or a Fortune 100 CEO. When we take him out, this could be the end of Brigade 910."

"What will that mean for what you're up to? For Octavian?"

"I think it's finally going to force Octavian into some mistakes, flush him out into the open. If the group collapses, then his precious revolution slips away, and he loses the pretext he needs to bring about a police state. I think losing Gaines is going to force Octavian to do something rash."

"Who is he, boss?"

"God only knows, kid." Peterson shook his head. "He's someone who reached out to Bryson years ago, after he lost his family on Nine-Eleven. Someone from Bryson's military days. Someone who's been cultivating all of this for a long, long time, and now he's making his move. And if we don't figure it out in time, you won't recognize the country you're living in."

"Especially not from the inside of a jail cell or a coffin," Fullerton said.

"Which is why we're going to nail Gaines and seize the high ground. Force the son of a bitch to make some mistakes. That's how we got Gaines—we took out so many of his skilled subordinates that he got sloppy. Octavian will fall the same way. It's how you defeat these groups. Hollow them out."

Fullerton nodded. It had been a long war, going back to Brigade 910's first attack in 2018, nearly six years ago. And here was the tipping point, finally.

"How's that leg of yours?" Peterson asked.

"It's good to go," Fullerton replied. "Doc says it's all better."

"Good. Then the op's yours. Use the same team you used to collar Richards. No Luca, no McLain. Except this time, you'll have a lot more manpower behind you."

"No Luca?"

Peterson shook his head. "You know that he's family to me," he said. "But this is life and death. This is life and death, with national security at stake. It isn't about Luca's feelings. Chances are, we're going to lock Gaines up so tight that the closest Luca will ever get is watching his trial on television. This is the real world, not the goddamn wild west."

Fullerton nodded. "Copy, sir."

Fullerton knew how Luca felt, he wanted to scream it at the kid, he knew how he felt. When Fullerton was eleven, a stray bullet blasted through his older brother Jerome's back, right in the middle of the bedroom they shared in the Newark projects. One minute, they were roughhousing before bedtime, and the next, after Jerome stood proud after hip-throwing Fullerton, the bullet sliced through the window and struck him. Fullerton watched him cough up blood until he died.

And there was nothing Fullerton could do about it. He was too terrified to do anything but run screaming into his mother's bedroom, and in the weeks that followed, the police barely bothered to investigate. No one in the neighborhood would snitch, and that was that. Fullerton could grow strong, claw up from the streets and build himself up into a world-class law enforcement agent, but he'd never get to arrest the drugged-up degenerate who'd fired a bullet through his bedroom window that night.

Which was why Fullerton was into Johnny's quest for awhile, maybe even subconsciously egged him on. How could you not root for the dude? He was chasing down the most wanted man in America, who had murdered his father.

But the whole thing had gone too damn far. Luca had no idea who he was dealing with—but Fullerton did. And arresting Gaines now would save Johnny's life, because if Johnny rushed off to confront Gaines himself, he would surely die.

That's why Fullerton was racing to nail Richards like he did. The smart move *was* to string it out, to give Richards more rope to hang himself, perhaps more time to physically lead the team to Gaines without the risk of tip-off. But Fullerton knew that Johnny would be breaking down Richards's door to grab that phone and go after Gaines, and he couldn't let that happen. He couldn't let his best friend die. He couldn't lose a brother again.

"This is your op," Peterson said. "You've earned it. When this is over, you'll be known in the ranks as the man who apprehended Jack Gaines." Peterson laughed. "You'll be almost as famous as Luca."

Fullerton laughed himself. "What a lucky little punk he was that day," he said.

Peterson smiled for a moment more, but then he lasered a look into Fullerton's eyes. "Bring him in, Fullerton. Win this war."

Fullerton always kept his cool, but now the hairs on the back of his neck sprang to life.

"I will, sir. I'll get him."

Chapter 20

The next night, Fullerton crouched in the brush outside the lodge nestled deep in the Catskills in Phoenicia, New York. Of course Hyperion was holed up here; *of course* he was. It was always a place like this, some abandoned shack in some distant corner of the earth, steeled into a fortress within.

Fullerton peered through his night-vision goggles at the lodge, its spare wood frame and front porch burning green in the dark. Gaines had set up the simplest obstacle, the cleverest little tripwire: he'd propped the picnic table in front of the door up on the porch, and according to Lundquist and Miller over the radio, had done the same round back. And the lights were out inside.

Gaines had set it all up so beautifully. He'd rigged things so that *he* held the element of surprise, so that *he* was the one who'd lunge on them in the dark, probably with a machine gun and his own night-vision goggles. He'd opted for the rustic lodge over the elaborate compound, and it was the right choice. Fullerton and his forces could've rolled up to the edges of a compound, breached a wall, and crept around inside. Here, they'd be bursting through the windows, and Gaines would be ready for them.

Fullerton cocked his machine gun. He'd recommended firing a few rocket-propelled grenades at the place, but Peterson vetoed a kill mission. He wanted Gaines alive, to perp-walk him in front of his minions and crush their revolution for once and for all.

So Fullerton had led some sixty-five federal agents on a march through the woods at night, ditching their vehicles a mile short of the lodge so that Gaines wouldn't hear any traffic. Leaving drivers behind, they'd soldiered through the night, finally pouring through a clearing and surrounding the lodge. And now on Fullerton's mark, they'd blast flash grenades through the windows and go crashing inside, machine guns and shotguns drawn, to haul in the most wanted terrorist since Osama bin Laden. In an instant, the vehicles they'd ditched would come roaring up on their heels, and a helicopter would be hovering overhead. All on Fullerton's mark.

Fullerton gritted his teeth. He'd raided plenty of safe-houses over the years, broken down plenty of doors, dodged plenty of bullets. He'd fought off would-be assassins last spring, and had been stabbed on his last mission. Even with a fiancée fretting over him at home, he was ready to die.

He remembered something Iranian protesters had chanted after the 2009 presidential election, when he was a teenager: *I welcome death, I welcome death, but not subjugation, but not subjugation.* If braving bullets in that safe-house meant first taking down Gaines and then Octavian, then so be it.

Fullerton clutched his radio, took a short breath, and then clicked the transmitter. "Let's roll," he said.

At that, he led the agents out of the brush, some of them fanning out around the perimeter, others taking positions near the lodge's windows. Fullerton himself backed up beside a window. He paused a moment, then nodded at his comrades-in-arms. "Breach," he said into the radio.

Several agents fired stun grenades through the windows. Fullerton flinched as a grenade crashed through his window and exploded inside, and then he smashed open the rest of the window with the butt of his gun and hurled himself within.

Fullerton was in the stronghold now; several agents were, stalking through the pitch black with their night vision goggles and infrared laser sights. He peered through his goggles as he crept, the lodge enveloped in green mist.

Gaines could be anywhere—at the top of the stairs some of the agents were now starting to climb; secreted in a closet in one of the bedrooms; in the basement; in some hidden crawlspace not diagrammed on the blueprints.

Where are you? Fullerton thought, floorboards creaking beneath his feet as he marched through the green. The ground floor was bare, unfurnished, dusty and cobwebbed. Fullerton felt like spraying the floor with bullets; maybe he'd nail Gaines with a stray.

Just then, there was a ratcheting sound above.

Fullerton's eyes darted up, then around the ground floor; no one else had heard the sound, or was reacting to it like he was. But he'd heard it; for sure, he'd heard it.

The other agents continued their sweep of the ground floor, opening closets, looking for trapdoors, while still others ascended the stairs towards the bedrooms.

Must've been my imagination. Goddamn it, these ops are making me crazy—

There was a burst of machine gun fire, and an agent screamed.

Fullerton aimed his gun wildly, looking for the shooter. And then there was another ratcheting sound, followed by another burst—*ratatatatat*—and another agent screaming.

"We're under attack!" Fullerton yelled. "Where's the shooter? Where's the shooter?"

There was another burst, then another, then another, followed by agents returning fire at a shooter unseen. The raid exploded into chaos as agents ran through the lodge, some diving for cover, others kicking in doors, others spraying the lodge with bullets.

There was another burst from above, and a volley of bullets screamed through the air, strafing Fullerton, singeing into his back. Fullerton dropped as more bullets rained through the lodge, cutting down other agents, splintering the floorboards.

"Retreat!" Fullerton yelled. "Retreat!"

He began to crawl away, had to crawl away, realizing that they'd been ambushed, and that the ambusher was mechanized, that it wasn't human.

Chapter 21

Gaines gazed out at the Puerto Vallarta night, waves of moonlight lapping against the beach below. He stood for a moment in the floor-to-ceiling window regarding the Pacific, the ocean that had raised him, the ocean that would be waiting for him at the end of his revolution. The ocean with no memory.

He turned to Juliana, sleeping in their bed. He studied her for a moment, the way her raven hair fell on the pillow, the way she sighed as she turned in her sleep, reaching for him. For Gaines, the sun rose and set with her. But all he could do was steal nights like this every few weeks, rendezvous some place or another, until the Wilkins regime fell.

Gaines turned to the tablet computer gleaming on the desk, glared at the night-vision image of Fullerton and his storm troopers rampaging through the lodge in Phoenicia. Gaines had baited this trap, and now the fascists would get what they deserved as he watched from the comfort of this beach house in Mexico.

He heard Juliana stir behind him. "Jack," she called. "You're awake."

"Come take a look at this," Gaines said. "I want to show you something."

Juliana slipped on Gaines's shirt and crossed the room to him. She sat on his lap.

"Look," Gaines said, pointing at the figures glowing in green on the tablet screen. "These men on the screen. They've been sent to kill me."

Juliana's eyes widened, and then she turned to face Gaines. "To kill you?"

Gaines nodded, looking past her, glowering at the screen. "That's right. That's how the American government does its business. They sent this squad out in the middle of the night to storm into that house and kill me."

Gaines had killed people; she knew that. He'd killed civilians in the hundreds now, and if he'd had his way last year, it would've been by the thousands. But they were collateral damage. That was a filthy term, but the revolution was filthy business. Wilkins,

Bryson, and their plutocrat benefactors were fortifying America into a garrison state, shoving the yoke of fascism and slavery onto helpless citizens. *Someone* had to lead the resistance, and the blood of the innocent was on the fascists' hands—not Gaines's.

Fullerton and his thugs were the ones planning the true crime against humanity tonight—a government's targeted assassination of its own citizen.

"We don't have to live like this," Juliana said. "This hiding—this running. Sneaking like this." She caressed Gaines's face. "We can run away, Jack. Run away to a place where no one can touch you."

Gaines turned to her, cupping her face in his hands, and looked into her brown eyes. He closed his eyes for a moment as the waves surged outside. Those waves could take them to Fiji… Tahiti…

Then he opened his eyes and shook his head. "I can't," he said. "You know I can't. I have to destroy the Authority before it's too late."

He'd told Juliana everything: about Brigade 910, the revolution, everything. She was his only attachment on the face of the earth, his only confidante, the only person he could ever trust. He'd saved her life once, three years ago, when he was hiding out in Mexico for the first time. She was trapped in a brothel, trapped in a cruel world doing unspeakably cruel things to her, and Gaines had gunned down her pimp and set her free. He saved her life then—and she'd spent the next three years saving his.

He was fighting for the ones he couldn't save, the other Julianas whom the vile capitalist machine was pulverizing around the world, the dollar-a-day workers tortured by paramilitaries for organizing, the sex slaves tortured by mafia thugs for trying to escape, the dissidents tortured by security forces for raising their heads, for trying to stand up. That was the world—the torturers and the tortured, masters and slaves, and the slumbering masses between who let it all happen. And Jack Gaines, with a genius IQ, millions of dollars' of special ops training, and a pure heart, was the only one who could lead a brigade against the military-industrial puppeteers and drive a stake through the black heart of the whole motherfucking system.

And so he'd tipped off the Authority to his location through his conversation with Richards, and had rigged the property with cameras—and booby traps.

"Look at him," Gaines said to Juliana, pointing at Fullerton, crawling on camera. "We used to be close. As close as brothers." Gaines paused. "And he turned out to be a pig."

"What happened?" Juliana asked.

"He betrayed me. Either he was keeping it from me all along, or he had a change of heart at the end. Viceroy, we called him. He came up out of a real rough neighborhood in the U.S. He knew what we were fighting for." Gaines shook his head, glaring at Fullerton. "And he threw it all away. Got a lot of our people killed. Almost got me killed."

"And… he thinks you're in that house we're looking at?"

Gaines nodded. "He does. But I was waiting for him."

"Waiting?"

"Look." Gaines tapped the screen, and the perspective flashed to a dark room bathed in green. "This is the inside of the house. Watch this." He tapped the screen again, giving way to a different camera shot, with a set of telescopic sights superimposed on the image. He then swept his hand over the screen, causing the shot to swirl.

"Machine guns," he said to Juliana, turning to her. "Embedded in the walls all over the house, motorized, controlled by web commands from me. It's something I've been developing for awhile. And I've wired the place to explode."

Juliana nodded, then frowned. She caressed Gaines's face again. "We could leave tonight," she said. "We can live our lives somewhere. We can beat them another way, Jack. Any way but this."

Gaines stroked her hair, then kissed her. "This is the only way. It'll be over soon." He paused. "Go back to bed. You—you shouldn't have to see all this."

Juliana stood up. "Puerto Vallarta tonight," she said. "And then what? Phoenix tomorrow? Houston next week? Running, until someone finds you and kills you?" She turned away. "And how many more people have to die?"

Gaines adjusted the camera shot, cutting down still more agents with a sweep of his finger. "As many as it takes," he said, not looking it up. "I didn't start this war, Juliana. But I'll finish it."

He glanced behind him for a moment, in time to spy Juliana shaking her head and sinking into bed.

Gaines turned back to the screen. *I didn't make the world, Juliana. It was given to me this way.*

He studied Fullerton's team. *So Viceroy is a commanding officer now.*

Gaines scrutinized the agents with Fullerton. Luca wasn't with them. Something must have happened, some kind of falling out.

Which meant that little piglet Luca would live to fight another day. Gaines smiled at the thought. He wasn't even after Luca, wasn't trying to kill him at all. He was just keeping tabs on him, because he was so goddamn amusing. Luca was a pest, an overachieving punk who got real lucky in stopping Project Orion.

Luca didn't belong on this battlefield. He was no Wilkins, no Peterson, no Fullerton—and damn sure no Hyperion. Maybe Luca was a little smarter than the average agent, a little sharper of a marksman than the average agent—maybe. But really, he was a nobody, a tenacious little prick who made himself a degree better by sheer force of will, who had a knack for being in the right place at the right time.

Gaines smiled as he aimed for the kill shot as Fullerton crawled. When Luca came for him, he'd find himself in the *wrong* place at the *wrong* time. Just like Fullerton had tonight.

Chapter 22

It was a bloodbath.

Gaines's technology was far from perfect, Fullerton explained to Johnny afterwards, but even wild bursts from the weapons he'd embedded were effective in strafing dozens of agents. Fullerton had essentially led a Pickett's charge into an automated machine gun nest, where unseen snipers gunned down his men in the dark of the abandoned lodge. The agents fired wildly at their unseen assailants, which returned fire from all directions. Even as reinforcements poured into the lodge, no one could stop the carnage.

After taking multiple rounds to his bulletproof vest, and watching agents blasted through their skulls before his eyes, Fullerton and others had managed to evacuate. *We'll bombard the place from the outside*, he'd commanded.

But Fullerton had barely made it outside when the place exploded into a fireball. As he watched secondary explosions rip into the Phoenicia sky, he realized that the whole thing had been a complete trap, a house of horrors designed to kill them all.

All told, it was a worse disaster than the ambush that had wiped out Secret Service Director Chan and his men last spring. Twenty-three agents perished in the attack on the lodge, including Lundquist and Miller, and Congress had summoned Peterson to Washington for hearings.

And as Johnny lingered in the graveyard after Lundquist's funeral ended, leaning against a tree and looking at Fullerton, he knew there was only one move to make.

As the black parade drifted apart, Johnny crunched through snow towards Fullerton, a February wind misting around them. The partners regarded each other for a moment, clad in gray overcoats and black suits.

Johnny folded his arms. "I thought we beat them," he said. "I didn't think we'd be burying our guys again. And almost burying you."

"We're in a war, Luca," Fullerton said. You know that."

"I know." Johnny paused. "But I thought it was my war."

"Because you're obsessed, man. Because you can't imagine that this is about more than you and your pops."

"Which is why you and Peterson left me off the mission. I know." Johnny gazed out at the gravestones. "But you're wrong. I've always known this was about more than me. But I'm the only one willing to do what it takes."

Fullerton narrowed his eyes. "What are you trying to say?"

You know what I'm trying to say. After what happened up at that lodge, you have to know.

"I'm saying that we're going to do this my way from now on," Johnny said.

"Is that right?"

"That's right. Do you want to nail Gaines? Or sit back and watch him blow up more people all over the country?"

Fullerton shook his head. "Sorry, Luca. I'm not down with vigilante justice."

Johnny grabbed his shoulder. "Peterson's going to shut this thing down," he said. "They're going to tear him apart at the hearings, and he'll shut it down. You know how he is. He just lost two of his guys, and almost lost you, and he lost one of his best friends last year, Chan. And Peterson is always going on about how conservative the President is, how he's nervous about making any big moves. Well, now we won't be making big moves for awhile."

Fullerton shook Johnny off. "And if those are our orders, then we won't be making big moves."

"Bullshit. You and I are going to make big moves."

"How the hell are we going to do that?"

"We're going to take the fight to Gaines. You know what I've been up to all these months—I know you know. And you've kept it quiet. Why? Because you know I'm right. In your heart, you know I'm right."

Fullerton shook his head again. "Wrong, Luca. In my heart, I think you're fucked in the head. And if I've kept it quiet, it's because I didn't want you to get in trouble, because I thought I could lead you on the right path."

"I'm on the right path," Johnny said. "And now I'm going to lead *you* on the right path."

"To what? Insubordination? Murder?"

"No. To justice." Johnny paused. *How do I make him understand?* "Fullerton, listen. You know what I do when I'm not on the clock. I work at this job, and I do everything you and Peterson and Wolfe tell me to do, but in my own time, I do my own thing. I pound the pavement looking for Gaines."

Fullerton nodded. "Right. You chase him around the block when you should be spending your nights with your girlfriend, building some kind of life for yourself."

"It won't be much of a life if he kills me, will it?"

"I don't think he wants to kill you, man." Fullerton lowered his eyes. "I think he wants to kill *me*."

What are you talking about? "Kill you? Why?"

"I was undercover in Brig 910 for a minute. Got real tight with all of them, including our man Gaines. And then I flipped on them, got a lot of them busted in a shootout. Gaines… got away. And he's had a hit out on me ever since." Fullerton paused. "You remember the night Sigma and his boys picked you up last year? Well, I shot three dudes outside my pad that night. Except I don't think they were there to take me away, like they did with you. They were there to straight-up kill me."

I had no idea. "And you think that's any way to live?" Johnny asked.

Fullerton sighed again. "Of course it isn't. But Alicia knows how it is. She knows that she could get that knock on the door from Peterson one night, and I'll be gone. It's what I swore to do."

Johnny shook his head. "You didn't swear to get assassinated by some terrorist scumbag who's at large because Peterson doesn't have the balls to go after him. And neither did I. This asshole *planted surveillance* on me, man. Snapped pictures of me, my mom, my girlfriend. And what has Peterson done? *Nothing.* And it's not even his fault, because there's hardly anything he *can* do. Peterson's in a different spot now, all caught up in the D.C. game, trying to outfox Bryson or whatever, trying to politic the situation for Wilkins. He's taken his eye off the ops ball. He doesn't know what's happening on the ground like we do. And we're the ones who could die because of it."

Johnny studied Fullerton, watched him take it all in. He'd dropped a bomb on him, had just committed the law enforcement equivalent of treason—he'd advocated insubordination, maybe even mutiny.

Fullerton turned it over for a moment, started to speak, then bit his lip and paused again. Finally he shook his head. "No way, Luca," he said. "You'll get us both killed—or arrested. We can't go running covert wars and shit. That's not what this is about. We're supposed—we're supposed to be maintaining some kind of order. We're supposed to be standing for something, for the rule of law. Not settling scores."

Johnny arched his eyebrows. "And sending a commando unit into a country lodge in the middle of the night was upholding the rule of law?"

"Goddamn right it was. We weren't there to kill the dude unless we had to. He's the most wanted fucking terrorist in the country! We just should've—" Fullerton looked away for a moment, and for the first time in their friendship, Johnny thought he saw a tear slip down his cheek. "We just should've worked off better intel. *I* should've worked off better intel."

"You didn't get those guys killed, Fullerton. Gaines did—not you."

Fullerton turned to walk away. "Of course I did," he said, his back to Johnny. He sighed. "Of course I did, man. Of fucking course I did." He started to walk away, then turned to face Johnny after a few steps. "You go do what you need to do. I can't stop you, and you know I ain't got the heart to try. But you're going to get yourself killed. That's what I've been trying to stop all this time—my boy getting himself killed. But you're going to go your way, and I'll go mine."

It doesn't have to be that way, Johnny thought. *Just join me. Together—we can beat Gaines together. We can end this thing.* "Come on, Fullerton," Johnny said. "just hear me—"

"I heard you out already. And you got my answer." Fullerton studied Johnny for a moment. "Let me ask you something."

"What?"

"Are you ever going to let this go?"

Never. "When he's dead, Fullerton." Johnny mimicked slitting a throat. "I'll let it go when he's dead."

"I thought you'd say that." Fullerton nodded to himself. "And your girl—you ever going to tell her the truth?"

Not until it's over. "Why would I?"

"Because she has a right to know. For what you might bring down on her—and on you—she has a right to know. At least I let Alicia choose. I told her the deal, gave her the choice whether to ride with me or not. And now I'm going to marry that girl. Think about it." Fullerton paused. "There's this line in a poem I read once," he said. "I know you don't read, so I'll break it down for you. *Out beyond ideas of wrongdoing and rightdoing, there is a field. I will meet you there.*" Fullerton looked into Johnny's eyes. "If I had one wish for you—one thing I could give you in this whole world—it would be for you to meet me, to meet all of us, in that field." Fullerton studied Johnny for a moment more, then turned and walked away.

It's not that simple, Johnny thought, watching Fullerton leave. *Goddamn you, you know it's not that simple.*

"You're a bad man, Johnny Luca," a female voice called behind him.

Johnny whirled around to find Neely smoking a cigarette, clad in a puffy coat with a fur collar. *If it isn't my favorite pint-sized pain in the ass.* "What are you doing here, Neelah?"

Neely grinned. "Let's stick with Neely, Giovanni. Anyway, I *work* with you, remember? And I was at the funeral. What a fucking disaster that op was."

Johnny pulled up his collar as the wind whipped snow into his neck. "I'm talking about you standing here, right behind me. What are you up to?"

Neely held up her mobile; there was a microphone sticking out of a jack. "Parabolic, dude. Captures everything someone is saying and renders it as text on the phone." Neely puffed on her cigarette. "I was just reading your convo. I noticed you and Fullerton getting all heated, and I got curious."

"And when you get curious, you spy on people."

"Don't you?"

"And what are you going to do now, turn me in?"

"I could. I could." Neely nodded to herself, pondering the question as she took more drags. "Or I could join you in your little adventure."

This girl is nuts. Johnny strolled up to Neely and slipped the cigarette out of her hand, taking a drag himself. "You sure could," he said, smiling into her eyes. Then he flicked the cigarette into the snow. "But I don't ride with kids."

Neely didn't flinch. "You're about to start. Because you need me."

"*You*? What do I need from you?" Johnny laughed. "Look, you're a good kid, McLain. You were solid on that Richards op. But this isn't your fight."

"Any fight against terrorist assholes is my fight."

"Good—that's good. So go put in your time, rise through the ranks, and maybe you'll collar a big one someday."

"Or we could kill a big one now."

I can't believe I'm having this conversation. What is she, like seventeen?

Johnny wagged his finger. "It's against the law to be a vigilante," he said. "And you'll get yourself killed besides."

Neely rolled her eyes. "I'm much more of an asset than you think."

Johnny muffled a laugh. "Are you?"

Neely nodded. "For starters, I'm a straight up seductress. I can lure dudes to their deaths just by batting my eyelashes. Real *black widow* style." She smiled. "But besides that, I can handle a weapon way better than you, hack into any network, and can pull some pretty sick moves behind the wheel."

Where did we find this chick? "I don't have time for this. So I'll pretend we didn't have this conversation, and you pretend you didn't listen in. Go spy on someone else."

Neely shook her head, then suddenly charged at Johnny and hip-tossed him into the snow.

What the fuck! Johnny thought as he went airborne and was slammed onto his back. Regaining his bearings, he swept his leg around Neely's ankle, dropping her on her stomach, then rolled to his feet.

I really hope no one saw that.

Johnny stepped away from Neely. "What the hell is wrong with you?" he asked.

"I'm not—" Neely caught her breath, then kipped up onto her feet. "I'm not afraid of anything. I'm not afraid to die."

Johnny narrowed his eyes, and in that moment, he believed her.

"Maybe you aren't," he said. "But I'm not going to get you killed."

"You don't know the shit I've seen, dude," Neely said. "I can help you."

Johnny shook his head. "See you at the office, McLain. Do me a favor, and stay out of my business."

Johnny turned and trudged his way through the cemetery. This was his fight. He'd asked Fullerton to join him. But if Fullerton wasn't down, then Johnny would fight it alone, to the death.

Chapter 23

"The time has come to confront the enemy within," Bryson said, addressing a lecture hall of national security professionals. "I speak not of the terrorist enemy within our borders, but the enemy within our government who enables him."

Wilkins glared at the flat screen television in the Situation Room. *Unbelievable hypocrisy*, he thought. *Chilling, sociopathic hypocrisy.*

He turned to Peterson and Sharpe—and Bragg, whom he'd invited as well. "Unbelievable," he said.

"He's making his move," Peterson said.

"We find ourselves at a crossroads, an inflection point," Bryson went on. "A moment when our economy is at the lowest point of a generation-long slump, when rising powers and non-state actors threaten and overtake us abroad, and when an anarchistic band of thugs tears us apart inside our borders. A moment when elements of our government—including the President himself—encourage, tolerate, and tacitly support these thugs. And at times, even actively support them."

The hairs stood up on Wilkins neck. *This man tried to kill me last year. Tried to make my wife a widow. Tried to make my children fatherless. And there he is, a free man, calling me a traitor in front of my country.*

"We don't have to watch this," Sharpe said.

"Of course we have to watch it, Will!" Wilkins yelled. He lowered his head and massaged his temples for a moment, then righted himself and reached out for Sharpe's elbow. "I'm sorry." He turned to the others. "I'm sorry."

"Don't apologize," Bragg said. "Get even."

"True, the enemy nearly assassinated our President last year," Bryson continued. "Last May 27, just like December 7, and September 11, and other tragic days, should live in infamy. We should always support our President at a moment of crisis, especially when he nearly gives his life in service to his country. But with the benefit of perspective, let this be the moment when we finally face the uncomfortable truth: It was President Wilkins's own policies and words that emboldened Brigade 910 in the run-up to its Project Orion offensive, and what resulted was the cruelest form of blowback, blowback that nearly took the lives of the President and thousands of innocent civilians. President Wilkins tried to ride the Brigade 910 tiger, and is still trying to ride it today. But the tiger is shaking loose, and is now rampaging through our cities. And it's time we ask ourselves: Where does this stop?"

"It's an inflection point, all right," Bragg said. "As of today, we have to assume that Bryson is running for president, and is aiming to take you down hard. And either we move fast to outflank him, or we'll still be putting these fires out in October and November."

Bryson's harangue continued. "Reed Wilkins has done nothing—I repeat, for absolute clarity—*nothing* to make this country safer, and in fact, he's made us *less safe*. Reed Wilkins is a man who supports radical social policies, radical economic policies, a man whose sympathies lie with the anarchists tearing our cities apart, instead of with the men and women trying to stop them. For the President, Brigade 910 is a win-win. On the one hand, he supports their goal of radical transformation of our great country. And on the other hand, whenever Brigade 910 commits an atrocity, the President uses it as a pretext to seize more power, to wrap himself in the flag, to claim more writ to do whatever he pleases—which happens to be the enactment of the very radical agenda that Brigade 910 advocates. I stand before you today as someone whom the President removed from office based on what he called my 'rampant abuse of civil liberties.' And yet, under the Wilkins-Sharpe-Peterson regime, the so-called abuses have intensified. Look no further than the appalling Gestapo raid on an uninhabited country home last week. Acting on the barest of intelligence, Wilkins sent our agents in full-bore, right into a buzzsaw, a booby-trapped house of horrors. And for what? Surely not to catch any terrorist. But simply to make a show of force, to demonstrate that Wilkins and his lackeys were in charge, that they were doing everything they could to make us safe. And all they accomplished was getting twenty-three good agents killed, and terrifying the poor folks living in that small town. An atrocity."

"You have to hit back, and hard," Bragg said. "This may be the most scathing speech I've ever seen a former administration guy deliver."

Wilkins nodded. He felt himself drowning again, as he did for much of the first half of last year. He was growing grayer, and his night terrors had returned. Delilah tried to comfort him, but she didn't know, she just didn't know what was at stake—what could happen to three hundred fifty million people if Wilkins made a false move.

"The raid was a mistake," Wilkins said. He looked at Peterson. "I don't mean that as a criticism, Hunter. But you gambled. It was a gamble, and we lost." He glared at Bryson, gesticulating on the screen. "We lost, big time. And we're going to have to cool it for awhile. Maybe for a long while."

"As in, until November?" Peterson asked.

"Maybe so." Wilkins lowered his eyes. *The old reelection trap.* "Maybe so."

"Last year, in addressing the nation after the failed Project Orion attacks," Bryson said, "President Wilkins referred to 'unknown interlopers who pull the strings of terror and hide in the shadows.' This was an unconscionable lie, the most vile sort of misdirection ever to come out of the Oval Office. If anyone has pulled the strings of terror, it's been Wilkins and his administration, firing up anarchists with his advocacy of a radical agenda and then acting baffled when those same anarchists attempt to cause mayhem in America."

"Then what's the plan?" Sharpe asked. "Beat Bryson at the ballot box? And if Bryson wins, then what? We all accept living under Octavian, and go home?"

Wilkins punched the mute button. "I'll tell you what the plan is," he said. *Here goes nothing.*

"The Gadsden Brigade."

Wilkins studied the others. *Let's see if any of them understand.*

Peterson's eyes widened. "I don't believe what I just heard," he said. "I need to hear you say that again."

It would be Peterson. Of course.

Wilkins smiled. "The Gadsden Brigade, Hunter. They're real."

"But how…" Peterson shook his head. "It's just a legend. How can that be?"

"The Gadsden Brigade?" Sharpe asked. "What are you talking about?"

"The Gadsden Brigade," Wilkins said, "is not something you'll find in a history book. The Founding Fathers recruited them in 1789 to defend the republic against anyone who would overthrow the government and impose tyranny from within. At different times, they've been known as the Gadsden Brigade, at others the Constitutional Guard... but they've always been there, flying under the old Gadsden flag, the 'Don't tread on me' snake. They're an elite special forces group. Only the President himself can deploy them."

Sharpe furrowed his eyebrows. "You know I'll believe anything you say," he said. "But this is a hell of a story."

"How many brigades are we up to now?" Bragg asked. "Brigade 910, the Gadsden Brigade, any others we should know about?" He threw his hands up. "I'm sorry, Mr. President. I don't know what else what to say."

"I know this is a lot to take in," Wilkins said. "But believe me, they're—"

"My father," Peterson interrupted, not paying attention. "My father was an old Secret Service agent. Worked Kennedy's detail. He told me about the Gadsden Brigade—and I searched every corner of the government for them. Never really found anything, though. Just some traces here and there." He leaned forward in his chair. "But if the Gadsdens are real, they can help us."

Wilkins shook his head. "No they can't, not yet. I've been in touch with their commander, General Union McCallister. The Gadsens are living in exile."

"Exile?" Bragg asked. "Why?"

Wilkins sighed. "There's a lot to tell, boys. As usual, an awful lot." He looked down for a moment, three years of the American presidency bearing down on him, grinding into his shoulders, his back. *Why do I always find myself telling my closest confidantes things I can never expect them to believe?* "The last president," Wilkins said, "deployed the Gadsden Brigade to Central Asia in 2018. He deployed them there because someone tricked him into believing that there was a group of rogue U.S. officers holed up there,

Apocalypse Now-types who were recruiting soldiers to turn on the U.S. government and go revolutionary when they came home. Officers plotting terror attacks against the U.S. government. So the Gadsdens deployed, and walked right into a trap. Just like your men walked into a trap the other night, Hunter. Just like our friend Chan walked into a trap last year." Wilkins's shoulders dropped for a moment. *Chan should be here with us right now.* "There were assassins waiting for them, and there was an ambush. A lot of the Gadsdens were wiped out, maybe half. The rest scattered, living on some of the harshest terrain in the world. Suddenly they found themselves hunted men, not able to cross borders, not able to return to the U.S. Exiled. It was June 2018."

Peterson perked up. "June 2018," he repeated. "Right before—"

"Iowa," Sharpe said. "Right before the Iowa attack."

Wilkins nodded. "Right before the Iowa attack. Right before the Authority was formed, before we started living through this nightmare that we can't seem to wake up from."

"And let me guess," Bragg said, "The man who tricked the last president was a senator named Alexander Bryson."

"Exactly. Bryson posed as the front man for a group of generals concerned about this phantom threat based in Central Asia. He'd already made a name for himself exposing and slamming domestic radical groups, anarchists and so forth. He linked this Central Asia mission with the domestic terror threat, said we were going to have a big domestic terror problem on our hands if these officers and their brainwashed soldiers started coming home and linking up with these radical groups. Bryson was a decorated soldier who lost his family on Nine-Eleven—and the last president was gullible. So he authorized the mission."

Bragg nodded. "Which led to the Gadsdens being decimated and exiled, and cleared the path for the very thing Bryson warned about: the rise of a domestic terror threat. Along with a police state to combat it."

Sharpe nodded along, the realizations building to a crescendo in the Situation Room. "And Bryson already had the first Anti-Subversion bill in the bag—his office turned out a draft bill within days of the Iowa attack," he said. "And before anyone knew what was happening, we had the Authority on our hands, with Bryson as the first director."

Wilkins arched his eyebrows. "And the man responsible?"

"Octavian," Peterson said.

"Octavian," Bragg repeated. "He was one of the military men that Bryson was fronting for back in 2018. He drew up the whole thing. The whole goddamn thing."

"The leader of the Gadsdens," Peterson said. "McCallister, you said? You've communicated with him? How?"

"He reached out to me a few nights ago," Wilkins said. "Somehow, he found a way to reach out to me. Right here, right in the Situation Room. One of the Secret Service agents woke me up one night and told me there was an urgent request for a video conference. And there McCallister was, right on that screen over there, on an encrypted video connection."

"He just… popped up on a video screen the other night," Sharpe said. "After all this time. And you believe him? You believe *in* him?"

With all my heart. "I do. Because the first thing I did was work my channels at DoD and Central Intelligence." *My channels. I'm the President, and I have to find loyal channels in my own government.*

"And McCallister's story checks out?" Bragg asked. "Why didn't anyone ever tell you about the Gadsden Brigade?"

"Why do you think?" Wilkins said. "Because I wasn't meant to know about them—ever. Hell, I'm not even supposed to be alive right now, remember?"

"So what do we do now?" Peterson asked.

Wilkins leaned forward. "Get Octavian."

"Does McCallister know who he is?"

"He's got some ideas," Wilkins said. "It's a short list. And Hunter, you'll be running down those leads."

"Yes, sir."

"And besides that, we need to prepare the way for the return of the Gadsden Brigade to the United States. It's time to bring a gun to a gun fight. If Octavian and Bryson are going to try and take this democracy down, try to set up the fascist dictatorship of their dreams, then they're going to have to beat the one group that's been stopping their type for the last two hundred fifty years."

"And how do we bring them back?" Bragg said.

"Deliberately," Wilkins said. "Slowly, carefully, without making waves. Leave that to me."

The others nodded and murmured their assent.

Wilkins studied them for a moment. Sharpe and Bragg weren't quite buying it, not yet. Sharpe was the analytical lawyer, trying to sort out the facts, identify the weak points in the story. And Bragg was the tough guy from Brooklyn, the cynic whose BS detector always was ratcheted to the end of the dial.

But Peterson believed. Peterson still had the wonder in him, the boy who fell asleep dreaming of his father's tall tales, the man who scoured the government for scraps of its deepest secrets. *We need that idealism now*, Wilkins thought. *It might just save our lives.*

"Hunter," he said. "I have a message for you to give to someone."

"Who?" Peterson asked.

Someone I've never met. "The young man who saved my life. I want you to tell him…" Wilkins measured his words. "I want you to tell him that I said thank you. And that we shall meet in the place where there is no darkness."

Peterson perked up, puzzled. "Sir?"

"He may not understand. But someday he will."

Peterson smiled. "I'll tell him."

Wilkins found himself thinking about Luca a lot lately, as they all headed into a final, deadly, decisive phase of this conflict, as they jumped off the cliff that could finally awaken them from this six-year-long nightmare. Luca was just an ordinary guy, a hard worker, someone who read up on the President's eventual would-be assassin when no one else would, and ended up stopping her at just the moment she was going to pull the trigger. He was just a regular guy, someone who got up in the morning and worked hard every day, and made himself into something more just by putting in a little extra effort. And in a moment of truth, he found a courage he never knew he had.

That's America, Wilkins thought. *That's what we're fighting for, who we're fighting for. And I'll pledge my life, fortune, and sacred honor to keep us free from anyone who would dare threaten this country.*

Chapter 24

Johnny stroked Lizbeth's hair as they lay in his bed, a single candle flickering on the night table beside him, bouncing light across the dark, throwing her face into relief. "Your article was awesome today," he said.

Lizbeth beamed, her emerald eyes shimmering in the candlelight. "You think so?"

Johnny nodded. "I know so. You're already a Pulitzer winner."

Lizbeth giggled. "Hardly, Gio. But you're sweet." She punched Johnny's arm. "You can be pretty sweet when you're not being all douchey about the Yankees. Who knew?"

"Don't get used to it—it's spring training, baby!"

They laughed. Lizbeth had just written an article detailing the Authority's abuses of its surveillance powers, highlighting a few things even Johnny himself didn't know about. She was right about the Authority. As soon as Johnny and the rest of the team crushed Brigade 910 and busted Octavian, the American people had to dismantle the agency for once and for all.

"Anyway, we've got way more stories in the pipeline about the Authority," Lizbeth said. "Do you see that investigation they're running out of the Manhattan D.A.'s office? Trying to link the Authority to the terror attacks last May?"

Johnny thought of Justine. "I heard something about it," he said.

"Well, it's *crazy*. They might be finding all kinds of sick stuff, these insane connections. It's like that prosecutor who said the CIA killed Kennedy." Lizbeth paused. "Between you and me and the candle, I think the Authority has really shady ties to Brigade 910. Dudes at the top. Your boss's boss's bosses."

"And you're going to try to prove this?"

"I'm going to do my job—investigate, and report what I find. Objectively."

Johnny nodded. "Just don't start investigating *me*."

Lizbeth arched her eyebrows. "I would never dream of it, Luca."

"You know," Johnny said to Lizbeth, "you're doing such a good job over at *Rebellion* that you should just forget about that story about the dude who saved the President. Just keep turning out stuff like this, and we'll be millionaires."

"Billionaires, babe," Lizbeth said. She studied Johnny. "What is it with you and that story, anyway?"

Oh, nothing. "What do you mean?"

"What do I mean? You've been trying to shut it down from day one. You're hating on this dude. You don't want him to get the recognition he deserves."

You're damn right I don't. "He's probably boring, you know. He's probably way into video games and fantasy baseball. What kind of story would *that* make?"

Lizbeth rolled her eyes. "You're just projecting your dorkiness onto him. Not everyone is a loser like you." She chuckled. "Sorry, I meant hottie. Dreamboat. Sexy. Not everyone is as *sexy* as you."

"I don't need this abuse." Johnny flipped over on his side, turned away from Lizbeth. "I'll have you know that I've won three fantasy baseball championships."

Lizbeth tickled him until he turned back towards her. "You're so weird about this story. I mean, if you did an awesome job cleaning a gun at work, or fixing the polygraph machine, you'd want someone to know about it, right?" Lizbeth paused. "Or whatever it is you do."

Johnny narrowed his eyes. "Do you think I do anything else?"

"I do, actually."

"And what do you think I do?"

"Why don't you tell me?"

"Because there's nothing else to tell."

Lizbeth nodded. "Right. There's nothing else." She looked into Johnny's eyes. "And you're telling the whole truth, like always?"

Don't make me do this. "That's right." He paused. "You think I'm not?"

Lizbeth shook her head, her eyes still trained on his. "I couldn't. Because you've never lied to me once. And I've known you a whole seven years now. I trust you more than anyone else on the planet." Lizbeth caressed Johnny's face. "But tell me something, Gio."

A chill splashed across Johnny's shoulders, then tumbled down his spine. "What?"

"Where do you go all the time?"

The question floated up into the candlelight, lingered for a moment, and then opened up the first chasm between them in seven years, the first millimeters of distance.

"I don't understand the question, Lizbeth."

"It's kind of a simple question, though. Because you work what I think is a nine-to-five job, but you keep the weirdest, randomest hours. And sometimes you bail at the last minute. And sometimes you disappear for hours, maybe even a day or two. And sometimes you show up with bruises on your face, welts on your back. Or with your arm in a sling."

"I got hurt playing softball. I told you that."

Lizbeth nodded. "And the rest?"

"I train with the guys—with the agents. Martial arts, hand-to-hand stuff. It gets rough sometimes." *And sometimes I get my face smashed into a shower door by a Russian mafia thug who killed my father.*

"And when you're no-showing on me, disappearing for awhile—that's all training, too?"

"Maybe it is. Or maybe I'm just losing track of time." Johnny pulled Lizbeth close, snuggled her up to him. "What's wrong?"

Lizbeth looked up at him and closed her eyes, content in the embrace for a moment. Then she pulled away. "Gio, listen." She looked up at the ceiling. "We're... supposed to be building a real thing here. Whatever that means. We're supposed to be building a grown-up relationship, because we've known each other forever, and we're in love, and we trust each other. But you're still a mystery. Just like you were before. Back when we weren't dating, when I hardly even saw you and missed you all the time. You're a mystery. And I don't want to date a mystery." Lizbeth turned to face Johnny. "I want to date *you*, Gio. I want to date you, *all* of you. I want to know who you are, what you do. I want to share it all with you, help you, celebrate with you, whatever. No secrets."

The words were dancing on Johnny's tongue, a year and a half of the secrets that Lizbeth hated, the murder, the intrigue, the revenge, the near death. *At least I let Alicia choose*, Fullerton had told him at the cemetery. *I told her the deal, gave her the choice whether to ride with me or not. And now I'm going marry that girl. Think about it.*

"The night we kissed," Lizbeth continued, "you told me that you came a long way to see me that night. Well, I came a long way to see you, too. I stuck my neck out for you, Gio. I gave up a different life to be with you. Because I wanted a life with you." She traced her fingertip through Johnny's hair, down along his jawline. "Just meet me halfway. Partners, Gio. We're partners in this. Remember that."

Johnny nodded. There were two moves here. Tell her everything, or—stop living a life that made him keep secrets. Stop chasing killers, stop gunning for revenge. Wrap up his obligations with the Authority and then just *let it all go.*

Johnny thought back to his father's wake, more than three years ago now. On the night before the funeral, after all of the mourners had left the funeral home, he knelt before the coffin, alone in the room. Lizbeth, Billy, and the rest of his friends were waiting for him outside, waiting to take him to restaurant and help him forget. Johnny looked down at the body—the last time he'd ever see his father—and started to cry. But just then, he heard Lizbeth giggle outside, laughing at some joke that Billy had cracked. Johnny took a hard look at the body in the coffin, and then he knew. It wasn't his father. It was a lifeless body, buffed up, made up, shiny and glossy and fake. Wherever Giovanni Sr. was, it wasn't in that room, wasn't in that coffin. There was no life in that room—and outside, where Billy and Lizbeth were laughing, there was life.

Johnny gazed at Lizbeth. *This* was where there was life. Out there, wherever Gaines was—there was death. And any move Johnny made in that direction would just be a commemoration of that death. Here in this apartment—in this bed—*this* was life.

Johnny pulled Lizbeth close and kissed her on the lips. "We're partners," he said. "And I'll never forget that."

They didn't say more. And as they melted to sleep, the chasm widened that much more, millimeters of distance giving way to centimeters, cracking open by the second.

Chapter 25

Reed Wilkins was galvanized by thoughts of the Gadsden Brigade.

It was 1:00 A.M., and Delilah was sleeping beside him. In his military career, and as President, Wilkins had seen it all, from the sun bouncing off the Bosporus in Turkey to the full moon glowing in the glaciers of Iceland, and all the majesty and wonders of the world between. But all he wanted out of life was here in this bed, the tranquility of a night with Delilah, getting to watch her sleep, getting to hold her as he fell asleep with her.

And that's why he was alive with thoughts of the Gadsden Brigade. Because after years of total war with Bryson and Octavian, he'd finally found the fighting force that could finish them for once and for all. Wilkins could at last shower the nation in peace, at last enjoy his days and nights with Delilah without cringing in terror at the thought that America was about to plunge into permanent fascism.

Peterson and Sharpe—and Chan, rest in peace—were damn good. And Bragg was a fighter, staking his livelihood on the crusade of a lifetime.

But General Union McCallister was a soldier, and that's what it was going to take to end this thing.

Two weeks ago, the head of Wilkins's Secret Service detail had approached Wilkins in the Oval Office, had told him that there was an ultra-secure transmission coming through in the Situation Room, a transmission from a source they'd not received in years. The agent explained that Wilkins alone had the authority to receive the transmission.

So Wilkins had gone down to the Situation Room and accessed the transmission via fingerprint and retinal scans. And there was McCallister on the screen, clad in camouflage and standing at attention. After Wilkins ordered him at ease, McCallister proceeded to explain who he was, the unit he led, how they had been exiled and had finally managed to gather in a secure location and develop the resources to establish a line of communication with the White House. How they had followed the rise of both

Bryson and Brigade 910 while in exile, had followed the bombings and the growing police state, and finally the attempt on Wilkins's life last spring. How night was falling in America, and how they could stop the night.

Stop the night. Those were the words that resonated with Wilkins, the words that jolted him to the realization that this McCallister was telling the truth, that something supernatural had welded them together at this moment in American history. That God himself had willed it.

About a year ago, in a dream, Wilkins's late mother, rocking in a chair on their old porch, had told him, *That sun is falling so hard now, I'm scared there's gonna be night forever. Don't let it fall. You can do anything, honey. You're my boy. And I know if you're facing down the night, you can keep the sun in the sky.*

And at a midnight meeting at Arlington Cemetery with Chan and Peterson last year, it was Wilkins himself who had said, *We're in the twilight of republics and the rights of man, and night is falling. We can't let it. We can stop the night.*

Wilkins and McCallister together would strike Octavian down. They would stop the night.

Wilkins sat up. He had to talk to McCallister, had to plan their next moves.

He slipped a leg out from under the sheets, then pivoted out of bed. He'd taken two steps when he heard Delilah call behind him:

"And just where do you think you're going, Mr. President?"

Wilkins smiled in the dark. "Just going to down to fix myself a sandwich, Mrs. Wilkins."

The First Lady sat up and clicked on a lamp, and light burst through the bedroom. She rubbed her eyes. "I suppose this is better than creeping in a closet at one in the morning, Reed. But something tells me that you're up to more than fixing a sandwich right now."

"And how do you know about my old habit of creeping in that closet?"

Delilah was referring to Wilkins's practice of sneaking out of bed and into the walk-in closet in the bedroom, where he'd pull open a trap door and bound down a stairwell that took him to a chamber. The chamber led to a secret tunnel beneath Washington.

"I'm your wife," Delilah said. "I know more about you than *you*."

Wilkins smiled. "That closet is a top-secret matter of national security, you know."

"Well, I have a confession to make. I've known about it since the first night you used it. You're not as smooth as you think you are."

"It's a federal offense to question your President's smoothness." Wilkins smiled. "Well, then I have a confession to make, too. I'm not going down to make a sandwich."

Delilah nodded. "I know that's right. So who are you meeting?"

"Someone who can win this war for us, baby."

"And does he have a name?"

"Union McCallister. General Union McCallister."

Delilah laughed. "Sounds like someone out of a Western."

"Acts like one, too."

"And you trust him?" Delilah paused. "Because it's hard to trust anyone these days."

"I do trust him, sweetheart."

Delilah smiled. "Then go to your meeting, Mr. President. Go do whatever it is you do. Be careful, or I'll kill you."

Wilkins returned the smile. "Yes, ma'am."

Moments later, after navigating through the darkened residence and setting at ease his Secret Service detail's cacophony of "Sir, are you all right?", Wilkins was in the West Wing basement, at the doors of the Situation Room. He snapped them open, slipped inside, and then locked them shut.

He switched on the lights, and the Situation Room brightened to life. Wilkins had waged war for the right to use this room, had nearly paid for it in blood. It was like capturing a hill on a battlefield. He'd recaptured his Situation Room, and now he'd use it to project power against Octavian.

He approached a retinal scanner mounted on the wall, a box the size of a thermostat. The two electric eyes scrutinized his own in under a second, and a blue task bar beamed from left to right.

Verified.

Wilkins then laid his index finger on a fingerprint scanner cut into the wall, and a second later there was a beep. Verified.

A computer embedded in the conference room table then flashed to life. Wilkins sat down at the table, then swiped his finger across the tablet screen, navigating first to the video conferencing application, then to the IP address from which McCallister had contacted him. He tapped the IP address.

The main video conference screen on the wall flashed on. INITIALIZING, it read. And then a moment later: SECURE TRANSMISSION ESTABLISHED.

And a moment after that, General Union McCallister was onscreen, clad in camouflage and standing at attention for the President. Wilkins returned the salute.

McCallister's short brown hair, dusted with silver, was parted at the side and swept back. On the right side of his chest was a patch that read "McCallister", and on the left was a patch that read "U.S. Army"; one star ran down the center, between the patches. Behind McCallister was flat grassland, stretching all the way to a mountain range sloping at the top of the screen.

"General," Wilkins said. "I want you to know that I've got my top man closing in on Octavian. And I'm working the necessary channels to arrange your transport back to the U.S. You and your men are almost home."

McCallister smiled. "That's the best news I've heard in a long time, Mr. President."

"What time is it where you are? It's one thirty here in Washington."

"Twelve thirty, sir. Lunchtime."

Eleven hours ahead, Wilkins thought. *That's east of Afghanistan. Maybe Kyrgyzstan, eastern Kazakhstan.* "I need to know if we can win this thing once we get you back here."

"I swear it." McCallister sharpened his eyes. "This is the moment we've been trained for, sir. Defending against a coup—or reversing a coup, if we have to. We'll have to root out traitors, identify who's loyal. And if we end up in a civil war scenario, we'll have to fight. We'll have to build loyal units and fight."

"A *civil war* scenario?"

McCallister nodded. "That's what Octavian's preparing for. Our intelligence indicates that he's built up his power centers. He's swayed some important generals to his side who are prepared to turn on you when the time comes, who are prepared to deploy heavy weapons and hard power to back up Octavian if necessary. He's got Brigade 910 wreaking havoc all over the place. And most importantly, for the day-to-day policing, he's got his Authority shock troops and his intelligence apparatus. He's developing secret police capability, something straight out of East Germany."

A chasm exploded open in Wilkins's stomach. *A civil war.* "And how... how would this civil war play out, exactly?"

"The most likely scenario would be urban warfare. Our cities would be under occupation, essentially. The cities are where the opposition to Bryson is the strongest, and if Bryson and Octavian make any move on you, there will be massive demonstrations in the cities, the biggest we've seen yet. Maybe the biggest in our history. And when that happens, Octavian will shut them down."

"How?"

"Truck-mounted non-lethals, microwave weapons, which could bring hundreds, maybe thousands to their knees without a shot fired. Paintball guns to identify protesters even after they've run away. Photo-tagging technology—Authority agents can snap pictures of protesters and then feed them to smart streetlamps that have cameras inside, cameras that can talk to each other and follow dissidents all over the city. And then once they identify dissidents, they can shut down their bank cards, jam their internet, remotely access cameras and microphones on their computers. Octavian can neutralize the opposition over a period of months, maybe even weeks."

Good God, Wilkins thought. "And that's where you come in," he said.

"Affirmative, sir," McCallister replied. "That's where the Gadsdens come in."

"Explain."

"If this scenario plays out—if our cities are occupied—we'll embed with the opposition. Cultivate rebel units, teach them how to carry out acts of sabotage, how to keep the resistance alive. Show them ways around the technological dragnet. Get them ready for street fighting."

"If it comes to that."

"If it comes to that. Or we can just outmaneuver Octavian and arrest him. But the hour is at hand."

"I know it is," Wilkins sighed. "Believe me, I know. You should know... Bryson offered me a deal not too long ago. Kind of a ceasefire. He lets me live, lets me round up the rest of Brigade 910, and I stay out of his way." Wilkins shook his head. "And I turned it down. If we don't catch Octavian in time, then we'll be in a civil war. And if that happens—General, you'd better win. You and your men had better be as good as you say you are. Or we're all dead."

McCallister looked into the screen with absolute confidence. "We're up to this challenge, Mr. President. Whatever it takes."

You'd better be. "Who is Octavian, McCallister?"

"Someone from Bryson's past. Someone who reached out to him after September Eleventh and saw someone he could mold, someone he could use as a vessel for his ideas. And as the conditions in the U.S. have deteriorated over time—our debt, our unemployment, our unrest—he's gotten stronger. He didn't cause these things, but he's preyed on them. And now we're at a tipping point where not enough kids can find a job, there are riots in every city, hardly anyone remembers what it's like to live in a country that isn't a surveillance state—and at the same time, Octavian's reached the height of his power. He's in a position to make a move, to plunge us into a new Dark Ages and set himself up as emperor." McCallister paused. "But sir, maybe it's not just him. Maybe he's part of a group, some kind of cabal—"

"There's only one," Wilkins argued. "One mania. One obsession with power. Hitler was only one man, Stalin was only one man, no matter what they represented or whoever followed them. There's one Octavian." *All along, it's felt as if I've been matching wits with one adversary.* "McCallister," he said. "Where are you?"

McCallister turned to his side and swept his arms over the landscape. "The steppes. Kyrgyzstan. We've had to live off this land for years, win the trust of the locals. Carry out some missions for them, and for us. And now we've secured our position."

Wilkins nodded. "Thank God you have. And soon you'll be home. Home to fight the war of our lifetimes."

"We're ready, Mr. President."

"So am I, General. I'll be in touch again soon."

Wilkins cut off the transmission. *I'm not sure we can win that civil war. We have to get Octavian. That's the only way.*

Chapter 26

Attorney General Wilson Sharpe held up his umbrella, fending off an evening thunderstorm as he waited beside the canal under the Key Bridge. A moment later, a shape in a trench coat emerged through the sheets of rain, walking up to him.

"You're late," the man in the coat said.

"I was held up," Sharpe said. "Keeping up appearances."

"We're past the point of keeping up appearances. This is a fight for our lives."

Lighting streaked from the clouds, bathing the face of Alexander Bryson in light.

"I know," Sharpe said. "I'm doing the best I can."

"That's not good enough, Sharpe. Considering there's a grand jury investigating me."

"But that's a state investigation, I can't stop it—"

Bryson pulled a revolver from his pocket and pistol-whipped Sharpe, knocking him to the ground. He cocked it and pressed the barrel against his temple.

"Listen to me," Bryson said. "If you disappoint us again, you're dead. You came to me, remember? Begging us to get you out of your little whore problem, talking about how you thought Wilkins was endangering the country. And then when you get your chance to do right by us, you blow it."

"I'm sorry," Sharpe said, rubbing his head. "Please..."

Bryson pressed the barrel harder into his temple. "You make sure this Manhattan grand jury comes out the right way. Is that clear?"

"It's clear!" Sharpe was pleading. "It's clear!"

Please kill me, Sharpe thought as he writhed in agony. *God, please kill me, please…*

Sharpe *had* come to Bryson, a year ago. The "little whore problem" that Bryson mentioned was a prostitute who'd died during a night of partying with Sharpe. Sharpe hadn't done anything to her; she'd been using drugs. But he hadn't made a clean break, hadn't covered it up the right way; he'd tried to save the girl's life instead of calling in a fixer to make her go away.

There'd been paramedics and police; Sharpe left before they arrived. But since then there had been whispers, swelling to a murmur, and the murmur could lead to some sort of investigation. Scandal and ruin—and incarceration—awaited.

Sharpe needed to sell his wares, needed to trade something valuable to save himself.

So he approached Bryson. After all, Wilkins *was* endangering the country. Sharpe had opposed the Total Information Awareness Act in the beginning, but as Brigade 910 intensified its reign of terror, it became clear that signing the damn law was the only way to stop them. But Wilkins was stubborn, stubborn for reasons he wouldn't tell Sharpe—his best friend—consorting instead with Peterson and Chan and shutting Sharpe out of the whole thing. It wasn't until months later—after the attempt on the President's life—that Wilkins had told him the truth.

So Sharpe approached Bryson. He leaked information to him, and on Bryson's orders, he leaned on Wilkins in private to sign the law.

Bryson made Sharpe's problem disappear into the foggy mists of the capital. But he wanted more. He wanted servitude from Sharpe, and if he refused—he'd be assassinated. His wife, too. *A car bombing*, Bryson told Sharpe. *You'll both die. And what has your wife done to deserve that? Nothing.*

Sharpe had no idea that Bryson had intended to kill Wilkins. But even after the assassination attempt, even after Wilkins had taken Sharpe into his confidence, Sharpe had continued paying fealty to Bryson, feeding him information to save his life.

But as Sharpe massaged away the pain from Bryson's pistol-whipping, for the first time in his life, he wished he was dead.

He wobbled to his feet. "The Gadsden Brigade," he mumbled.

Bryson narrowed his eyes. "What did you say?"

"The Gadsden Brigade. Wilkins has been in touch with the Gadsden Brigade. And he wants to bring them back into the country."

"Do you even know who they are?"

Sharpe shook his head. "No. But Wilkins does. He explained the whole thing. Says he's been in touch with General McCallister.

Says you were the one who drove them out in the first place."

Bryson nodded. "And what has McCallister been telling him?"

"Wilkins didn't say. He just said that he's been in touch with him, that he knows about the Gadsdens now, wants to bring them back."

Bryson aimed the gun at Sharpe for a moment, then pulled it back and smiled. "Good work, Sharpe. You've still got a chance. Get rid of this New York DA investigation, and we'll take care of you. We can make you anything, if you deliver. Fortune 100 CEO Sharpe. Secretary of State Sharpe. Chief Justice Sharpe." Bryson waved the revolver. "Only don't disappoint me. I'm not nearly so patient these days."

He about-faced and marched away, the rain pounding his umbrella.

Sharpe pulled out a handkerchief and dabbed the side of his head. Blood.

I think I know, he thought.

There was one secret he didn't leak to Bryson, one delicious detail he was keeping all to himself, the greatest treasure of all.

"I think I know," Sharpe said softly as he watched Bryson walk off.

I think I know.

Octavian.

I think I know who Octavian is.

Chapter 27

Johnny whistled as he strolled into the convenience store. It was mid-March, the weather was getting warmer, and the Garden State—even Johnny's urban corner of it—was blooming to life. A breeze carried blooming flowers in fragrant whispers as the last snows melted away in thawed-out currents, the sky shimmering in every puddle, blue and white bursting from under gray.

Johnny yanked open the glass door of the refrigerator and grabbed a bottle of water. He was a sucker for the springtime, just like everyone else. The weather was awesome. The Yankees had signed a couple of top free agents over the winter and were looking good in spring training. And in a few weeks, he'd be turning twenty-six, and would be treated to his usual week-long birthday party.

"Take a walk, man," the shopkeeper said. "We don't need no Yankees in here."

Johnny laid the bottle of water on the counter and adjusted his Yankee cap. "You Met fans are everywhere, aren't you?" he said. He shook his head as he glanced at the Middle Eastern man's Mets cap.

"This is our hood, man. Let's go Mets. This is the year!"

Johnny laughed. "Thirty-eight years without a championship, buddy. Not since nineteen eighty-six. My *dad*, man. My dad was a *kid* the last time your squad won. But he was smart enough to be a Yankee fan." Johnny paid for the water. "Me, I was born in ninety-eight. The Yankees won a hundred twenty-five games that year. The best team of all time."

"And you know how is the team, always buying all the players! Corrupt!"

God, these Met fans are idiots. "Check that out, man," Johnny said, pointing at the television behind the counter. A local news broadcast was showing the highlights of the Yankees' spring training game that day. "Now *that's* a team. They could beat you wearing tuxedos. All class." Johnny grinned. "But least we can agree on one thing: Boston sucks!"

The man tore off Johnny's receipt and handed it to him. "You're right about that, my man. Boston suck the *ass*."

Boston suck the ass indeed.

"We now return to our top story," the anchorwoman reported on the broadcast. "A Jersey City woman was found dead in her apartment this morning, the victim of an apparent home invasion robbery gone wrong. Police found her with an execution-style bullet wound in the back of her skull…"

"Yeah, this story, man," the shopkeeper said. "This girl live right up the street."

Johnny arched his eyebrows. "Up the street?"

"The victim, Justine Newell," the anchorwoman continued, "worked as an assistant district attorney in the Manhattan district attorney's office."

My God, Johnny thought, dropping the bottle of water.

"My man, you all right?"

My God, my God, my God.

Johnny clenched his fists, felt his knuckles cracking, the cords across his shoulders stiffening into steel wire.

"You know her, man? You know her?"

Johnny burst out of convenience store and tore up the street.

Chapter 28

Johnny pulled the bandana over his face as he watched his target drift into view.

He was in Irvington, behind the wheel of a rusting Chevy he'd stolen in Newark earlier that night, glowering at a middle-aged white man as he strutted out of a housing project high-rise. It was Sergeant Buchanan, the man who'd betrayed Johnny's father by selling him out to Brigade 910, walking to his car after wrapping up his collection rounds—extorting tribute from drug dealers and other malcontents in exchange for keeping them out of prison. It was Sergeant Buchanan, whom Johnny had stalked for a year, whose every step was known to Johnny before he even took them himself, and who was now out of luck.

The stout, mustachioed Buchanan fiddled with the inside pocket of his coat—he had a habit of fingering the cash envelopes inside, maybe out of OCD or some way of getting off—and then zipped the coat tight. He popped open his car door and plopped his heft in behind the wheel.

Buchanan pulled off the curb and headed down the one-way street. Headlights off, Johnny trailed behind him, settling into the right lane less than a car length behind.

They approached an intersection. Buchanan rolled through; Johnny turned right. He sped through a devastated side street, past young men milling outside crumbling apartment blocks, handguns in their waistbands.

Johnny knew these streets; he and Fullerton had obliterated a Brigade 910 safehouse out here once, had blown it up after a shootout. Johnny shot someone through a door that night, had probably killed him.

He hung a quick left, now parallel to Buchanan, who was one street over. Except Buchanan would be catching all the traffic lights, and Johnny had time to lay the trap. He zoomed to the end of the street, turned left, then raced to a stop sign. Buchanan would approach the intersection in a moment.

Across the street from Johnny was an apartment building with a side door that he had pried open earlier that night, with a side stairwell leading up to the roof.

Johnny pulled his hood over his head as he waited, his heart now battering the inside of his chest. *They killed Justine*, he thought. *They killed Justine, and there's no turning back now.*

He readied to make his move, the move he'd planned for a year now, the move that had played out in his head every night since he'd nailed down Buchanan's Irvington routine.

Buchanan approached, and Johnny surged through the intersection.

He smashed into Buchanan's passenger side, his front end crumpling into the passenger door in a symphony of shattering glass and crunching metal. An airbag exploded in Buchanan's face; Johnny had no airbag.

He had to move fast. He bolted out of his car and raced towards Buchanan's car, brandishing a baseball bat as he approached the driver's side. He smashed the window once, cracking it and spraying glass on Buchanan. Buchanan cringed, then pulled a gun.

Do or die, Johnny thought.

He smashed the window a second time, blasting it open and pouring shards on Buchanan. Johnny reached in and unlocked the door, then opened it and ripped the gun out of Buchanan's hand. He yanked Buchanan out of the driver's seat, threw him onto the pavement, and walloped him in the back with the baseball bat. "Who the," Buchanan gasped. "Who the fuck are—"

"Shut the fuck up," Johnny said, splaying him on his stomach and snapping a handgun against the back of his head. "Hands behind your back, or I'll blow your fucking head off."

"If you want the money, it's in my pocket—"

"Hands behind your back, or Suzie loses her father right now."

Johnny felt the terror burst through Buchanan, who slid his shaking hands behind his back. "Kid," Buchanan said. "Tell me who you are. Let's talk about this."

"Shut up." Johnny handcuffed him, then yanked the big man to his feet. "You'll get your chance to talk, Sarge. Now fucking move."

He grabbed the back of Buchanan's neck with his left hand and jammed the gun into his back with the right, frog-marching him towards the apartment building. Johnny left the wreckage strewn behind them; no one called the cops in Irvington.

A few steps from the door, Buchanan heaved himself backwards, throwing Johnny back. Johnny wound up and cracked his gun into the back of Buchanan's head, splattering him on the ground.

"Try me, motherfucker," Johnny said, pulling Buchanan to his feet. "The next one'll be a bullet."

He slammed Buchanan through the door he'd unlocked earlier, and the two poured into the base of the building's stairwell. Someone had left the light on, a spartan bulb glowing against the peeling wall, throwing into relief the rotting wooden stairs and the heap of needles and vials lining the floor. Johnny grabbed a chain off the floor and lashed it into the light, blasting the ground floor into darkness.

"Move," Johnny said, jabbing the gun into Buchanan's back and forcing him to climb three flights of stairs in the dark.

They came to the corrugated metal double-door that folded open to the roof, which Johnny unlocked earlier that night. He bashed it open, then pushed Buchanan up the last step.

Johnny bounded after him, stepping over Buchanan onto the roof. He dragged him along the pitch, then horse-collared the back of his neck, forcing him to his knees with his back to Johnny.

Johnny pushed his gun into the back of Buchanan's head. "Detective Giovanni Luca," he said. "It's time to answer for Giovanni Luca."

"I don't know what you're talking about," Buchanan said, struggling to breathe.

Johnny grabbed a fistful of hair. "Don't bullshit me, Sarge. I know every fucking move you make—I know everything about you. And I know you got Detective Luca killed."

"He committed suicide. He wasn't killed. He killed himself."

Johnny drove a knee into his back, forcing Buchanan to scream in agony. "You believe that story, asshole? You think he killed himself, you dumb fuck?" Johnny pulled back his knee. "I got bad news for you, Sarge. He was murdered. The guys you sold him to—they killed him."

Buchanan stiffened, then seemed to choke back tears. "Luca was a good cop," he said. "I'm just a scumbag, a degenerate. I shake people down for money, I make my own on the side. But Luca was good. He wouldn't do what you're doing right now, kid."

Johnny bit his lip. "But you sold him out anyway, right?" He pressed the gun into the back of Buchanan's skull.

"Yeah, kid. I sold him out." Buchanan paused. "But I didn't know it was going to be a hit job, like you're telling me. I swear on my kids, I didn't know it was going to be a hit." Buchanan started to cry. "I swear to God, kid, I thought I was selling out some drug investigation, helping some yo boys beat a drug rap. I didn't know I was getting a cop killed." Buchanan wept. "Oh, God."

Johnny thought of Ivanov, how he'd told Johnny he was "right with God." His face hardened into stone. "God won't help you now," he said. "But I'll send you to him. Maybe he'll help you then."

"Please, kid, I got a family of my own—"

"I want you to see something." Johnny dragged Buchanan to the edge of the roof, then glared at the alley below. "Take a look at that street down there, all the fucking misery down there. And you come around and stick them up for money." Johnny pulled a second gun out of an ankle holster, checked the chamber, then holstered the first gun. "Take a look at that street, Buchanan. It's gonna be the last thing you see on earth."

"Please don't, please—"

Johnny pulled the trigger.

The hammer struck the firing pin; nothing. No bullets.

"Must be your lucky night," Johnny said, pulling back the gun as Buchanan collapsed into a crying heap. He drove a knee into Buchanan's back again. "You get to be my messenger, Sarge. You're going to tell them all that I'm coming for them. They'll know who I am. All those contacts you have with Brigade 910—

you better start blowing them up. Tell them I'm coming for them. Tell them the only way I'll let them live is if they talk. Tell them that I want Jack Gaines—Hyperion—or they all die. Open mouths get fed, Sarge. Tell them open mouth mouths get fed." Johnny pushed Buchanan onto his stomach and stood over him.

"Luca," Buchanan gasped. "Luca… was a good cop…"

"And I'm a bad cop. So listen to me. I don't give a fuck about you or your family. You betray me, and you're dead. Every phone call you make—every text message you send, every email—I follow them all. So don't fuck with me."

"Anything you say," Buchanan said, weeping. "I'll do anything you say."

You're goddamn right you will. "Good dog." Johnny knelt beside Buchanan, reached under his collar, and pulled out the police shield hanging from his neck, so that it was showing over his clothes. "You'll have to find your own way home, Sarge. I'm thinking you might have to buy your life with that cash in your envelope. But don't worry—you got your shield showing now. Even these kids you call 'yo boys' ain't crazy enough to cap a cop."

Johnny stood up, then bounded back into the dark of the stairwell.

Chapter 29

Johnny glanced at himself in the rearview mirror as he zipped in and out of traffic on the highway later that night. Sometime in that whole Buchanan scrap, he'd picked up a nasty cut on the side of face, near his eye. God only knew how.

He'd left Buchanan on the roof, then fled out of the back of the building and sprinted for a few blocks. He then jacked another car a few blocks from the scene, dumped it in Newark, and took a train home.

And now he was out on the road again, driving his own car, out to take care of more business.

Johnny shook his head at the sight of himself in the mirror. *Christ, what am I becoming?*

I really wanted to know you, Johnny, Justine had told him, the morning they'd broken up last year. *And I think I'm going to miss you more than any guy I ever met, and I hate it.*

They'd killed her; Johnny was sure of it. An execution, made to look like a home invasion gone wrong. Maybe Gaines had dispatched his Brigade 910 thugs to pull the job, or maybe Bryson had sent his Authority shock troops to do it. But however they did it, they'd murdered a prosecutor brave enough to investigate their crimes, and had sent a message to the Manhattan D.A.'s office and any other concerned citizens who might raise their heads. The message: *Back the fuck off.*

A tear streaked down Johnny's cheek as he drove. He looked down for a moment, and there he and Justine were, sitting at a restaurant in New York on Valentine's Day last year, her blonde hair falling past her shoulders as she shimmered in her black and white dress. *I think this is the nicest Valentine's Day I've ever had*, she'd told him.

Johnny pounded the steering wheel. Goddamn it, Justine was in *law school* a year ago. And somehow she got mixed up in this. She was probably so excited to get this case, her first big case out of school, investigating high crimes against the public, all in the name of democracy. That was the passion Johnny had adored in her, the passion that her future husband would've fallen in love with.

And for that passion, they'd killed her. Gaines had killed her, Bryson had killed her, that motherfucking Octavian had killed her. This sick machine had eviscerated Justine.

And that's why Johnny couldn't wait anymore, couldn't sit on his hands and wait for Peterson to play diplomacy and strike deals in his shiny new bureaucratic job in D.C. Yet again, the bad guys had shown their hand: for all the chess moves, all the dancing around, all the goddamn *politics*—the radical Brigade 910 on one side, the fascist Authority on the other side—they were all murderers, serving one Octavian. Murderers.

And you can't negotiate with murderers.

So Johnny would take the fight to them, and finish it for once and for all. He had the training. He'd take the fight to Gaines—and end this nightmare.

Because sooner or later they'd come for Johnny. His mother and his brother, too—and Lizbeth. Lizbeth, who'd told Johnny a few of weeks ago that she wanted to get involved in the Manhattan D.A. investigation. Lizbeth.

Johnny turned off at the exit for Nutley. He drove through the north Jersey town, the suburbs sleeping now at 1:00 A.M. How many sleepy suburbs had he driven through at this hour during this war? How many more would it take?

He pulled up to a garden apartment complex, similar to his mother's, and cut off the engine. The answer to that question could be inside that building.

Johnny walked across the lawn to the front door, and then caught a break when a couple of drunk girls stumbled outside. He slipped through the door.

He walked up to the second floor, down to the apartment at the end of the corridor. He braced himself, then pounded on the door.

Johnny heard stirring within. He pounded again.

A moment later, the door opened, and Neely McLain stood at the threshold.

She grinned. "This better not be a booty call, Luca," she said. "Because you're not my type." She studied Johnny. "What the hell happened to your face? And how did you find out where I li—"

"You're not the only one who can hack a file, McLain," Johnny said. "I need to talk to you."

"About what?"

"About that conversation we had after the funeral." Johnny paused.

"What about it?"

Johnny paused. "Are you as good as you say you are?"

Neely threw her head back. "Better."

Johnny looked into her eyes. "Prove it to me."

Chapter 30

"The first thing you should know about me is that I'm an orphan," Neely said, passing Johnny a glass of bourbon. She clinked her glass against his and took a gulp. "The only thing you need to know, I guess."

Johnny gulped the drink. "I'm sorry to hear that," he said.

"Don't be. It's all a long time ago now." Neely said. "Twelve years, actually."

God, she was just a kid. "What happened?"

Neely looked past him. "It's not a story I tell all the time, Luca." She sighed. "But I guess we're in the same boat on this one, with your dad and all." She looked at Johnny, her eyes dipped in sorrow. "That's in your file, too."

Johnny stroked the cut on the side of his head. "I figured."

He glanced around her apartment, which wasn't at all what he expected. It was a tidy little space, with a small piano in the corner of the room, and two overflowing bookshelves pouring tomes into stacks on the floor. Most were in English, some in Arabic. There was a print on the wall of an old painting, of a girl from the 1800s reading a book.

"Anyway, I told you my full name is Neelah," Neely said. "And that I'm Syrian. Well, think about that. Syria, twelve years ago."

Johnny considered the question. "There was a civil war."

"Right. A civil war. And my parents… were activists." Neely gulped her bourbon. "They were both educated—they were doctors. God, my mom—" Neely smiled. "She was so smart." She looked back up at Johnny. "So my parents supported the resistance. They treated people who got injured when the army shelled our town, and they did… more. They held meetings in our house. Half the time they were just taking people in who were on the run, or wounded, or who'd just lost their whole family. But besides that… they got political. And one night, the soldiers broke down the door."

Johnny touched her elbow. "Neely—I'm sorry."

Neely shook him off. "That's not what this is about—getting you to feel sorry for me. I'm just telling you what my deal is." She looked past Johnny again. "Anyway, I guess they weren't taking prisoners that night. They'd planted a microphone in our house weeks before, someone told me later… and they didn't need my parents for anything. They just wanted to get rid of them. They wanted to liquidate them, I guess that's the word you hear sometimes. Liquidate." Neely drew her gaze back into focus, back onto Johnny. "So they pounded at the door, and my mom told me to hide under the bed. That's what I remember the most—the way the door pounded. One minute it was normal, we'd just finished dinner, and I was getting ready for bed, and the next… the door was half-busted off the frame, splintered. So I ran under the bed, and a few minutes later I heard the shots. They got my parents, and both of my brothers—my brothers were fourteen and fifteen. And then one of the men found me under the bed." Neely cupped the bourbon with both hands, like a cup of coffee, and Johnny thought it was to keep her hands from shaking. "He dragged me out from under," she said. "He was only about eighteen himself. Pimples on his face. He looked over his shoulder for a second, started to yell something to his commander, and then he stopped. And he looked at me and whispered in Arabic, 'Hide under the bed, sister.' He fired two shots at the wall—and left. They all left." Neely shook her head. "Thank God for small favors, I guess."

Jesus Christ, Johnny thought. *That's worse than death.*

"I must've hid under there for maybe three hours, scared to death they'd come back," Neely continued. "And when I came out, I… found the bodies. I don't think I had any tears left at that point. I threw up, and I fainted. I was eight." Neely threw back some more bourbon. "When I woke up, I went to our neighbors' house. They were our best friends—my dad used to say I was going to grow up to marry the little boy who lived there. They were our best friends, but they were too scared to come check on us that night. How could they? But when I knocked on their door, they took me in… they hid me. Within a week, they'd smuggled me out to a different town, and then out to another, and before I knew it I was living in a refugee camp in Turkey." Neely forced a smile. "Typical refugee story, I guess. Eventually I ended up here. Some adoption program, some outreach program, whatever it was.

My parents who adopted me… *they're* my parents now. And I love them more than life itself." Neely smiled, and this time it wasn't forced. "They nicknamed me Neely."

Johnny smiled back. Neely was from a different world, a world he couldn't possibly understand. He reached back for the only words that could bridge that divide, words that could reach out and actually touch her. "Neely," he said. "If you've been through my file, then you know that my father was killed. Killed for investigating Bryson."

Neely nodded. "I know."

"And they just killed this girl… a prosecutor. Someone who was investigating Bryson. Someone I used to know… someone I used to be close with."

Neely nodded again, solemnly.

Johnny threw back some bourbon. "That's why I'm here right now. They're killing us, while we sit around and wait. And I'm tired of waiting."

"You're after Gaines."

Johnny figured that Neely knew it all at this point, had probably known it all along; there were no secrets. "Right. I'm after Gaines. And Fullerton won't back me up, Peterson won't back me up. It's just me, chasing bad guys in the dark. And you're the only one who's offered to help. But I need to know if you're for real."

Neely slammed the glass on the table. "You're goddamn fucking right I'm for real."

The slam startled Johnny, but he righted himself. "Prove it, McLain."

Neely squared her jaw. "I've done some bad shit, Luca. I'm not the sweet suburban girl my parents think I am. Before Wolfe recruited me, I was hacking for some bad dudes, helping them launder money, steal from banks, all that. And I've used a gun before. That's all I'll say." Neely paused. "Wolfe found me. I came up on his radar as part of some Brigade 910 investigation. I fit some kind of a profile for him. Good with a computer, a sharpshooter just like you, and I'm not afraid of anyone or anything, not afraid to die. He helped me out of the charges I was facing, helped me keep the whole thing a secret from my parents—

they think I'm off at college—and fast-tracked my training. He introduced me to Peterson, and Peterson told me what we're up against, why we're running out of time." Neely looked into Johnny's eyes. "Let me tell you what I'm about, Luca. It might sound familiar to you. I want revenge. And unlike you, I'm not afraid to say it. I know that Peterson and Fullerton work on you, try to tell you that's not the way, how you're supposed to be after justice and all that. Well, that's good. Good for them. But that's not how I operate. In my country… everybody knows everybody. That's how it is in an Arab country. And I know that the guy who found me—who let me live that night—was executed eventually. It might've been for sparing me, or maybe just for being sympathetic to people generally. But he was executed by his commander. And the commander, the guy who sent them all in, the guy who killed my parents and my brothers—he's still alive. He's living like a king in Iran. Some big mafia guy now. And I'm going to get him."

"Get him? In Iran?" Johnny asked.

Neely nodded. "That's right," she said. "Someday, after we've wiped out this fucker Octavian, I'm going to go to Iran. And I'm going to knock on the right doors, and I'm going to make the right moves, and I'm going to get close enough to kill that son of a bitch. If I'm lucky, I'll slit his throat. And if not, I'll double-tap him in the head. That's what I'm about—revenge." Neely helped herself to more bourbon. "And if you're after the same, I can help you. I know what these dudes did to your dad, and what they must've done to you. And I've got the tools to help you get what you want—with none of the lecturing the bosses lay on you."

"And with good drinks," Johnny said, holding up his glass.

Neely smiled. "Top shelf, playa." She leaned forward. "So you need to ask yourself, are you going to keep running around without the benefits of Neely Incorporated? Or are we a team?"

Neely Incorporated. He studied her, then held up his glass. "We're a team."

"Good," Neely said, clinking the glass. "Then let's do this job right."

Chapter 31

"What about General Canfield?" Peterson asked.

Colonel Rutherford studied the piece of paper in front of him, then shook his head. "I can't believe you'd even ask me that," he said. "Canfield took shrapnel in Afghanistan, for goodness sake."

"Colonel, we're going to find ourselves saying that about a lot of the names on this list. But our profile of Octavian is someone who warped over time, a patriot gone wrong. Someone who went haywire. A hero in the 2010 Afghan surge could be a maniac in 2024."

"Impossible, Peterson. The man is a hero, plain and simple. He almost died for this country. I ain't fixin' to cast suspicion on a man who served with valor."

Peterson snatched the piece of paper away from Rutherford. "All of these men served with valor—but one of them is Octavian."

"And how do you know that?"

Peterson started to answer, then shook his head. He didn't know that.

He'd grown close with Colonel Shay Rutherford over the last year. Rutherford had given sanctuary to Luca and Fullerton in the darkest hours of Operation Reichstag, starting with the night Luca was tortured and Fullerton nearly murdered. And he'd fortified his army base in New Jersey into a fortress that sheltered Peterson's counter-assault force in the days before Operation Reichstag—the squad that plunged into the heart of darkness last May and smashed Bryson's master plan.

Rutherford was a stranger a year ago, pressed into Peterson's service by President Wilkins. But now he was a friend, a damned close friend. And today Peterson had visited Rutherford on the base, bearing the list of officers that Wilkins had compiled on General McCallister's advice.

Peterson looked Rutherford in the eye. "I don't know that someone on that list is Octavian," he said. "But the President is confident."

"Because McCallister said so."

Wilkins nodded. "Right. Because McCallister said so."

"And the criteria is what? Someone who was a C.O. to Bryson before? Someone who's been mouthing off against the U.S. of A. over the last few years? A good soldier who got all disgruntled?"

"He's someone Bryson trusted in the years before Nine-Eleven. And after Bryson lost his family on one of those planes, Octavian—whoever he is—approached Bryson about doing something to crack down on the terrorist problem. He turned Bryson into who he is today."

"And all this intel comes from McCallister?"

I know how this must sound, Peterson thought. "That's right."

"But you've never spoken to him. And the President… just knows him as this general who shows up on a video conference link from out in Central Asia somewhere."

Peterson grinned. "You enjoy making a jackass out of me, Rutherford?"

Rutherford grinned back. "You do a mighty fine job of it yourself, Peterson."

"Then what do you suggest?" Peterson asked. "Wait, don't tell me. I've got it. We've got Total Information Awareness in the toolbox now, right? Well, we've only got about two hundred million suspects right now. We could probably run surveillance on them all. Hell, we're probably doing it already."

Rutherford laughed. "I hate to break it to you, Mr. Director," he said. "But you might have to."

"You think it's that bad, eh?"

"Needle in a haystack, partner."

Peterson leaned back in his chair and glanced around Rutherford's office. The walls were bedecked in framed military honors and artifacts from his posts over the years, many of them inscribed in Arabic. Rutherford had risen through the military ranks, Peterson through the civilian ranks, and now here they were, desperate to save the world and still just one agonizing inch short.

Peterson looked out at Rutherford, sitting ramrod straight across the desk. "You ever think about packing it in, Colonel?" he asked.

"Never," Rutherford said. "You?"

"Never." Peterson sat up. "But I'll tell you something. The President's been talking a lot about nightmares lately. Not his own nightmares, but how we've all been living this nightmare for five, six years now, and we can't seem to wake up from it. And I'm starting to feel the same way. I can't remember what it's like to have a normal life anymore."

Rutherford nodded. "That's what war's like. Twenty-four-hour ugliness. And you spend months, years in that ugly, until you reckon you're never gonna see anything else, never gonna lead a normal life—never gonna wake up from the nightmare. And a lot of people don't." Rutherford leaned forward. "But I'll tell you what the key is, Peterson. Small wonders. Little flashes of beauty you won't see in a nightmare. The look on a little kid's face when you pass him candy in the middle of a dirt road in some village. The sound of your wife's voice on the sat phone. Lookin' at your little daughter take her first steps, even if it's on the computer." Rutherford smiled. "So you need to ask yourself—what are your small wonders? What keeps you out of the nightmare?"

Peterson nodded. It had been years since he'd asked himself anything resembling that question. He was a workaholic; he knew that. But now he was a workaholic drowning in a black ocean, gurgling beneath the waves, trying to wrench himself back above the water, back into the light.

"That's a good point you've got there," Peterson said.

Rutherford shook his head. "That wasn't a rhetorical question. What do you have, Peterson? What's gonna get you through this?"

"My wife passed away—you know that. Lost her a long time ago. And we didn't have any children. That's just how it is."

"Yeah, but you've got something going on. You think there's some kind of firewall between the civilian side and the military side, but I can plug into the rumor mill whenever I want, Director. And I happen to know there's something going with you and your secretary, Miss Cynthia."

Peterson smiled. Maybe there was; maybe there wasn't. He hadn't even properly *kissed* her yet, hadn't even taken her out on a real date. But good Lord, he would take her on a proper date, if he could. He looked down. In another life, maybe.

"Look at you smiling," Rutherford said. "You just gave yourself away. I couldn't have you as a soldier in my unit. The enemy could read the battle plan off that face of yours." Rutherford laughed.

"You got me," Peterson said, laughing. "So do me a favor and get a move on with that list. Just pick a *name*, for God's sake. Just pick a guy at random, we'll say it's Octavian, and then we'll go lock him up. Case closed. And then I could at least buy this girl a nice dinner."

Rutherford chuckled. "That's the wheels of justice for you. Thank the Lord I'm not a civilian."

Peterson sighed. "I never thought I'd end up here, you know. I started out as a Secret Service agent, just like my dad. God, I looked up to that man. He served under Eisenhower and Kennedy. He quit not too long after Kennedy was killed."

"And did he have any theories on that?"

"He sure did. But he kept it to himself, for years and years. And then when one day, when he was old—when he was dying, actually—we got on the subject somehow. And I'll never forget what he told me. He said, 'That was the most false-flag bullshit that ever was. The whole thing was a goddamn frame-up, ordered by all those bastards on the inside.'"

"Christ almighty."

"But he didn't know that, really. He just *felt* it. He didn't have any actual theory about what happened. But he knew something was wrong, knew all the way down to his soul that something was wrong about the whole thing. But what he could he do? He took it to his grave. He couldn't change the world, not that part of it, anyway. He couldn't beat the machine."

"And now here you are, the loyal son walking in the footsteps, and you really *are* mixing it up with a bunch of bastards staging false-flag attacks, trying to kill our President. You're fighting the machine."

"But that's not what I meant by telling you that. I'm just—"

"I know you didn't mean it that way. But life's got a whole rhythm to it, a poetry you can't even control sometimes. The thing your daddy felt was real—he just had no idea how to fight it. And now you're fighting it, and you might just win. There's a poetry in that, the kind of poetry I believe in." Rutherford smiled. "You've got more small wonders than you know."

He squared his jaw just then, and seriousness flooded his face. "Can I trust you with something, Peterson?"

Peterson sharpened his eyes. "You know you can."

"Between you, me, and the flag, I think our Commander-in-Chief has lost his marbles."

"How's that?"

"This Gadsden Brigade thing—I think it's fools' gold. There's something about it that just isn't right."

"But you had to have heard of them before. *I've* heard of them, and I'm a civilian. Even my dad heard of them, and that was back in the sixties."

"I've *heard* of them. But I don't *believe* in them. It's just a legend. Legends don't start suddenly coming true. The President's in his darkest days right now, going through his toughest times. And suddenly this white knight McCallister starts appearing to him on a video screen, from some undisclosed location in Lord-knows-where-istan?"

"You think he's making it up? Seeing things?"

Rutherford shook his head. "Of course not. He's talking to the fella, all right. But who in the blue hell is he?"

"You're the military man. You tell me."

"Union McCallister is a retired brigadier general. Served with distinction in Iraq and Afghanistan. But there's no evidence he was ever involved in special ops, not ever."

"But that's what a clandestine group is. You know that. The Gadsden Brigade is like a sleeper cell, on the side of good. How many times could they ever have been deployed in our history? Or have they *ever* been deployed in our history?"

Rutherford threw up his hands. "Damned if I know. But fine. I know for a fact that McCallister is a living, breathing human being who served in Uncle Sam's army. And I know that he disappeared about six years ago, which matches up with Wilkins's side of the story. But that's not as peculiar as you all think it is. Some guys—they're just born fighters, or they're loners. And when they retire, they don't get some desk job someplace, don't go serving on the board of some corporation. Some guys *do* disappear. You know why? Because they go S.O.F., that's why: soldier of fortune. They could make millions. And I'm telling you, based on all my experience serving this country, that it's more likely that Union McCallister is some soldier of fortune than the leader of some super-elite special ops unit."

Peterson felt a burning in his stomach, and in that moment, he realized the whole appeal of McCallister and whatever he was selling. He *needed* McCallister to be real, and so did Wilkins. Because if he was a fake, then they all really could be at the end of their rope—and hanging from one, before long.

"And his men," Rutherford continued. "Who in tarnation are they? We know who McCallister is. But who's in the unit? How many are there? And how are we supposed to get them all back here?"

"I don't know," Peterson said. "You'd have to ask the President. I know as much as you do. He..." Peterson paused. "He's keeping this one really close to the vest."

Rutherford nodded. "And there's the rub, as Willy Shakespeare says. I'm not trying to rain on y'all's parade here. I'm just trying to keep our wits about us. We all need that right now. It's life and death—and that's the type of situation I know best. Life and death."

The Gadsdens are real, Peterson thought. *I can feel it, the way Dad could. They have to be. They just have to be.*

We need them to be.

Chapter 32

Bragg looked across the *Resolute* desk at Wilkins as the two sat in the Oval Office. "It's March, almost April," he said. "And Bryson still hasn't jumped into the race."

He glanced around the office. Bragg had been visiting the Oval Office since Barack Obama was president, but the majesty of the room never failed to awe him. Behind Wilkins were three tall windows made immortal by Kennedy during the Cuban missile crisis, when the young president had stood in the dusk agonizing over the fate of humanity. No doubt Wilkins had suffered the same agonies of late.

Behind Bragg was the fireplace, where Wilkins sat with foreign heads of state. Off to the left was the east door, which led out to the Rose Garden, where Wilkins had held court with the press following his veto of the Total Information Awareness Act last year. To the right were the northwest door, which led to the West Wing, and the west door, which led to Wilkins' study—the heart of the Wilkins presidency.

Power flowed through this single room, power of a sort that Bragg had never felt anywhere else, power that Wilkins could concentrate and beam to the ends of the earth with a phone call or the slash of a pen, power that could exercise dominion over billions in all the remotest corners of the planet. Today Bragg had come to help Wilkins concentrate that power against Bryson and Octavian.

"Maybe he won't jump in after all," Wilkins said.

"Or maybe he'll go third party. After America gets a good dose of Taylor Quade running against you, there might be an opening for Bryson then."

Wilkins laughed. "Taylor Quade—good lord. We're risking our lives to fight for democracy, just so I can run an election against Taylor Quade? Goodness gracious."

"Quade's catching on. He's polling well in hypothetical matchups."

"I don't doubt it. He's a very well-dressed man, after all. Suit's a little empty, though."

Bragg chuckled. "Look at you, shifting into campaign mode. You bring half the energy to this election that you're using on our Octavian project, and you'll steamroll Quade." Bragg paused. "But Bryson. What's he up to? What's he waiting for?"

"Damned if I know. I can't figure it out myself. Maybe he's given up on the presidency—and he just wants my head." Wilkins looked out the window for a moment, then turned back to Bragg. "But what's the endgame? We've always assumed that the plan was to get Bryson in the White House. They tried to kill me and screwed it up, but they'd beat me in the election and take down the whole system from the inside. So what's the plan now? Use Quade as a Trojan horse?" Wilkins shook his head. "That just doesn't seem right to me. It's not a strong move. Octavian and Bryson—they make strong moves."

"Maybe they're planning another Operation Reichstag?"

"We would've picked up something on it. Peterson's been busting Brigade 910 operatives left and right. And besides, it's too obvious. They tried that already."

Then there's only one move left to make, Bragg thought. "You're right," he said. "That's not how they'll come at you. But I've got a radical idea."

"What's that?"

"*We* go at *them*."

"We're trying, Bragg. You know that."

"But I'm not talking about a decapitation strike against Octavian—not if we don't know who he is yet. I'm talking about engaging these guys head-on, you demolishing Bryson in a big speech, me exposing him in the press. Why should we wait?"

"Because we're trying to avoid false moves, that's why. You know that. We'd be leading with our jaws."

"Leading with our jaws how? We've got the Operation Reichstag file. We have a mountain of documentary evidence that Bryson tried to orchestrate the worst terror attack in American history, a massive false-flag attack."

"The documentary evidence isn't as much of a mountain as you think, and it isn't airtight. And keep in mind that Moloch is dead.

He was the only real witness we had, and he conveniently caught a bout of depression and killed himself."

Damn, he's gun-shy, Bragg thought. "But we can't sit around and wait to see what these guys are going to do next. We're trying to figure out their endgame, as if it's up them, as if this is supposed to happen to us. I've got a better idea—we'll make it happen to *them*. *Our* endgame. They don't have to be the ones flying this plane."

"They're flying it as long as we don't know who Octavian is," Wilkins said. "I wish that weren't true, but that's the way it is." He paused, then smiled. "You and Peterson, the both of you. Cowboys."

"You need us," Bragg said. "Let us off the leash. Enough with the holding pattern, already. You saw the way Bryson tore you apart in that speech a few weeks ago. *Fight back*."

Wilkins started to speak, then stopped.

I've got him thinking, Bragg thought.

"I can't tell you or your reporters what to write, or not to write," Wilkins said. "But hypothetically speaking… if you were to go down this road, I'd ask you to go slow. Nice and slow, real gradual, so we could test the waters a bit. Hypothetically speaking, of course. Because the President can't talk to a media bigwig about what to publish."

Bragg smiled. "Of course. And gradual sounds like a good approach to me, Mr. President. Hypothetically speaking."

"And I might just be interested in making a speech about all this, after all."

"I'll have the editorial on the speech polished and ready to go." Bragg studied Wilkins.. "Can I ask you something?" he said. "Something that might be a little close for comfort?"

"You media types are all the same," Wilkins said, rolling his eyes. "Fire away, Bragg."

"You trust this McCallister?"

Wilkins set his jaw. "With my life."

"But how?"

"Because sometimes, it's just instinct. How did you know to start developing those media platforms of yours? Did someone put up a PowerPoint showing you how much market share you'd get, how much profit you'd make? Or did you take a leap of faith?"

"It was a leap of faith, but it was based on fact. I had a vision. I had some reason to believe that I'd found a market, some way *in.* I didn't have a PowerPoint in front of me, no, but I knew the lay of the land." Bragg paused. "And with all due respect, all you have is someone who pops up on a video screen.

"I have a lot more than that, Bragg. There's a lot I don't tell you or Peterson, or Sharpe, or even my wife. The Gadsden Brigade is for real, and what Octavian and Bryson did to them is real, too. And we're going to get them back here."

Delusions, Bragg thought. *This is worse than overwork, worse than depression—this is mental instability. Our President is losing it, right before my eyes.*

"I trust you," Bragg said. "You know that, I hope. If I didn't, I wouldn't be here—I couldn't be here. I'm staking the integrity of my publications on a man who I think is the last hope for this country." Bragg thought of the bomb that exploded in his office in Chicago. "I'm risking my life."

Wilkins nodded. "There's a 'but' coming. The more flattering the intro, the faster that 'but' comes."

Bragg smiled. "*But*, Mr. President, I'm a professional skeptic. It comes with the territory. And I'm skeptical of this one." Bragg leaned forward and laid a hand on the *Resolute* desk. "And I think you should be, too. Because we're banking on a fairy tale, and Bryson and Octavian are banking on bullets and bombs."

"Sharpe says they'll wade in blood," Wilkins said. "I don't doubt it." He massaged his temples for a moment, then righted himself and locked his eyes onto Bragg's. "But here's what they don't realize, Bragg. I'll wade in blood, too. *Theirs*."

Bragg swallowed hard. *He's losing touch with reality.*

He rose and extended his hand to Wilkins. "Then let's get to work," he said. "Let me go after Bryson. We're not going down without a fight."

Wilkins rose and shook Bragg's hand. "We're not going down," he said. "Period."

Chapter 33

Gordon Bragg's helicopter took off from the White House helipad as Bragg sipped from a tumbler full of single malt.

Even at sixty-one, he still marveled at how far he was from the Brooklyn streets where he grew up—at the moment, two hundred fifty miles in distance, and forty years in time. From getting his ass kicked by the Italian toughs in Bensonhurst for having a funny-sounding name, to a silver Mercedes helicopter ferrying him to and from sit-downs with the President of the United States—who was now the *second* black president in American history, a fact which would have been incomprehensible to the guinea punks who used to kick Bragg's teeth in. He was light years from home.

Bragg looked out the window of the helicopter as it ascended above the capital. From the red-brick tenements of Brooklyn to the majesty of the National Mall from above—the Capitol standing sentry to the east, the lawn stretching to the Monument in the west. From there the reflecting pool shimmered to the steps of the Lincoln Memorial, where Martin Luther King had thundered his dream.

Bragg had been everywhere in the world—London, Paris, Beijing, Tokyo, Rio, Cape Town; everywhere. And this swampy southern town, whose stunted office buildings weren't half as tall as those in Rosslyn, Virginia, was the most beautiful place he had ever seen. The city was the seat of power of the most awesome nation in the history of the world, every inch of it a monument to that power.

Bragg turned on the LCD monitor that filled the wall across from his seat. He had his own cabin on this silver hulk that whirred above Washington: leather seats, hardwood floors, a full bar.

Bryson flashed on the screen, and Bragg glowered.

He was replaying the speech Bryson had given a few weeks ago, in which he'd declared that *Reed Wilkins is a man who supports radical social policies, radical economic policies, a man whose sympathies lie with the anarchists tearing our cities apart, instead of with the men and women trying to stop them.*

Like Bragg had told Wilkins that day, it was the most devastating speech he'd ever seen a former administration official deliver against a sitting president. Wilkins would have to launch a line-by-line counterattack, and Bragg would have to back him up.

Bragg wondered if the President was up to the task. He seemed like he was beginning to lose his mind, counting on that McCallister to ride in as a white knight. The Commander-in-Chief was cracking.

This was Wilkins's Cuban missile crisis. Bragg was born during the real thing, back in October 1962, something his father never failed to remind him of growing up. The senior Bragg worshipped Kennedy—"That man saved the world back in sixty-two," he'd always say—but Gordon didn't share his father's admiration. Kennedy was a milquetoast wimp who almost got hundreds of millions of people killed. He was feckless, a weakling who yanked American missiles from Turkey in order to buy a few years' peace from the Soviets, condemning millions in Central Europe to continued slavery.

At least Wilkins had spurned Bryson's deal. But did he have the guts to go all the way? And now it was fair to ask—could he muster enough sanity?

Bragg fixed his gaze on Bryson, studying his body language, the gestures, the ice in the eyes of a man who tried to kill thousands of civilians last year.

And as Bragg stared in, it hit him. *That's it,* he thought. *That's it.*

He grabbed his tablet and began scribbling notes with his stylus.

I have to take this to Wilkins, he thought.

There was only one man who could be Octavian, and Bragg had just figured out who it was.

Chapter 34

Johnny cocked his handgun and laid it under the driver's seat. "You in position?" he asked into his wireless headset.

"Affirmative," Neely said.

"Good. Any minute now."

Johnny peered outside, raindrops pattering on the windshield and streaking down in rivulets. He was sitting in an abandoned lot in north Jersey, grass sprouting through cracked concrete, long-bankrupt strip mall stores standing fallow in the yellow glow of the lot's light towers. He was waiting for an informant.

Since Johnny's assault on Buchanan several weeks ago, the corrupt cop's terrorist buddies had been much more talkative, and Johnny and Neely were closing in on some who could lead them to Gaines. It was now clear that the Authority, under Peterson, had inflicted massive damage on Brigade 910 over the last year, and increasingly Gaines relied on stooges to carry out his orders. Lots of them were rich-boy faux-revolutionaries who were losing their nerve, some of whom had already come begging for mercy after Johnny had served notice through Buchanan that he'd kill anyone who didn't cooperate. In fact, he'd already gleaned one investigative nugget that had eluded Peterson and Fullerton: Gaines had operated out of Puerto Vallarta the night of the failed raid on the upstate lodge, and had used a computer program he'd written himself to gun down Fullerton's men.

But there had been other unexpected developments. Over the last couple of weeks, three of Johnny's informants had turned up dead: one from a drug overdose, another by suicide, the third by car accident. Someone was on to the whole thing now, and the end couldn't be far off. The same thing, after all, had happened to Giovanni Sr.'s informants over the last few weeks before the end.

Tonight, Johnny was meeting up with a man named Kronos, some Greek wannabe mafioso who was slinging drugs for Brigade 910 and had intel on Gaines's circle. Neely was camped out on the rooftop of one of the abandoned stores, clutching an automatic rifle mounted on a bipod.

"You sure you can handle that thing?" Johnny said into his headset.

"You want to see me squeeze one off?" Neely asked. "Put one right through your windshield?"

Johnny rolled his eyes. "No thanks, McLain."

"Come on, Luca. I'll shoot one into the passenger seat. Just to show you how I handle it."

"No thanks, munchkin. I believe you."

"Call me munchkin again, Luca, and I'll blow your nuts off from this rooftop. Even though these telescopic sights might not be strong enough to find them."

Johnny laughed. "You could see them from space. Don't worry about that."

Just then, a blue BMW came gliding through the lot. "Showtime," Johnny said into the headset.

The BMW pulled up next to Johnny's SUV, and the driver powered down the window.

Johnny lowered his passenger-side window and faced the driver of the other car. "Hands on the steering wheel," he said. The driver complied.

Johnny scrutinized him: mid-to-late thirties, black hair slicked back, olive skin, clad in black. *He's headed to the fucking club after this. Right out of a goddamn movie.*

"You Kronos?" he asked.

The man nodded. "Right. And you're Luca."

"That's right. Your boss knows me very well."

"You have Hyperion's attention. And he'd like to—"

"I know you blow him every night, Kronos, but his name is Gaines. Don't give me the Hyperion bullshit. Gaines."

Kronos's eyes blazed for a moment, but then he nodded and composed himself. He cleared his throat. "*Mr. Gaines* would like to make you an offer."

"He's not in a position to negotiate. Dead men don't make deals."

"But Mr. Gaines is alive, Luca. And right now, he knows where you are, but you don't know where *he* is. So he can make any deal he wants. And dictate the terms, too."

Johnny narrowed his eyes. "And how do I know you really talk to him?"

Kronos grinned. "Because I just watched a video of your pig father getting what he deserved."

Johnny reached for his gun.

"Don't let him get to you, Luca," Neely said in his headset. "Focus."

"Mr. Gaines told me he'll give you your own private screening," Kronos continued. "It's a good little flick. I watched it while I fucked a hooker last night."

"What does Gaines want?" Johnny spat.

"To meet you. Tonight."

Johnny swallowed hard. *No way.* "Then tell him to come here."

Kronos shook his head. "No, Luca. We'll take a little drive to go meet him."

"Don't do it," Neely said in the headset. "Don't fall for that."

"No deal," Johnny said. "We're not taking any little drives. Go tell Gaines that he can come to me and beg for his life on his knees, or I can go find him and put a bullet in his fucking head."

"Good," Neely said.

"Or maybe he'll find *you*," Kronos said. "Or your mother."

Johnny nodded. "And maybe I'll find yours. Helena Kronos, sixty-three years old, works in a bookstore, lives in Woodbridge." Johnny grinned. "But don't worry, Kronos. I won't touch her. I'll just throw your body through her living room window tonight."

Kronos arched his eyebrows. "Mr. Gaines has another offer for you."

"Tell me."

They must be trying to figure out what I'm made of. Trying to see what kind of a man I am, where my breaking point is.

"If you stop your vendetta," Kronos said, "if you forget about revenge for your father, if you stop hunting Mr. Gaines, he'll make you a powerful man."

I must be getting closer to this son of a bitch than I thought. "Powerful," Johnny said. "And how's he going to do that?"

"He'll hand you every Brigade 910 lieutenant wanted by the Authority. He'll get them all in one place, and the arrest is yours to make. You give the intelligence to your people, lead the team, and bust the whole group." Kronos, still gripping the steering wheel, leaned out the window. "You hear me, Luca? He'll give up his revolution. This whole war, six years of bombings and attacks, all over—if you leave him alone. And you'll be the biggest hero in America."

"I wouldn't sell out my parents for that," Neely said into the headset.

I know Gaines. And if there's one thing I know for sure, it's that that fucker will never, ever give up that "revolution" of his.

"But I'm already the biggest hero in America," Johnny said. "And I also know that the revolution won't be over until Gaines is dead or in jail." He paused. "Any other offers?"

Kronos shook his head. "No. Which means I'll be leaving now. Mr. Gaines likes to hear bad news right away."

Johnny nodded. "Well don't mind me. I'll just follow you, and I can talk to Gaines about it myself."

"It doesn't work that way, Luca. Because if you tried, you might run into some obstacles. The kind that would have me throwing *your* body through your mother's window tonight." Kronos paused. "So no deal, then?"

Johnny shook his head. "No deal."

Just then, Kronos looked in his rearview mirror.

"Two, right behind you," Neely said. "Driver's side."

Johnny's eyes darted at the side mirror, and there they were, two goons charging with guns drawn. He ripped into reverse and slammed the gas pedal.

The truck surged backwards, and the goons dove out of the way; Johnny had been aiming for them. He whipped out behind Kronos's car, blocking his exit for a moment.

Out of the car, Johnny thought, *out of the car if I want to live—*

He popped the door open and jumped out, handgun drawn. One of Kronos's men, face swaddled in a bandana, squared up for an Uzi shot.

Johnny shot first, nailing him in the shoulder.

Gunshots exploded behind him, shattering glass, eviscerating metal. It was Neely, gunning down Kronos's car from the roof, pinning the Greek inside. Kronos peeled backwards and smashed into Johnny's truck, then lurched forward and zoomed off under a hail of Neely's gunfire, a final shot blowing out his rear window as he escaped.

Fuck. He whirled around to face the second shooter and smoked him with one shot, splitting his cranium and blasting his brains across the lot.

Johnny turned now to the first shooter he'd hit in the shoulder, twitching on the ground, thrashing for his Uzi, which was far out of reach.

"Don't worry about this little fucker," Neely said in the headset. And with one shot, she capped him through the neck, splaying him in a pool of maroon.

"We need to get the fuck out of here," Johnny said.

"No shit," Neely said. "I'm on the way down. Swing around back."

Chapter 35

"That was a hit, plain and simple," Neely said, smoking a cigarette as Johnny drove. "He offered you a deal, and when you turned him down, it turned into a hit. That came from Gaines."

"But that deal was bullshit, McLain," Johnny said. "I would never accept it. Gaines had to know that."

"Maybe not. He doesn't know you, not like you know him—or like you think you know him. Maybe he thought he could make a trade with you, like a ceasefire or something. No more attacks from Brig 910, and you lay off him."

"Neither of us would stick to that deal. He'll never stop trying to burn down this country, and I'll never stop trying to kill him."

"And now he'll never stop trying to kill you. He reached some kind of a breaking point with you, some kind of a red line. You're becoming a real problem to him now. And he wants you out."

Johnny gripped the steering wheel more tightly. "Then it's just a matter of time, now. One of us lives, and one of us dies."

They were boring through the Lincoln Tunnel, on the way to a "fixer" Neely knew in the city who would take care of Johnny's truck. A constellation of yellow lamps illuminated the roadway ahead, glowing off the clinical tile on either side, as a battalion of citygoers raced towards midtown.

"Luca, do you believe in God?" Neely asked.

I can't remember the last time someone asked me that. "Never met him," he replied.

Neely squinted. "Well, I believe in Him. There is no god but God, Luca. Remember that."

Johnny nodded. "Copy, munchkin."

"I know you don't give a shit, or you don't think about it much. But growing up where I did, you learn what that means. Bashar Assad wasn't God. Gaines isn't God, Octavian isn't God. God is love, God is justice. And that's why no wicked dude can hold power forever. Because justice will come for him in the end."

"But there are plenty of wicked dudes having their moment right now."

"Well, sometimes my automatic rifle can speed up the process." Neely took a drag on her cigarette. "Are you an atheist?"

Who knows anymore? Johnny sighed. "I don't know what I am. I believe in right and wrong, I believe in justice. My mom, she's the religious one."

"You could use a little religion at a time like this, with what we're up against. A little religion to keep out the fear. I'm not afraid of anyone, not afraid to die. I fear only God, Luca. God is great." Neely turned to Johnny. "Luca, what do you know about the end of the world?"

Johnny glanced at Neely, then turned back to the road, the truck surging through the tunnel. "I know the first sign of the apocalypse would be if you stopped talking for five seconds."

Neely grinned. "Good one, asshole. But maybe we should be thinking about it."

What's she talking about now? "Why?"

"Because if we can't stop Octavian, then maybe the end of the line won't be too far behind."

Johnny groaned. "Look, the dude is trying to be some kind of dictator, but I don't think he's trying to end the world."

"Oh no? You haven't seen him challenged yet. I know a thing or two about this, what happens when a dictator is challenged. Assad was a little dictator, a nothing. But when people rose up against him, he bombed towns with warplanes, tortured and murdered children, used chemical weapons. And now Octavian is about to get his hands on thousands of nuclear warheads, enough blow up the planet like a thousand times over." Neely shook her head. "What would Hitler have done with that kind of firepower? What would Gaddafi have done?" She paused. "What's Octavian going to do when someone challenges him?"

Johnny considered the question for a moment, then shrugged. "How about some music?" he said.

Neely rolled her eyes. "Allow me," she said, firing up some hip-hop.

Chapter 36

Lizbeth glanced at the lamb shank sitting on Johnny's plate on her dining room table, languishing cold in red wine sauce beside yellowing mashed potatoes. She blew out at the candle on the table and looked down at the text message glowing on her phone: "I'm sorry, sweetheart. I'll explain."

But you won't, she thought, sipping her wine.

He hadn't explained a thing in a year. And now, as Lizbeth drank her wine and gazed around the room she wanted to share with him, the life she wanted to share with him, it occurred to her that she knew nothing about the man she wanted to marry.

Nothing that counted, anyway. She'd known him for eight years now, knew the name of his first fantasy baseball team, his favorite book, his favorite song. She knew how to make him laugh, how to make him smile, how to rub his back in just the right way so that he'd fall asleep beside her.

But she didn't know what stalked the nightmares he had every night, what made him toss and turn and sometimes scream. She didn't know where that scar on his shoulder came from. She didn't know what he did for a living, where he disappeared to all the time. She didn't know what he obsessed over, what made him smolder inside.

Smolder. It was a word that Lizbeth had come to associate with Johnny this past year. Something was burning inside him, consuming him, consuming them.

Johnny Luca had made himself unknowable. And Lizbeth loved him anyway, still tried to find a way in.

She scooped up Johnny's plate, crossed the room to the garbage can, and dumped his dinner in the trash. *What a waste*, she thought.

Lizbeth had planned this dinner all week, researching the recipe, tracking down the right ingredients, picking out the perfect wine. Tonight was going to be special, not least because she knew that her cooking would blow Johnny away.

But instead, he no-showed, and not for the first time.

But it'll be the last time, Lizbeth thought.

I came a long way to see you tonight, he'd told her that night last year under the tree. *And I'd like to tell you all about just how far I came.*

Now it was time to see what the words were worth. Either Johnny would keep that promise to tell her everything, or it was over. Either their life together meant more to him than keeping all of those goddamn secrets, or Lizbeth would knock the two of them back to the way they were before—her life and his, wandering apart, lonely and incomplete.

How did we ever live before we found something so perfect? Lizbeth had asked Johnny a few months ago.

A tear rolled down her cheeks. *I don't know,* she thought.

Lizbeth loved Johnny more than life itself, more than whatever she'd written in that silly letter to him in college, more than she could ever express. He was her soulmate.

But if loving him was going to be impossible, she'd leave him. She would.

Chapter 37

"This is your moment, Gov," Ricky Howser said to Taylor Quade as they stood backstage, cheers reverberating through the arena as Senator Blair onstage fired up the crowd of twenty thousand.

"Our moment, Ricky," Quade said, slapping his campaign manager on the arm. He turned to his wife Abby, and their daughters Katie and Victoria: "Our moment, girls."

Quade beamed, reveling in the history of the night. As of tonight's primaries, Taylor Quade, Governor of Indiana, had amassed enough pledged delegates to be anointed with his party's nomination at the national convention and challenge Reed Wilkins for the presidency of the United States.

"Remember your themes," Howser said.

Quade counted on his hands as if reciting for a teacher in school. "Wilkins sucks, change is coming, and we can win this war on the terrorists and get the country on its feet with strong and principled leadership," he said. "Relax, Ricky. That's what teleprompters are for."

"You never know when one of those things'll freeze up on you, champ."

"Not me. I'm the chosen one, Ricky. This is our time."

Quade smiled at Howser, his campaign manager since his first run for Congress eleven years ago. They'd served three terms on the Hill together, followed by a miracle run for governor and a tremendous upset against the incumbent. Now Quade was white-hot, fresh off a landslide reelection the year before and riding on the highest approval ratings for any governor in the nation.

Howser was hard-boiled, grizzled, an old hand in the business of politics. His sleeves were rolled up, revealing hairy, thick arms. His brown hair was rumpled, graying, thinning. He was growing softer and rounder by the day, and he always smelled like stale coffee. For some reason, he reminded Quade of a chewed-up cigar.

Quade turned to Abby and the girls. "Show time," he said.

"Good luck," Abby said, smiling.

"Good luck, Daddy," nine-year-old Katie said.

"Go kick some ass, Dad," fourteen-year-old Victoria said.

"*Victoria*!" Abby chided.

"Let her go," Quade said. He smiled at Victoria. "You've got a mouth on you like your old man, sweetheart."

The soon-to-be first family, all blonde. Abby was pretty enough, in a middle-America-can-relate-to-her kind of way. She was in her late forties, maybe a little plumper than she used to be, but she had a tough schedule taking care of the girls and making appearances on the campaign trail.

The girls. Victoria was growing up fast, tough and aggressive like Quade, with a ruthless streak he could be proud of. All she needed was the right dusting of charm; that would come with time, especially as she grew more beautiful. Quade felt closer to her than anyone else on earth.

Katie was sweet like her mother, charming like her. In the months ahead, Quade would introduce her to the country, and the country would fall head over heels in love with her. She'd just gotten braces, though she probably didn't actually need them. *Quade* needed her to have them, to sell the image—so Katie got braces. They seemed to hurt her, which Quade felt bad about sometimes.

Quade looked into Abby's eyes, and they shared a knowing look. They'd been married for seventeen years now, some of them spent actually in love. They went to law school together, and there was something about struggling through all-nighters together, agonizing over the bar exam, fretting over paying bills, and raising two young children that bonded a man and a woman together for life, even when there was nothing else left but the memories and the kids. She was the mother of his children and the First Lady of Indiana. She'd suffered the humiliation of Quade's affairs, the ones that the palace guards in the media covered up for him. Of course, when she had an affair of her own with a lawyer in Indianapolis, Quade had the man investigated for fraud and sentenced to twelve years in prison. There would be none of that.

But now Quade and Abby had a deal. He would be President, and she would be First Lady, and together they'd raise Katie and Victoria and make the world the way they wanted it to be.

As for how he wanted the world to be, Quade still wasn't sure. It didn't really matter—policy didn't matter, legislation didn't matter. All that mattered was a free world led by Taylor Quade, from which all good things would flow. Quade would take care of his fellow citizens, protect them, soothe what ailed them. And in order to make that reality, Quade would let two hundred million eligible voters project onto him whatever they wanted to see.

And so Taylor Quade, Governor of Indiana, forty-nine years old, stood before a black curtain as a crowd of twenty thousand chanted his name: "We want Quade! We want Quade!" Quade was caught between the moment when he was just a man, and the moment in which he was the presumptive nominee and the next president. Back here behind the black curtain, there were steel rods and stage light towers and painted concrete walls; out there, there was confetti and video screens and bunting. Taylor Quade, six feet tall, slim and elegant, his blue eyes shining, his light brown hair coiffed, awaited his moment.

"So it is now my honor to introduce to you the Governor of Indiana," Senator Blair said onstage, "the man who will deliver us from Wilkins's America, the next President of the United States, Taylor Quade!"

Quade glided to the stage as the crowd roared, the lights pouring down on him. Some shrank under those lights; others shone. Quade glowed as he soaked up the cheers.

"My fellow Americans," he said as the words filled up the glass teleprompter tilted towards him like a distant lectern, "tonight I stand before you holding articles of faith that you have placed in my hands. I stand before you as the bearer of your message to Washington, that we can stand strong against our enemies and preserve our identity as guarantors of freedom; that we can feed our hungry and care for our sick and yet still promote prosperity for all; that we can transcend the rancor that divides us and join hands in the fellowship and humanity that binds us. I stand before you as the proud nominee of our party, and as the man who will end the thuggery and ineptitude of the Wilkins administration!"

The crowd erupted as more words filled the teleprompter. Quade loaded his delivery, and in that second, he weighed the words on the screen. What did they mean, after all? What did any of this mean?

Quade raised his hands to silence the crowd, then smiled. What did it matter?

Chapter 38

Johnny put his key into Lizbeth's door, the April night heavy with the explaining he had to do. Two nights ago, he'd stood her up, out chasing phantoms, getting into a shootout and nearly getting himself killed. Again, again, again.

Johnny sighed. He'd be twenty-six in a week. When would enough be enough?

He regarded the door for a moment. Lizbeth lived in Hoboken, he lived in Jersey City; a fifteen-minute drive. A year ago, when he was deep in the heart of Operation Reichstag, blowing up safe-houses with Fullerton, getting tortured by Sigma, this was all he ever could have asked for—to be coming home to Lizbeth at the end of the night.

Remember that, Johnny thought as he turned the key in the lock.

"For a year, Reed Wilkins resisted the Total Information Awareness Act," oozed Taylor Quade's words from Lizbeth's television. "For a year, he coddled the most radical elements in our society, gave them aid and comfort, gave them time to consolidate their power and grow—to metastasize, like a cancer. And then Congress did what he wouldn't—overrode his veto and passed the act. And in the time since, the President has wielded his newfound power like a tyrant desperate to cover his tracks, crushing protests in Chicago, launching a commando-style raid on a country home in a quiet upstate New York village, cracking down on—"

Lizbeth powered the television off and turned to Johnny. "Quade," she said, rolling her eyes.

Johnny smiled. "Not a fan?"

"Do I have an IQ over seventy?"

Johnny hadn't given the election much thought, really. But of course he'd vote for Wilkins. After all, the dude *did* save the country from a fascist overthrow last year. And besides, Wilkins could appoint Johnny as Secretary of Fantasy Baseball once they'd taken out Octavian.

Lizbeth crossed the room and took Johnny's hand. "Let's sit," she said. "We should talk."

Uh oh. That was why she'd asked Johnny here tonight, to talk. And the way she asked, the way she took his hand tonight, she wasn't going to take any excuses this time.

They sat on her couch silently for a moment. Johnny glanced at the digital photo frame on the side table, cycling through pictures of Lizbeth with her parents, her sister, her college friends—Johnny and his old roommate Billy included. He smiled when the frame shuffled through Lizbeth's last few months with Johnny.

Lizbeth turned his face towards her and looked into his eyes, her own green eyes sharpening behind her rectangular glasses. "So what's going on with you, sweetheart?"

Where do I begin? "What do you mean?"

"You know what I mean." Lizbeth frowned. "Is this normal for us now? You bail on me, and have nothing to say?"

"I told you. Something came up the other night. And I'm sorry. It doesn't make it right. But something came up, and I had to go take care of it."

"And what was it?"

Johnny didn't answer. *You deserve to know.*

"It's a simple enough question," Lizbeth said. "You were going to come here for dinner, and then… you didn't. And since I know you're not stupid enough to cheat on me, there has to be some explanation." Johnny could tell she was struggling to keep back a tear. She looked down. "At least I *hope* you're not stupid enough."

This sight of Lizbeth, fighting back tears wondering if he was cheating on her, broke something inside Johnny.

"My father," he said.

Lizbeth looked up. "What about him?"

Johnny ran his hand through his hair, clutched his scalp. "Someone killed him, Lizbeth."

Lizbeth put her hand to his arm. "What are you talking about?"

"He didn't kill himself. He got mixed up in something bad, something really serious, and someone killed him and made it look like he shot himself."

Lizbeth stroked his face, then locked his hand in hers. "You know this… for sure?

Johnny nodded. "I've known it for about a year now."

"And how do you know?"

"He left a diary. My mom gave it to me last year, told me I had to read it. It turns out he was working a case, and the case… took a wrong turn, I guess. He found out some things he wasn't supposed to find out. And then someone killed him. If you read the last few diary entries…" Johnny looked down. "If you read the last few, you can see that he knew it was coming. And no one could help him."

Lizbeth took it all in. And then she threw her arms around him and pulled him close, hard, kissing him all over his face and his head. "My God, why didn't you tell me?" she said, holding him tight. "A whole year, Gio, you've known this a whole year—"

"Lizbeth—"

"Shut up," she said, holding Johnny even closer now. "Just shut up."

Johnny closed his eyes, sinking into her embrace. He remembered kneeling before his father's grave the morning after he found out, after a night spent crying on his mother's couch. There was no one to hold him that morning as he knelt before the grave, as he vowed to get even with those responsible. And tonight, just for this moment, he allowed himself to fall into Lizbeth's embrace.

"Who else knows about this?" Lizbeth asked.

"My mother," Johnny said. "A few other people."

"Paul?"

"No. My mother didn't want him to know. She thought he was too young."

"Gio…" Lizbeth stroked Johnny's hair. "What was he investigating?"

How do I put this? "Corruption. There was a mole… a mole inside his department. And it led to something more, much more. And my dad kept following it, even when the bosses told him to back off."

They fell silent for a moment. What else could Johnny say? How the hell was he going to tell her about Brigade 910 and Octavian?

"So when you disappear all the time, like the other night," Lizbeth said, "That has something to do with this?"

Johnny sighed, then slipped from her embrace and sat up. He took her hand. "It does." He looked away for a moment, then turned back to Lizbeth. "Because I know who killed him."

"Who?"

"I can't tell you, sweetheart."

"Back to the secrets again," Lizbeth said. "And what are you trying to do, catch him yourself?"

"No." Johnny shook his head. "I'm trying to kill him."

"What?" Lizbeth's eyes widened in shock.

It's simple enough. "I know who he is, and I spend my time trying to track him down. So I can kill him."

"So you can kill him." Lizbeth closed her eyes. "Where were you the other night?"

"Meeting up with people who might know where he is."

"So you can kill him?" Lizbeth got up from the couch and paced around the room. "That's murder."

"Murder is what *he* did, Lizbeth," Johnny said. "I think you know the difference."

Lizbeth narrowed her eyes. "The *difference*," she said. "You're going to hunt him down and kill him. If you know who he is, and where he is, why don't you call the police?"

"That didn't do my dad any good!"

"Gio, listen." Lizbeth studied him for a moment. "I don't know who you are right now. This… this isn't you. You *know* this isn't you. You're not a killer."

Johnny thought back to the shootout with Kronos and his men the other night. *If only that were true.*

"This is crazy," Lizbeth continued. "Gio, you know I'd do anything for you, right? I would die for you, if I had to. I would do *anything* for you. But I can't follow you down this kind of path."

I know. "I'm not asking you to."

"But you are. If we're together, then we're together all the way. You support me, I support you. That's what this is all about." Lizbeth wiped away tears. "But I can't sit at home wondering if you're out killing someone—or getting killed." She crossed the room back to him, sat beside him again. "I can't pretend like I know what this is like for you. I don't. I never… knew anyone who was killed. So I don't know how it feels. But I hear you scream in your sleep sometimes. And now I know why." Lizbeth took Johnny's hand again. "But you know this isn't the way. This *can't* be the way."

Johnny kissed her hand, then slipped loose and stood up. "It's the only way," he said. "What am I supposed to do?"

"Call the police." Lizbeth was pleading now, like Johnny's mother did that night last year. "Or tell your bosses. Tell *anyone* who can deal with this the right way."

"Lizbeth, the guy who did this—I can't call the cops to bring him in. I can't call the *feds* to bring him in. I have to do it myself."

"What are you talking about?"

I said too much. Johnny pointed to Lizbeth's front door. "Someday I'm going to walk through that door, and it's going to be over. I promise. This whole thing is going to be *all over*, and we're going to have a life together. Someday soon, I'm going to walk through that door and tell you that it's all behind us."

"Or someday your mom will knock on the door and tell me that we lost you." Lizbeth started to cry, then steadied herself. "And if you make it back—if you walk back through that door—how much blood will you have on your hands then? Who will you be?"

"I'll be me. Who else would I be?"

"You should go." Lizbeth got up and walked over to him, then kissed him one more time. "God, I love you more than anything." She embraced him, buried her head in his neck, and Johnny felt warm tears on his skin. Lizbeth stepped back. "But you're going to have to do this without me. And I never thought I'd say that."

One last chance to let it all go. One chance to call the cops, like she said, or let Fullerton and the guys chase their leads and find Gaines. One chance to lead a normal life.

"Then I should go," Johnny said. "But I'm telling you, I'm going to walk through that door soon. And we'll never have to worry about this again."

"It might be too late then," Lizbeth said, crying. "But you've made your choice."

Johnny started to reply, started to walk over, take her in his arms, tell her he was forgetting the whole thing, that he would let it go.

But then he choked back the words. She was right. He'd made his choice, and now he had to live with it, to see it through to the end, to whatever end there was. He turned and walked out of the apartment.

Chapter 39

"Bragg's done a pretty good job of hammering Bryson in those publications of his," Wilkins said to Peterson and Sharpe as they sat in the Oval Office. "So good, actually, that Quade's the man now." Wilkins grinned. "And Quade, fellas, is what I call a layup."

Peterson grinned back. "I like to think of him as a hanging curve," he said. He shrugged at Sharpe. "But I'm a baseball fan."

Wilkins laughed; Sharpe smiled faintly.

Wilkins narrowed his eyes. Sharpe hadn't been himself lately. He was quiet, withdrawn, melancholy. Last week he'd rambled and stammered through testimony before the House Judiciary Committee, and there were rumors that he often sealed himself in his office at Justice for days at a time. And as he sat here in the Oval Office this morning, he looked as if he hadn't slept in days, his eyes glazed over, an uncharacteristic five o'clock shadow cast across his profile.

We're all cracking up in our own ways, Wilkins thought as he studied the men in the room. Sharpe was falling apart. Peterson didn't have a life outside this—hadn't had a life outside this for eighteen months now. And Bragg, who was running late to this morning meeting, was staking his fortune and legacy on this, veering from responsible entrepreneur to man obsessed with taking down Bryson.

That was the word: *obsession.* The four men were now obsessed with destroying Octavian, with tearing down the Octavian latticework. They'd all marched off to halt the would-be emperor like doughboys off to war, and now that exuberance had rusted over to grim duty as they sank into their trenches. This was now a war of attrition, consuming them, wearing them down by the day.

"I guess there's been a change of plans," Peterson said. "Bryson can't be president now—Bragg made him too radioactive." He looked intently, almost pleadingly, at Wilkins. "That's something, you know."

Maybe so, Wilkins thought. Peterson was trying to show a sign of progress, any sign. Those were few and far between these days.

"That was their plan all along, to move Bryson into the White House, for him to get his hands on all the levers of power," Peterson continued. "So now Bryson's out, and Quade's in. Is Quade their boy?"

"Does it matter?" Wilkins asked. "Let's say he's not their boy. If he's sitting in this chair, is he going to stop them?" Wilkins shook his head. "Not only can't he stop them, but if he's sworn in on January 20, they'll be controlling him by January 21."

"Then you'd better get the stump speech ready, Reed," Sharpe said.

Wilkins arched his eyebrows; Peterson turned to Sharpe. Those were the first words he'd spoken all morning, and he'd called the President by his first name.

Wilkins weighed the words for a moment, then smiled. "The man's right," he said, gesturing towards Sharpe. "Will here couldn't run an election worth a damn, but he's right about that one. I'm going to have to beat Quade at the good old ballot box. Give him the old one-two." Wilkins threw a couple of punches. "It's a democracy, after all."

"Can't you dump that miserable Greenaway from the ticket?" Peterson asked.

Al Greenaway was Wilkins's bumbling idiot of a Vice President, some career Beltway hack the party had forced upon Wilkins to balance the ticket. *Can air balance anything?* Wilkins had joked with Peterson, then on his Secret Service detail.

Al Greenaway, the man who would've been President if Wilkins had been assassinated last year, the man Bryson would have annihilated in this year's election if all had gone according to plan.

Wilkins shook his head. "I can't dump him," he said. "Sign of weakness."

Peterson sighed. "Well, maybe neutralizing Bryson put Octavian back on his heels a little bit," he said. "Maybe the real fight now is the election, after all. Not bullets and bombs, but the election of 2024."

"Followed by another assassination attempt in 2025 if Reed wins," Sharpe said. "Another Operation Reichstag, and another assassination attempt."

Sharpe was right, and for a second, Wilkins wanted to hate him for it.

Just then, the northwest door opened, and Bragg stepped inside.

"You're late," Wilkins said.

"I know," Bragg said. "I'm sorry." He held up a leather briefcase. "I was just putting the finishing touches on it."

"The finishing touches on what?" Wilkins asked. *What's he up to?*

Bragg crossed the room and sat between Peterson and Sharpe. "Our breakthrough. Goddamn it, finally, our breakthrough." He held up the briefcase again. "The definitive report on Octavian's identity."

Wilkins had fought in the Gulf War; he'd run tough campaigns for governor and president; and he'd survived an assassination attempt last year. But a chasm exploded in his stomach now in a way it never had before.

"You'd better get talking," Wilkins said.

Chapter 40

"It can't be," Wilkins said.

"Believe it," Bragg said.

"I won't."

"We need to hear him out," Peterson said.

"I've heard enough, and I say no."

"Conclusive evidence," Bragg said. "We have conclusive evidence that Union McCallister is Octavian."

Impossible, Wilkins thought. He raised a fist to slam it on the *Resolute* desk, but caught himself. Instead he pointed his finger at Bragg. "How can you have conclusive evidence on someone who barely exists?"

"Because he *exists*, Mr. President. He's left his footprint in this world. Enough for me to investigate."

"To *investigate*?"

Bragg nodded. "That's right. I knew you wouldn't investigate him—so I did. This McCallister situation has seemed off to me from day one, and now I can prove it." Bragg looked grave. "I'm not trying to lead a witch hunt here. I just want the truth, before they kill us. And I think I've found it."

"Tell me everything you know," Wilkins said, dismayed. He pointed at Sharpe. "Will, listen up, because you'll be opening an investigation immediately. And you—" Wilkins turned to Peterson—"get ready to saddle up, if you need to."

All eyes fell on Bragg as he drew his leather briefcase up to his lap and fished out several file folders. "Union McCallister, the man who you've been talking to by videoconference," he began, "used to be the leader of the Gadsden Brigade, like he's telling you. But somewhere along the way, he betrayed the Gadsdens, betrayed his country, and now he's out for himself. He's a disloyal soldier, and he's been trying to overthrow the government of the United States."

Wilkins felt the blood bolt to this face.

"Octavian is someone from Bryson's military past," Bragg continued. "We've known that since the beginning. Well, here's their military past together." He tossed a folder onto the *Resolute* desk. "Alexander Bryson served under McCallister's command in the Gadsden Brigade. That's right, our man Bryson served in the Gadsden Brigade too, years ago."

"How the hell can you know that?" Wilkins asked. "I didn't even know the Gadsden Brigade *existed* until a couple of months ago, and you didn't know until I told you. And now you've put together a file on them?"

"Damn right, I did. Because I know where to look, and I have the connections inside DoD. They know I'm loyal, that I'm not some Russian spy or something. There've been questions about McCallister inside the brass for a long time, concerns that he was a lunatic who could try something like this. And they've been trying to take him out themselves." Bragg gestured to the desk. "Look at the documents for yourself. They're originals. Ask the Joint Chiefs."

I knew Bragg was a goddamn loose cannon, Wilkins thought. *And maybe, just maybe, this son of a bitch has saved all our hides.* "And what am I going to find in this file?" Wilkins asked, tapping the folder.

Bragg sharpened his eyes. "That McCallister was a top soldier, and he served in the group we know as the Gadsdens. The Gadsdens aren't a standalone group who just wait to assemble when some dictator threatens the Constitution, guys. They're made up of Special Ops from other groups who get called on as the Gadsdens if there's a crisis. The rest of the time, which is really all of the time, they're out on missions. McCallister was a Ranger, and he rose in rank over the years." Bragg surveyed Peterson and Sharpe for a moment, then continued. "But he started going his own way some time in the 2000s. He started running his own covert operations, covert operations in Africa and Asia. He got into drug trafficking, started making connections with narco mini-states, started providing training and mercenary manpower for their militias. He turned out to be goddamn good at psy-ops, at ginning up fringe groups and fomenting unrest. He made money off of this, guys. Big money. Enough money and connections to order himself up a mercenary division in any backwater country that he found himself in. But no one knew, not at the time."

"And where's the Bryson connection?" Peterson asked.

"Bryson was a protégé. First, it was legit, two good soldiers serving under the flag. But after Nine-Eleven, McCallister led him on unauthorized counterterrorism raids, rendition, waterboarding, all that—so Bryson could get revenge for his wife and kid. He was turning Bryson, exploiting him. And eventually, Bryson came back stateside and started up his civilian career, on the way to being elected senator and everything else." Bragg paused. "I've got my own theory about what happened."

I knew you would, Wilkins thought. "And what's that?"

"Bryson is McCallister's Manchurian candidate. He brainwashed him when they were serving together, twisted his mind over his family getting killed, and turned him into some kind of lunatic ultra-nationalist. And then he sent him back here, a charismatic guy who could get himself elected to high office and make things happen."

Peterson narrowed his eyes. "You're giving McCallister a hell of a lot of credit," he said. "But he's just a man, just one man. An Army Ranger who went off the grid and started training paramilitary groups for drug lords in God knows where. And now we're supposed to believe that he's about to overthrow the government?"

"You're underestimating what one man can do, Hunter," Bragg said, "and you know it. Hitler was just a man too. He was an art school reject, a nothing. Never won more than thirty percent of the vote. But he knew where the pressure points were, knew how to acquire power and project it, and then how to consolidate it. Look at Jack Gaines and what he's managed to do with Brigade 910. He's just one man, but he sees all the angles, knows how to maximize the power of that group of misfits he leads." Bragg sliced the air with his hand, the Brooklyn in him coming out. "But now think about it another way. Look at Los Zetas in Mexico. They were special forces who decided they wanted a piece of the action. So they hired themselves out as muscle for the cartels. And then they *became* a cartel, the strongest cartel, with all that training and hardware they had. And today, they're still the strongest. They could seize the Mexican state if they wanted to." Bragg spread his arms out wide, as if he were back at that press conference a few months ago, laying down the law to the "court eunuchs" in the media. "Now who's to say they haven't *already* seized the Mexican state? And who's to say there isn't one leader, one Octavian, who made it happen?"

"But this is America," Wilkins said. But he immediately felt foolish. *America, all right. The America of Bryson and Octavian and Operation Reichstag.*

"Right, this is America," Bragg said. "So in America, what was McCallister's move? It's all right there in that file, Mr. President. He did the same thing here that he did in some of those other countries—reaching out to fringe groups, anarchists, all kinds of miscreants. He spread that money around, and he struck gold in this country—because he was dealing with an America completely different from the one we grew up in. Fifty percent youth unemployment, cities and states going bankrupt, debt slavery, you name it." Bragg looked Wilkins in the eye; he was hitting his stride now, the Bragg of the board room, of the press conference. "But that's only one side of it," he continued. "That's the radical side of the equation. Just by knowing the right pressure points, he stoked unrest, fomented terrorism and unrest. Which created an opening for the other part of the equation."

"The Authority," Peterson said.

"Right. The Authority. The radical terrorists drove people into the arms of the fascist Authority. And that's where Bryson came in—a charismatic leader who'd lost his family to terrorism. He was the perfect face for the Authority. And now just enough of the silent majority supports the Authority, which gives it legitimacy. The Authority itself is loyal to Bryson, and he's loyal to McCallister. And now McCallister has a goddamn dagger aimed right at the heart of our democracy."

Wilkins gulped. *I'm responsible*, he thought. *I brought him into my closest confidence, made arrangements to bring him back into the country…*

"But why?" Peterson asked. "What the hell does he want?"

"Power," Bragg said. "Not money, not glory or fame, not some kind of nationalist revival. Just power. Getting out of bed in the morning and knowing that he controls three hundred fifty million people, that he can deploy the strongest military in the history of the world, that he can project so much power that every person on the planet would feel it."

Peterson narrowed his eyes. "You sure know a lot about him."

Bragg returned the look, then reached into his briefcase and pulled out another folder. He passed it to Peterson. "Pentagon behavioral analysis of McCallister, describing everything I just said and a lot more. It turns out that he's set up his own little fiefdom over in Central Asia somewhere." Bragg turned to face Wilkins. "Mr. President, the story you heard about the Gadsdens is that someone duped them into going on a mission, then had most of them killed. But that's wrong. No one duped them. The Pentagon sent them on a mission to take out McCallister, and they were all killed, every last one. The men he has around him now—they aren't Gadsdens. They're mercenaries, or fanatics like he is. The Gadsdens don't exist anymore—they're all dead."

Wilkins's insides turned to water. At this very moment, on Wilkins's orders, McCallister and his men were mobilizing to travel overland out of Kyrgyzstan into Tajikistan, then across Tajikistan and into Afghanistan. In Afghanistan, they'd board air transport, and would first fly to Turkey, and then finally back to the United States. Wilkins remembered Bragg's words from a moment ago: *He made money off of this, guys. Big money. Enough money and connections to order himself up a mercenary division in any backwater country that he found himself in.*

"There's more," Bragg continued.

There always is, Wilkins thought. "Tell us," he said.

"McCallister's got a real following now, and I'm not talking about Bryson or the soldiers he's holed up with. I'm talking about organized crime."

Wilkins arched his eyebrows. "What do you mean?"

"Well, we know that mafias can control countries. We know that at a certain point, a mafia has more money and more weapons than the state they're up against, that they can overcome the state itself and take it over. They control southern Italy, huge chunks of Mexico and Latin America, parts of Eastern Europe and Central Asia. They're creeping across Western Europe, laundering money through real estate and even through political contributions to presidential candidates. The world economy has been in a depression for fifteen years now. And the mafias are the strongest they've ever been, capturing entire states, threatening to capture more."

Wilkins nodded. "That's right. But what does that have to do with McCallister?"

"He's recruiting these mafias to his cause, getting them to believe in him, to invest in him. When he moved past drug trafficking and started getting political, starting sponsoring terrorism here in the U.S. through Brigade 910, the other cartels backed away from him, thought he was crazy and bad for their business. But now they think he can win. They're starting to think the government is going to fall in this country, and that they can do a hell of a lot of business with whatever comes next—whoever comes next." Now it was Bragg who started to bubble over with outrage. "It can happen here," he continued. "The mafia got Kennedy elected in nineteen sixty, and they probably killed him, too. Or look at Russia today. The mafia didn't make a dime under the Soviets, not when they were selling people cigarettes and TVs. But they made billions in a free-for-all under Yeltsin, and once Putin took over, they had a strongman they could deal with. And now Russia—with as many nuclear warheads as we have—is a mafia state. Most of the former Soviet countries—mafia states. And now these same kinds of scumbags are bribing politicians in Greece, in Spain, in France, buying votes for them, even contributing to presidential campaigns. All of these European countries that literally have gone bankrupt in the last fifteen years are now starting to buckle, starting to come under the influence of these guys, who have more money than God." Bragg bored a look into Peterson and Sharpe's eyes, then turned back to Wilkins. "And now they've got their eyes on us. And McCallister—Octavian—is their man."

Bragg's words hung in the Oval Office, thick as smoke after a bomb explosion. Wilkins lowered his head and wondered what other presidents must have heard in this office over the years: the Confederates seizing Fort Sumter; the Germans invading Poland; the Japanese bombing Pearl Harbor; the Soviets building missile bases in Cuba. And now this, a threat aimed right at the heart of America's democracy, and Wilkins himself had invited McCallister into the country.

Wilkins looked up. "We have to stop him."

Bragg nodded. "We do."

"But how?" Peterson asked.

"I can think of a way," Bragg said. "Drone strike."

"Are you out of your mind?" Wilkins threw up his hands. "Good lord, a *drone strike.* We don't even know where McCallister is."

"But you talk to him by videoconference."

"But I've never known where he was, exactly where he was." Wilkins paused. "And now he's on the move."

"What do you mean?" Peterson asked.

"McCallister and his men… are headed this way. Traveling in convoys through Central Asia right now. And then flying back here."

Bragg gritted his teeth. "You ordered this?"

Wilkins nodded. "I did. I… deployed the Gadsden Brigade."

"You've deployed the exact opposite," Bragg said. "We have to alert the Pentagon."

Alert the Pentagon, Wilkins thought. *I started out thinking I was deploying the only force that could save us, and now I'm alerting the Pentagon to stop them.* "You're right," he said. He turned to Peterson and Sharpe. "He's right. I at least have to detain them until I figure out what the hell is going on here."

"But they're going to think it's an ambush if the army swoops in on them in the middle of Central Asia," Peterson said. "And then it becomes a kill mission anyway."

"Maybe so." *There's no right move here*, Wilkins thought. *But I have to find one.* "I'll handle this. I started this, and I'll decide how to finish it. But right now, I need to think about all of this. Bragg, I'm going to review these files and decide how to take out this son of a bitch. Peterson—be ready to make a move when I tell you to. But for now—you all should go."

Bragg, Peterson, and Sharpe rose to leave.

Not so fast, Sharpe, Wilkins thought. "Will, you stay," he said. "Bragg, Peterson, we'll be in touch."

Bragg and Peterson nodded, then left the Oval Office.

Wilkins waited for the door to close behind them, then leaned across the desk to address Sharpe.

"What are you thinking?" he said. "Cat's had your tongue all morning."

Sharpe ran his hands through his hair, which was getting as gray as Wilkins's now, and Wilkins saw that they were shaking. *He's in agony*, Wilkins thought.

"Sounds like we have our man," Sharpe said.

"You think so?"

"Well, it's like Reagan used to say: trust, but verify."

"You think we can verify?"

"It's all in files, Reed." Sharpe gestured to the desk. "They won't lie."

They won't lie. I'm just going to hate reading them.

"Christ, Will," Wilkins said. "What the hell am I going to do? This son of a bitch is on the way back to the country, and I'm the one who cleared a path for him. I just wanted to believe in something, something good. I wanted to believe in it so much that I let myself get blindsided."

"It's the first time you got blindsided in all these years… the first time you weren't ten steps ahead. You're only human—for God's sakes, you're only human." Sharpe laid a hand on Wilkins's shoulder. "How are you never going to be a little slow, never going to be a little late? You're doing all that you can. But these sons-of-bitches are goddamn *determined.* And you and me… we just want to live in peace. To lead a normal life."

Wilkins nodded. *That would be nice. Me and Delilah and a bunch of grandbabies.*

"Why us, Will?" he asked.

"What do you mean?

"I mean, don't you ever ask yourself that? Why us?" *He has no idea what I'm talking about.* "Look at us. We started in law school together. God, how many years ago was that now? More than thirty, in ninety-three, wasn't it? You probably didn't think you were that old." Wilkins grinned. "I seem to recall your Fresh Prince 'do at the time."

Sharpe laughed. "You just better keep yourself away from the late night snacks around the White House, Uncle Phil."

Wilkins slapped his belly. "I'm your commander-in-chief—fit as a fiddle. I'm built to last. Bryson can't stop me, bullets can't stop me. So take that Uncle Phil talk somewhere else." *God, it's good to shoot the breeze, even just for a second.* "Good lord, law school. How many all-nighters did we pull that first semester? Thinking our lives would be over if we flunked contracts, or torts?"

"Don't forget civil procedure."

Wilkins chuckled. "Oh, I haven't. I might've forgotten everything I *know*, but I damn sure haven't forgotten the class." He shook his head. "And look at us now. The President and the Attorney General. But why us?"

"There's that question again. What do you mean?"

Wilkins gazed across the room, almost beyond Sharpe. "I remember how all of this started," he said. "One night, maybe a year and a half ago, I called Peterson down to Arlington cemetery. Peterson and Chan. And I told them, 'We're in trouble. Trouble of the worst kind.' Because I knew, I *knew*, that Bryson was going to assassinate me for vetoing his crazy law. And then the next thing I knew, it wasn't just Bryson trying to kill me. It was Bryson, pulling the strings of Brigade 910, controlling the terrorists *and* the Authority, trying to overthrow the government. And now it's Octavian—McCallister—gathering forces, getting ready to make his move. And if we lose, we die. We die, and everyone in this country is a slave."

Sharpe considered subject, and Wilkins thought he looked wistful. "I know why it's you," he said. "It's because you're good enough, Reed. Sometimes these moments find you. Buchanan could've been president during the Civil War, but it was Lincoln. Hoover could've been president during World War II, but it was FDR. And you—you're up to this challenge. That's why it's you. Because it's destiny. Because you're good enough, tough enough, to beat these bastards."

Or maybe just crazy enough to fight back, Wilkins thought. He rose and shook Sharpe's hand. "Your lips to God's ears," he said. He pulled his best friend into an embrace. "Your lips to God's ears."

Chapter 41

Johnny glanced at Neely as she sat in the passenger seat of the SUV, bathed in the glow of the streetlight that spilled inside. Her hair burned with more orange than usual tonight, and the spikes on her bracelets twinkled. On her t-shirt was an image of three brightly-colored piñatas beating a man hanging upside-down from a tree.

Johnny thought of Fullerton. He hadn't spoken to him in ages, not since that morning at the cemetery a couple of months ago, not since Fullerton said they'd have to go their separate ways. The honorable fuck, he'd actually meant it. Wolfe had stuck Johnny at his desk and tasked him with shuffling papers while Fullerton continued working in the field. Johnny figured that Fullerton and the remainder of their old team were still taking doors, still nibbling at the case against Gaines.

But Johnny and Neely were doing more than nibbling. They were ripping through Gaines's entire organization, barreling straight towards Gaines himself. And Johnny found himself wishing that Fullerton were along for the ride, that they could take this last door together. They were best friends, after all.

Johnny lowered his head. And Lizbeth was his girlfriend, or at least he'd thought so. But she'd asked him to leave the last time they were together, had also told him they'd have to go their separate ways. The price of nailing Gaines was getting goddamn high.

"You're all dressed up tonight," Johnny said to Neely. "You have a date?"

Neely rolled her eyes. "I'm married to the sea, Luca."

They were reconning Kronos tonight. The Greek had holed up at a friend's apartment in Brooklyn after the shootout, but Johnny had intercepted his text messages. He'd had no trouble tracking Kronos down, and tonight he and Neely would repay him for the ambush in the abandoned lot. If Kronos stepped out of the apartment, they'd grab him.

"What's your deal, anyway?" Johnny asked. "Who are you dating these days?"

Neely groaned. "I told you. I don't have time for that stuff."

"You don't have time for a *relationship*. I know. You're a big, bad federal agent who doesn't like to get close to anyone. I get it." Johnny waved his hands, feigning wonderment at the presence of celebrity. "But you have to go on *dates*, at least. There's a normal human being in there somewhere."

"Of course I go on dates. Not like it's any of your business."

"It's my business, all right. We're partners." Johnny stroked his chin. "I know your type, actually. Lawyers."

Neely nodded matter-of-factly. "You're right, for once."

Yeah right. Johnny laughed. "Come on. You were blasting bad guys with an automatic rifle last week. Something tells me you might find lawyers boring."

"But that's the whole point. The more boring the dude, the better. Someone who can balance me out, help me to relax. Someone to help me pretend I have a normal life." Neely grinned. "And besides, I value intelligence. Which is why it's tough to hold a conversation with *you*."

Smartass. Johnny shook his head. "But you shouldn't date lawyers. They're nerds." He drummed his fingers against the steering wheel for a moment. "And besides. Dating a boring dude—how is that any fun?"

"I'd have to ask your girlfriend." Neely winked. "God, Luca. '*Dating a boring dude—how is that any fun?*' A retarded caveman could string together a better sentence." She chuckled to herself. "If you *must* know, that's how I keep my feet on the ground, I guess. You see the Neely that's shooting a gun, or running surveillance like this, or hacking files or whatever. My parents, they see the college girl getting A's. And my friends—they see the girl partying with them." Neely pulled out a pack of cigarettes, slammed it into her palm, and unsheathed a cigarette. "I won't tell the boss if you won't," she said, firing up her lighter and taking a drag.

"Christ, you'll stink up the whole goddamn truck," Johnny said, edging down the passenger-side window.

"Right, and now that you opened the window, this whole Brooklyn street is going to hear all about my dating life." Neely angled the cigarette towards the sliver of open window. "You see, it goes like this: With my friends, I'm the girl who gets drunk and gets high and dances all night. With my parents, I'm a good student. With Peterson, I'm the loyal federal agent. And with you..." Neely considered it for a moment. "With you, I'm a fucking *outlaw*." She laughed to herself. "So yeah. The guys I date, yeah, they can be lame. I just move in and out of their lives when I feel like it. Sometimes it's nice for a guy to cook you dinner or mix you drinks at his place. Sometimes it's nice to play house for a night." Neely shrugged. "And sometimes it's nice to be an outlaw."

They fell silent. The Brooklyn street's redbrick tenements hulked over them to the right, with terraced row houses lining the block to the left, across the street. The row houses yielded to a convenience store on one counter and a liquor store on the next, their signs burning red in the April night. And straight ahead, at the corner across the street from where Johnny and Neely were parked, was a schoolyard. A lone teenager was hurling a rubber ball against a concrete wall, running across the lot and fielding the rebounds, then firing the ball back at the wall.

"So what about you?" Neely asked. "How's it going with what's-her-name?"

Good question. "Lizbeth. I don't know how it's going."

"Shouldn't you know?" Neely blew smoke out the window. "Who should I ask, then?"

"You mean it's not in that file you stole?"

"No. Nothing in the files about commitment phobia or small penis size."

Johnny laughed. "Shut *up*, McLain," he said. "I'll tell you what the deal is. I told Lizbeth the truth, sort of. At least about my dad, anyway. About what happened to him. She always thought it was suicide, remember. Everyone does." Johnny studied the teenager slamming the ball against the wall in the schoolyard, chasing it down and whipping it back. "I told her that someone killed him, and that I know who is, and that—"

"And that you're going to kill him," Neely said.

Johnny nodded. "Right."

Neely took a drag. "Let me guess. She's not a fan of that plan."

"No, she's not a fan." Johnny paused. "I mean, why should she be? How could anyone be?"

"No one could be, I guess." Neely looked into Johnny's eyes. "Unless they know what it's like."

"Right. And she doesn't."

"So what does that mean for you two?"

Johnny sighed. "She asked me to leave when I told her about it. She said I was going down a road that she couldn't follow me down."

"And you're going to go down it anyway."

"I have to."

The two fell silent again. Johnny began to wonder if he and Lizbeth actually could have a life together after all of this, or if that was a lie he was telling himself, something to convince himself that everything would be all right.

"Luca," Neely said, cutting through the silence. "I want you to have something."

"What?"

Neely reached into a bag and pulled out a scarf. "This." She handed it to Johnny.

Johnny took it in his hands. It was checkered in red and white, soft cotton with white fringes. He looked up. "A scarf."

Neely shook her head. "That's no scarf, man. That's a *keffiyeh.* A Syrian keffiyeh. It was my dad's."

Johnny's eyes widened. "Your dad's?"

"Right. It was my dad's. It's all I have left of him, actually. And when I kill the creep who took him and my mother away from me, I'll be wearing it." She brushed her hand over Johnny's. "But I want you to have it for now. Until you kill the guy who took *your* father from you. Until you do what you need to do."

Johnny put his hand to where Neely's had been. *Until I do what I need to do.* "I can't accept—"

"You can, and you will. We're in this together. And I want…" Neely closed her eyes, then opened them. "I just want you to have it, that's all."

Johnny ran his hand over the scarf. It was cool, soft. "Thank you, McLain."

We're in this together. Neely could never know just how warm those words felt. Or maybe she was the only one who *could* know—

"Kronos," Neely said.

Johnny's eyes darted up, and there Kronos was, skulking out of one of the row houses across the street.

"Let's roll," Johnny said.

Kronos whipped out a car remote and pushed a button. A Mercedes parked up the block flashed as it unlocked.

"Damn it," Johnny said. "Fucker was too quick for us. Let's tail him, see where he goes. We'll find a better spot to grab him."

"You sure?" Neely asked.

"Positive."

Johnny watched as Kronos, again clad in his club-wear, strolled up the block to the Mercedes. He opened the driver's-side door, dropped behind the wheel, turned the key in the ignition—

And then the car exploded, a wall of orange flames screaming into the night as it vaporized Kronos.

Chapter 42

We're at the end, Johnny thought as he raced through the streets. *No more games, no more dancing around it, this is it. Gaines is coming for me, and I'm going after him. We'll collide soon, real soon.*

Johnny ignored Neely as he blew through stop signs, weaved in and out of traffic, blazed up Eighty-Sixth Street past the dancing lights and Chinese letters of shops and restaurants. The Brooklyn streets still crackled at this nine-o'clock hour, and Johnny's psychotic driving fit right in.

He ignored Neely's uncharacteristic appeals to reason, that maybe it wasn't so smart to peel out from the scene of a car bombing, that someone would make their plates and then the cops would make *them*. But Neely was green, too green to know the rules of the game—Johnny had filched a government vehicle from the field office, and any local cop who ran *those* plates would back off once he realized the Authority was involved, even if a car bomb had just exploded. Johnny didn't doubt that Neely had done her share of running from the law, but in this truck, they *were* the law.

He wrenched the steering wheel with one hand as he sliced through traffic and sped towards the Verrazano Bridge. He had to dump the g-ride back at the office, had to get back home, had to *plan*. Gaines was coming, and he had to plan.

Johnny recalled an entry from his father's diary: *Everyone who assisted in my investigation last spring is now dead, as of last night. I believe I will be killed within days.*

Giovanni Sr. turned out to be right. At a certain point, his killer—Gaines—decided to move against him, and started by killing off the informants, burning the bridges between them. The instant that car bomb exploded tonight, Johnny knew what was happening.

He steered the SUV onto an on-ramp for the Verrazano and got stuck in a glue-trap of traffic. The bridge connected Brooklyn to Staten Island, where Johnny had started all this madness by assaulting Ivanov a few days before Christmas. The bridge's two inverted horseshoe-shaped towers stood above, lights twinkling along massive cables that dipped from one tower and then ascended towards the next.

Giovanni Sr. used to drive him and Paul over this bridge all the time; their grandparents lived in Brooklyn. *Top or bottom?* he'd ask. The bridge had two decks; Johnny loved the lower deck, which felt more like a tunnel, and Paul loved the top, which offered views of the Manhattan skyline.

But the memory didn't make Johnny smile. Instead it burned like acid, like every other memory of his father that Gaines had corroded. Maybe Paul could still smile, but not Johnny, not as long as he wore the truth like a millstone around his neck.

Johnny would deliver justice to Gaines, and he'd take back everything the son-of-a-bitch stole—the memories, Johnny's friendship with Fullerton, his relationship with Lizbeth—everything, except his father's life.

Chapter 43

Octavian clutched the photograph of President Wilkins between his thumb and forefinger, pursing his lips as he scrutinized America's last democratically elected commander-in-chief.

Wilkins was raising his right hand as he took the oath of office: *I do solemnly swear that I will faithfully execute the Office of President of the United States. And will to the best of my ability, preserve, protect and defend the Constitution of the United States.*

Preserve, protect, and defend, Octavian thought. Wilkins swore to preserve this fat, spoiled, debt-addled disgrace of a country crawling with dependents begging for scraps. To protect a country where less than half the citizens paid taxes and barely half of them worked. To defend a country whose people were fit to be ruled.

Maybe there was a time when the American people were fit to rule themselves, to beam a beacon of self-government for the whole world to wonder at. But no more. These people were begging for a master, and Octavian would be that master.

He glowered at the picture of Wilkins, his right hand raised as he stood before the Chief Justice in January 2021. *I was moving against you even then.*

From Wilkins's first day in office, it would all come down to one choice: sign the Total Information Awareness Act, or die. Octavian and Bryson had laid the foundations for the superstructure, had poured the concrete. A willful president would not stand in the way.

Octavian and Bryson had whipped up Brigade 910, had formed the Authority. They controlled the radical left and the radical right, and had deployed their denizens inward, eating towards the center like termites. There would no center anymore. *Strategia della tensione.*

The strategy of tension clarified the question, purified the populace. The radical left—Brigade 910—drove the people into the arms of the radical right, the Authority. And the Authority would rule.

And as for those who would not be driven into the arms of the Authority, who would not beg for protection—for those who resisted—Total Information Awareness would give Bryson the machinery to identify and brand them as enemies of the state.

America was fit for a master, and Octavian deserved to be that master.

The American people were unworthy of their freedom in a way they never had been in their history. They weren't the same citizenry who had smashed the Germans in World War I, who had destroyed fascism in World War II and obliterated communism in the Cold War.

The financial meltdown of 2008, and the perpetual depression that followed, revealed their mediocrity. The depression had bared America's rotten core for the world to see—for the Octavians of the world to see. Americans didn't want freedom; they wanted *sustenance.* The master-of-the-universe bankers, the CEOs in the boardrooms, the bloodsucking bureaucrats, the overeducated thirty-somethings, the underemployed twenty-somethings, the moochers barely surviving on their welfare and their disability checks—they all wanted the same thing. Government as Daddy.

When the economy collapsed for good in 2008, Octavian saw the same scene play out at every level of government, from the halls of Congress to the councils of the smallest towns. Banks that had gambled the wealth of nations on insanely risky credit instruments? Bailed out, because they were "too big to fail." Auto manufacturers that had posted the largest losses in recorded history? Bailed out, in exchange for fealty to the government. A federal government in more debt than every other country combined? Taxes raised, to continue gorging Leviathan. An unemployment crisis of a magnitude not seen since the 1930s? Expand unemployment and disability benefits—so the unemployed could subsist but never find a job, and reward Daddy Government with their votes.

Everyone had their hands out—corporate welfare for well-connected companies, mortgage relief for people who bought homes they knew they couldn't afford, free higher education, free health care, free contraception.

But nothing was free, they'd all learn. And Octavian would teach them.

Octavian was the sort of man who took whatever was there for the taking. And when he decided he wanted an entire country, he found it ripe for the taking. He found daylight between the rights enshrined in the Constitution and what people actually wanted out of their government—warm, wonderful daylight. Octavian would step into that breach, and would rule.

Why? Because he could.

There was no other reason, really. Octavian wasn't out to restore the faded glory of the nation, the way Bryson was. He didn't get off on torturing the innocent, the way Moloch did. It was so much simpler than that.

Octavian was fit to rule, and the American people were fit to be ruled. They *wanted* to be ruled. The more Octavian reached for power, the more it flowed into his grasp. The more he probed with a bayonet, the more mush he found.

If it weren't me, Octavian thought, *it would be someone else. There always is. There's always an Octavian after the fall of a republic.*

Only Wilkins could stand in the way. Wilkins, who was an accident of history, who should never have been elected, who had eked out a victory over Octavian's chosen horse in 2020 and slipped into office by a bare majority. Wilkins was a throwback, the sort of man America used to elevate to the presidency when it was still the land of dreamers and innovators and rugged individualists. As Octavian seethed on Election Night 2020, it occurred to him that Wilkins's election was destiny, the sort of destiny that only happened in America. The people—the dwindling number who still had backbones—had thrown Wilkins up as the last hope against some unseen enemy. And now there would be a fight to the finish.

Wilkins had gotten lucky in November 2020, and luckier still that afternoon in May 2023. His luck would run out now.

Octavian would give the American people Taylor Quade, the president they deserved. Then Octavian would pump so much dependency down their goddamn throats that they'd gorge themselves to death. And he'd rule over the zombies who remained.

Octavian laid the picture of Wilkins on the table. The most delicious irony, of course—what Wilkins would agonize over in the days and months ahead, until Octavian finally had him executed—was that it was *Wilkins* who had let Octavian in, who had taken him into his confidence. The President was so desperate to believe in a hero, that he'd opened the door to his worst enemy.

Octavian regarded the photograph for a moment, and then tore it to pieces.

Chapter 44

Sharpe tapped each of his pants pockets, right and left, as he stood at the threshold of Hunter Peterson's office. Each pocket held an object that would set everything right, that would finally end this nightmare.

Sharpe was a traitor to his country, and to his best friend. He'd fed secrets to Bryson from the beginning, and for what? To avoid scandal. To salvage his marriage, his political career. Because Sharpe couldn't own up to a night with a prostitute, Reed had nearly been assassinated, and now tyranny was at their door, coming for all of them.

What a small man I've been, Sharpe thought. *What a small man I am.*

He knocked on Peterson's door. There was a pause, a moment heavy with eternity. *He has to be here*, Sharpe thought. *It's after hours, but he's here, I know he's here—*

The door opened, and there was Peterson. "Will," he said, surprised. "What are you doing here?"

"We need to talk," Sharpe said.

Peterson nodded. "Come in. Sit down."

Sharpe followed him inside and closed the door as Peterson sat at his desk. "I'll just be a minute, Hunter. I don't need to sit."

"All right, then." Peterson looked up at him, perusing him with his investigator's eyes. It was eight o'clock, and downtown Washington was asleep but for a few drunk bureaucrats out for weeknight kicks. "So what's up?"

"There's going to be a coup, Hunter."

Peterson arched his eyebrows. "I know. We've known that for a long time."

Sharpe shook his head. "You don't understand. There's going to be a coup *now.* Over the next couple of days. And you have to stop it."

Peterson leaned forward. "What are you talking about?"

Sharpe reached into his pocket and fished out a USB drive, then reached across the desk and laid it in front of Peterson. "Take this. *Read everything on it.* And then do what you need to do."

Peterson glanced down at the flash drive, then back up at Sharpe. "I don't understand."

"You will. Once you read those files, you will. You'll understand everything you need to know about Octavian."

"Everything… I need to know… about Octavian."

Come on, Peterson. Snap out of it. Wake up. Be the man Reed needs you to be right now.

"That's right," Sharpe said. "When you're finished, and once you've figured everything out, go up to New York and get your agents ready. Take over the New York field office in the World Trade Center and do what you need to do."

Peterson looked into his Sharpe's eyes. Already he seemed surer, ready to spring into action. "I understand," he said. "And you? What about you?"

"I'll do what I can." Sharpe headed towards the door. He opened the door, but stopped at the threshold—he had to stop, for one more thing. He looked over his shoulder. "Do it for our country, Hunter," he said. "And for the president we serve."

Chapter 45

Sharpe headed out into the downtown night and hailed a taxi.

"The Tidal Basin, please," he said to the driver.

The driver nodded and started to drive. Sharpe looked down; a typical DC taxi driver could spot a Cabinet official in his cab, and he wanted no attention, not tonight, not now. Not for this.

The driver dropped him off a few minutes later, and Sharpe paid the fare and got out. He strolled towards Tidal Basin, an April chill biting his face.

The cherry blossoms were out, splashing pink along the waterfront. Sharpe smiled. *After all these years, this is still the most beautiful thing I've ever seen.*

He trailed along the water's edge, deeper into the night, farther from the streets, from pedestrians. After a few minutes he was alone in the black, moonlight shimmering on the water, the Jefferson Memorial in the distance.

Sharpe walked up to the water's edge. *This is the Washington I remember.*

He'd taken Mary on their first date here, for a lantern walk during the Cherry Blossom Festival. Two years later, he proposed here.

And now everything was finished, all finished.

Sharpe reached into his pocket and pulled out a handgun. *What a small man I've been. What a small man I am.*

He pulled out a silencer, then fitted it to the gun. The spring night was so perfect, so still, he couldn't stand to shatter the quiet.

Sharpe turned around, the water at his back now, right at his heels. He stuck the gun in his mouth. *Public, this has to be public, maybe if they find me in the morning, it'll buy Reed and Hunter some time.*

A tear streamed down Sharpe's face. *Forgive me*, he thought, *God forgive me—*

Sharpe pulled the trigger.

Chapter 46

Hunter Peterson stared at his computer, the monitor beaming white in the den of his townhouse in Alexandria. *Of course,* he thought. *Octavian. Of course.*

He bolted to his feet, the urgency surging through him. He couldn't stand another second in this house. *Three people on earth*, he thought. *Three people on earth know what I know. Me, Sharpe, and him. Octavian.*

Peterson paced the room, the bluish glow of false dawn streaming through the window. He'd been up all night, poring over the materials that Sharpe had provided. Sharpe had drafted a detailed report, and attached files, so many files, files that constructed a mosaic, tile by tile, until they yielded up the face of the man bent on destroying the republic—Octavian.

Octavian ruled an international crime organization that spanned four continents, and he was about to make his play for absolute power. He controlled Alexander Bryson, he controlled Taylor Quade, he controlled so many players in the underworld and legitimate world that Peterson nearly retched at the thought. He'd consolidated his grip over the underworld in the last year, blasting all of his rivals off the battlefield in a crime spree that ringed the globe—gangland shootings in Asia, car bombings in Africa, even an assassination that Octavian had personally served up himself in South America while posing as an honored dinner guest.

Octavian headed drug syndicates, human trafficking syndicates, arms trafficking syndicates. The money was pouring in, crashing in, an ocean of money, filthy money that was finding its way into legitimate investments, gobbling up companies, perpetuating itself.

The world was in a global depression, its democracies had seized up, and its citizens were squabbling over a shrinking pie, gridlock rendering governments unable to govern. And wherever there was the smallest chasm between the institutions of a state and the reality on the ground, Octavian's power rushed to fill the vacuum. First in the developing world, then in a crumbled Europe, and now—finally—in an America on the brink of collapse.

Octavian had stoked revolutions in distant corners of the earth, had propped up subservient governments in mineral-rich nations, had unleashed militias through the developing world that were, unbeknownst to them, coalescing into his army. He'd used terrorist groups where he had to, skull-cracking security forces where he had to, smooth-talking huckster presidential candidates where he had to.

And now the bastard's hour is at hand. Follow the money, if anyone had ever bothered to follow the money—

But how can you dare to follow the money when you're a slave to it?

Every company that Octavian had rescued through shadow banking, every dictator that owed his life to Octavian's militias, every political candidate who had won office through Octavian's contributions—who among them would ever demand to know where the money came from, who would investigate the shell companies, who would expose the monstrous machine that now powered the motor of the world?

And now he wants us, Peterson thought. *The richest prize of all—control of the United States of America, and everything that comes along with it. Absolute, unbridled power, more important to this maniac than money, more important than God. Because once he has this power, he will be God, which is all he wants, all he's ever wanted.*

And he's here, goddamn it, he's <u>here</u>. He's here, and he's about to make his move.

There's going to be a coup now, Sharpe had said. *Over the next couple of days. And you have to stop it.*

Peterson lowered his head. *I have to stop it*, he thought.

Do it for our country, Sharpe had told him. *And for the president we serve.*

Peterson looked glanced up at the wall, at the photos he'd brought down from his old house in New Jersey—his father Hank posing with Presidents Eisenhower and Kennedy, of Peterson himself posing with every President from Clinton to Wilkins.

Peterson thought of his early days in the Secret Service—the road trips, the drunk nights in Podunk bars with his buddies, the overtime burned investigating two-bit counterfeiters, the little thrill he got out of "confessing" to women that he was a Secret Service agent. *Those were the good old days*, he thought. *Not the kind that are meant to last forever, but the kind you think of at a time like this, the kind you'd give anything to slip back into for just an hour, just a minute, just one more drink with the boys.*

Somewhere along the way it became a career, at some point he became professional. And somewhere along the way, he met Patricia.

God, Peterson thought. *Tricia.* No pictures of her on the walls. *My wife, the only woman I'll ever love, and not a picture of her, not one. Because I can fight Moloch on the roof of the World Trade Center, I can hunt down bad guys and risk my life, but I can't stand to look at a picture of the wife I lost six years ago.*

Peterson was forty-three then, and Tricia was thirty-five. They'd been married nine years.

He was thirty-two when he met Tricia, working the Bush detail at the tail end of W's second term. She was working at a coffee shop in DC, going to grad school to study literature. And Peterson… he smiled at the thought now, smiled in the middle of his dark den in Virginia. Peterson had read *The Great Gatsby*, then *The Grapes of Wrath*, just to impress her, just to have something to talk to her about before he worked up the courage to ask for her number.

The guys ribbed Peterson mercilessly, but it worked. He and Tricia dated, and it wasn't long before it blossomed into love. Peterson proposed after two years, and they were married six months later.

I'm trusting you, old man, Tricia had told him the night he proposed, nuzzling up to him in the dark of his bedroom that night, the two of them wearing only a sheet. *Protect me. Protect the family we're going to raise, the world we're going to make together. And I'll protect you.*

In the end, he couldn't protect her, not from the cancer that stalked her. They were trying to have their first baby together when Tricia was diagnosed. And then she started to slip, farther from Peterson, farther from the world they'd made together, until she was gone.

Peterson surveyed the empty room this morning, the ghosts on the wall, the white ember of the computer monitor, the bookshelves with dusty copies of *The Great Gatsby* and *The Grapes of Wrath* jammed in there somewhere.

I never wanted to be Authority Director, never wanted to face down this horror, never wanted to risk my life every waking second of every day.

I never wanted this. But that's not the point.

Protect me, Tricia had said. *Protect the family we're going to raise, the world we're going to make together.*

Peterson approached the computer. *Protect the world we're going to make together.*

I can do that, he thought.

Peterson sat back down at his desk and looked over the executive summary that Sharpe had prepared for him. *I'll have to commandeer the New York field office, like Sharpe said. If Sharpe's right about all this—we can nail Octavian in New York. We'll have to wait until the time is right, track his movements all day today if we can. And then we'll swoop in and nail his ass to the goddamn wall.*

Peterson looked out the window. Gold was burning through blue, a new day fighting to be born.

The world we're going to make together.

We'd better be ready, Peterson thought. *Me, Rutherford, Wolfe, Fullerton, Luca, McLain, every last one of us.*

He glanced out the window again, at the wisps of sunrise streaking through the sky. *Tonight we take down the superstructure. Tonight we bring Octavian to justice.*

Chapter 47

What they don't know about me, Gaines thought, *is that I actually believe in this revolution.*

Gaines was leading a revolution. The pigs who wanted to kill him—President Wilkins, Attorney General Sharpe, Authority Director Peterson—called him a terrorist. *He's only out for himself,* they said. *He's just a cult leader, just out to manipulate his pathetic little group, just out for money and power. He just wants to see the world burn.*

On the last point, they were right, almost. Gaines *did* want to see the world burn—the world *they* had built. The world of a thousand have-nots for every have, the world of slavery, of misery, of exploitation, of poverty beneath serfdom. The world that forced Juliana into a brothel because her family had been born a few pennies too short.

Wilkins, Sharpe, Peterson—they manned the battlements defending that world, pulled the levers of a machine chewing up six billion people for the love of a few captain-of-industry grandees and the fat Westerners whom they bribed with bread and circuses.

Gaines was one of those Westerners, and also the son of one of those captains of industry. Jack Sr. sat on the board of a few scumfuck multinationals that expropriated and enslaved the indigenous as they ripped resources from the ground in the most distant corners of the earth. And now Jack Jr. knew all the tricks—the off-the-books money that funded paramilitaries to murder people who tried to organize, the bribes to dictators and their henchmen, the contributions to politicians who would turn brother against brother, who would promote a strategy of tension to keep the weak divided and helpless.

Gaines learned all of this young, heard it around the dinner table, on the yacht, in the back of limousines. If he was grateful to his father for one thing, it wasn't the money—it wasn't the pampered life—it wasn't the education at the shiny schools. It was for Jack Sr. telling him how the world worked, how it was the civilized against the uncivilized, and how the uncivilized deserved to get screwed as long as they lived like animals.

Growing up in the Gaines household was a living death. Not that his parents were cruel—just the opposite. They were sweet and loving. They gave young Jack whatever he wanted, even things he didn't know he wanted until they gave it to him. Gaines hungered for nothing, struggled for nothing, labored for nothing; everything was his at the point of a finger. Teachers cowered before him, umpires and referees cowered before him. No one dared challenge Jack Gaines Jr.

Maybe it was because of his genius-level IQ, maybe it was because he was sensitive like his mother instead of hardy like his father, but it all started to feel empty to him early on. Gaines was an only child. As for friends—he was never alone, but always lonely. He drew boys to him with his athletic supremacy, and drew girls to him with his good looks, but he didn't feel close to a single human being growing up. He was too taciturn, and he had a way of always saying the wrong thing.

Reading filled the void, and when Gaines was a teenager, it was Marx and Trotsky who spoke to him. He became obsessed with the notion that the world was an arena that pitted slaves against their masters, that the Gaines family lived comfortably through the exploitation of others. When Gaines went skiing with his family, he felt no rush hurtling down the mountain; when he read the canon of revolutionary Marxism, life burst inside him, for the first time ever.

Somewhere along the way, something else began to kindle in Gaines—*rage*. He was hungry to puncture the bubble in which his parents had encased him, and he seized the chances his prep school offered to travel abroad—to Honduras, to Indonesia, to Zambia. Everywhere he saw the machine, his father's machine, chewing up human beings and spitting out their remains like fertilizer.

Gaines was admitted to Harvard, and he marched off to college like a dutiful son. At least there he could study under the world's best professors, could take in all the courses, all the books, that could teach him how to grind the machine's gears, how to overthrow the system.

But studying wasn't enough, could never be enough. That first year, Gaines slipped farther and farther away from his classmates, from the reality around him. Maybe because it was no reality at all: it was a construct, designed to civilize Gaines and the other students and train them to be good dogs in service of his father's machine. They would all be taught to play the game by the rules, to oppose the system from within, and therefore to never prevail over it.

So Gaines constructed his own reality: *revolution.*

He knew of anarchist groups popping up around the country as it wallowed in a recession that Jack Sr. and his pig friends had created. He was deep underground, spending his nights tapping away at message boards, linking up with others who saw no way to save the world other than by destroying it.

Gaines dropped out of Harvard after a year to join the army. At that point, the die was cast. He wasn't joining the army to serve his country or to get his life in order, but to acquire the training necessary to start a war.

And what training he received: brilliant and able-bodied, he joined the special forces. The army spent millions providing Gaines state-of-the-art training in weapons handling, hand-to-hand combat, demolition, execution of raids, survival in harsh environments, and blending in with indigenous populations. He saw action in Africa and in South and Central Asia, abducting or killing high-value targets.

He never disobeyed an order, never strayed from the script, even as he found the missions more and more repugnant. He killed whom he had to kill, even the ones he thought were innocent—which was just about all of them. They were collateral damage, not in any U.S. government war, but in Gaines's coming revolution. With each passing day, he marched one step closer to launching that revolution, and he didn't care about whom he killed along the way.

He cared instead about the Pakistanis, Afghans, Somalis, and Malians he lived among, the innocents whom the U.S. imperial superstructure was annihilating every day. He burned with rage at the Pakistani weddings immolated by drone strikes, the Afghan three-year-olds addicted to opium, the Malian families feeding themselves off garbage heaps, the Somali children whose ribcages stretched their skin. And he vowed to lay their imperial oppressor low.

After six years, Gaines received an honorable discharge. He was twenty-five years old, and the year was 2020.

He returned home to find that the revolution had ignited without him. Brigade 910 had declared war on the American regime, bombing soft targets in the nation's cities. The economy was as depressed as ever, and recruits—the young unemployed, mostly—were legion. Alexander Bryson and his proto-fascist thugs were baying for the revolutionaries' blood, forming the Anti-Subversion Authority and driving ever more recruits into the arms of Brigade 910 with their heavy-handed tactics.

The moment had come. Gaines stepped into the breach, linking up with a Brigade 910 cell in New York under the command of Sigma, a former CIA operative, and adopting the code name Hyperion.

Jack Gaines had been awkward, solitary, friendless; but Hyperion was a *leader.* Hyperion was a natural, a commander of the wayward, a Harvard-educated super-soldier who could lead his cell into battle. For the first time in his life, he had friends—blood brothers and blood sisters who had pledged their lives to toppling their capitalist overlords. Jack Gaines had always been too serious, had always said the wrong thing—but Hyperion blazed with passion, could mesmerize recruits with his perorations against the imperialist enemy.

The campaign continued into 2021. The bombings continued, the sabotage continued, the recruiting continued—and so did Bryson's overreaction. Brigade 910's ranks swelled.

Gaines was now the right hand of Sigma. Sigma was the first mentor Gaines had ever had, and meeting him had been one of the three most consequential events of Gaines's life.

The other two came in 2021: meeting Juliana in Mexico, and meeting Viceroy in New York.

Gaines met Juliana first. He'd been running drugs over the Arizona border, and he went to ground in Mexico, boring all the way down to Guadalajara. Walking the streets one night, he saw a hoodlum slapping around a girl in an alley. Gaines had seen this scene play out plenty of times in his travels, and he'd always stiffened his lip and walked on. But this time his hand went to the gun holstered at his hip. And a moment later, he'd gunned down the pimp and freed Juliana.

Later that year, he met Viceroy at a Brigade 910 meeting in a Bronx basement. Viceroy was a black man who'd scrapped his way through the Newark projects, a couple of years younger than Gaines, a natural leader with every reason to join the revolution against the capitalist tyranny that had condemned his family to poverty.

Sigma was a mentor, the father Gaines had never had; and Viceroy was a comrade-in-arms, the best friend Gaines had never had. Viceroy confided in Gaines about the night a stray bullet ripped through his bedroom window in Newark and killed his brother. *I've been after them ever since*, Viceroy told him. *At first I didn't know who "they" were—but now I do.*

Sigma and Gaines tasked Viceroy with recruiting new revolutionaries, peeling away the disaffected. He was perfect in the role.

As 2021 carried on, the revolution collided with Detective Giovanni Luca.

Pig or not, Luca was only a local cop, just a citizen. Just a citizen who could've minded his own business in his little town in New Jersey, who could've stuck to locking up teenagers on bogus drug charges or whatever else he did for a living, who could've enjoyed his barbecues and ballgames and all the other distractions the imperialist regime offered him.

But instead, Luca decided to interfere. He arrested a young revolutionary named Ryan Colgate and interrogated him. After Colgate was transferred to federal custody—and after a Brigade 910 revolutionary liquidated him for his betrayal in talking to the police—Luca sank his teeth into the case. He was a man on fire, drilling through every lead in the case, headed straight towards the heart of Project Orion. And that was unacceptable.

So Gaines liquidated Luca. He hired a heavy named Sergei Ivanov to abduct the detective and bring him to Gaines, and then Gaines delivered the revolution's justice to him. Even as he did, he felt a twinge of regret. Luca was just a citizen; if he had half a brain, he'd be standing with Gaines instead of acting as lapdog for the imperialist regime.

In 2022, Gaines was jolted by the shock of his life. Viceroy was a pig—an Authority agent named Julius Fullerton. The whole time, he'd been feeding intelligence to his masters, and they launched a raid against Gaines and his cell. They killed several, and nearly killed Gaines himself.

There were more shocks in 2023. Luca had a son, a son who'd grown to be the most vile pig of all, a jackboot in the Authority. Like the father, he was a nothing, a local rube. But teamed with Fullerton, the younger Luca perpetrated a one-in-a-million upset, an accomplishment so far beyond his abilities that Gaines wanted to punch the wall thinking of it now—Luca hurled a spear at Project Orion and somehow struck the bullseye, nearly destroying the revolution in the process.

And appallingly, this Giovanni Luca, Jr.—Johnny Luca, they called him—had been coming after Gaines ever since. *Luca* was stalking *Gaines*, raiding safe-houses, beating his men, collecting intelligence. Luca—who didn't belong in this game, who couldn't play on this level, whose proper place was beneath the sole of Gaines's shoe—had willed himself so much farther than Gaines ever could have expected, like a worm slugging his way through the dirt. Luca was now at the gates—but would advance no further.

Johnny Luca had threatened the revolution as no one ever had before. For that, he would die.

Today was Luca's twenty-sixth birthday. He might survive the day. He wouldn't survive the next.

Gaines turned around to face his bound-and-gagged guest, the bait that would lure Luca to his execution. "It's zero hour," he said.

Chapter 48

Johnny rubbed his hands together as he stood outside his mother's apartment building. It was April now, but still cold, a stiff chill slicing the air.

He thought back to the night in December he camped under Ivanov's porch for four hours. That was a different cold, a dead cold, a blueblack cold that crystallized his veins. This afternoon's was lighter, sweetened with the first notes of spring.

He rang his mother's bell again. *Hopefully she's got some hot chocolate ready.*

April 6, 2024, his twenty-sixth birthday. A year ago his mother had given him his father's diary, had cast him hurtling towards the truth. *She wanted me to quit the Authority*, Johnny thought.

And now Johnny had pulled within striking distance of Gaines, and Gaines knew it. Three more of Johnny's informants had gone quiet over the last week, and Johnny knew for sure that at least one of them had been murdered, blown to bits in a car bomb just like Kronos. This was playing out exactly like his father's diary, except Johnny knew that Gaines was coming. And better yet—Johnny was coming for *him.*

A *tap* cut through the quiet, a plastic bat hitting a plastic ball. Two boys no older than eight—brothers, probably—chased the ball in the courtyard.

Johnny smiled. *It's getting to be that time of year.*

He waited a moment more for his mother to open the door, then fished out the key to her apartment. *Maybe she's out shopping.*

He turned the key in the door and pushed it open, crossing inside. "Mom," he called. "It's the birthday boy."

Johnny pulled the door closed and ascended the stairs, his feet drumming and creaking across the wood. Just beyond the stop of the stairs was the kitchen table, and beyond that, a stenciled banner that read "Happy birthday!"

He reached the top of the stairs. "Mom? I—"

"You can't be here," she called behind him.

Johnny whirled around, and there was she was, sitting on the couch. She wasn't her normal, smiling, joking self.

"What do you mean?" Johnny said, crossing the room to her.

Marissa stood up. "You need to leave."

"Mom." Johnny narrowed his eyes. *What's going on here?* "Talk to me."

Marissa held his gaze for a moment, her blue eyes red at the edges. She'd been crying. She stepped towards Johnny, clutching her tablet computer, then thrust the device into his hands. "How could you?" she asked.

Johnny looked down at the screen, and his eyes widened at the headline glowing at the top. *Jesus Christ.*

"LOCAL SERGEANT MURDERED," the headline screamed. "Sergeant Thomas Buchanan Found Shot Execution-Style."

Buchanan, the mole in Giovanni Sr.'s department, the corrupt cop that Johnny had ambushed in Irvington last month.

A chill fluttered up Johnny's spine, then exploded across his shoulders, radiating to the tips of his ears. "You think I did this?" he asked.

Marissa grabbed the tablet back. "I *know* you did this."

Johnny folded his arms. "What kind of person do you think I am?"

"Not the boy I raised, that's for sure. You're someone else, something else." Marissa choked back tears. "What kind of person are you? You're the kind of person who stood here a year ago and told me you were going to murder people. And now you're actually doing it."

"No I'm *not*!"

"Your father wrote about Buchanan in his diary. Buchanan betrayed him, sold him out. And now he's dead." Marissa pointed at Johnny. "Lizbeth came to see me, Johnny. She told me what you do in your spare time, how you spend your nights. You're a criminal. And now it looks like you're a killer." Now Marissa began to sob. "You were *out*, Johnny. Last year, you were out. You got together with Lizbeth, this incredible girl who loves you more than anything, more than life itself. You were out, you survived that gunshot, you were—"

"What gunshot?" Johnny asked.

Marissa wiped her eyes and curled the edges of her mouth into the saddest smile Johnny had ever seen. "The one you took in your shoulder, kiddo. The one that left the scar."

The only people on earth who knew about that gunshot were President Wilkins, Peterson, Fullerton, the members of Johnny's strike team, and the politicians who'd visited Johnny in the bunker beneath the Empire State Building last May. Johnny narrowed his eyes. "There was no gunshot, Mom."

Marissa nodded. "You know, they say the guy who saved the President's life took a bullet in the shoulder."

"Good for him," Johnny said. "People say a lot of things. Like you, actually. Calling me a killer. You think I'd just execute this guy, like they're saying in that article?"

Marissa looked down as she considered the question. Then she looked back up, tears streaming from her eyes. "Yes, sweet pea. I do."

Unbelievable. "Then you're right. I can't be here."

"Johnny—"

"No, you said it. I—I need to leave." Johnny stormed past his mother towards the bathroom, blood surging to his face. He needed to cool off, collect himself. He slipped into the bathroom and closed the door behind him.

Buchanan's dead, Johnny thought as he flipped on the faucet and splashed water on his face. *And Mom thinks I killed him.*

Johnny ran his hands through his hair. He then opened the bathroom door and took a step towards the living room, but stopped in front of Paul's room.

He stepped into his brother's room and closed the door behind him. Marissa had tidied up the room, but Johnny couldn't help but smile at the propaganda plastered all over the walls. *The people want the regime to fall!* blared one poster showing revolutionaries clashing with the police in Tahrir Square during the Egyptian revolution of 2011. *Down with the dictators!* screamed another, this one showing protesters hurling rocks at the Authority during a riot last year.

I should go. I need to sort this out, need to figure out how to make this right with Mom, how to make it right with Lizbeth. And I need to figure out what the hell happened to Buchanan.

Johnny stepped towards the door, turned the doorknob and started to pull the door open. But something danced across the corner of his eye just then.

He turned around and stood at the entrance of Paul's room, and there it was: a backpack on the floor by the side of the bed.

Johnny squinted. Wires protruded from the bag, wires that looked like component cables for a television. But he knew what they were, knew what they were as he stepped back inside the bedroom, as he knelt beside the bed and took the bag in his hands.

What the fucking fuck, Johnny thought.

Detonators. There were detonators in the bag.

Johnny unzipped the bag, rustled around inside, and then gasped.

Pictures of Buchanan, Kronos, and the dead informants. Directions to their homes, pictures of their homes. Maps of their neighborhoods.

"What the fuck is going on," Johnny said out loud. He shoved everything back in the bag, zipped it up, and darted back into the living room.

"Johnny," Marissa said, "I don't want you to lea—"

"Paul," Johnny said. "When was the last time he was here?"

Marissa looked surprised. "Over the weekend. He came to visit. Why?"

Johnny held up the backpack, forcing himself to stay composed. "He left his bag."

Marissa reached for the bag. "Well, I'll call him, tell him he can pick it up the next time he comes—"

"I'll take it to him." Johnny pulled back the bag. "I'm going up to visit him at school, anyway. And it's got some books in it."

Marissa nodded. "Okay, you take it." She paused, then embraced Johnny. "I don't want to believe these things about you," she said. "Just remember, Johnny. I love you. Lizbeth loves you. She wants to be your wife, this amazing girl." Marissa laid a hand on his shoulder. "It's like I told you on Christmas day. Revenge is like poison. Don't let it ruin your life. I loved your father, even after we broke up. But he's gone. He was gone when you thought it was suicide, and he's gone now that you know it was a murder. He's not coming back, and nothing's going to change that. You don't have to walk among the dead like this. There's *life* with Lizbeth, with me, your brother, your friends. Come back to us." Marissa kissed Johnny on the forehead, then stroked the crucifix at her neck. "And remember, any sin can be forgiven. Any sin."

Johnny shook his head. "I'm not asking for any forgiveness. And I didn't kill anyone." He walked past his mother to the top of the stairs, then turned around to face her one last time. "But I swear to God, I'm going to find out who did."

Johnny bounded down the stairs and out the door.

Chapter 49

Oh, Will, President Wilkins thought as he sat at his desk in the Oval Office late in the afternoon of April 6. He closed his eyes for a moment, shuddering. Then he opened them, and there was the headline screaming across the top of his computer, blaring from his favorite publication, Gordon Bragg's *Rebellion*:

ATTORNEY GENERAL FOUND DEAD IN APPARENT SUICIDE

Wilkins closed the page. *Why?* he thought. *Why?*

Then he squared his jaw. *How?*

They'd found Sharpe a few hours ago, dead from a self-inflicted gunshot wound. But self-inflicted gunshot wounds in this game, in this city, had a funny way of being inflicted by someone else.

Bragg had been the first to call. "I want you to hear this from me, and not from the FBI or someone else in the media," he said. "It's Sharpe. I don't know how to say it."

"Say it," Wilkins had said, already expecting something horrendous.

"They found him at the Tidal Basin. He shot himself. We've lost him."

And for the first time in his presidency, Wilkins had lost it, had finally allowed himself to be human. He hung up the phone without a word, dropped his head onto his desk, and sobbed.

But even that moment couldn't last. Wilkins composed himself and called the head of the FBI, ordering him to ensure that Mrs. Sharpe and their children had round-the-clock FBI protection in the days ahead. Then he called his secretary and asked her to clear his schedule for the day. Eventually he'd have to talk to Sharpe's deputy, who'd be serving as interim Attorney General, and at some point would have to issue a statement or face the press. And by nightfall, there would be Senators at the White House, peddling various suggestions for Sharpe's replacement.

They killed him, Wilkins thought a few moments after he'd spoken to his secretary. *They killed him and made it look like suicide.*

He called Bragg back. "I want answers," Wilkins said. "Get to the bottom of this, Bragg. Someone murdered Sharpe. Find out what happened."

Hours later, Wilkins sat at his desk, stupefied. Delilah had come over to console him, Garrett and Gabrielle had called him, but duty called; it, always called. Wilkins had conferred with the interim Attorney General, put out a brief statement, and had already fielded a call from a Senator about a replacement.

What was it Woodrow Wilson said about this city? Wilkins thought. *Southern efficiency, northern charm.*

There had been calls from Peterson, but Wilkins avoided them. He didn't need to hear any more condolences. Just for one day—just for today—he wanted to shut it out, wanted to lull himself into a fantasy that he was serving out a normal presidency.

From the beginning, Sharpe wanted to make a deal, reach an accommodation. *He wanted me to sign the Total Information Awareness Act, to negotiate, to spare my own life and avoid bloodshed. That's who he was. A peacemaker. But I had to push ahead, and I killed him.*

Just then, there was a commotion outside the Oval Office.

Wilkins heard voices arguing, and then a moment later, a crash—the sound of someone being slammed against the wall.

The door opened, and there stood Alexander Bryson.

"Bryson," Wilkins spat.

Bryson grinned, those ice blue eyes twinkling. "Wilkins," he said. "I came to offer my condolences."

Wilkins stood. "You can offer them from prison."

Bryson threw up his hands. "And what crime did I commit?"

"Assassination of the Attorney General. And my Secret Service detail can arrest you right now."

Bryson smiled, and this time it was no grin. It was the same smile Bryson wore in this room a year ago, when he'd grabbed a portrait of the First Family, smashed it against the side of Wilkins's desk, and flung it to the floor. *Wait for tonight, Mr. President*, Bryson had said. *Wait for a special report on the news. You'll know my power then.*

"Your detail might have a hard time arresting me," Bryson said. "Because my Authority agents have them under arrest right now, in handcuffs right outside this door."

Wilkins stepped towards Bryson. "*My* Authority agents," he said. "Peterson's."

Bryson shook his head. "You sure have missed a lot over the last few hours." He looked out the door behind him, nodded at someone in the hallway, and then turned back to Wilkins as Authority agents crossed into the Oval Office. They carried machine guns.

"Take Mr. Wilkins into custody," Bryson directed them. "Reed Wilkins, for your role in staging the Project Orion attacks last year, you're under arrest for treason, conspiracy to commit murder, and providing material support to a terrorist group."

"*My* role in staging the attacks!" Wilkins thundered as the agents approached him, brandishing their weapons. "*My* role! You lying son of a—"

One of the agents wrenched his arms behind him and handcuffed him.

What the hell is happening, Wilkins thought, *what the hell*—

"I have the full Project Orion file," Bryson said. "And the American people are about to learn that you drew up the attacks to bring about a police state in the U.S. And President Greenaway will address the American people tonight, and either President Greenaway or Taylor Quade will oversee your prosecution."

The room began to spin. "President Greenaway…" Wilkins said.

"You're under arrest for *treason*, Wilkins. You're unfit for office, and Greenaway has assumed your office under the Twenty-Fifth Amendment." Bryson pointed at Wilkins. "What was it you said to me last year? *I would caution you to address me as Mr. President, you treasonous son of a bitch. Because I'm your President, until I'm not.*" Bryson nodded. "And now you're not. You'll never see this room again." He stepped towards Wilkins and laid a hand on his shoulder, feigning reassurance. "But don't you worry. We'll be keeping you under house arrest—until the day we take you out and kill you."

The Authority agents began to lead Wilkins away. He yielded for a couple of steps, but then stiffened, stopping short before

Bryson. "You won't win," Wilkins said. "You can't beat us—not all of us. You won't win."

"We've already won. Sharpe's dead. Who else do you have—Bragg? He can't help you now, not with a pen and a computer. And Peterson? He'll be in custody by the end of the night. We didn't find him at Authority headquarters today—he's not in Washington. He's up to something, isn't he? But it's too late. We'll get him before the night is out, and what I have planned for him is a little less comfortable than house arrest." Bryson leaned in close. "And his death will be a little less comfortable than yours."

Come on, Peterson, Wilkins thought. *We need you now.*

Wilkins struggled to look over his shoulder, to catch a fleeting glimpse of the Oval Office, of his presidency, as the agents hustled him towards the door. "All for Octavian," Wilkins called to Bryson behind him. "Was it worth it? To destroy your country, all for the worship of one man?"

Bryson motioned for the agents to stand Wilkins in place. "Why don't you ask Octavian yourself?" he asked.

Wilkins narrowed his eyes. "Ask Octavian?"

Bryson nodded. "That's right. You can ask him yourself. When you meet him tonight."

Chapter 50

Johnny fastened the holster to his hip. Two hours ago he'd found a backpack full of detonators in his brother's bedroom, and now he was going to do something about it.

The day's last beams of sunlight tumbled through the window, the Hudson River gleaming in swirls of orange as the sun plunged behind the skyline beyond. Most prominent in that skyline, as ever, was One World Trade Center, reaching 1,776 feet into the sky. It was the sum of Johnny's dreams when he was a surveillance technician living in that Newark studio, before he was an agent—to serve in the New York field office, to work on the most critical counterterrorism cases.

Johnny looked around the apartment. Two months after he'd moved in, boxes were still strewn about, and framed prints were propped up on the floor, angled against the walls.

I never moved in here. I never settled in, never started my new life. I never left that studio in Newark.

Johnny picked his Glock up off the glass coffee table, along with a loaded magazine, and shoved the magazine into the gun's grip.

Confronting my own brother with a loaded gun. And who the fuck knows where it goes from there?

Johnny holstered the gun, then walked over to the kitchen counter. He picked up a roll of double-sided tape.

He thought back to something he'd read in his father's diary:

I stick a fresh piece of double-sided tape on the inside edge of my report drawer whenever I open it. It's not a superstition. It's because one time about ten years ago, somebody stole a report out of my drawer and destroyed it. It turns out some big drug dealer scumbag I'd been putting the heat on had paid off some lowlife to destroy evidence. The prosecutor had been making a big deal about nailing this guy, and I almost lost my job when we lost the evidence.

So it's real simple– I open the drawer, peel off the tape I'd slapped on there the last time I closed it, and stick on a new piece. It's really small, just a little pinch. It's enough for me to tell if someone tampered with the drawer or not.

Johnny started pinching pieces off the roll. Giovanni Sr. had a file cabinet to protect; Johnny had an entire apartment to secure.

He started with his night table drawers. Then it was his bureau drawers. Johnny pinched off more pieces and "secured" his medicine cabinet, his kitchen drawers, the bathroom door, the sliding doors of his closet.

Johnny threw on a jacket, covering the holstered gun, and grabbed his brother's backpack. He then secured the front door with its slice of tape and headed out.

The elderly security guard, snoozing at his desk in the lobby, roused at Johnny's footsteps. Johnny held up a hand. "Don't let me wake you," he said. "A bomb just exploded in my apartment, but I got out in time. So you can go back to sleep."

The old man grinned. "Good thing you sniffed it out with that guinea nose of yours," he said. "You could've been blown to bits!"

Johnny rolled his eyes.

He descended into the parking garage, his sanctuary of concrete and oil slicks, the reason why he'd picked out this particular apartment building—it was a dead zone for mobile signals and GPS, and even better, it connected with a train station buzzing with trains bound for New York City.

But tonight Johnny would drive. He'd drive an hour out to Paul's campus, to bring him his backpack and confront him about the vigilante killings. And God only knew where that would lead.

Johnny dropped into his truck and drove off.

My God, what the hell have they done to you, Paul?

The sun disappeared as Johnny drove, the last streaks of orange drifting from the sky, yielding to the black of night.

Whenever Johnny got in trouble when he was a kid and sat in his room crying, or steaming, his baby brother always seemed to come along asking to play a video game or some wiffleball. Neither of them knew at the time how perfect that was. But Johnny knew it now. Did Paul?

Johnny sighed. Something had changed in Paul over these last couple of years, the same way something had changed in Johnny. Paul burned inside the way Johnny burned inside.

And then, as Johnny rocketed along the highway that night, he knew. He knew what had happened to his brother, why he'd found detonators in his bag. He didn't want to believe it—he wouldn't believe it until he faced his brother tonight—but he knew.

Johnny turned off at his exit. He drove through the small New Jersey town, first along a main street of antique shops, taverns, a diner, and a general store, and then into the wooded outskirts. The truck dipped down hills and crested back up, picket fences and front porches easing by on the left, farmland stretching across the valley below on the right.

He followed the signs for Paul's college, winding deeper into the woods until they gave way to the campus, guarded by a tall wrought-iron gate. He signed in at the gatehouse and parked his car.

Johnny got out of the car and headed towards Paul's dorm. As Johnny walked along the paths of the wooded campus, he thought back to his own college years—to a boy and a girl under a tree as snow swirled around them—to a boy and a girl about to kiss. *Billy cut in that night*, Johnny remembered as he walked, *and then Lizbeth and Dick started dating, and then Dad died. I didn't kiss Lizbeth until three years later, and by then I was in too deep with all of this, too deep to be the man she deserved.*

Paul's dorm came into view. Paul had a girlfriend of his own now, Julia. Would he lose her now too, the way Johnny lost Lizbeth? All because some maniac killed their father three years ago?

Johnny approached the dorm. No need to be covert about this, he figured. He'd knock on Paul's door, ask his roommate to give them a minute, and then find out what the fuck was going on. If it had to get any more real than that, he had the gun. A gun—for a conversation with his brother.

Johnny heard hooting and hollering as he approached, drunk students laughing.

"And then I told him," Paul yelled in the distance, "'Maybe because monochloramine doesn't disassociate into ions, you fucking jackass!'" Johnny heard a beer can smash against a wall.

Paul and his friends were partying behind the dorm building, in a picnic area at the edge of the woods, far back from the university's main path.

"Luca man, you're crazy!" One of the partiers yelled back.

"You're the fucking chemistry man, dude!" He threw his own empty can against the wall. "The fucking chemistry man!"

Must be some party, Johnny thought as he crept forward.

And just then, his brother came into view: nineteen years old, gulping his beer as he stood on a picnic table, raising his arms to call everyone to attention.

"I'll show you how fucking crazy I am!" Paul yelled. "Check *this* out."

He gestured at two of his friends, who rushed forward holding fire extinguishers.

Johnny squinted. *What's he up to*?

"I own you all, bitches," Paul said, pulling his phone out of his pocket. He then pointed it at a trash can in the distance, crouched and turned away from it, and pushed a button.

The trash can exploded in a pop and fell over, on fire.

The party crowd erupted in cheers as Paul's appointed deputies put out the fire. "I love you Paul Luca!" one girl screamed. Paul bowed.

Johnny glanced down at the backpack he clutched in his left hand, then shuddered.

He slung the bag over his shoulder and strolled forward, clapping as he approached the group. "Good show," he called out to Paul.

Paul gulped at the sight of his brother. "Johnny," he said, dropping his beer. "What are you—"

"You didn't invite me to the party," Johnny said. "And it's my birthday."

"You want a beer, dude?" one of Paul's goon friends asked.

Johnny held up his hand. "Not tonight." He surveyed the group for a moment. "Guys," he said. "I need to talk to Paul for a minute. Alone."

Everyone turned to Paul, who considered the question. Then he nodded. "Give us a minute," Paul said. "I'll catch up with you guys later."

He hopped off the picnic table as his friends stumbled away, taking their beer with them. "Is everything okay?" he asked. "Is something—"

"You tell me," Johnny said, whipping the backpack at his brother.

Paul caught the bag against his chest, and then his eyes widened. He looked down for a moment, scrutinizing the bag as he clutched it.

And then he looked back up, and the eyes that met Johnny's were not Paul's.

"I guess both of our masks are off now," Paul said.

Johnny's hand went to the bulge under his jacket. "Our masks?" he said.

"You can take your hand off the gun, Johnny. Unless you're going to shoot me."

Johnny narrowed his eyes. "Or arrest you."

Paul smirked. "Like the pig you are." He laughed to himself, shaking his head. "My big brother, a pig."

"And my little brother, a terrorist."

Paul's face hardened. "Says the agent for the Anti-Democracy Authority. A fucking fascist. *You're* the terrorist."

Jesus Christ, it's true. They got him, they turned him, Paul is one of them.

Johnny gestured towards the backpack. "And you're a murderer."

Paul laughed. "A murderer. Of who? A few drug dealers? A dirty cop?"

Johnny shook his head. "No. They were more. They were enemies of your revolution, right? Someone told you they were enemies of Brigade 910, and you killed them. They wound you up like a toy, and you killed people."

"And don't you do the same? Your boys ran people over with armored trucks in Chicago a couple of months ago. Tear gas, rubber bullets, the whole thing. People died—civilians died. And you—God knows what *you* do, how many doors you break down in the middle of the night." Paul clenched his fists. "After everything Dad said about the Authority. And you fucking *joined* them."

That cut Johnny all the way to the bone. "Paul, it's not what you thi—"

"No, it's not what *you* think. They killed Dad, Johnny." And just then, Paul let his age show, no longer the steely-eyed terrorist, but a nineteen-year-old way in over his head. He choked back a sob. "They *killed* him. It wasn't suicide. He was investigating the Authority, shady stuff about how they were going to overthrow the government. And then they killed him and made it look like he killed himself." Paul righted himself. "I'm sorry I had to tell you. But it's the truth."

No, I'm sorry. I'm sorry you had to find out. I'm sorry it happened. Every day since the day they killed him, and every day for the rest of my life. I'm sorry it happened.

Johnny looked into his brother's eyes. *I have to convince him.*

"The Authority *did* kill Dad," he said. "That cop you killed—Buchanan—he was in on it. He spied on Dad, fed them tips. And then one night, someone named Sergei Ivanov smashed a club over Dad's head, knocked him out, and took him away… to be killed."

Paul dropped the backpack. "How do you know that?"

"Because I read Dad's diaries."

"He left diaries?"

Johnny nodded. "He did, Paul. Two of them. Mom gave them to me, and now I can give them to you. But what I want to know is—how do *you* know about him getting killed?"

Paul studied Johnny for a moment, and as the brothers stared each other down in the moonlight, Johnny thought anything was possible. Paul could break down crying—or bolt off into the woods—or whistle for a gang of Brigade 910 assassins to ambush Johnny—or pull out a gun.

"Someone came up to me last summer," Paul said. "I was here for the summer semester, and someone came right up to me when I was walking to class, someone I'd never met before. He told me that he knew my father was dead and that he knew who was behind it, and then stuck a piece of paper into my hand."

Last summer. They turned him right after we stopped Project Orion. "And then the next thing you knew, they were telling you the Authority killed Dad and that you had to join the revolution to stop them."

Paul nodded. "Right. And I did. Because someone has to avenge him."

Johnny shuddered. *Paul wants the same exact revenge I want, he just had the guts to take it one step further. He's killed for it.*

"You're right about one thing," Johnny said. "I'm a pig, all right. I work for the Authority, even though I know what they did to Dad. I break down doors, arrest people, beat them up. But I know something you don't." Johnny gazed up at the moon for a moment, and just then thought back to a lakeside vacation when he was twelve years old, before his parents divorced, he and seven-year-old Paul running around in the moonlight as fireflies flashed around him.

"I know how Dad died that night," Johnny continued. "I know that Ivanov took Dad to a safehouse—a Brigade 910 safe-house—where a bunch of your revolutionaries were waiting. And then a man named Jack Gaines, who you call Hyperion, stuck a gun under his chin and pulled the trigger."

Paul glared at Johnny, his lips trembling, his body quaking. "*Liar*!" he bellowed.

Johnny shook his head, calm now, calm and exhausted and ready to give it all up, to forget about revenge for his father. "It's the truth. And the reason why Hyperion killed Dad, even if he doesn't know it himself, is because the Authority and Brigade 910 are one. It's all a show, Paul. Your revolution isn't real. Someone started this whole thing, some asshole who calls himself Octavian. Octavian wants to overthrow the government, to become a dictator. And he started up Brigade 910 to make everyone afraid of terrorism, and then created the Authority to help start a police state. That's what this all is. You're playing a part in a show. And I might be a pig, but I'm trying to stop them. The unit I'm in—we're trying to stop Octavian."

Johnny would be the revenge-obsessed vigilante no more. The same obsession had consumed his brother, had made him a killer and the target of killers, and Johnny had to save him.

Paul stared at Johnny, stared until the last of the convulsions swept through him, until his eyes were again the vacant orbs that had stunned Johnny a minute ago. "You're the one playing a part in a show," he said. "The pigs have been lying to you. Either that, or you're lying to me. Which you're pretty good at, right?"

Johnny arched his eyebrows. "What's that supposed to mean?"

"What is it that you call yourself?" Paul feigned wondering. "A surveillance technician? First for the FBI, and then you had to admit it, to cover your tracks—a surveillance technician for the Authority. And you sit down to Thanksgiving dinner, to Christmas dinner, and look me and mom in the eye and tell us that you clean guns for a living, fix surveillance equipment, whatever, and don't worry—I got a black eye because some box fell on my head in the closet. And meanwhile, you're just a goddamn fascist punk, one of Bryson's storm troopers who's going to turn this country into a dictatorship if we don't stop him. And you know what the best part is?" Paul shook his head. "The two of you *knew*, you and Mom, you *knew*. You *knew* that Dad was murdered, and you *kept* it from me, all this time. And you *work for the Authority*, Johnny. You swallow all their lies, and then you come out here, for what? To get me to believe you? Your bosses killed Dad. And I'm the one doing something about it."

Brainwashed. They brainwashed my brother. "You're doing something about it, all right," Johnny said. "You're killing people, dancing on Gaines's little string."

"And what are you going to do about it?"

Good question. "I'm going to get you out of here. Because now that they've used you, they'll kill you too. Guaranteed. They'll kill you next, and then me." *Gaines doesn't need Paul for anything else, so why not kill him next?* "We need to get out of here, Paul."

Paul shook his head. "I'm not going anywhere. And don't think of trying anything with whatever you've got under your jacket. I have my own, and I'll bet I'm faster than you are."

I'll bet you're not.

"You know what sucks?" Paul went on. A few tears escaped his eyes. "I fucking love you. You and Mom. I love you both, more than anything. But I'm on my own in this thing."

"I love you too, Paul. You're not on your own. Come with me. Let's get out of here, go somewhere safe."

Paul shook his head again. "You're the one who's getting out of here tonight. And wherever I go, don't worry about me. I'll do what's right for Dad."

The brothers studied each other for a moment, and then

suddenly Paul bolted off into the woods.

"No!" Johnny yelled. He coiled up for a chase, but didn't spring forward. His body sagged. Even if he caught Paul, he'd have to tackle him, and anything could happen if they were rolling around on the ground while carrying loaded guns.

Johnny sat on a picnic bench, his head in his hands. *God, if you're really there, I need you now.*

He rubbed his temples. *I have to get home to Lizbeth. I have to tell her everything, tell her the whole truth, tell her how much I love her.*

I'm trying to stop them, Johnny had told his brother. *The unit I'm in—we're trying to stop Octavian.*

Johnny had saved himself with those words, had saved himself from vigilantism and vengeance and obsession. Now he had to save his brother—and rejoin Peterson and Fullerton in saving the country.

Chapter 51

"Is the helicopter ready?" Peterson asked.

Rutherford nodded. "On the roof."

"Good. And your men?"

"Ready to seal off the exits on my order."

Peterson turned to Wolfe. "And our unit?"

"Kleibeck, Austin, and McLain are on the way," Wolfe said. "No word yet from Fullerton. And we've held off on contacting Luca, like you said."

I sent word out too late, Peterson thought. *I didn't want Bryson's thugs picking up on any unusual movements in the unit, and now we may have to do this without Fullerton.*

As for Luca, Peterson would reach out to him at the last minute, and pray that he could make it in time. Peterson had to be careful deploying Luca; Bryson's hounds would be sure to pick up on any sudden moves that he made.

"Then it's almost time," Peterson said. "We'll land on the helipad on the roof of the target building and apprehend the subject. Rutherford's men will seal off the exits." He forced a thin smile. "And then we'll grab a couple of beers and call it a night."

Peterson fell silent. Things were falling apart, and quickly. Sharpe was dead, supposedly by suicide. Bryson and had crew had "suicided" plenty of victims over the years, but Peterson couldn't rule out that this was an actual suicide. With the way Sharpe was acting last night, the way he was talking… anything was possible.

Once the news about Sharpe broke, Peterson knew it was time to leave Washington immediately. The wind had rustled the leaves, and now the hurricane was coming. He tried to contact Wilkins, but couldn't get through. Peterson would have to go this one alone.

As Sharpe had suggested the night before, he'd quit Washington for New York and had commandeered the New York field office. And now he was sitting in Moloch's old office at the top of the World Trade Center, where he and Moloch had beaten each other bloody less than a year ago.

Peterson looked out the window at New York City. Night had

fallen, and electric light washed through the canyon of skyscrapers, beaming tribute to the World Trade Center above.

Below, the city bustled as ever. *Nobody knows what we're about to do.*

"You're sure he's there?" Rutherford asked.

Peterson nodded. "Positive. I've had eyes on him all day. I know exactly where he is."

"And you're sure we can just land the helicopter on his building?"

"Well I don't think he's got guys up there with surface-to-air missiles, Colonel. They're not going to shoot down a helicopter in the middle of New York. He has no idea that we're coming."

"Then it's time," Wolfe said.

A pit cracked open in Peterson's stomach. "Just about. Get in touch with Luca. Tell him we need him."

Chapter 52

Johnny turned his key in the lock of his apartment door and pushed it open. *Some birthday.*

Just a few hours ago he was standing outside his mother's apartment building, freezing his ass off and watching those kids knock that ball around. And now here he was, and Buchanan was dead, and Paul was a terrorist assassin.

The old Johnny Luca would mix himself a Jack and Coke right about now. But the new Johnny Luca is going to drink the goddamn Jack straight.

Johnny grabbed the bottle, hoisting it to his lips. *Maybe it's time to apply to be general manager of the Yankees*, he thought, swigging the booze. He closed his eyes as the whiskey spidered inside his chest, singeing him all the way down. *I could be GM of the Yanks. I saved the President's life, after all. Can't I put that on my resume?*

Johnny studied his unsettled apartment, just as he had earlier tonight. It was time to move in here, after all. It was time for him to knock on Lizbeth's door and tell her the whole truth, tell her how wrong he'd been not to, tell her how he was putting death behind him and choosing life, a life for the two of them.

Partners, Gio, she'd told him. *We're partners in this.*

Johnny raised the bottle to his lips again. *I'll drive over there tonight. She'll still be awake. Tonight, after I calm down a little—*

Wait a second.

Still clutching the bottle, he strode towards the door to his apartment and pulled it open. He squinted at the door frame for a moment, studying a speck of the upper-left corner. *What good is putting double-sided tape on the door*, Johnny thought as he picked on a stripped slice of adhesive, *unless I can see if it pulls away when I open it?*

He peeled off the rest of the tape on the door. *This is so paranoid and stupid. Thanks, Dad.*

Johnny slapped himself in the forehead. *Now I have to take the tape off all the other stuff I put it on. Stupid, Luca, stupid.*

Johnny kicked the front door shut and crossed to the bedroom. He grabbed the doorknob and focused his eyes on the upper-right corner. He pulled.

The tape was already stripped.

Johnny raised his eyebrows. *That's funny.* It was like a high-school chemistry experiment that went wrong. *But Mr. Sanchez,* he thought back to junior year, *you said the tape was supposed to pull apart there.*

Johnny chiseled off the tape strips and then pivoted into the bathroom. He snapped open the mirrored medicine cabinet.

Stripped.

What the hell? I definitely didn't touch this or the door after I taped it up.

Johnny raced to the kitchen drawers. All stripped.

Now the blood rushed to his face. *The tape is supposed to peel apart*, he thought, the back of his throat clenching, *if no one has opened the drawer.*

Johnny crept to the living room closet. He felt his stomach open up.

Come on, he thought, laying his hand on the doorknob. *Give me a piece of double-sided tape pulling apart, so I can forget the others.* Johnny pulled the door open.

Stripped.

Johnny gasped. A bead of sweat slithered down his forehead.

He blinked, but it was still there: a pinch of tape on the wall, another on the door. His shoulder muscles heaved, his torso clinched. His hair stood up on end, his skin pulsed, his whole body about to lunge—

And then a peace cascaded over Johnny, almost like a hand on his shoulder and a whisper in his ear. *Someone's been in here. In the last couple of hours. And I'm going to walk over to that kitchen counter, real calm, and grab my gun.*

He strode towards the counter, one step, two steps—

The television on the living room wall flashed to life, and there was Jack Gaines, glowering on the screen.

Johnny dropped the whiskey bottle, and it shattered at his feet.

"Luca," Gaines called from the screen.

Every cord in Johnny's body snapped taut, locking him in place.

"Don't act so surprised," Gaines continued. "You knew this was coming. You knew that if you pushed me enough, it would come to this. And just like your pig father, you kept coming. And now you'll get what he got."

Johnny grabbed the gun and glared at the image of Gaines. The camera was zoomed in tight, so that only Gaines was visible in the frame. *This has to be a recording. He can't be watching me, this has to be some kind of a recording—*

"Maybe this is a live video feed, and maybe not," Gaines went on. "Maybe there's a camera in your apartment right now, maybe not. It doesn't matter. Either way, I'm watching every move you make. I've watched every single move for the last year. I know everything about you. Marissa. Paul. Lizbeth. I could've taken any of them away from you whenever I wanted, but I stayed out of your way. Because all I want to do is live and let live. That's what the revolution is, Luca. Live and let live. But that wasn't good enough for you."

Live and let live.

"I could've taken everything from you," Gaines said. "But I didn't. And how did you repay me? By trying to take everything from *me*." Gaines wagged a finger. "And that's the worst thing of all. I hate you, Luca. I hate you for so many reasons. But what I hate most of all is that you're so goddamn *ungrateful*."

Johnny's finger curled around the trigger, but there was no one in the apartment, no one to shoot, just an image on a screen. His heart bashed against his chest, over and over and over, and he began to feel faint.

"I'm a man who keeps my word," Gaines continued. "You know that. So I'll make you a promise. You're going to die tonight, Luca. Which is a gift you don't deserve. What you really deserve is a life sentence, a life of crying over your pathetic father, of wishing you could see him one more time, of going to bed wondering where I am and dreaming about what you'd do to me if you ever had five minutes alone with me. You deserve a life sentence of destroying every relationship you have because you're so obsessed with your rotting corpse of a pig father. You deserve to end up as what you really are, which is nothing. You're nothing, and no one. You're just another small man who gets a little bigger with a gun in his hand. And I'm Hyperion."

The camera began to pan out, and Johnny saw that Gaines was standing in front of a window around sunset. *It's a recording.*

"I'm going to give you three gifts tonight," Gaines said. "It's your birthday, after all. First, you're going to get your big chance. You're going to meet me." The camera panned out further, revealing some of the view out the window behind Gaines—there was an abandoned lot, a few decrepit buildings—maybe warehouses—and in the distance, a bridge.

"Second," Gaines said, smiling, "you're going to get to spend some time with an old friend." The camera panned out further, until a second figure drifted into the shot, slumped against a brick wall, his hands tied behind his back. *It can't be, please God no—*

"Viceroy," Gaines continued. "You and Fullerton, working one last mission together." Gaines reached down and horse-collared Fullerton, jerking his face towards the camera.

Johnny grimaced at the sight of his partner. A laceration sliced across his shaved head, and one of his eyes was swollen shut. The other eye was glazed over, thoughtless, lifeless. God only knew what torture Gaines had already visited upon him.

"The two of you can share the third gift," Gaines said. "Death." He threw Fullerton back to the floor, then kicked him in the chest. He turned back to the camera, murder burning in his eyes. "So here's your next move, Luca. You're going to turn yourself over to me, so you can answer for your crimes. Go to Penn Station. And Brigade 910 will take you into custody." Gaines grinned. "That's right, pig. Right out in the open, in public. You're not getting the chance to pull any of your moves in the shadows. I'm in control tonight. If you cause a scene at the station—Viceroy dies. If there's a shootout at the station—if my men get arrested—if you get arrested—Viceroy dies. If there's a sudden train derailment—Viceroy dies. *Slowly.* And if you don't show up, I'll keep going until I find someone you *do* care about." Gaines smiled. "Just remember, Luca. This is how you wanted it. Remember that, as I'm killing you tonight."

The screen went black.

Johnny shuddered. *A plan. A plan, a plan, I need a plan.*

He pointed the gun towards the television, then swung around wildly, aiming at walls, at shadows. But there was no one there. It was just Johnny and an empty apartment. And outside—his death.

A plan, a plan, he needed a plan.

Johnny holstered the gun. Whoever was here, they must have set the television on some kind of timer. Or maybe rigged it with a motion detector?

One thing was for sure—he wasn't sticking around to find out.

Johnny raced towards the television and grabbed the DVR. There it was—they'd left a USB stick in one of the ports. He plucked it out and shoved it in his pocket.

A plan, a plan.

Johnny picked up a remote and pressed a button, flicking off the lights in apartment. He was alone in the darkness.

Hang on, Fullerton. Just hang on. I'll get you home to Alicia.

Johnny darted through the darkness towards the closet in his bedroom. What was it Peterson told them last year, the night before they saved the President's life? *Free your minds in there, and you can do this.*

Johnny stepped into the closet and closed the door behind him. He stood motionless for a moment in the black. *How did it ever come to this? We beat them, just last year, we beat them.*

Johnny lowered his head. *But I had to keep pushing. I couldn't leave things alone. And now I'm going to get myself and Fullerton killed.*

Johnny clenched his fist. <u>*No*</u>. *Not tonight. We're not dying tonight. Hang on, Fullerton. I'll get you out of there.*

Johnny laid his fingertip on the biometric sensor of his gun locker, waited for a beep, and then yanked the doors open. An automatic light illuminated his arsenal.

There was a shotgun, a machine gun, a couple of handguns, ammunition, and a bulletproof vest. Johnny felt his face flush. *It's not a drill this time. Someone could bust in any second. I need to get the hell out of here.*

He strapped on an ankle holster, then grabbed a handgun from the locker and slid it into the holster.

A plan was coming together.

Johnny grabbed a duffel bag and started loading it up: first the machine gun, then ammunition, and then finally the Kevlar vest.

He zipped up the bag as the plan rocketed along synapses through his brain, points of light colliding and converging, burgeoning towards critical mass. There was only one way he was getting through this night alive, and he had just figured it out.

Free your minds in there, and you can do this.

Johnny slung the bag over his shoulder. *Let's roll.*

He marched out into the dark apartment, through the black and then out the door into the hallway, into the light. He raced through the corridor and then took the elevator to the parking garage.

Time to put that train station to use.

He hustled through the parking garage, cloaked in misty orange light. Hauling the duffel bag, he approached a pair of glass doors that gave way to a vestibule, which in turn fed into the train station. The lights were out in the vestibule.

Johnny dropped a shoulder into the crash bar of one of the doors, then pivoted inside. *There should be a train in a few minutes,* he thought as he stepped into the black, *it'll get me into lower Manhattan in about ten—*

A fist crashed into his face, and then a pair of arms wrapped around him and speared him into the wall.

"Cuff him!" yelled the one who'd speared Johnny.

"Just hold him down!" yelled the other one.

Johnny thrashed against the one holding him down, buying himself a nanosecond to reach for the ankle holster, but then another punch crunched into his face, stunning him.

"Flip him over," he heard one of them say. "I'll cuff the pig."

An arm cinched around Johnny's neck and twisted, the torque wrenching him onto his stomach. The thug drilled a knee into his back. "Cuff him!" he yelled. "Cuff him!"

Just then, Johnny heard a door crash open, followed by the sound of some metallic burst. The punk with the knee in Johnny's back slumped against the wall.

Silencer shot. But who—

There was another metallic burst, and the sound of a second body hitting the floor.

Johnny rolled onto his back, then kipped up, drawing his gun. "Who the—"

"Kid," a voice called as a flashlight clicked on. "You need to get out of here."

The light revealed the face of the elderly security guard.

"You," Johnny said. "How did you—"

"I'll bet you're glad I stayed awake this time." The old man winked. "You have to catch that next train and get lost."

Johnny rubbed his face, then yanked up the duffel bag. "How did you… how did you know?"

The old man's face brightened, and now he didn't look the part of a bumbling, narcoleptic security guard. He looked confident, capable—professional. "Peterson's had me watching you since the beginning," he said. "I know I let you down last year. I owed you one." He gestured to the bodies on the floor. "This here was some kind of decapitation strike. They're after you tonight, big time. These two were in your place earlier." The old man beamed the light towards the door that led to the train station. "There'll be more coming. And I can't hold them all off. Take the train and head over to the World Trade Center, to the Authority field office. Peterson's looking for you."

Why? Johnny swallowed hard. "What's going on?"

The old man's face went grave. "A lot, kid." He grabbed Johnny's shoulder, then pulled his hood over his head. "Whatever you do, *hide your face.*" He looked into Johnny's eyes, and where Johnny had seen confidence earlier, he now saw terror. "Get yourself to the city and meet up with the boss."

Chapter 53

The glass elevator began to climb towards the top of One World Trade Center. Johnny looked out over lower Manhattan.

It was quiet, tense, barren. A few taxicabs glided through the streets, tumbleweeds drifting through the canyon of skyscrapers.

Electric light rippled through the reflecting pools of the September 11 memorial below, pools that had been poured into the concrete footprints of the buildings destroyed by terrorists in 2001. *Out of death, we harvested life,* Johnny thought.

It was something his father used to say. "Out of death, we harvested life. They knocked the buildings down, but we built something even more beautiful, even stronger. Out of death, life."

As the elevator ascended the tower, the view stretched into a cityscape, New York City gleaming out to the horizon. The Empire State Building and the Chrysler Building stood to the north as the Hudson River swirled through the west in ribbons of moonlight.

And somewhere below, there were violent protests in Times Square.

The whole world had changed tonight, and Johnny had caught a glimpse of it walking from the train station to the World Trade Center earlier.

PRESIDENT WILKINS UNDER HOUSE ARREST, a news ticker screamed in LED red across the front of a building. VICE PRESIDENT GREENAWAY ADDRESSES NATION, SAYS WILKINS "ACCUSED OF GRAVE CRIMES".

As Johnny walked on, a video screen fronting a different building showed highlights of Greenaway's speech. GREENAWAY: I HAVE TAKEN THE OATH OF OFFICE, read the news graphic below. WILKINS UNFIT FOR OFFICE WHILE UNDER ARREST, 25TH AMENDMENT INVOKED.

And then:

LEGAL EXPERTS: HOUSE ARREST UNCONSTITUTIONAL

PROTESTS ERUPT IN WASHINGTON, NEW YORK

The news broadcast then cut to footage of clashes between

protesters and the Authority in Times Square.

And now, Johnny thought as the elevator stopped at the ninetieth floor, *Peterson's planning to do something about it.*

"Luca, come in," Wolfe's voice had crackled over Johnny's two-way, just a few minutes after the old man had sent him on his way earlier. "This is mission critical. Come in."

Johnny had answered the call, and now here he was, stepping off the elevator. The great seal of the United States Anti-Subversion Authority, cut in gold trim on the glass-paneled wall, greeted him.

Johnny opened the door and stepped into the lobby. "Luca," Agent Austin called from behind bulletproof glass at the receptionist's desk. "Come in." A buzzer went off.

Johnny yanked on a white ballistic door and stepped into the office.

Peterson greeted him with a nod. "Follow me," he said.

Johnny followed him through the field office, striding past a maze of cubicles. They crossed into a large office, what had to be the SAIC's office. At the far end was a wall of windows, the skyline twinkling beyond. And outside, a balcony—the balcony where Peterson and Moloch had clashed at zero hour last May.

Johnny stepped into the office, where Peterson had assembled the team: Wolfe, Kleibeck, Austin, Rutherford, and Neely. And now Johnny would have to break the news that Fullerton wouldn't be joining them—nor would Johnny.

Johnny nodded at each member of the team in turn, at Rutherford—who had sheltered him and Fullerton after Sigma had nearly killed them both; at Wolfe, Kleibeck, and Austin—who had helped save the President's life last year; at Neely—keeper of Johnny's secrets, co-avenger of his father's murder.

"So I guess you all know what's going on," Johnny said. He gestured towards the windows. "Out there."

"We do," Peterson said. "A coup. There's been a coup." He looked at Johnny. "They have the President. And soon they'll be coming for us."

"But you have a plan."

"I do. We're going to arrest Octavian tonight, Luca."

Johnny's eyes widened. *You did it. You cracked the case, boss. I knew you wouldn't let us down.* "Octavian?" he said.

"That's right. There's a helicopter ready for us on the roof. We're going to fly across town and storm his building."

Johnny looked around the room for a moment. Wolfe, Rutherford, Kleibeck, Austin, Neely—even Neely—were all grave, solemn, silent. And Peterson… he was measuring his words. He wasn't commanding the room with confidence. Instead, he seemed as if he were praying with each word. They were badly outnumbered, Johnny knew. They were alone against the world tonight, and the team needed him.

He looked Peterson in the eyes. "Fullerton," he said. "Gaines has Fullerton."

Neely gasped—a first. "Jesus Christ," Wolfe said.

Shock registered in Peterson's eyes. "How do you know?" he asked.

Johnny pulled out the USB stick. "I have a video."

Peterson turned to the others. "Give us a minute," he said. "I need to talk to Luca alone."

The team filed out in silence.

They're all terrified, Johnny thought.

Peterson waited until the last of them left, then closed the door. "Show me the video," he said.

Johnny popped the USB into a computer on the SAIC's desk, then stepped back as Peterson watched. And there it all was, Gaines against the brick wall, then the camera shot widening to reveal Fullerton and a sliver of window behind Gaines, a bridge and a row of warehouses behind him.

Just remember, Luca, Gaines said on the video. *This is how you wanted it. Remember that, as I'm killing you tonight.*

Peterson's arm lashed out at the computer mouse, pounding off the video. "My God," he said. He lowered his head. "Julius."

Johnny had never heard him call Fullerton by his first name before. "Boss," he said. "We have to save him."

Peterson turned towards Johnny. "The helicopter's on the roof. We have to—"

"*We have to save him.*"

Peterson looked away for a moment, then turned back to face Johnny. "I bet you're going to tell me you have a plan."

Johnny nodded. "I do."

"What plan could you have?"

Well, this will sound completely insane. "The background. Look." Johnny reached over Peterson to play the video again, racing it forward to the moment the shot widened, when the window behind Gaines became visible. "Right there. The bridge, and the buildings. We can make his location off of those."

"You're out of your mind," Peterson said that. "How are you going to do that?"

"I'm not. But I know someone who can."

"Who?"

"A friend." *An old friend.* Johnny stepped back and folded his arms. "Boss, listen. I know what you guys are about to do. I know what we're up against tonight, what this all means. I know if we don't get Octavian, it's all over." He looked away for a moment, out the window, out at the city glowing outside. Then he turned back to Peterson. "But we can't leave a man behind. We can't leave *Fullerton* behind."

Peterson didn't yield. "You mean you can't leave *Gaines* behind."

"It's not about that—"

"Of course it is. It's a trap, Luca, can't you see it's a goddamn trap?" Peterson stood up. "You're walking into a trap. You think Gaines did this himself? Bryson set the whole thing up. This is his big move—to wipe all of us out tonight."

"But I *have* him," Johnny said. "Gaines messed up, and I *have* him. I can figure out his location, and beat him at his own game."

Peterson shook his head. "From that little bit of video! From a second, a split-second."

"You can do anything in a split-second, anything *with* a split-second. You know that." Johnny laid a hand on Peterson's shoulder. "This is *Fullerton* we're talking about here. We can't leave him to die, to get tortured in some rat hole and then die alone." Johnny bit his lip. "And Gaines. Sure, you know I want Gaines, I've wanted him since the beginning. But it's bigger than me, bigger than my dad. Gaines is the most wanted terrorist in America. And no matter what you do with Octavian tonight, Gaines is still going to be out there, bombing buildings and killing people." *And recruiting people like my brother, robbing them of their lives. No. No more.* "I'm going to put a stop to all of it tonight. I'm going to get our boy back, and I'm going to collar Gaines. Not *kill* him, boss. I'm going to bring him in. Because I've been thinking about all of this. I don't want revenge, I don't want death. I don't want to pay death for death." Johnny gestured towards the windows. "Look out there. There's *life* out there, even tonight, even with the whole country on the line. There's still life. Fullerton tried to show me, all this time, he tried to teach me to choose life over death. And I can't let him die. I have to give him his life back. He did the same for me once. And I owe him."

Peterson studied Johnny for a moment. "Life over death," he said. "I don't think any of us are going to get to make that choice tonight." He paused. "But maybe there's always a choice. I don't know." He crossed the room to the windows and looked out at the city. "It was right out here," he said. "Moloch and me, beating the hell out of each other. If he'd landed one more punch, or I'd missed one, maybe it would've gone differently. Just one punch, and Operation Reichstag would've gone ahead. There wasn't much choice in that."

"But there was," Johnny said. "You wanted it more. That was the choice. The good overcame the bad."

Peterson turned back to face him. "We're going to find out tonight if that's right. We'll find out if the good overcomes the bad. Or if it just comes down to who has more money and guns." He paused. "You think you can bring Fullerton home?"

I'm not sure. "I have to try."

"Right. You have to try." Peterson reached into his pocket and pulled out a USB stick of his own. "Take this."

Johnny arched his eyebrows as he took the USB. "What is it?"

"It's everything you need to know about Octavian. If we don't make it tonight, it's up to you. You and Fullerton." Peterson's voice trailed off. "If we don't make it, there'll have to be a rebellion. It's the only way. I don't know how, and I don't know by who, but there's going to be an uprising, a rebellion. And you and Fullerton will have to join that rebellion. I always said there was something special about you two, right? You're indestructible together. So bring him home.

"I'll bring him home," Johnny said. "And we'll all be throwing back beers tomorrow, and having a good laugh at Octavian, Bryson, and Gaines sharing a cell together."

Peterson nodded. "You should get going. Good luck, Luca."

"Good luck to you too, sir." He turned and headed towards the door.

"Luca," Peterson called behind him. "One more thing. The President has a message for you."

Johnny turned around. *The President has a message for me?* "What?" he asked.

"He told me to tell you, 'We shall meet in the place where there is no darkness.'"

Johnny threw up his hands. "What does that mean?"

Peterson shrugged. "You'll figure it out."

The two shared a final look, and then Johnny turned and left.

Chapter 54

It's so much worse than I thought, Johnny thought as he walked near Times Square, toting his duffel bag. He was headed towards Hell's Kitchen, where his friend was waiting. *So much worse.*

"I am a subversive, make your move!" boomed a crowd of thousands, bathed in the light of the Times Square video screens above. "I AM A SUBVERSIVE, MAKE YOUR MOVE!"

The Authority made its move, black-clad riot officers plunging into the crowd with truncheons and tasers as some of their comrades hung back and fired tear gas canisters. The balaclava-clad protesters engaged them head-on, punching and kicking, weathering truncheon blows and tasings as they bashed against riot shields, tackled officers, and wrenched their weapons from them. The crowd surged back and forth in response to the tear gas explosions, fighting not in formation, but in waves of rage, baying against tyranny, against usurpation. Several of the protesters were busting up chunks of street and sidewalk with hammers, then hurling the missiles at the Authority officers. Poisoned smoke rose above Times Square as tear gas canisters burst, spewing their contents into the night.

Above it all was a replay of now-President Greenaway's speech on one of the video screens, its audio blasting on loudspeakers:

"We face now a constitutional crisis of the gravest magnitude," he said. "I am confronted with evidence that Reed Wilkins, whom we elected as our President, conspired last year to engineer a series of false-flag of terror attacks that he codenamed Operation Reichstag. The plot included a staged assassination attempt against Mr. Wilkins himself in New York City. Based on my reading of the evidence, this appears to have been calculated to overthrow our democracy and bring about a police state in the United States. Mr. Wilkins, who had pretended to oppose the Total Information Awareness Act and had even gone so far as to veto it, planned to use the Operation Reichstag attacks as a pretext to assume dictatorial powers."

Bullshit, Johnny thought. *And everyone in this crowd knows it. They all know it's a goddamn lie, even if they hated Wilkins before, and now they're rising up against the lie. They're rising up to save their democracy.*

But how many people outside of New York were rising up tonight? And how many had Bryson and Greenaway convinced?

"The Anti-Subversion Authority has placed Mr. Wilkins under house arrest," Greenaway continued. "He is being held at a secure location, and he will be accorded all of the protections of our Constitution. During this time of unprecedented crisis, the Cabinet secretaries and I have advised the Speaker of the House of Representatives and the President pro tempore of the Senate that Mr. Wilkins is unable to discharge the powers and duties of his office while under arrest. I therefore have assumed office as Acting President under the Twenty-Fifth Amendment. I humbly ask all Americans to consider the words of former President Gerald Ford, who assumed office following President Nixon's resignation during the Watergate scandal: 'I am acutely aware that you have not elected me as your president by your ballots, and so I ask you to confirm me as your president with your prayers.' I also am acutely aware that you have not elected me, but I do ask you to confirm me with your prayers during this difficult time. All Americans, of course, will have the opportunity to choose their president in the election this November."

Johnny felt like hurling a stone at the screen at the sight of Greenaway, a lapdog hack who was doing Bryson's bidding.

The protesters in Times Square couldn't possibly win, Johnny recognized; the Authority officers were already overwhelming them with brute force. The protesters had hammers and stones; the Authority officers had gas masks and truncheons. The officers hulked over fallen protesters, clad in black body armor, jackboots, and visors.

This was Bryson's America, Bryson's Authority. It was clear that he was in charge down here. Peterson was up in that tower right now drawing up plans, but he was Authority Director in name only—his power was gone, his time was up. Johnny guessed that either Greenaway had reappointed Bryson or Bryson had started issuing orders, and it was do or die now. Johnny looked to the sky, hoping to see Peterson's helicopter above. *Come on, boss. Get him. Get Octavian and end this nightmare.*

Then Johnny looked at the video screen again, and saw a nightmare all his own.

ARREST WARRANT ISSUED FOR VIGILANTE AGENT, beamed a news graphic. ROGUE AUTHORITY AGENT ACCUSED IN MURDERS OF NEW JERSEY DETECTIVE, TERROR SUSPECTS.

The video then cut to a still photograph of Johnny.

Fantastic.

Johnny again took in the sight of Authority agents clashing with protesters. *Hmm. A warrant out for my arrest. I might not want to be around hundreds of federal agents right now.*

Johnny drew his hood over his head, then turned tail and got the hell out of there. He started to run, but then slowed down. *Flow of traffic, Luca. I'm wearing a hoodie and carrying a duffel bag while World War III is going on in Times Square right now. I might not want to be running.*

As he walked, protesters rushed past him, brandishing hammers and pieces of rock, off to pour into the melee at the square. Riot police stormed past.

Johnny walked past a block-shaped bin, sealed on top but with bottle-sized openings on the sides, an LCD screen gleaming on the front panel. It was a bomb-proof recycling bin, one of hundreds that the mayor had installed all over the city to take away at least one weapon in Brigade 910's arsenal: explosives hidden in garbage cans. They'd supposedly been tested in the New Mexico desert to withstand bomb blasts, and they were "smart" to boot, with the LCD screens carrying advertisements.

Except tonight there was no advertisement, but rather the visage of Johnny Luca.

A chill bolted down Johnny's spine. WANTED FOR MURDER, the bin read. CONSIDERED ARMED AND DANGEROUS.

Well, the last part is right.

He looked up the block, and there was another bin at the corner, flashing Johnny's mug in LCD pixels.

I need to get the hell out of the city.

He hurried his pace, the sounds of the ruckus at the square

behind him dying down. Bryson had played this one beautifully. If Johnny didn't die at Gaines's hands tonight, he'd be arrested. And even if he avoided arrest, he could never show his face again, could never visit his family, could never see Lizbeth.

Johnny had been planning to drive Lizbeth's place tonight, to tell her what a fool he'd been, to tell her how he was choosing life over death and wanted a life with her, life and life and life, until they grew old together.

Now, he didn't know if he'd ever see her again. And all he wanted was just one brush of Lizbeth's fingertips over his, just one breath of her scent, one echo of her laughter.

Johnny came upon a row of red-brick tenements, fire escapes zigzagging down the sides of the buildings. He stopped in front of a black wrought-iron fence a few doors down, made sure the house number was right, and then took a deep breath.

He approached the front door and slipped into the vestibule just as a tenant was leaving. Johnny turned his face to avoid eye contact and crossed into the building.

Goddamn walkups, he thought as he laid his foot onto a wooden step. *Everything about this dude is a pain in the ass, right on down to his apartment building.*

Johnny scaled the staircases, one flight, two flights, three flights. Finally, he was standing before his buddy's door.

Johnny knocked. There was shuffling within, followed by the clicking of the door as it was unlocked. And then the door opened.

"An arrest warrant, eh?" Billy Hawkins said. "I always thought that if you were going to get arrested, it would be for indecent exposure!"

Chapter 55

"I'd never get busted for indecent exposure," Johnny said, hustling Billy inside and closing the door behind them. "No one would ever call *that* exposure indecent."

Billy threw up his hands. "Well, you're the expert!"

Johnny, accused of murder and on the run from a coup regime that was trying to kill him, couldn't help but chuckle. Billy, in all his corpulent, blond mop-top, red-bearded glory, was his college roommate, the only guy who'd ever believed that Johnny could win Lizbeth over back in the dark days of Dick the Red Sox fan. His business venture in Miami had washed out, and now he was back in the city. And more to the point, he was a computer genius with an odd knack for winning "view from your window" contests on various blogs.

Johnny took in the sight of Billy's closet-sized studio. *And I thought my old place in Newark was a goddamn mess.* The floor was a minefield of crushed beer cans and pizza boxes, with a few plates of crusted-over meals on the coffee and end tables. At the far end of the room, there was an exposed brick wall, with an anarchist "A" symbol spray-painted in white.

This could be my last night on earth. And I'm spending it in this fucking hovel.

"Icelanders," Billy said.

Johnny squinted. "What?"

"I met a bunch of people visiting from Iceland at a bar last night. And I brought them all back here and partied until like six in the morning."

Johnny nodded. "And hooked up with the hot blonde, of course."

Billy smiled. "I hook up with the hot blonde in *every* scenario."

Fat fuck's probably telling the truth. "So how did you hear about the warrant?"

"It was breaking news on the *Transvestite Guineas with Small Dicks* listserv," Billy said, grinning. "You're a pillar of that community, after all." Then the grin evaporated. "It was on the news, actually. Kind of a side story to all the stuff going on at the White House."

"I didn't do it, Billy."

Billy nodded. "I know you didn't, dude. I knew it couldn't be true." He folded his arms. "What kind of trouble are you in?"

"The worst kind of trouble. Life and death." Johnny heaved a breath. "Listen. There's been some kind of coup tonight. Do you know who Alexander Bryson is? The guy who used to run the Anti-Subversion Authority?"

Billy nodded. "I do."

"Well, if I'm right about what's going on, he's overthrown the government tonight. And he put up Greenaway as his stooge. And me…" Johnny paused. "I'm mixed up in it, me and other people I work with. I can't tell you how. But my back is against the wall, and I need to get the fuck out of the city tonight. But I need your help first."

Billy nodded again. "Anything, dude. Name it." He grinned again. "Well, not a hand-job. But most things."

Johnny pulled one of the USB sticks out of his pocket. "It's not a hand-job, asshole. I need your help with a video. One of those 'view from your window' things you're so good at."

"But those things are one in a million—"

"And you get them every time." Johnny looked into Billy's eyes. "This whole night's one in a million, dude. But I can't go down without a fight. And right now, you're that fight." Johnny grinned, then tossed the USB stick to Billy. "No pressure, though."

Billy caught the USB. "Of course not."

Johnny crossed the room to the window and drew the shades down as Billy popped the USB into his laptop. He closed his eyes as Gaines's voice drifted through the room.

"What the fuck," Billy said behind him.

Billy didn't sign up for this, Johnny thought as he stood before the window. *He's not mixed up in any of this, not with Gaines, or Bryson, or anyone else. But he's all I have right now.*

"Who the fuck is this guy?" Billy called across the room.

Johnny turned to face him. "His name is Jack Gaines," he said. "He killed my father."

"He killed… but I thought your dad… I mean, he committed—"

"He didn't kill himself. He was murdered. That guy you saw in the video—he killed my dad. And he made it look like suicide."

"But why?"

"It's best if you don't know, dude."

Billy ran his hands through his mop-top. "And the other guy? The one who's tied up?"

"He's my partner. And I have to save him."

"Your partner."

Johnny walked across the room and laid a hand on Billy's shoulder. "What, no jokes about me having a life partner?" *I've actually shell-shocked him into not calling me gay.* "I'm a federal agent. That's all I'm going to say. And that guy you saw who's tied up, he's my partner. He saved my life twice. And I need to get him out of there."

"I see." Billy ran his hands through his hair again, then rubbed his beard. "Well, you're in luck, ginzo. I think we can crack the case."

Please let that be true. "Really?"

"Give me a few minutes."

Johnny couldn't sit, he couldn't stand, he could only pace as Billy drummed away on the keyboard. Every minute was a lifetime, maybe Fullerton's lifetime. Every sixty seconds carried the possibility that Gaines could execute Fullerton.

Penn Station. They're waiting for me at Penn Station. Because Gaines wants me out in the open? He's afraid of me in the shadows?

It's a trap. But what kind of trap?

The kind Bryson would set up. It's a sting operation, and not even Gaines himself knows it. Bryson must've set this up somehow. Gaines must really think his little Brigade 910 jerk-offs are going to "take me into custody." But really Bryson is going to have something like twenty Authority agents swoop in and arrest me. Fucking idiot Gaines has no clue that he's dancing on Bryson's string.

But I'm going to tell him. Tonight, when I'm cuffing him. I'm going to tell him that his "revolution" is one big lie. He devoted his whole life to burning down the country, and he's Bryson's puppet. Something for him to think about when he's locked up in prison for the rest of his life.

"Get over here," Billy said. "I did it. I figured it out."

Johnny leapt towards Billy. "Show me," he said.

Billy feigned cracking his knuckles, as if he were a master pianist about to commence a performance. Then he pointed at the screen. "Your boy Gaines gave you a big gift," he said. "The bridge."

"What about it?"

"What about it, he says. That's the Ben Franklin Bridge, which connects Philly and Camden. I mean, that little landscape just screams northeast to me, some kind of old industrial zone. And that bridge—I've driven over that bridge before. Look at those blue trusses, those V-shapes kind of crisscrossing like that. I know the bridge. Here." Billy pulled up a picture of the Ben Franklin Bridge, and it was an exact match to the image in the video. "I mean, this guy has to be to a fucking idiot to let that in the camera shot. Now we have it narrowed down to Philly or Camden."

That's my boy, Johnny thought, smiling.

"For a minute there I thought the camera might be on the Philly side," Billy went on. "But the buildings aren't quite right. Remember that girl Becky I worked my magic on for awhile back in college? She was from Philly. I drove out there a few times, hung out with her, met her family, all that—until her dad kicked me out of the house one night for saying something stupid. Anyway, I got a feel for the place. I'm kind of an architecture nerd, and these buildings just don't look like Philly to me. So we're on the Camden side here, and the bridge is only a few blocks away, you can tell. At this point, it's just a question of picking up on little landmarks and getting the angles right." Billy pointed at the screen. "Now look. You can see the outline of a stadium, the edge of a stadium, in the upper-left corner there. That's a minor league baseball stadium. It hasn't been used in years, but it's an old ballpark. And here, in the foreground—those are light rail tracks, the River Line, I think it's called, running parallel to the bridge. And those buildings across the street—boarded-up warehouses, you can see the boards in the windows. And there are all kinds of other little things you need to notice here—the slopes of the roofs, the positions of the street lamps, even where that dumpster is. So there are lots of details here, just in this little still image. And if you keep Googling and using street view, and if you're a total stud with skills like me, you can figure it out eventually. Which is what I did." Billy called up a window and lined it up next to the paused video. "Here's the street view from where I think the building is," he said. "It's a perfect match."

Johnny was ready to spring into action. It was a perfect match, all right. Billy had done it. And now it was time to roll.

"Here's the building where Gaines shot the video," Billy said. "This is where you need to go." And there it was, a boarded-up warehouse in the middle of nowhere, in an abandoned industrial area. "It's a war zone down there," Billy continued.

"Maybe," Johnny said. "But I'll be ready." He rolled up his jacket to flash his handgun.

"Is that going to be enough?"

"Trust me. I've got a hell of a lot more hardware than this." Johnny gestured towards his duffel bag. "All right, dude. I have to do my thing now."

He crossed the room in silence, yanking his duffel bag onto the couch and unzipping it. Johnny cinched a layer of Kevlar over his clothes. He grabbed the machine gun, inspected it, then slung it across his chest. He ran his hand over the last item in the bag: the red-and-white keffiyeh that Neely had given him.

Johnny wrapped the scarf around his neck, then zipped up his jacket and turned to Billy. "It's time," he said. "Now Billy, if you really want to serve your country, I need two things from you."

"What's that?" Billy asked.

Johnny held up one finger. "One, I need some Jack, ASAP." He held up a second finger. "Two, I need your motorcycle."

We're right by the Lincoln Tunnel. I can zip out of here real quick.

"Mat... Matilda?" Billy said.

"Yeah, dude. I need your bike, even though I'm not calling it Matilda."

Billy gulped, then shook his head and grabbed a bottle and a set of keys from the kitchen counter. "Why do I feel like it's not a great idea to hand you liquor and a motorcycle key at the same time?" he asked, passing them to Johnny.

"I'm carrying a machine gun and riding out to face a dude who wants to torture me to death," Johnny said. "You're worried about a little booze?"

He swigged the liquor, closing his eyes as it blazed through his chest. He hoped it wasn't his last drink of Jack Daniels on earth.

"All right," Johnny said. "I'd better go. I need you to do one more thing for me, Billy."

"What?"

"Lizbeth and my mom—tell them I'm innocent. And tell them I love them. Paul, too. Tell him I love him." *Paul knows I'm innocent.*

"I will," Billy said, throwing a meaty arm around Johnny. "Good luck. Come home safe."

Johnny returned the embrace, then stepped out the door.

November 18, 2021, Johnny thought as he bounded down the steps. *And now, two and a half years later, I have the chance to make it right.*

Gaines, you son of a bitch, I'm coming for you.

Chapter 56

Peterson cocked his machine gun. "This is it," he told his assembled men. "Let's move."

Of the original group, Kleibeck, Austin, and Rutherford remained. Peterson had redeployed Wolfe and McLain by ground.

"You sure you can fly that bird?" Kleibeck asked Austin.

Austin cocked his gun. "Don't worry about me," he said. "Just make sure you can shoot straight."

"Remember, I want him alive," Peterson said. "If we can help it."

"Sometimes you can't," Kleibeck said.

"He's right," Austin said. "When you're dealing with a scumbag like this, sometimes your finger slips."

Damn right it does, Peterson thought. *But we need him alive. Otherwise, it'll look like an assassination. We need this monster to stand trial for his crimes.*

Just then, the door burst open, and in marched a group of armed Authority agents.

Goddamn it.

"Sir," the agents' leader called, addressing Peterson. "Tell your men to put down their weapons. You all need to come with us."

Peterson narrowed his eyes. "And why would we need to do that?"

"Director Bryson has summoned you to Washington."

Peterson nodded. *Director Bryson.* "But I'm the Director, young man."

"President Greenaway has dismissed you, sir."

"But Wilkins is the President." Peterson hoped the others would pick up on the charade.

The agent shook his head. "Not anymore, sir. He's under house arrest. Vice President Greenaway has assumed office."

"And Bryson is summoning us to Washington," Rutherford said, picking up on Peterson's charade. "I'm a colonel in the United States Army, son. Who is he to summon *me*?"

"He's summoned you all on suspicion of sedition. You all need to put down your weapons and come with us."

Bryson's sent green boys to bring us in, Peterson thought. *He must be short on manpower right now, with all of that chaos down at Times Square.*

"We'll come along quietly," he said. He turned to Austin and Kleibeck, then nodded at them. "Gentlemen, present your weapons."

And in an instant, Peterson whirled around and opened fire, Austin and Kleibeck blasting their guns behind him. Together they gunned down the five Authority agents. Four of them dropped dead instantly, the fifth hitting the floor and twitching. He reached for his weapon—until Austin shot a bullet through his eyes.

"Christ, these were my men," Peterson said. "Just kids."

"This is war tonight, sir," Kleibeck said.

War. "Let's get to the roof."

Blood surged to Peterson's face as his heart crashed against his chest. He was an automaton rushing through the office, then out into the hallway and up the stairwell, his boots clanging on the metal steps. He was a mind in a body not his own, a mass of nerves and limbs pulling him up the last few flights to the roof.

Peterson and the others spilled out onto the roof, guns drawn. The black helicopter stood on the helipad, doors removed on Peterson's orders. It was unguarded; Bryson hadn't deployed agents up here yet, but they'd be coming. They had to move.

Peterson led the charge towards the helicopter, and the others followed in formation. He jumped in and fitted himself with a headset. The others piled in, doing the same, with Austin jumping into the cockpit and firing the aircraft to life.

"Austin," Peterson called through the headset as the helicopter took off, rotors whirring. "Four Thirty-Two Park Avenue."

"Copy," Austin called.

The helicopter ascended from the World Trade Center helipad and headed north. Four Thirty-Two Park Avenue was the second-tallest building in the city, a luxury apartment tower, and Octavian would be in the penthouse. In just a few minutes, Austin would touch down on the tower's helipad, and then they'd climb down to the penthouse level and blast their way through the windows.

A matter of minutes, Peterson thought as the helicopter soared through the city.

Air surged through the helicopter as it rocketed along at one hundred fifty miles per hour. They flew past one skyscraper after another, each a beacon of electric light in the black night, each a monument to the power and innovation of man, the sort of power and innovation that only liberty could unleash. *New York City will never submit. Not to Octavian, not to anyone. This city will not be subjugated.*

Times Square came into view, and Peterson could see smoke rising, waves of protesters crashing into their oppressors, mayhem and tear gas explosions throughout. *We can't save you now. But maybe in a few minutes…*

The helicopter approached Octavian's tower, a perfectly symmetrical rectangle scraping the firmament and hulking over the city.

"Rutherford, send up your men," Peterson said into the headset. "Austin, put it down."

"Copy," Rutherford said, then issued his own orders through a radio.

"Copy," Austin said.

"Four on the roof," Kleibeck said.

Four armed men were guarding the roof, preparing to open fire on the helicopter.

"Authority agents?" Rutherford asked.

"Doesn't matter," Peterson said. "Kleibeck, fire."

Without a word, Kleibeck fired off a machine gun burst, cutting two down immediately.

The third agent aimed at the helicopter and shot off a burst, the bullets slicing into the frame and rocking the aircraft.

"Christ!" Austin yelled.

"Put it down!" Peterson commanded. "Kleibeck!"

Kleibeck aimed and fired as the helicopter approached the helipad, nailing the third agent as the fourth squared up with a weapon on his shoulder.

"That's a goddamn rocket launcher," Kleibeck said. "They're going to shoot us down over the city!"

"Not tonight," Peterson said. "Come on!"

Kleibeck squinted into the telescopic sight as the agent aimed a surface-to-air missile. Kleibeck's finger curled around the trigger; the agent raised the launcher; and a bullet cratered through the agent's forehead, splattering his brains as his lifeless legs flew out from under him.

"Put this goddamn thing down," Peterson said.

"Copy," Austin said.

"So much for the element of surprise," Kleibeck said as the helicopter hovered over the helipad and touched down.

"There's no surprise when you land a goddamn helicopter on a roof," Peterson said. "Let's move. Down the ladders and through the windows."

The group rushed off the helicopter and ran towards the steel ladders leading down to the penthouse level. *It would be nice to take the elevator down instead*, Peterson thought as he ran, *but we aren't exactly welcome guests.*

They dove towards the ladders, rolling onto their stomachs and swinging their legs out behind them, then got their bearings and descended, landing on the patio outside of the penthouse.

The four stood before a panel of floor-to-ceiling windows, and there were more of Octavian's guards inside, charging towards the windows and aiming their weapons.

Peterson and the others opened fire, shattering the windows and cutting down several of them. "Inside!" he yelled. And then he recalled Wilkins's words from their meeting at Camp David: "We die if we don't!"

They charged through shards of broken glass into Octavian's luxury living room, blasting the agents they hadn't hit in the first wave. Peterson's group took control of the room, as several of the palace guards lay dead or dying—a foothold in the compound of Octavian himself.

"Where the hell is he?" yelled Austin.

"Sweep!" yelled Kleibeck.

"No!" yelled Peterson. "Stay together!"

Just then, Gordon Bragg walked into the living room.

"Peterson," he said. "What's going—"

Peterson aimed his machine gun at him. "Hands up, Bragg," he said. "You're under arrest."

Bragg raised his hands, his face frozen in shock. "Under arrest?"

Peterson nodded, keeping the gun trained on him. "That's right, Octavian. Move a muscle and you die."

"My men are headed this way," Rutherford said. "They're in the hallway."

"You hear that, Bragg?" Peterson said. "It's over. You're on your way to prison. And then you'll be tried for treason."

"There's been a mistake," Bragg pleaded, the shock on his face now yielding to terror. "We thought you were Bryson's men, coming to arrest me like Wilkins. We have to stop Brys—"

"No more talking, Bragg. Austin, put the bracelets on."

Just then, there was a commotion in the penthouse, and in walked Rutherford's men. *Thank God,* Peterson thought. *Thank God. We did it. We caught him.*

"We need secure transport," he said to the new arrivals.

There was no response.

Bragg's terrified face curled into a sneer.

And then two of Rutherford's men gunned down Austin and Kleibeck.

They weren't Rutherford's men at all, but instead more Authority agents, and were now pointing their weapons at Peterson and Rutherford.

"Put *your* hands up," Bragg said. "Move a muscle and *you* die."

God, no, Peterson thought.

An agent slipped behind him and disarmed him, and another agent did the same to Rutherford.

Bragg smiled. "Nice work," he said to the agents. "Now step aside."

Suddenly, he whipped a gun from his waistband and shot Rutherford in the head. The colonel collapsed.

Peterson nearly threw up. *No, no, no.*

Bragg turned towards him. "Don't worry," he said as Authority agents handcuffed Peterson. "You won't die tonight. We're going to have some fun with you first."

Chapter 57

"Go ahead with everything that we discussed," Bragg directed the agents as they led Peterson away in handcuffs. "Make sure you keep the NYPD away from the building. Director Bryson will control the messaging to the press. And I want transport to Washington. I have an appointment to keep."

"Yes, sir," the senior agent said. The agents filed out with Peterson in tow.

Bryson would control the messaging, all right. And tonight the press would report that Peterson had gotten word of Wilkins's arrest and realized that the game was up, that he was going to be implicated in Wilkins's plot to overthrow the government last year. So he'd responded by commandeering the New York field office and then moving against Bragg, who'd been one of the few voices in the media brave enough to criticize the Authority over the last year.

And tomorrow, Bragg's publications would start the process of conceding that Bryson was a patriot all along, that it was Wilkins and Peterson who'd been trying to turn the Authority into an American Gestapo.

Would the public believe it? Bragg beamed at the thought. Of course they would. They were all terrified now. They'd believe anything if it meant that life could get back to normal, if they could keep their jobs and have food to eat, if there weren't tanks rolling through the streets.

It's all over, Bragg thought as he surveyed the wreckage of the luxury penthouse. *Democracy made its last stand tonight, and it's all over.*

It had all ended with the whimper he'd expected, though he never imagined that Peterson would piece it all together in time. *Sharpe*, Bragg thought. *It must have been Sharpe. The way he was looking at me during that meeting in the Oval Office—he knew. He knew, and he told Peterson. And then he killed himself, the fool.*

Bragg's shoes crunched against broken glass as he walked through the living room. There were dead bodies in here, many dead bodies. Peterson had put up a hell of a fight.

He looked down at the corpse of one of Peterson's agents. His blue eyes were open, wide open in terror, terror that Bragg had inflicted.

Bragg smiled at the corpse. "I'm Octavian," he said.

He was Gordon Bragg, billionaire founder of *Rebellion* and a dozen other publications dedicated to the destruction of the fascist superstructure. And he was Octavian, overlord of an international criminal empire and perpetuator of that superstructure.

He was Gordon Bragg, college dropout and entrepreneur extraordinaire, who had powered some of the greatest technological advances of the late twentieth and early twenty-first centuries through his innovation and largesse. And he was Octavian, a street hood from Brooklyn who had plowed his billions into arms, narcotics, and human trafficking.

He was Gordon Bragg, who liked to tell interviewers about how he never would have escaped those Brooklyn streets without a loving family supporting him. And he was Octavian, whose father had repeatedly beaten him unconscious when he was young, and who never forgot the primacy of physical force as he grew older.

He was Gordon Bragg and Octavian, a man with all of the money in the world but never enough of the power he craved.

Bragg kicked away shards of glass and stepped out onto the patio. His city lay below, those Brooklyn streets ten miles to the south.

He hadn't escaped those streets so much as he'd conquered them. The Gordon Bragg of magazine profiles and adoring biographies had been bullied by street hoods; the *real* Gordon Bragg *was* a street hood, running a vicious gang that made its money through armed robbery and drug trafficking. The "official" Gordon Bragg enrolled in Harvard to flee those streets; the *real* Gordon Bragg enrolled in Harvard because he could, because he had a genius-level IQ and wanted to dedicate his life to the acquisition of power—power in the world beyond the streets, power in the legitimate world.

What Bragg learned in his year at Harvard was that the street world and the legitimate world were exactly the same. People plotted against each other just the same, betrayed each other just the same, worked every angle for every advantage just the same—

and yielded before the more powerful just the same. It made no difference if the players were using guns and knives, or money and nepotism—everyone hustled. And it so happened that Bragg could hustle better than anyone else.

When he left Harvard and started racking up his millions, on the way to his billions—as he started to move among the circles of the corporate titans, of the captains of industry—it all became even clearer, so much clearer. The world was a war of all against all, and the only currency was power—not money, but power. The masses were toys in the hands of plutocrats, plutocrats in boardrooms who gave orders that were carried out in distant corners of the earth. And Gordon Bragg deserved to reign as the greatest plutocrat of all.

First he'd been a street hood; then a successful businessman; and then he learned how to synthesize the two. He moved between worlds, from the boardrooms to the backwaters and back again, from skyscrapers in New York to mining towns in the Congo. Bragg saw the way corporations ruled the developing world through bribery and arms trafficking, and he learned how to leverage those networks to his advantage. In time, he set up his own networks, funneling weapons to paramilitaries and investing his profits in narcotics and human trafficking.

And in the second decade of the twenty-first century, Bragg became a media mogul—and more importantly, a celebrity.

Celebrity inoculated him against any and all scrutiny of his dealings or private life. The press might drive itself into a frenzy over what his wife Courtney—safe at home in Malibu tonight—wore to the Oscars, but no one would ever question how he made his money so long as he set up philanthropic foundations and hosted charity galas that stroked the fancy of his Hollywood friends. No one would ever peer behind the curtain of Bragg's life as long as he cozied up to the coastal elites, to the politicians and reporters in the northeast corridor, to the producers and movie stars out west. By making a stand against Bryson and taking up legion other progressive causes, Bragg had certified himself as a "good" rich man, and the chattering classes would never challenge him. When he called reporters "court eunuchs," he meant it—

because they were unwitting eunuchs in *his* court.

But it wasn't just the money that made Octavian's rise possible; it wasn't the guns, the drugs, the corruption; it wasn't the celebrity. Ultimately, it came down to two characteristics of the world that emboldened Bragg to make his final moves.

First, he discovered that the world was blind, willfully blind, to where money came from. The companies he rescued, the politicians he bankrolled, the charities he funded, none of them ever dared ask where it all came from, or what it all came from. In an age of austerity, of perpetual global depression, no one probed, no one challenged—they just took what they could get.

Second, Bragg realized that most people lacked the courage to confront unspeakable horrors. Most people wanted to go about their lives, to get their daily bread, to keep their jobs and roofs over their heads. They were too weak, too afraid, to challenge a monster in their midst.

Bragg smiled as he gazed out at New York City. Finally, the American people would get the government they deserved. They had paved the way for his coronation, for his ascendancy to the seat of power. By their weakness, their dependency, their pettiness, their greed, they had destroyed their own democracy, ruined their own republic. Representative government and self-rule had broken down, and now Octavian would rule them all, would give them a Taylor Quade to make them feel good about themselves and would *rule them all.*

Bragg turned back to the wreckage of his penthouse and grinned at the corpses. *Wilkins and Peterson are in custody, and Sharpe is dead.*

Who's going to stop me now?

Chapter 58

The motorcycle rocketed along the highway. Johnny had been on the road for an hour and a half; he was close. Close to Fullerton, close to Gaines.

The highway was empty, quiet, the motorcycle's headlamp a solitary beacon in the black. *It's too quiet*, Johnny thought as he raced along.

It was after two a.m. now, but something was off. The highways were barren, tense, the way they were in the days after Operation Reichstag last year. Giovanni Sr. used to tell Johnny that this was what it was like after Nine-Eleven.

Something's happened up in New York tonight. But what?

He tightened his grip on the handlebars for a moment. *Simple enough. Either we won, or we lost.*

The questions bubbled through his brain as he raced along. Where would Johnny go once he freed Fullerton and collared Gaines? Was there a country left to go back to?

He swallowed hard as the exit approached. *No time for questions.*

Johnny slashed to the right and whipped through the exit ramp. He bore into the heart of Camden, flanked by abandoned homes, their doors boarded up, their windows blasted out. Grass sprouted through the sidewalks.

He was blocks away now, just blocks—

Two figures popped out of the shadows and yanked a chain taut across the street.

The motorcycle struck the chain and dive-bombed into the pavement, hurtling Johnny up the block.

I'm dead, he thought as he launched airborne and then struck the asphalt, rolling over and over and over, his cranium bashing into the street. *They killed me, they killed me and I'm dead—*

He blinked. He wasn't dead; he was breathing; his heart was beating; he could see the moon glowing above.

He reached for his gun, but he couldn't move, couldn't even bend his arm to draw the gun at his hip. Blood streamed down his head, poured into his eyes.

And now there were footsteps pounding the pavement behind

him, growing closer by the nanosecond. They were running towards him, and he couldn't move.

Johnny's head sank backwards. *Don't go down. Get up, get up—*

Machine gun fire crackled suddenly, and a pair of footsteps died out. Then there was another crackle, and another pair of footsteps died out, a body crashing next to Johnny.

Johnny forced his hands to his face, wiped the blood from his eyes—and there the corpse was, his face swaddled in a red bandana, one of the two who had pulled the chain across the street.

He heard more footsteps, slower now, one deliberate *clack* after another, approaching him. And finally there was a figure looming over him, toting a machine gun.

"You hurt?" the man asked him.

I must be dead. This can't be real.

"Ivanov?" Johnny said to the man standing above him.

The man studied Johnny for a moment, then smiled—somehow, amidst the carnage, he smiled. "You remember," he said. He leaned down and pulled Johnny to his feet.

Johnny's legs buckled, but Ivanov held him up. "How…" Johnny said. "What are you doing here?"

"Gaines send the word tonight," Ivanov said. "He tell everyone to get ready for Luca Junior, that tonight he would kill you. So I drive here and get ready."

"Why?" Johnny asked. "I don't unders—"

"You didn't kill me that night," Ivanov said. "You give me my life. And now I do the same for you."

I'm right with God, Ivanov had told Johnny that night. *No one knows, I straighten up and I'm right with God.*

"Right with God?" Johnny asked.

Ivanov nodded. "Right with God, my friend." He let go of Johnny and stepped back. "Bones broken?"

Good question. Johnny's body was a bundle of bruises, his head was bleeding, and he'd probably broken ribs. For all he knew, he'd fractured his skull. "I don't know. But I can walk. And I'm still breathing."

Ivanov studied Johnny, then nodded. "Then you walk." He gestured up the street. "Is just a few more blocks."

"Right. I'll walk." Johnny unzipped his jacket and fingered the trigger of his machine gun. "And you?"

Ivanov held up his own gun. "Me? I guard road. More will come."

There was more to say, so much more. But tonight wasn't a night for why or how—it was a night for life or death. And time was up.

Johnny surveyed Ivanov for a moment longer, then nodded and started to limp up the street.

"Johnnny Luca Junior!" Ivanov called after him as he walked. "Go get your justice!"

Chapter 59

Johnny limped up the street through the wasteland, the warehouse growing closer with each step. Ivanov was blocks behind him, guarding the road. And Jack Gaines was inside the building in front of him.

Johnny looked up at the crumbling brick building. It was two stories tall, and all of the windows were busted out.

All of them except one.

One window was intact, up on the second floor, off to the far right. That's where Gaines had shot the video, and that's where Johnny was guessing he was now.

He stepped into the warehouse, machine gun drawn. Industrial bulbs beamed yellow light overhead; this was no abandoned warehouse, not tonight.

He could see the second floor from down here, lined by metal railings above. Johnny guessed he was right below Gaines now.

He padded through dust and debris, ducking out of sight of the railings, the musty air invading his throat. A stairwell, there had to be a stairwell somewhere.

Johnny crept through the warehouse. If a guard popped out, he'd blast him; he'd lose the element of surprise, but this was life and death.

He stepped over broken pallets, keeping close to the wall. And there it was, a metal flight of stairs leading up to the second floor.

Johnny glanced up, his heart pounding. *Go get your justice*, Ivanov had told him. He took a deep breath.

He laid his right foot on the first step, then propelled his left onto the second, then his right onto the third, all in silence. Stealth was life; a clang or a creak was death.

Johnny laid the weight on step after step, the weight of Giovanni Sr.'s death, of Fullerton's life, each second bursting with the possibility it could be Johnny's last, Gaines's last, Fullerton's last. Finally, he ascended to the top, at the mouth of the corridor. And at the end of that corridor, around the corner, were Jack Gaines and Julius Fullerton.

Johnny skulked down the hallway. *I could shoot him where he stands. One shot, right through the head. Game over. Go get your justice,* Ivanov said.

No. I have to bring him in. I told Peterson I'd bring him in. This isn't about me. It's about Fullerton, it's about our mission.

Johnny began to tiptoe as he approached the end of the corridor. *Bring him in to who? What if Peterson's dead? What if there's still a warrant out for my arrest?*

Enough questions. Questions can get me killed.

Johnny backed against the concrete wall as he came to the end of the hallway. He took one final breath, then peered around the corner.

There Gaines was, his back to Johnny, standing over Fullerton near the window. Fullerton was slumped against the wall, unconscious, his hands bound behind his back.

Johnny ducked back around the corner. *Fullerton had better be only unconscious. Because if he's dead, I won't be able to control myself.*

His heart pumped against his chest, exploding with each beat. He gulped; he couldn't breathe; he had to breathe, he *had* to breathe.

One shot. One shot ends this.

Johnny swung around the corner and raised the gun.

"Take the shot," Gaines said, his back still to him. "That's what you pigs do best."

"Not this pig," Johnny said. "Put your hands up, Gaines."

Gaines shook his head, still facing the window. "I don't think I will, Luca." He laughed to himself. "You really are something, you know that? You *found* me. Of course you did. Of course you did." The laughter evaporated as he turned around to face Johnny. "But it's over now. You've taken all of this as far as it's going to go."

Johnny kept the gun trained on Gaines as he stood face-to-face with his father's killer. Gaines was the figure in the mug shots writ large, the pixels on the video made flesh—a little taller than Johnny, a little broader, with wavy blond hair and blue eyes. *Jack Gaines. I got him, Dad. I got him.*

Johnny's heartbeat slowed; his breathing regulated; calm radiated through him. He had Gaines dead-to-rights. "I think we'll take it a little farther," he said. "Put your hands up. You're under arrest."

Gaines's eyes flared with fury. "I'm under arrest. *You're* arresting *me*. Hyperion." He glared at Johnny. "And what's the charge?"

Johnny returned the glare, smashed back the volley. "Mass murder of civilians. Material support for a terrorist organization." He narrowed his eyes. "Murder of a police officer."

Gaines shook his head. "All wrong, Agent Luca. All wrong. You should've taken Pig Senior's advice and gone to law school." His glare intensified. "Collateral damage isn't a crime. Fighting a revolution against fascism isn't a crime. And handing out justice to a fascist animal isn't a crime."

This guy is a fucking lunatic. He really believes this stuff. The whole world is black and white to him—he's the white, and we're all the black. He's the most dangerous type of person there is—a true believer.

Johnny peered through the sights of the gun. *I should take the shot. Finish him off right here.*

"You're no revolutionary," Johnny said. "You're a terrorist. You hide while you blow up kids with car bombs. You brainwash my brother to go kill people for you. You send a college girl to kill the President because you don't have the guts to do it yourself." Johnny shook his head. "Look at you, holed up in a warehouse in the middle of nowhere. This isn't much of a revolution, is it? You're just a coward, a common criminal, a *nothing*. I read all about you, asshole. Daddy's a big-time CEO, and he doesn't love you because you're a fucking misfit loser. And now you need to show the world how special you are." Johnny looked into Gaines's eyes. "But you're not special. I want you to think about that every night before you fall asleep in your cell. There is absolutely nothing special about you. You've just taught yourself how to kill people."

Gaines's expression didn't change. "And what does that make you, Luca? The hero?" He shook his head. "Look at you, with that gun in your hand, with all that gear you're wearing. You're an agent for the Anti-Subversion Authority. Did you ever stop to think what that means? Ever stop to think who you serve?" Gaines spat. "You're a storm trooper for a dictatorship that is inflicting *misery* on the rest of the world. I'm talking about white phosphorus burning skin off people's bodies in Iraq. Twelve-year-olds in Africa with their arms hacked off for trying to escape working in diamond mines. Children in Afghanistan addicted to opium and then forced to work in poppy fields. People making a dollar a day, living on trash heaps, getting blown up and maimed in explosions from the local chemical plant. And the trafficking and slavery, all of the slavery and exploitation in this miserable fucking world. All inflicted by this rotten, amoral, imperialist dictatorship." Gaines took a step towards Johnny. "And you, holding that machine gun for them. They're using you, like the little empty-headed tool that you are. There's so much you're going to learn before you die tonight, Luca. So much you'll wish you never knew."

Except I won't be dying tonight. "Not another step," Johnny said. "Hands up, or I'll kill you."

"'Hands up, or I'll kill you,'" Gaines mimicked. "Welcome to the new world order. 'Hands up, or I'll kill you.' So take the shot. Neutralize the threat. Isn't that what you pigs do with terrorists?" He smiled. "Or is there something else you're after? Something I took from you? I've lost track. I've taken so much from you already."

The hairs on the back of Johnny's neck hardened into bristles. *Don't let him get to you, Luca,* Neely had told him that night they confronted Kronos. *Focus.*

Johnny narrowed his eyes. "All I'm after is you. And Fullerton."

"But you can't have him." Gaines took another step towards Johnny. "Viceroy, we called him. When he was one of us."

"He was never one of you." Johnny glanced at Fullerton, who was still unconscious. His eyes lasered back towards Gaines. "He pretended, you stupid fuck. Because they had to stop you. And now I'll finish the job."

Gaines stretched his arms, as if preparing for a workout. "There's so much you don't still don't know. But don't worry, Luca. I'll give you a history lesson tonight."

"Let me give you one first," Johnny said. "A lesson I've been waiting to give you for a long time. Your revolution is bullshit,

Gaines. Everything you fought for is a lie. Your old buddy Sigma—he used to take orders from someone he called Octavian, right? I met him once, the night Fullerton put a fucking bullet through your boyfriend's head. You want to know who he was?" Johnny grinned. "It was Shepherd Moloch. The Special Agent in Charge of the New York Authority field office. I saw him myself, giving orders to Sigma."

Gaines paused a moment to swallow that down. "You're lying, pig."

Now you can have the sleepless nights. Tonight, and every night for the rest of your miserable, worthless fucking life. "Your little revolution is bullshit. Bryson planned it all from the beginning. He dreamed it up so that he could terrify everyone, so that he could take power for himself, to trick people into thinking they needed him to keep them safe from scumbags like you. All so that his boss, someone that *he* calls Octavian, could be a dictator. And what's your part in this? Who's Jack Gaines?" Johnny shook his head. "You're nothing. You're just a little puppet on Bryson's string. You murdered all these people for your revolution, and you played right into Bryson's hands. I want you to think about that every night for the next fifty years, when you're rotting in solitary. You got fucking played, Gaines."

Gaines glared at Johnny for a moment, the realizations convulsing through him, and then he charged.

Johnny aimed; his finger curled around the trigger and began to squeeze, but before he could, Gaines caught his arm and forced it up. Johnny raked the ceiling with machine gun fire as he struggled to shake Gaines off.

Gaines punched Johnny in the face, and he went down, hard. He tried to right the gun, but Gaines kicked it clean out of his hands across the room.

Not tonight. I'm not dying tonight.

Gaines dove towards Johnny, but he rolled away and kipped up, cracked ribs and all. Now Johnny had the high ground.

He laid a kick into Gaines, then another, each laced with fury, with vengeance. He reared back for a third, but Gaines caught his leg and wrenched him down.

They were both on the floor, Johnny flat on his back, Gaines struggling to get to his feet. Johnny edged sideways, squared up, and kicked Gaines flush in the face.

The two inched away from each other, gathering their bearings, and then got back to their feet at the same time. Gaines licked blood from his lips, then smiled as he lowered into fighting formation. "Get what you came for, Luca," he said. "Do it for Daddy."

I'll get it what I came for, Johnny thought, lowering into formation himself. *I'll get it, I'll get it—*

The two charged each other. Johnny ducked Gaines's roundhouse kick, then pivoted towards him and lashed a punch into his face, rocking Gaines back on his heels. Johnny snapped off a kick, but Gaines blocked it. Johnny then tried to sweep Gaines's legs, but Gaines jumped, then swung high with another roundhouse kick.

This one connected, and Johnny reeled. Blood gushed down the side of his head. He raised his hands to defend himself.

Gaines smiled, his mouth full of blood. "You can't win, Luca," he said. He circled Johnny, a vulture eyeing his prey. "I'm going to teach you tonight, like a dog. You can't win."

Johnny kept pace with the circling, his hands raised in defense. He felt himself limping, felt his ribs throbbing, felt his head gushing. "Come teach me," he said.

Gaines measured him for a moment, then rushed straight ahead and launched an airborne kick, his foot blasting through Johnny's defenses and smashing right into his face.

Johnny's feet flew out from under him, and his head bounced against the floor. *Hang on, Fullerton, he thought, hang on…*

A kick smashed into his ribs, then another. The pain swirled through his torso, then coursed through him, shooting through to his extremities, up to his head. Gaines's thugs had beaten Johnny back in his building, then they'd ambushed him on the road to the warehouse, and now Gaines himself was pouring it on, finishing him off. Johnny's body wilted.

A knee plunged into his back, and then a pair of hands yanked his own hands behind his back, then zip-tied them. Johnny blinked in and out of consciousness.

Gaines hoisted him to his feet, then hurled him against the brick wall, where he landed next to Fullerton.

Johnny tried to sit up, to right himself. He strained against the zip ties, then surrendered. He couldn't free himself.

One shot would've ended this, would've ended everything.

He turned to Fullerton. He was still breathing. But how much longer would either of them be breathing?

"So I'm nothing, you say," Gaines called from across the room. "And the revolution is nothing. Well, now we'll find out who *you* are. We'll find out what *your* obsession is worth."

Johnny looked up. Gaines was standing behind some sort of lectern, sweeping his hand across a tablet computer.

Just then, a motorized beam lowered a flat-panel television from the rafters.

Johnny followed its descent with his eyes. *What else does he have hidden up there?*

"I told you I'd teach you a lesson tonight," Gaines said as the screen came to rest. "And now you're going to learn."

He tapped the tablet a few more times, and a video loaded on the screen. "Look what I found in the archives," Gaines went on. "You see, when the revolution sentences a criminal to death, we like to film the execution—which is exactly what we did for your pig father."

Please God, no, Johnny thought as he looked at the screen.

"You're going to watch every second of this," Gaines said. "And if I see you look away, Viceroy dies." He tapped the tablet again, and the video began to run.

Giovanni Sr.'s hands and feet were handcuffed to a chair that was bolted to the floor, similar to the way Sigma had bound Johnny when he tortured him last year. Barely conscious, the detective had a black eye, and there was dried blood on his face. He strained against the handcuffs.

Johnny felt tears streaming down his cheeks.

Brigade 910 members came into view on the screen: Ivanov, a few of Gaines's henchmen, and then Gaines himself.

"For crimes against the revolution, and for collaborating with the corporatist conspiracy, Brigade 910 sentences this fascist to death," Gaines said onscreen. He brandished a handgun, then stuck it under Giovanni Sr.'s chin.

Johnny choked back sobs. *Please kill me. Kill me, kill me, don't make me watch this—*

Gaines, onscreen, looked into the camera. "Viceroy, step forward and accept the honor of executing this pig," he said.

Viceroy.

A second later, Fullerton stepped into the frame. He took the handgun from Gaines, his hands shaking.

"Prove your loyalty to Brigade 910," Gaines said. "Do your duty."

Johnny's heart began to pound. The back of his throat sealed shut; he couldn't breathe. Chills exploded through his body.

Fullerton looked at Giovanni Sr., then back at Gaines, his face contorted in hesitation, his hands still shaking. And then he turned back towards Giovanni Sr. and jammed the barrel of the gun under his chin. His hand shook again, but then it steadied.

No. No, no, no—

Fullerton pulled the trigger.

Chapter 60

"So you came for revenge tonight," Gaines said, drawing a handgun. He walked towards Johnny, then spit blood on him. "And now you can have it. He's right next to you, Luca. I even did you the favor of knocking him out cold."

Johnny couldn't stop shaking. Fullerton was next to him, *right next to him*. The man who killed his father, right next to him.

Gaines held up the gun. "Look familiar?" he asked. "It's the same gun. The same gun Viceroy used to kill Detective Luca." He cocked the weapon. "And now you can kill him with it."

I can kill him.

Gaines aimed the gun at Fullerton. "Just say the word, and I'll pull the trigger. One after the other. You kill him, and then I kill you." He smiled. "Just think. For a few seconds between the two shots, you'll know that you accomplished what you set out to do."

Go get your justice, Ivanov had told Johnny.

Gaines aimed the gun at Johnny. "I don't have all night, Luca. I could do you an even bigger favor and shoot you first. So you wouldn't have to think about any of this anymore."

Johnny thought back to the morning after he finished the diary, the morning he knelt before his father's grave. He'd been so exhausted, and all he wanted to do was collapse on the ground and sleep it all away, and now—

There was an explosion downstairs.

Gaines raised his eyebrows. "What's going—"

There was another explosion downstairs, followed by machine gun fire.

Flashbangs. And now someone's shooting their way in.

He heard footsteps charging up the metal stairs, *clang-clang-clang*, and more gunfire.

Gaines holstered the handgun and ran towards the machine gun he'd kicked away from Johnny, grabbing it just as a stun grenade dropped into the room, exploding in light and smoke. Two more grenades dropped in and exploded.

Machine gun fire sliced through the smoke and raked the room; Gaines rolled out of the way and returned fire, then smashed the window behind him with the butt of the gun.

Neely and Wolfe emerged through the haze, Wolfe squaring up to reel off more shots, Neely running towards Johnny and Fullerton, sliding between them.

"We need to get out of here," Neely said, slicing Johnny's hands loose, then Fullerton's. She yanked on Fullerton. "Can he—is he—"

"He's alive," Johnny said, adrenaline bursting through him, snapping him to his feet. He unholstered the handgun strapped to his ankle.

"Luca," Neely said, "you have to carry Fuller—"

Wolfe and Gaines exchanged bursts of fire, then Gaines scooped up his tablet computer and jumped out the window.

Johnny, gun drawn, rushed past Wolfe to the window. Gaines was crumpled in a heap outside, but his goons were already helping him to his feet, shielding him. Johnny aimed his handgun and cut down one of them, then twisted aside as they returned fire. He peered back down, and Gaines was fiddling with his tablet computer.

Holy shit, Johnny thought, connecting the dots.

He turned to the others; Wolfe had slung Fullerton over his back. "Booby traps!" Johnny yelled.

A car screeched up to Gaines and his goons. Johnny leaned out the window again and opened fire, cutting down two more of the Brigade 910 thugs, then squared up for Gaines himself. He zeroed in on the target, caught him in his sights, and squeezed off the rounds.

Johnny nailed Gaines in the leg, flooring him.

But then another bodyguard yanked him away and threw him into the back of the car, which sped off.

No, Johnny thought, blasting off more rounds, shooting out the back window of the car and then the road behind it as it raced away. *No, no, no.*

And then he heard a ratcheting sound above.

He turned to Neely and Wolfe. "*Run*!" he screamed. "*Now*!"

They ran; Johnny ran; bullets rained down from the rafters, screaming as they strafed the floor.

Gaines had rigged the rafters with gun turrets, just as he had in the safe-house in upstate New York, and now the entire warehouse was a death trap.

Neely and Wolfe tore down the hallway as the turrets continued blasting away. Johnny was a few steps behind them, just a few steps—

A bullet smashed into his back, knocking him to his stomach.

Kevlar, the bullet had buried itself in the Kevlar. Johnny crawled away as the turrets strafed the floor, splintering the surface, exploding in cement dust.

He ducked under the metal railing, grasping the floor with both hands, swinging over the ground level below. And then he let go, falling away from the mayhem above and crashing to the floor below.

Johnny felt his leg muscles slice to ribbons, his sides explode. Neely and Wolfe, still carrying Fullerton, had now made it safely down the stairs, joining him on the ground level.

"This place," Johnny gasped, forcing himself to his feet and clutching his ribs. "This place is going to blow. For sure."

"Then let's fucking move!" Wolfe yelled.

Sounds like a plan, Johnny thought, tearing after them with his remaining strength.

They ran out of the warehouse as more bandanna-clad henchmen swarmed in. Johnny fired first, hitting two; Neely fired next, hitting the other two.

Wolfe, Fullerton still over his shoulder, charged towards a black SUV, then yanked the back door open and threw Fullerton inside. Johnny followed Neely towards the truck, jumping in as Wolfe dropped behind the wheel.

"I think you know what happens now," Johnny said as Wolfe fired up the truck and peeled out.

And a moment later, the warehouse exploded behind them, rattling the windows of the truck as Wolfe raced into the night.

Chapter 61

Wilkins stared into the darkness above him, into the black that enveloped the bedroom in the safehouse where they were keeping him. It was two a.m. now, maybe three, and his presidency had ended only hours ago.

That sun is falling so hard now, I'm scared there's gonna be night forever, his mother had told him in that dream. Don't let it fall.

I failed, Wilkins thought as he lay flat on his back, his stomach quaking. *Night's fallen, and I've failed.*

It had all happened so suddenly. Bryson had burst in, followed by his agents, and before Wilkins could get his bearings, he was in the back of a truck, blindfolded.

Wilkins had tried ordering the agents to stop in the name of their president, but he quickly realized the futility of that. So he sat in the back of the truck as it glided along highways, then rumbled down what Wilkins reckoned were backroads. After about two hours, the truck stopped, and the president's jailers hustled him into the safe-house, removing first the handcuffs, then the blindfold.

Wordlessly they led him through the dark home, creaking along old wooden floors. Wilkins could make out a hearth, a dining room table, some sparse furnishings.

Then his jailers, carrying machine guns, escorted him upstairs to a bedroom. Still silent, they deposited him inside and closed the door behind him. Wilkins could hear a click as a guard locked the door from the outside.

The walls were clinical white, unadorned. In one corner was a bed, in another a desk.

Wilkins, who had woken up that morning besides Delilah in the White House, found himself alone in a bedroom in an old country home God-knew-where.

He crossed the room to a window; it was barred. And outside was black, as far as the eye could see. He really *was* out in the country somewhere.

Wilkins considered trying to open the door, but he didn't dare. He knew it was locked. And if it wasn't, who knew what could happen—the guard could lose his cool and shoot him, and then all hope would be lost.

Wilkins sat on the bed. Hope of what, exactly? He was under house arrest. He was fifty-eight and had aged more in the last two years than he had in the first fifty-six. He was alone, without Delilah, without Garrett, without Gabrielle, and completely cut off from the outside world. There was no hope.

So he'd tried to sleep, but he couldn't stop shaking. And now here he was, still trembling after three o'clock.

We're in the twilight of republics and the rights of man, and night is falling, he'd told Peterson and Chan. *We can't let it. We can stop the night. We can stop the night.*

Night's fallen, Wilkins thought as he stared into the darkness. *Chan's dead, Sharpe's dead, and Peterson…* Tears streamed down Wilkins's cheeks. *If Peterson had stopped the night, I wouldn't be here right now.*

There was a knock on the door.

Wilkins sat up straight against the headboard. The door creaked open, and in stepped a guard. Without a word, he flicked on a light, then stood at attention.

Gordon Bragg stepped into the room.

Could it be? Wilkins thought. *Did Peterson pull it off?*

He jumped to his feet. "Bragg," he said. "Tell me won. Please God, tell me we won. Have you come to get me out of—"

"It's not worth saving, you know," Bragg said.

"It's not… worth… saving." Wilkins narrowed his eyes. "What do you mean?"

"The country, Wilkins. It's not worth saving. So you can rest now. I came to tell you that you can rest."

Wilkins studied Bragg, his shoulders thrown back, his face twisted in a grin, his eyes gleaming with mockery. *It can't be*, he thought. *It can't be, it can't be, it can't be.*

And then he shuddered, the truth exploding through him.

"Octavian," Wilkins said.

Bragg nodded slowly. "That's right. But I think you figured it out a little late."

Wilkins clenched his fists. *I can kill him with my bare hands*, he thought, measuring the distance between them. *I can crush his voice box before the guard shoots me, and we can die here together. And then this nightmare will be over, all over.*

Bragg nodded at the guard, who pointed the gun at Wilkins.

"I told you that it's not worth saving," Bragg said. "So don't make any false moves. It's over now. You can rest."

Wilkins unclenched his fists, shaking. *I have to survive. I have to survive, for Delilah and the kids.*

"This country," he said to Bragg. "This country gave you so much. It gave you everything."

Bragg's eyes now flashed with contempt. "This country gave me *nothing*," he said. "What does it have to give? This country *takes*, everyone here takes. And that's what I did. Everything I accomplished, everything I have, I *took*. And now I took this whole country, right out from under you."

The room began to spin. Wilkins tried to steady himself, tried to stand firm. "That day in the Oval Office, when you told us who Octavian was…"

"I told you the truth. I told you everything you needed to know about Octavian. Everything I told you about McCallister, just apply it to me, and you have the whole truth." Bragg smiled. "And now here we are. Here's your big chance. You've got me right here in this room, just like you always wanted. You've got Octavian. What are you going to do about it?"

What am I going to do about it? I'm going to kill you, Bragg, I'm going to lunge towards you and end this—

And then Wilkins's eyes darted towards the barrel of the gun pointed at him.

"Just tell me you give up," Bragg said. "I came here tonight to accept your surrender. No one's ever going to read about this in a history book, but we'll always know the truth. Reed Wilkins, the last democratically elected president of the United States, surrendered to Gordon Bragg, Octavian." Bragg paused. "I can give you your life, Wilkins. Because Bryson wants to kill you. He wants to put you on trial and have you executed. But I think you deserve better than that." He looked at Wilkins curiously. "The truth is, I respect you. You might be the only person in this country I actually respect. You're a throwback to what this country used to be. Patriotic, strong, brave. *Brave*, Wilkins. You almost took a bullet for what you believe in. But it was for nothing, all for nothing—because what you believe in isn't worth fighting for. Take a look around. At some point, we'll let you have a television in here, we'll let you see what the outside world is like. And you'll look at it in a different way, after tonight. This country doesn't deserve democracy, can't handle democracy. The system doesn't work anymore. Congress can't even agree on the name of a post office, let alone matters of state. And why not? Because everyone wants their piece of the action, their ride on the gravy train, without putting anything in.

"This is a country of dependent little children squabbling over their toys. And you might think that I'm trying to punish them for that—but I'm not. I don't have an ideology. I'm not trying to revive the lost glory of America, or trying to impose some kind of Aryan supremacy or anything like that. I'm just taking what's there for the taking. This is a country of celebrity-obsessed, weak, selfish little children who can't make hard choices, can't be trusted to make hard choices. Look at what the last six years have taught us, Wilkins. Look at what I was able to accomplish just by whipping up those Brigade 910 punks, that pathetic bunch of tinfoil anarchists. And overnight, the country handed the Authority a blank check—a blank check to eavesdrop on every conversation it could, break down as many doors as it had to, beat up however many college kids were necessary. Think about it. They were *begging* you to sign the Total Information Awareness Act—you had to veto it. And then they passed it over your veto!"

Bragg smiled, almost benignly. "You're defending a country that doesn't exist anymore. Maybe it existed twenty years ago. Maybe it didn't even exist then—maybe fifty years ago, when we were growing up. But it's over now. They're going to elect Quade, Wilkins. Imagine that. *Taylor Quade*. A therapeutic, feel-good president who'll tell them how much he cares, how he'll make sure the government gives them everything they need to survive." Bragg held out his hand. "So surrender now, and just live your life. And eventually, when we work all of this out, you can see your wife and your children again. You don't have to bow down or anything like that. Just shake my hand and tell me that you give up."

Wilkins looked at Bragg's hand. *Delilah and the kids… I can see them again… I can grow old with them…*

Bragg's hand was life—surrender was life.

But not a life worth living.

"Pull that hand back, before I break it," Wilkins said. "You won't win, Bragg. It doesn't matter if you kill me. There's going to be an uprising—a rebellion, like the name of that magazine of yours. And the American people—the American people *I* know, the American people *I* believe in—will rise up and stop you. And you'll be the one who surrenders."

Bragg considered Wilkins's response for a moment, then shook his head, more plaintively than anything else. "You're wrong, Wilkins," he said. "And since I'm a man of my word, I'll make myself clear right now. You're going to die. You'll never see the outside of this house. You won't even appear in court or get any kind of real trial. Because the people will be too afraid to question Bryson and Quade, too worried about themselves, too obsessed with getting on with their normal lives. They'll be petrified. And eventually, they'll forget about you." Bragg shook his head again. "And you—you'll never see your family again. What a fool you are. What an idealistic fool." Bragg's expression brightened. "But at least we'll provide you with good accommodations here, like a former president deserves. Peterson won't be so lucky. He landed a helicopter on my roof tonight— tried to shoot his way in, on some kind of crazy kamikaze mission. And now he's in custody. Let's just say his accommodations won't be as comfortable as yours."

Wilkins grimaced; Bryson had told him the same thing. "Just remember," he said. "You can kill us. But we're just men, just two men. You'll never put down the rebellion, Bragg. Remember those words, the day you finally lose. *You will never put down the rebellion.*"

Bragg smiled. "I already have," he said.

Octavian turned and left the room, leaving Reed Wilkins to his house arrest.

Chapter 62

The armored SUV wound along a back road, burrowing through the black of night, its headlights spilling white light on the cornfields that lined the road. Wolfe had been driving along cornfields for a while now; for how long, Johnny couldn't be sure. He was floating somewhere behind time. The world inside the car—Wolfe in front, Fullerton to the left, Neely to the right—was all shadow and mist.

His father's killer stirred beside him, lapsing in and out of consciousness in fits and starts. Johnny's hand kept going to his holster. One shot could've finished Gaines, and now one shot could finish Fullerton. *Go get your justice*, Ivanov had said.

Ivanov was dead. At some point during this drive through another dimension, Johnny had asked Wolfe if anyone had been guarding the road to the warehouse as he and Neely approached. *There was*, Wolfe said. *He waved a gun at us, and McLain shot him.*

Ivanov died for me, Johnny thought. *And I couldn't do the job.*

He glanced at Fullerton, still stirring. Johnny started shaking. *My best friend. My partner and best friend. And it was him, all along. He did it. He did it.*

"The headscarf," Neely said, almost as if calling out to Johnny to rouse him from a dream. "You wore the headscarf."

Johnny turned to face her, first in puzzlement. But then he felt around his neck, and there it was, the *keffiyeh* she'd given him.

"I did," he said. "But I don't think I deserve to wear it." He started to unwrap it.

"Are you kidding?" Neely said, grabbing his hand to stop him. "You saved Fullerton's life." She smiled, almost gazing at him. "My dad would be proud, Luca. I know I am."

Johnny shook his head. "You guys saved his life, not me."

"You went in after Fullerton when no one else would," Wolfe said. "You found him, and you bought us enough time. We were just your reinforcements."

"Don't worry about Gaines," Neely said. "His time will come. We'll bag him." She looked into Johnny's eyes, and he knew that by "we," she meant the two of them. "We saved Fullerton. That's what counts."

That's what counts.

The SUV rumbled on, bouncing along a road that parted a sea of cornfields. The first tendrils of dawn streaked across the sky.

Here in this truck, for just these few hours, the four of them were safe. They were *all* behind time, here in the middle of nowhere, away from Octavian, from Bryson, from Gaines. They were huddled together, and they were safe.

"How did you guys know where to find me?" Johnny asked.

"Peterson sent us after you," Wolfe said. "He decided he didn't want you going after Gaines by yourself, so he told us to try and track you down."

"We got a late start, but I used some of my special talents," Neely said. She grinned. "And eventually we figured out that you went to your buddy's place."

God only knows what those "special talents" must be.

"Your buddy Billy's something else," Neely said. "He asked me for my number."

Of course he did.

"Peterson," Johnny said. "Did he—do you know if he—"

"It doesn't sound good," Wolfe said. "It's all over the news. The team landed a helicopter on Gordon Bragg's roof tonight and went in guns blazing—"

"Gordon Bragg? Why?"

"Bragg is Octavian," Neely said. "That flash drive the boss gave you—he gave us copies, too. He told us the files can prove that Bragg is Octavian."

"But those websites he runs, those magazines—they're all opposed to Bryson. Lizbeth writes for one of them—*Rebellion*."

"None of this makes any sense," Wolfe said. "But the news is saying that Bragg survived the attack, and that Peterson is in custody. Greenaway is saying that Peterson was part of Wilkins's plot, whatever that means. This is all so crazy." Wolfe's voice was breaking. "Austin and Kleibeck—I don't know if they made it. And Peterson and the President are under arrest."

"And there's a warrant out for me."

"Right," Neely said. "And I'm sure there'll be warrants out for us too, eventually. Waff, man. Waff."

Johnny raised his eyebrows. "Waff?"

"W-A-F. We are *fucked.*"

Couldn't have put it better myself.

They fell silent as the miles rolled behind them.

There's going to be an uprising, Peterson had said at the World Trade Center earlier tonight. *A rebellion. And you and Fullerton will have to join the rebellion. I always said there was something special about you two, right? You're indestructible together. So bring him home.*

Johnny glanced at Fullerton. *I brought him home, boss.*

He pulled a piece of paper out of his pocket. He studied it for a moment, then crumpled it up and let it fall to the floor.

"What's that?" Neely said.

"It's nothing," Johnny said. "Just a stupid letter I wrote."

"What kind of letter?"

Johnny sighed. "A letter I wrote to Lizbeth a few days ago." Johnny shook his head. "And I'll never give it to her now. Who knows if I'll even see her again."

"You will, Luca. You know you will. We'll all make it home someday."

"Maybe we will. And maybe we won't. And if we don't—McLain, let me tell you something. If we don't make it home, then I wasted my time. All of that time I spent on Gaines—I wasted my time." Johnny punched his open hand. "I should've been building a life with Lizbeth. And now it might be too late. Remember what I'm telling you, McLain. Revenge, it's not everything. You can't let it be everything. There's more to life—"

"Lead Mag," Fullerton said, struggling awake.

Johnny's mouth hung open, and in slow motion, he turned to face the man who murdered his father.

"You're awake," Johnny said, trembling.

"Where… where are we?" Fullerton asked.

"Western Pennsylvania," Wolfe said. "A couple of hours outside Pittsburgh. Luca here saved your life tonight."

Fullerton, still dazed, managed a smile at Johnny. "I knew you would, man," he said. He struggled to sit up. "I told Gaines you would."

Johnny nodded, in a stupor. He felt drunk; he felt the truck begin to spin. He closed his eyes, and there was Fullerton, sticking the gun under his father's chin and pulling the trigger.

My gun, Johnny thought. *I'll pull out my gun and shoot him. Stick it under his chin and pay him back for what he did.*

"We're going to have to split up in a few minutes," Wolfe said.

"Split up?" Fullerton asked. "What do you mean? Why?"

"Because that's the boss's plan. There's a lot you've missed, Fullerton. Everything, basically. Octavian and Bryson have taken over. The President's under house arrest, and the boss... We don't know what happened to him. He tried to raid Octavian's place tonight, but I don't think it worked. The news is saying that he's in custody."

"Christ," Fullerton said. "But why would we split up?"

"Because we're better off on our own. If they pull over this truck, they've got us—all of us. But if we split up, at least a couple of us can make it to where we need to go. Hopefully all of us."

"Make it to where we need to go," Johnny repeated. "And where's that?"

"Find a way to get yourself to a computer when I drop you off," Wolfe said. "And read what's on your flash drive. We need to go out west and meet up with a group called the Gadsden Brigade."

"Who the hell are they?"

"They're a special forces unit. The Gadsdens are a group that protects the country against coups from within, from anyone who tries to overthrow the government and set up a dictatorship. And we need them now to start up the rebellion."

"The rebellion. Christ." Johnny massaged his temples. "And do we have any idea where these people are?"

"No. They've been living in exile. Bryson had them exiled a few years ago. And now all we know is that Wilkins deployed them awhile back. He was trying to get them into the country. And if they make it back, we have an idea of where they might be headed." Wolfe paused. "The three of you—you have to review those flash drives like trained investigators, the trained investigators that you are. And then destroy them."

"And what are we supposed to do when we split up?"

"Fend for ourselves. Until the time is right."

Johnny nodded, then fell silent. Until the time was right. When that would be, of course, was anyone's guess.

Wolfe drove on for a few more minutes, and then pulled over. "This is it," he said. "We should start to split up now. Luca, you should go first." He turned around to face Johnny. "Are you going to be all right? I know you took a hell of a beating tonight."

It was true. Johnny had sustained head injuries, cracked or broken ribs, and God knew what else. His entire body felt broken. But he told Wolfe the same thing he'd told Ivanov tonight, the only thing he could say, really:

"I can walk. And I'm still breathing."

Wolfe considered that for a moment, then nodded. "Keep one of your weapons on you," he said. "Take this." He handed him a full magazine. "Hopefully, you won't even need that much. Otherwise, do what you can to get more ammunition." Wolfe reached onto the passenger seat, then handed Johnny a debit card and a mobile phone. "Take these, too. The card is loaded with enough money for you to live on. And the phone has a prepaid SIM card. I know you know this, but don't even think of calling your girlfriend or your family. When the time is right, we'll reach out to you. Don't worry about how. Leave that to me and McLain." He paused. "Now, you're going to want to be on the move. Head west—that's all I can say. Head west, and stay away from big cities. There are going to be protests, and you don't want to get mixed up in all that—not yet."

Johnny took the debit card and phone, then nodded. "And you guys?" he asked. "What's next for you?"

"We need to make sure Fullerton is okay, after everything he went through tonight. And then we split up. Until—"

"The time is right."

Wolfe nodded. "Right. Until the time is right."

Johnny climbed past Neely and popped open the door. "Stay safe, guys," he said. "Good luck."

"Luca," Neely said, embracing him. "We're going to win this thing. We'll spring the boss loose, and we'll win this thing."

"We will," Wolfe said, shaking Johnny's hand. "Remember that, every night you're out here on your own. We'll win."

Johnny nodded, then stepped out of the truck.

"Luca," Fullerton called from inside the SUV, holding out his hand. "You saved my life, man. I won't forget that. I swear, I'll never forget that."

I won't forget it either. He shook Fullerton's hand and looked into his eyes. "See you on the flip side," he said, then closed the door.

He looked up at the sky as the truck sped off. It was dawn now, a new sun rippling through the sky in waves of orange.

Johnny turned back to the road, looking after the SUV as it raced to the horizon. *I won't forget, Fullerton. Believe me, I won't forget.*

He watched the truck for a moment longer, then plunged his hands into his pockets and started walking up the road.

Epilogue: Chapter 1

A week later, Neely crouched on a fire escape in Hoboken, crowbar in hand.

She'd disobeyed orders, like she'd been doing all her life. Even when she was a little girl back in Syria, in the old days before the war, she never listened to her parents, never followed the rules, because she knew what was right.

She'd disobeyed Wolfe, had gone east instead of west, because there was something she had to do to set everything right. She'd gone all the way to this fire escape overlooking the Hudson River, because Johnny Luca had worn her father's *keffiyeh*. *Like I asked him to. He wore it.*

Neely raised the crowbar, then bit her lip as she angled it, about to break into Lizbeth's apartment.

Neely had hacked everything there was to know about Lizbeth pretty early on, but she'd revisited the file after splitting up from Wolfe and Fullerton, just to see if there was anything she'd missed the first time around.

There wasn't. Lizbeth was an okay enough chick, a good little Suzie homemaker type. She'd started out writing asinine articles about high school football, and had progressed to writing asinine political commentary, although she must have thought it was serious journalism. Lizbeth's heart was in the right place. And Neely guessed that she was pretty enough, too.

But that didn't matter. What mattered was the crowbar in her hands, and the letter in her pocket.

After Johnny left the truck that morning a few weeks ago, Neely had scooped up the crumpled-up letter he'd left behind and shoved it in her pocket. By now, she knew it by heart:

***

Dear Lizbeth,

You gave me a letter once, and you asked me not to open it until I knew what I wanted out of life. And I opened it the second I realized that what I wanted was a life together with you.

I'm not the writer you are, but I have a few things I want to tell you.

I've been thinking a lot lately about what it means for us to have a life together. It means a life of love, and respect, and trust, and a lot of laughing and partying, until we get old. It means that I meet you halfway, like you asked. It means that we're partners.

That's not how I've acted since we've been together. That's not the guy I've been. I've kept things to myself, bottled up inside, and I've kept secrets from you. I've tried to be two people—someone who could be a good boyfriend for you, and someone who's been off chasing shadows, all alone.

And now you know why I've tried to be two people. You know about my dad, and you know what I've been trying to do, why I've been away from you—even when I've been in the same room as you, sleeping in the same bed with you, why I've been away from you.

And what I want to tell you is that I don't want to be away from you anymore. I don't want to be two people—I know who I am, and what I want. And what I want is to be your man for the rest of our lives. Partners, like you said.

After you asked me to leave that night, I realized what I've been doing all along. All of this time that I spent trying to make things right for my dad, all of this time I spent chasing shadows—I've been choosing death over life. I don't want that anymore. All I want is life, life with you. And I know—I know—that's what my dad would want for me.

So I'm holding out my hand to you now, and I hope you take it. I hope we can walk down this road together, towards the life we're going to build, towards the world we're going to make together.

After all, just like you said in your letter, I'm pretty sure you're my soulmate, and I'm pretty sure I'm yours. It's a forever kind of thing.

It reminds me of a line in a poem I read once:

"Out beyond ideas of wrongdoing and rightdoing, there is a field. I will meet you there."

(Okay, I'm lying. I didn't actually read it, but a good friend told me that line once.)

I hope I can meet you in that field, sweetheart.

Love,
Gio

***

Neely wrinkled her nose at the recollection of the poetry quote. *Rumi. You've been holding out on me, Luca.*

She jammed the crowbar into the base of the window and started to pry, jimmying until she heard the lock crack. She then yanked up the window and climbed into Lizbeth's kitchen.

She won't be home from work for awhile yet. Plenty of time to hide.

Just then, a hand slammed on a light switch across the room, and there was Lizbeth, holding a butcher knife.

Well, that was bad intel.

"Who are you?" Lizbeth said, trembling. "I'm not afraid of you, whoever you are."

Really? Neely tried not to roll her eyes. *Really.*

"Please," she said, advancing on Lizbeth and coming upon her within a few strides. Lizbeth didn't even move the knife. Neely grabbed her wrist and squeezed lightly, then disarmed her and stepped back. *She's pretty enough. I guess.*

"Tell me who you are," Lizbeth said. "I'll call the police."

Neely grinned. "Why? You never saw a girl with orange hair before?"

Lizbeth trembled even more. "I told you, I'm not afraid of you."

God, I should stop torturing the girl. Even though it's kind of fun.

"I'm friends with your boyfriend," Neely said.

"Johnny," Lizbeth said immediately. "You know him?"

"Do I know him?" Neely laughed to herself, then raised the crowbar for emphasis. "We're tight, Lizbeth."

Lizbeth stared at her. "Why should I believe you?"

"See for yourself." Neely held out Johnny's letter, close enough for Lizbeth to see.

"That's his handwriting," Lizbeth said. "Why are you here?"

To do the right thing. "To give you this letter." She handed it to Lizbeth. "And to tell you that he's innocent. And safe."

"Thank God," Lizbeth said, tears flowing down her cheeks as she took the letter.

What a wimp. "Whatever you've heard about him on the news is a lie," she said.

"I know. I know." Lizbeth wiped her eyes. "How do you know him?"

Neely considered how to answer the question. "There's a lot you don't know about him. And I don't have time to tell you everything. All you need to know is that we're both federal agents. And Johnny, and the rest of us, we're on the run."

Lizbeth nodded, trying to take it all in, even though it was obviously overwhelming her. "But he's safe?"

Neely nodded back. "He's safe." She paused. "There's something else you should know about him, too."

"What?"

"I know you've been working on this story, trying to figure out who saved the President's life last year. So I want you to take a look at something." Neely fished a photograph out of her pocket and handed it to Lizbeth.

She watched Lizbeth as she scrutinized the photo. She had just handed over the only known photograph—the only evidence on the planet, photographic or otherwise—of Luca saving President Wilkins's life last spring, an item she'd pilfered from Peterson's files a few months ago.

"Oh… my… God," Lizbeth said, recognition electrifying her face, her eyes. "My God, my God, my God. It was him." She looked up at Neely. "It was him. It was him."

It sure was. Neely smiled, despite herself. "It was him, Lizbeth. All along, it was him. And now you see why he wanted to keep it a secret—why we all wanted to keep it a secret."

"I do." Lizbeth pressed her hands against her thighs, trying to steady herself. "I do."

"I need to get going. Read that letter I gave you." Neely paused. "And there's one more thing."

"What?"

How can I make her understand?

"There's an uprising coming," Neely said. "An uprising against Bryson, against Greenaway, all of them. Everything they're saying about Wilkins is a lie. Just like they're lying about Johnny, they're lying about Wilkins, too. Bryson's the one who's tried to set up a police state, not Wilkins. And now there's going to be an uprising."

Should I tell her about Bragg? Should I tell her that she's really working for Octavian?

Neely chased the thought away. That intel was too much for one person, for one citizen, to handle. It would be like handing over the country's nuclear launch codes to a person on the street.

"I know you're a writer," Neely continued. "I know you write for Bragg, for *Rebellion.* But what you've written so far doesn't really cut it. Johnny needs you. *We* need you. Think about everything that's happened—think about Bryson, about the coup against the President, about what this uprising means. And then think about how you can help, about what you have to give." Neely looked into Lizbeth's eyes. "Think about who might be out there reading your articles."

Lizbeth returned the look, understanding. "I will," she said.

Neely studied Lizbeth for a moment longer. And then she climbed out the window and slipped down the fire escape.

Epilogue: Chapter 2

Bryson is the key, the man thought as he aimed the rocket launcher in the dead of night.

Bryson had been the key all along. Octavian was a fanatic, a megalomaniac, a man obsessed with power. But not Bryson; he was never in this for power. He'd gotten into this for family—for the wife and daughter he lost on September 11. He'd gotten into this for justice, which had corroded into revenge; for love, which had warped into hate.

Bryson had sworn the oath of the Gadsden Brigade, and somewhere within him was a soldier of the constitutional guard. He might be Director of the Anti-Subversion Authority again, but his heart still burned for the words "Don't tread on me." It had to. It had to.

The man squared up, aiming the rocket launcher at the mansion nestled in the hills of the Virginia exurbs. It was a fortress; Wilkins may have humiliated Bryson last year by sending agents to raid his home, but in the time since, Bryson had fortified it and added guards. And now that he was Authority Director again, it was guarded by the finest Authority agents.

But that was no matter. The man's unit had subdued the guards in a nighttime raid, then secured the perimeter, fanning out around the compound.

So here the man was, about to fire a rocket at Alexander Bryson's home. The rocket would register its payload into a wing of the mansion and blow it to smithereens.

No one would die in the blast; the man had made sure of that. His unit had confirmed that no one was in the home, and Bryson's guards were safely away from the blast zone. No one would die—not tonight, not yet. There would be a rebellion soon, and people would die then—but not tonight. Tonight was a token gesture, nothing more.

But he'll know it was me. He'll know it was me, and he'll know that we're here. He'll know that we're pouring over the border now, that more of us are coming, that he can't stop us from coming. He'll know that we're here, and that he'll have to face me in the battlefield if he wants to defend his Octavian.

The man turned to one of his subordinates. "We're finally home," he said.

Then Union McCallister fired the rocket at Bryson's mansion, smiling as it whistled towards its target and exploded on impact.

Epilogue: Chapter 3

He'd made it as far west as Indianapolis, and now he knew everything, finally, he knew everything.

Somewhere in western Pennsylvania, Johnny had reviewed Peterson's flash drive, then destroyed it as Wolfe had ordered. He'd been on the move since, hitchhiking, staying in motels. And he was on the move again tonight, walking along the White River as the Indianapolis skyline glistened in the distance.

Gordon Bragg was Octavian. Bragg—publisher of *Rebellion*, Lizbeth's boss, the man whose jet they were going to ride on—had funded Brigade 910 from the beginning, had co-opted Bryson, and now had launched a coup and overthrown President Wilkins.

And Paul... Paul had joined Brigade 910. He was out there somewhere tonight, maybe on campus, maybe in hiding. Gaines had gotten to him, had brainwashed him, and now he was out seeking his own revenge for Giovanni Sr.

And Fullerton. Fullerton had committed an unspeakable crime, and now there'd have to be justice.

Johnny was headed west. West to where, he had no idea. All he knew was that on Wolfe's mark he'd be liaising with the Gadsden Brigade, with a general named Union McCallister, and that there was going to be a rebellion to take the country back.

The presidential election was in six months, and Wilkins was under house arrest. Greenaway, the new President, would be running for reelection as Bragg's brain-dead lackey, while Bragg's real horse, Taylor Quade—governor of the state in which Johnny now stood—would be running to cement Bragg's rule. If there was any hope left for the country, it lay in the Gadsdens' uprising—and either in freeing Wilkins from house arrest, or in a third-party candidate mustering the guts to challenge the Bragg machine.

I should be going east, Johnny thought as he walked. Back home. *Back to try and find Paul, back to Lizbeth.*

But he was heading west, and nothing could change that. If he turned around—if he tried to see Lizbeth one more time, just hold her one more time—they'd arrest him, or kill him.

But I'm going to make it home. I will walk through hell to make it home.

Johnny pulled the mobile phone out of his pocket and launched its browser. He'd read something incredible tonight, and he had to read it again, had to remind himself it was real.

"*We therefore declare a rebellion against the forces of tyranny in our midst,*" wrote Lizbeth in the concluding paragraph of the *Rebellion* editorial posted online a few hours ago. "*We declare a rebellion against the storm troopers of the Anti-Subversion Authority beating the protesters in our streets. We declare a rebellion against the surveillance state eavesdropping on our phone calls, reading our text messages, following our every move and monitoring our every thought, our every breath. We declare a rebellion against the overthrow of our democratically elected president, Reed Wilkins, and categorically reject any allegations against him until they are proven in a court of law or in an impeachment trial before the United States Senate. In the name of a generation rising to defend the freedoms won and championed by our parents and grandparents, we declare a rebellion against usurpation, against fascism, against those forces that have arrayed themselves against the universal rights of men and women to assemble, speak freely, and pursue their happiness in peace. We invite all Americans—of every generation, of every background, of every race, color, and creed—to join us in this fellowship of liberty, to band together under this banner of rebellion, to fight by our side until democracy and justice once again carry the day in our home, the United States of America.*

"*Out beyond ideas of wrongdoing and rightdoing, there is a field. We will meet you there.*"

A chill splashed at the base of Johnny's spine, just like the first time he'd read the editorial earlier tonight. *She knows. My letter... Neely... it had to be Neely. Lizbeth knows, and I have to make it home to her. I have to.*

Johnny Luca marched west, off to a rendezvous with the Gadsden Brigade, off to rebellion.

www.ingramcontent.com/pod-product-compliance
Lightning Source LLC
Chambersburg PA
CBHW030535310726
48979CB00010B/1922/J

* 9 7 8 0 9 8 9 1 7 7 5 2 8 *